Dear Reader,

Welcome back to the next story in the IT'S TRADING MEN! trilogy. We're in the second month of Trading Men on Trading Cards with the St. Marks Lunch Exchange group of single women in midtown Manhattan, and a new batch of hot hunks have just entered the dating pool!

I'm so excited to introduce you to Rebecca Thorpe and Jake Donnelly. Rebecca is the CEO of a very large philanthropic foundation, and at twenty-eight, she's not willing to settle for anything less than the perfect husband. So far, several have come close, but none have had that magic *something*.

When she sees Jake Donnelly on a Trading Card, she falls instantly in lust. He's completely wrong for her. Jake's a former NYPD detective, wounded in the line of duty, who lives in Brooklyn. He doesn't care about the social registry or where she got her degree. He's the man of Rebecca's most wicked dreams, and she can't wait to cut loose with Jake for one night of carnal indulgence. Only, they both soon realise that one night won't be nearly enough…

I hope you enjoy the fantasy and fun of *Have Me*, and continue on with *Want Me* in June.

As always, I can be reached at joleigh@joleigh.com. Hearing from readers is the best thing ever!

Love to you all,

Jo

HAVE ME

BY
JO LEIGH

First published in Great Britain 2012
by Mills & Boon, an imprint of Harlequin (UK) Limited,
Eton House, 18-24 Paradise Road, Richmond, Surrey TW9 1SR

© Jolie Kramer 2012

ISBN: 978 0 263 89373 1
ebook isbn: 978 1 408 96906 9

14-0512

Harlequin (UK) policy is to use papers that are natural, renewable and recyclable products and made from wood grown in sustainable forests. The logging and manufacturing processes conform to the legal environmental regulations of the country of origin.

Printed and bound in Spain
by Blackprint CPI, Barcelona

Jo Leigh is from Los Angeles and always thought she'd end up living in Manhattan. So how did she end up in Utah, in a tiny town with a terrible internet connection, being bossed around by a house full of rescued cats and dogs? What the heck, she says, predictability is boring. Jo has written more than forty novels and can be contacted at joleigh@joleigh.com.

To Yael. I strive to create heroines who
are as terrific as you.

1

Where R U???

REBECCA THORPE DIDN'T bother returning her friend Bree's text because there was no need. She was already walking up the pathway to the St. Marks church basement, the ready-to-be-frozen lunches she'd prepared in a large tote in preparation for the bimonthly lunch exchange. That wasn't what had slowed her pace though. She took her hand out of her coat pocket and stared again at the trading card she'd been toying with for the past fifteen minutes.

Ever since Shannon Fitzgerald had introduced the idea of using trading cards for trading *men,* the lunch exchange group, now numbering a whopping seventeen women, had been in a dating frenzy. The concept was simplicity itself: everyone involved recommended men they knew who were eligible and in the market. Whether they were relatives, friends or even guys without that perfect chemistry—for them at least—there was suddenly a bounty of prescreened, fully vetted local men. None of whom knew that they were members of this very select group.

On paper Gerard had seemed ideal. He was gorgeous, not only on the front of the card, either. Tall, dark, handsome, he'd gotten his degree from Cambridge, then had come to New York to work for the United Nations. He was urbane, sophisticated, dressed like a dream. And he'd taken her to dinner at Babbo, which was never a bad thing.

Sadly, like the other three men Rebecca had gone out with, courtesy of the trading cards, there had been no sizzle. Maybe she'd see Gerard again because he was fascinating, and they had many common interests, but the man she was looking for wasn't him. She'd known ten minutes into the date that the magic was missing, and while she'd been disappointed, she hadn't been surprised.

She was too picky. Or something. She couldn't spell out her criteria for *the one* but she certainly knew when she hadn't found it. She'd never had luck with men, and that had as much to do with her being a Winslow as it did with her taste, but the end result was that she hadn't truly connected with a man, not for the long haul, and the trading cards hadn't changed her luck.

So, with all due respect to the trading cards and to the whole idea of dating, she was done. No more cards for her, no more setups, no more blind dates, no more searching and no more hoping.

If she met someone in the course of doing what she loved, then great. If she didn't, she was fine with that, too. At twenty-eight she wasn't willing to say she'd never try again. She wanted to have a partner, maybe even have kids. But for now? Work was enough. Work was almost too much. It barely left time for her to visit with friends, go to movies, the theater, read a book. She was taking herself out of the game.

Determined and damn cold, she walked into St. Marks. The sound of women, of her friends, greeted her the moment she stepped over the threshold. There was a lot of joy to be had in her world, and only a part of it depended on a man.

"There you are," Bree said, grinning as she met Rebecca at one of the long tables. "Charlie bet me you wouldn't make it today. He said the donor dinner is getting too close."

Rebecca started stacking the lunches she'd prepared. "What did you win?"

"Something juicy that would make you blush."

Rebecca was glad not to have to hear the details. Charlie Winslow was her cousin, and while he was her favorite cousin, and she'd played an integral role in getting him and Bree together, there were certain things she'd rather not have in her memory. "As long as you're happy, I'm happy. And he's right. The dinner is driving me insane. I hate this part. I despise having to ask for money."

"Hard to run a charitable foundation without funds," Bree said.

"I know. But it defeats the purpose if I have to wine and dine the donors to the tune of several hundred thousand dollars. That money should be used elsewhere."

Bree, who looked adorable in skinny jeans with a gorgeous camel cowl-neck sweater, patted Rebecca's arm. "You could always serve them dinner á la soup kitchen. As a statement."

"I've considered it. But I really do need their money. Besides, the Four Seasons isn't known for its soup-kitchen ambience."

"Keep thinking about how much good the Winslow Foundation does. Then suck it up."

Rebecca laughed, as Shannon, the most important member of the lunch exchange, came plowing through the door. The redhead didn't know how to make anything but a dramatic entrance.

"I have new cards!" she said, lifting up a box from her family's printing shop. "Brand-new delicious men. You guys have outdone yourselves this time. Truly."

Rebecca pulled out Gerard's card, which had been in the second batch of trading cards. The first exchange had happened in February, a couple of weeks before Valentine's Day. As this was only the group's third exchange, it was too early to say how successful the new venture would be overall, but none of the dates had been disasters, and that was something.

She headed toward the front table where the cards were spread out for the taking, indecisive about putting Gerard back into the mix. For a moment, she was tempted. Tempted to forget she'd decided only minutes ago that she was done with all this. Maybe one more try? But that thought was dismissed the moment she remembered what she had waiting for her back at the office. Even if she wanted to try again, now wasn't the time. The dinner, which was more of a banquet complete with orchestra and dancing, was in just over a week, and if she found time to sleep between now and then, it would be a miracle.

Someone—Bree?—pushed into her from behind into the long table. "Hey, jeez." What was this, sale day at Barneys? Rebecca dropped Gerard's card on top of the pile and was in the process of getting out of the way when a tiny little tap stopped her.

She picked up the trading card resting against her hip. Then she stared. The name on the top was Jake Donnelly. The picture made all her female parts stand up and take notice. So to speak. Because he was the single most attractive man she'd ever seen. Ever. He wasn't the handsomest, but handsome was easy, handsome was proportions and ratios and cultural biases. No, Jake Donnelly was the man who fit *her*. She hadn't realized until right now that she'd carried a blueprint in her brain, made of exacting specifications down to the texture of his eyebrows.

They were on the thick side, dark. As dark as his hair, which was parted, long on the collar, unstudied, and, oh, who was she kidding, it was his eyes. They were an astonishing blue. Not pale, but a vibrant, piercing cerulean. The rest of his face was great, fabulous, a perfect frame; rugged enough that the parts of her that weren't transfixed by his eyes were doing a happy dance about the rest.

A happy dance? Okay, so it wasn't a sale at Barneys, it was high school and she was swooning over the quarterback. Even when she'd been in high school she hadn't swooned. This was unprecedented in every way.

She blinked. Took in a much-needed breath. Looked around. Just like in the movies, sounds returned, the picture in her hand wasn't the only thing in focus and she was Rebecca once more.

Almost.

She turned the card over, found out Donnelly had been recommended by Katy Groft. Rebecca made her way through the tightly packed crowd and sidled up to Katy, an NYU postgrad studying physics.

"Oh, you found Jake."

"Please tell me he looks like this picture."

Katy grinned. "Oh, he's even better."

"Oh, God." Rebecca didn't dare look to see which

category he fell in…marrying kind, dating or one-night stand. Not until she asked "Is he already taken?"

"Nope. You're in luck."

"Thank God. Because wow. He is…"

Katy sighed. "It pains me, it truly does. Because he's a sweetheart and he's funny, decent and very discreet. But he doesn't want a relationship at all. He's extremely private, too, so if that's going to bother you—"

"Private's good. Private and discreet is even better. Can you call him? Oh, he's probably at work now."

"Did you not read the back of the card?"

Rebecca felt a little blush steal across her cheeks. "Um…" She turned it over.

* His favorite restaurant: *Luigi's Pizza in Windsor Terrace.*
* Marry, date or one-night stand: *One night.*
* His secret passion: *No idea. But he's renovating his father's house in Brooklyn between jobs.*
* Watch out for: *Nothing, actually. He was great. I found him through my uncle whom I trust beyond measure.*
* Why it didn't work out: *Nothing scary here. Hot and fun. He's not sure what he's going to do with his life.*

Katy laughed, which made Rebecca tear her eyes away from Jake's picture.

"What?" she asked.

"Nothing," Katy said. "I'll call him right now."

"That would be very, very good."

THE SINK WASN'T COOPERATING. It was a heavy sonofabitch, and he couldn't just drop it into the new vanity, but the guy on the DIY DVD was talking too fast and Jake needed to rewind to get that last bit. He shifted the sink in his arms until it was balanced between him and the wall, unfortunately on his bad leg, then reached for his laptop. A second before his finger reached the touch pad, his walkie-talkie squawked. "Jake?"

Jake swore, which he'd been doing a lot this morning. This week. This month. It was his father. Again. About to tell him another idiotic cop joke.

Jake would have preferred not to hear another joke. Not while he was installing his old man's sink in the new master bath. In fact, not while he was still able to hear. But that's not how this gig worked.

He paused the DVD, lowered the sink to the floor and pressed the transmit button. "Okay, let's hear it."

There was a muffled giggle, a hell of a sound coming from a man who was sixty-three years old. "How many Jersey cops does it take to screw in a lightbulb?"

Jake sighed. This particular joke seemed to be stuck on repeat, as this was the third time he'd heard it in so many days. "How many?"

Now the laughter wasn't subdued and it wasn't only his old man laughing. The other two voices belonged to Pete Baskin and Liam O'Hara, all old farts, retired NYPD, bored out of their stinking minds and drunk on nothing but coffee and dominoes. "Just one—" his dad said.

"But he's never around when you need him," finished Liam.

The three of them laughed like asthmatic hyenas. The worst part about it? Someone had to be pushing the transmit button the whole damn time in order for Jake to hear it.

"Yo, Old Men?" he said, when he could finally get through.

"Who you calling old?" Pete yelled.

"You three. I'm trying to put in a sink. You know how much this sink weighs? I don't want to hear one more goddamn cop joke, you got it? No more. I swear to God."

"Yeah, yeah," Liam said. "Mikey always said you had no sense of humor."

"Well, I think he's damn funny looking, so I guess he's wrong about that, too."

"I can still whip your ass, Jacob Donnelly," his father said, "and don't you forget it."

Jake went back to the computer, replayed the section about the plumbing, then squared off against the sink. It hung off the wall, so the wheelchair wouldn't be an issue. In fact, the spigot was motion-controlled so his dad wouldn't have to touch anything if his hands were acting up.

Jake had already widened the door leading into the new master bath. It used to be a guest bathroom before his dad's rheumatoid arthritis started getting so bad. The wheelchair wasn't a hundred percent necessary yet, but soon his father wouldn't be able to make it up to his bedroom on the second floor, even with Jake's help.

He picked up the damn heavy sink and moved it over to the semipedestal, the plumbing all neatly tucked behind the white porcelain. It actually set easily, and since he'd been getting better with this plumbing business, he didn't find it necessary to curse the entire time he secured the top to the pedestal.

The problem wasn't the tools, but the pain. As soon as he could, he stood, stretching out the damaged thigh. The bullet had been a through and through, but what they don't say on TV is that it goes through muscle and tendon and veins and arteries on its quick voyage into, in his case, a factory wall. At least the thigh was less complicated than the shoulder wound.

Sometimes he felt as if it would have been better for everyone if the bastard had been a better shot. He rolled his left shoulder as his physiotherapist, Taye, taught him to do, then did a few stretches. This DIY crap had never been his bailiwick, but his dad needed the house to work for him, and the doctors had all thought it would be good for Jake to use his body to build something tangible.

Jake had realized when he was widening the wall that he actually liked remodeling. That was quite satisfying. The actual work itself though sucked like a Dyson.

But this was his life now. Crazy old men on the porch, fixing every problem the world had ever known. It didn't matter that it was March and as cold as hell outside; they kept on playing their bones, the space heater barely keeping them from hypothermia. Of course they had their cold-weather gear on. These men had been beat cops in so many New York winters the cold didn't stand a chance.

Thank Christ for electric blankets. 'Cause Mike Donnelly, for all his bluster, was getting on. It would be good when Jake had the new shower finished. Nothing to step over, nothing his crooked hands couldn't handle. Then he'd be able to jack up the heating bill to his heart's content, shower three times a day if he wanted.

In the meantime, there was plumbing to do. Jake limped over to the laptop and continued the how-to. Two minutes in, his cell rang. It was Katy Groft, which was weird. They'd gone out, it had been fine, but Jake had been pretty damn clear about his intentions. He wasn't one of those guys who said they'd call, then blew it off. None of that bullshit. "Hello?"

"Hey, Jake. Got a minute?"

"Sure."

"I'm sending you a picture."

"Okay." His phone beeped a second later. "Hold on." He clicked over to the photo, and what he saw surprised him even more than the phone call itself. It was... what's her name, the Winslow who wasn't called Winslow. Thorpe. That's right. Rebecca Thorpe. Ran some kind of big foundation or something, was always in the papers, especially the *Post*. What he didn't know was why Katy Groft would want him to see Thorpe's picture. "Okay," he said again.

"This is my friend Rebecca," Katy said. "Interested?"

"In what?"

"Her. Going out with her. You know, a date?"

He stared again at the phone, at the picture. Rebecca Thorpe was a beautiful woman. Interesting beautiful. Her face was too long, her nose too prominent, but there was something better than pretty about her. Every picture he'd seen of her, didn't matter who she was with, she seemed to be daring everyone to make something of it. Of her. Right now, looking at the overexposed camera phone photo, he had to smile. No choice. It didn't hurt that she had a body that struck all the right chords. Long, lean, like a Thoroughbred. "You do realize you called Jake Donnelly, right?"

Katy laughed. "Yes. I'm very aware of who you are. And who she is. And I happen to believe you two would hit it off well. I'm pretty clever about these things. And don't worry, she already understands you're not in the market for anything serious."

So this Thoroughbred wanted to go out with a quarter horse for a change of pace? "She knows I'm busted up, right?"

"Not a problem."

He gave it another minute's thought, then figured, "Sure. Why the hell not?"

"Great. How about the Upstairs bar at the Kimberly Hotel, tomorrow night at eight?"

It was his turn to laugh. "What is this, some kind of gag?"

"No. I swear. She's great. You'll like her. A lot."

He'd have to wear something nice to the Kimberly. But he hadn't worn anything nice in a long time. Before he got shot, that's for sure. "I'll get there a little early. Introduce myself."

"Excellent. You'll thank me."

"I'm already thanking you. For thinking of me. Although I'm still unclear why."

"You'll see," she said.

"Fair enough." He disconnected from Katy, but stared at the picture on his phone for a while. God damn, she was something else.

Katy had been only the second woman he'd been with since he'd been put out to pasture. She'd been great, and if his life had made any kind of sense, he might have pursued more than a onetime thing. But the only thing he knew for sure at the moment was that he was a broken ex-cop without a plan in the world except for rebuilding the house he was born in so his father could live out the rest of his days at home. After that was anybody's guess.

"Hey, Jake?"

He winced at the sound of his father's voice, tinny over the walkie. "Yeah, Dad," he said, his thumb finding the transmit button without his even having to look.

"How many cop jokes are there?"

He shoved his cell into his pocket. "Two," Jake said. "All the rest of them are true."

Laughter filled the mess of a bathroom, and Jake supposed that as far as problems went, having three lunatics telling him cop jokes all day was pretty far down the list.

2

Rebecca arrived at her building just before 6:00 a.m. She needed coffee and lots of it. Facing her to-do list was not something she was looking forward to but there was no getting around it.

Her suite on 33rd was a behemoth. The size itself wasn't the issue—it was the fussy ostentation that got to her, the image that nearly outweighed their purpose. There was an enormous fresh-flower display next to the huge mahogany reception desk. Warren, the receptionist, wouldn't be in until eight-thirty, and Rebecca's personal assistant, Dani, had been coming in at eight lately, an hour earlier than she had to. It was very, very still with no one else on the floor, but then that wasn't unusual. The air of gravitas was nurtured like a living thing in this fortress.

Rebecca didn't make a sound on the plush burgundy carpeting in the long hallway that led to her office. She swiped her key card, put her briefcase on her desk, her purse in her credenza drawer, and went to the small private room—the truest symbol of how much the founders had prized their creature comforts. She headed straight for the coffeemaker.

Once she'd finished with the prep and pressed the button for the machine to start brewing, she turned and leaned on the counter. There was a huge LED television mounted on the wall across from the deep and supremely comfortable leather chairs, museum-worthy paintings on the muted walls and a couch with such deep bottom cushions that it was more suitable to napping than sitting. Fresh flowers were here as well, replaced weekly by a service that understood decorum while making a point that when it came to the details, no expense was spared. It was as ridiculous as it was sacrosanct.

She was the first woman to ever run the foundation, and her ideas about modeling their business plan after the great philanthropic organizations like the Rockefeller Trust or the Carnegie Group continued to be an uphill war. Picking her battles had been one of her first and most important lessons.

That's why she tried hard not to resent the time and money being spent on the donor dinner. The guest list included most of the *Forbes* top-fifty richest people in the world. They gave millions so that after all these years, their endowments were in the billions. She needed to remember that and just do the job.

Preparing her coffee in her favorite mug soothed her, letting her prioritize the next few unencumbered hours. It wasn't until she took her first sip that her thoughts turned to Jake. And there was a problem.

Not her excitement, that was a pleasure and a rush. It wasn't like her to want a man purely for sex. She was, in theory, at least to quote her mother, above that sort of thing.

Guess not, Mom.

When she returned to her desk, instead of clicking

on her email, she got her purse from the credenza and took out Jake's trading card.

Oh, yeah. She wasn't at all sure why, but looking at him made her clench all kinds of important muscles. She hadn't even met him and his face started a chemical spike inside her. The exact same reaction had occurred each time she'd sneaked a peek at his photograph. She refused to acknowledge how often that had been.

The problem was, with this level of excitement over the two-dimensional image, how on earth was the very three-dimensional living man going to measure up?

It was all about narrowing her expectations. She could do that. It wasn't as if she wanted to fall in love with Jake or for him to love her. She hoped to like him, though, because she knew from experience that if he was a complete jerk, her attraction would vanish in an instant.

They were going to meet for drinks and that was to her advantage. She didn't normally indulge to the point of feeling buzzed, but when she did, she became more forgiving. And, if it came down to it, she could probably get him to not talk at all.

She put his card away, determined not to look at it again until after work. Not only was she slammed for time, but she needed to get home early enough to go the extra mile with grooming. Oh, the joys and pains of getting naked with someone new.

She clicked on her email icon, and the sheer number of new messages was enough to chase away any thoughts of sweaty sex. Especially when the first of the emails was from her father. That never ended well.

THE MORNING COFFEE WAS already made by the time Jake limped his way down the stairs. It was freezing outside.

Sitting in the kitchen, his father was bundled up in a thick wool sweater and had a lap blanket tucked around his lower half as he warmed his hands on his old NYPD coffee mug.

"The weatherman says we're in for a cold one tonight."

Jake nodded as he fixed his mug. Two sugars, half and half. He didn't drink until he slid onto the banquette in the breakfast nook. He needed to do something about the cushion covers. They were almost as old as he was and the regular washings had made them threadbare and pale. "I'm going to the city."

"Yeah?" his dad asked.

"Yeah."

"Date?"

Jake drank some coffee, sighing in satisfaction as it warmed him. "Yeah."

"I'll get Liam to spend the night, then?"

"Already cleared it with him. He's bringing over DVDs."

"Ah, shit," his father said, putting his mug down on the counter, then turning his wheelchair a few degrees so he faced Jake. "That means another goddamn Bruce Willis festival. Swear to Christ, Liam has, a whatchamacallit, a bromance, going with that guy."

"What's it matter? Pete's got a hard-on for his car."

"Yeah." Mike picked up his cup again. "Everybody's got something. Except you. What do you got a hard-on for, Jake?"

"What the hell kind of a question is that?"

"Watch the tone. I'm still your father. I'm wondering, that's all. You spent a lot of time wanting to be in vice, then all those years doing undercover work. I'm thinking there's gotta be something else now. Something, please God, more interesting than Bruce Willis movies."

Jake drank some more coffee, not sure how to answer the question. If he should answer at all. But no, he would. He and his dad had spent a lot of years being distant. What with the work, then with Mom dying of cancer, and Jake having to be so hush-hush about everything. He'd decided to fix up the house by himself because he wanted to know his old man. Wanted someone to know him in return. Now was not the time to back off. "I don't know, Dad. I got nothing. Just the house."

"That's not gonna last forever."

"Nope. But it's something to do while I learn how to be a civilian."

"I hear that."

Jake nodded in tandem with his father. It wasn't easy, this talking thing. But dying alone in a warehouse filled with drug dealers wasn't easy, either. He could do this. The worst that would happen? He'd look like an idiot. He already did that without trying. "I've got a date tonight," he said. "She a looker."

"Good for you," Mike said. "Nice woman?"

"Never met her. Comes highly recommended, though."

"Yeah?"

"She's a Winslow."

"*Those* Winslows?" His dad settled his cup snugly on his lap as he wheeled over to the nook. "What the hell does one of those Winslows want with you?"

Jake laughed. "No idea. Looking forward to finding out."

"Probably heard who your old man was. Couldn't resist."

"You keep telling yourself that. See what happens."

Mike awkwardly put the cup on the table, and Jake

held back his wince. It was getting harder for his father to hold the damn mug at all, as his fingers twisted and bent. But there was no use crying about it. There wasn't a cure, and the medicines and physical therapy could do only so much. Retrofitting the house was what Jake could do, was doing.

"You know Sally Quayle? Three doors down, her husband was killed in Afghanistan last year?"

"Oh, no, Dad. Come on. We talked about this."

"We did, and we agreed."

"I'm not goddamn Santa and I'm not the neighborhood fixer. In case you haven't noticed, I'm also busy."

"There's always time to do right. She's worried about being alone. Thinking of buying a gun."

"Ah, crap. You want me to go talk to her."

"I do. We all do. She needs to know how dangerous that could be. Go over her house security. Make sure she's safe, yeah?"

Jake sighed. "Yeah, yeah. I'll go over this week. After I get a good start on the new shower." Why was it the only time Jake sounded like he was from Brooklyn was when he was home? He'd had the accent scared out of him at St. Francis Xavier high school, but it always came back the moment he was in the neighborhood.

"This week is fine. And don't start anything too big on the shower this afternoon. You need to look your best tonight."

"I what?"

Mike sniffed. "You're my only son. And a certified hero. She should know who she's dealing with, this Winslow woman."

What could Jake say? "Sure thing, Dad. I'll shave and everything."

REBECCA PAID THE CAB DRIVER, then got out on East 50th Street at the entrance to the Kimberly Hotel. She'd chosen it because the rooftop bar had spectacular views of Midtown. Also she liked the way they made their gimlets here with a very unique lime cordial. It didn't hurt that their luxury suites were gorgeous, the feather beds to die for. Even if magic didn't happen between her and Jake, she'd enjoy staying the night by herself, and if that happened, she already decided she'd be utterly decadent with room service.

With that in mind, she went inside, her gaze lingering on the lobby's beautiful grandfather clock as she went to the front desk. She handed them her overnight bag and her coat to put in her room. Registration took no time at all and once her key card was in her purse, she went to the lobby restroom. She had to remind herself that whatever happened would be fine, that if he was an ass, she'd lose nothing but a fantasy. Still, she wanted that fantasy, so she freshened her lipstick, fluffed her hair, checked her breath and let her heart pump and her hopes soar as she caught the next ride up.

It was the express to the roof, not giving her much time to think, which was good. There were only three men in business attire aboard, none of them speaking, although she had the feeling they'd been in the same meeting. They all looked as though they'd been to the battlefield and lost and that drinks at the penthouse bar would be a just reward.

Her nerves hit what she hoped was their peak as they reached the thirtieth floor. It was all she could do not to take Jake's trading card out of her purse and hold on to it like a talisman. Not that she wouldn't recognize him. She'd practically memorized his face. He'd look good on the roof with the blue and white fairy lights under the glass domed ceiling, with the city skyline behind him.

Frankly, he'd look good in a crumbling boiler room. But as long as she was making this into some kind of romantic one-night dream date, she might as well have the proper setting.

Another thing she liked about Upstairs at the Kimberly was that the music wasn't deafening. They catered to a more mature crowd and had some respect for eardrums. It was a bar made for getting to know a person.

The elevator opened at one minute past seven. There were several areas where Jake could be. On the main floor, at one of the tables, at the light-bedazzled bar itself or on one of the leather couches to either side of the bar. She ran her hands down her black sheath dress as she walked into the middle of the room. She glanced to her right, and there he was. He'd scored a hell of a table, one close to the window that looked out at the Chrysler building.

It was too dark to see the color of his eyes, but she could tell he looked pretty much as advertised. Dark scruffy hair, broad shoulders with a well-fitting jacket, a light button-down shirt tucked into dark trousers. He saw her and stood, and yep, he had slim hips and long legs. Even at this distance, he was hotter than hell, and *please, please, let this not crash and burn in the first five minutes.*

She hoped he would be equally impressed as she crossed over to him. He took a few steps himself, careful to keep close enough to the table to prevent poaching. It wasn't until the third step that she noticed his limp.

Katy hadn't said anything. Meaning she didn't deem it noteworthy. Rebecca had no problem with that. It was an interesting detail, something to discover by layers.

"Rebecca," he said, and goodness, yes, that was a great voice. Deep and mellow and she thought about one of her recent not-so-wonderful blind dates that hadn't been helped by Sam's unfortunately high and sadly nasal tone.

"Jake," she replied as she took his hand. It was warm and large, and the shake just firm enough. He also knew when to let go. Big plus. He almost touched the small of her back as he held her seat, giving her the best view.

He sat across from her. The candles on the table gave a hint of his eye color, but she'd need real lights for that. Later. Now was for talking. And drinking because her heart was pounding a bit too hard for her to ignore.

Before they had a chance to start the opening volley, a waitress came to the table. Rebecca ordered her vodka gimlet and Jake ordered a bourbon and water. Nice. Traditional. Masculine.

The second they were alone, he leaned a little toward her. "I'm never great with openings," he said. "I've always thought there should be rules, a standard pattern that all blind dates have to follow. Like school uniforms or meeting the queen. It would make things so much simpler."

She thought about her trading card, and how that had helped, and wondered if Jake knew he was on a card, if he'd approve. She thought, yes. "You're right. It's an excellent idea and should be implemented immediately. What say we start with the basics. The front page of the questionnaire. I'm Rebecca Thorpe, I live in Manhattan and work in the East Village. I'm an attorney although I don't practice, and I was born and raised here in the city. I've known Katy for over a year, and she's terrific, so I trusted her when she told me we might hit it off. I'm not looking for love, or for more than an interesting evening, which I hope is what you're after, and…well. That's about it."

His laughter suited her down to her toes. It was genuine, easy, relaxed. His smile was even more delicious than his picture had implied. So far, so good. But now, it was his turn.

"I'm Jake Donnelly, I'm currently living in Windsor Terrace in Brooklyn, in the house where I was born. I'm staying with my dad doing some remodeling work. I come from a long line of cops, all the way back to when the Donnellys crossed over from Ireland. I've been with the police department since I graduated college. Well, until earlier this year. I have no idea what I'm going to do after I finish the renovations."

He leaned back as their drinks were placed on the table, then sought her eyes again. "And it appears we're both looking for a night to remember. How'd I do?"

"Great," she said, then she lifted her glass and clicked it against his. Jake was totally unlike anyone she'd ever dated. He was from Brooklyn, but he'd given up the accent for something far easier on her admittedly snobbish ears. She knew absolutely nothing about being a cop, about Windsor Terrace, about renovations. She was incredibly curious to know if his limp and no longer being a policeman were connected. And she couldn't imagine, not for the life of her, staying with her own family for more than about three hours. She and Jake were worlds apart, completely unsuited in every way but one.

He was *perfect*.

JAKE DRANK A LITTLE AS HE tried not to look as if he was scoping her out from head to toe. But screw it, he was. At least, as much as he could, given she was sitting.

Rebecca Thorpe was, to put it bluntly, off the charts hot. Her hair was golden and shiny in the glitter of the bar, her eyes smoky and intense. She was tall and slender, but the way her dress hugged her breasts made him say a prayer this night would end with him learning a lot more.

No mention of the Winslow name or the foundation she headed. Why not? Being careful? Probably, although why she would assume he didn't recognize her was a little baffling. Everyone who lived in New York knew of her family. They were like the Kennedys. Politicians, judges, private jets, private clubs, more money than sense if you asked him, but nobody did, and that seemed fair. He wouldn't know what the hell to do in a room full of Winslows, but being right here, right now with this one? It was his lucky day.

"I don't know where to start with questions," Rebecca said. "Do you miss being a cop?"

He'd left himself open for whatever with that intro, but he still wished she'd begun somewhere else. He shouldn't complain. At least she hadn't opened with the limp.

He was still self-conscious about the scars. Odd how the shoulder looked so much worse. The leg was no picnic, either. But it hadn't made anyone run screaming. Yet. What the hell, if it freaked her out, there was nothing he could do about that. He'd just get on home and read up on shower installations. "Yeah, I miss it," he said. "Hard not to, when it's the only thing I've ever done. I could have taken a desk assignment, but that wasn't me."

"Ah, so you were hurt on the job?"

He nodded. "Yeah. Shot in the thigh and the shoulder. They're not pretty, but I was lucky. Either one could have killed me, so…"

"I can't imagine. God, shot twice?" She shuddered, winced. "That's horrible. I'm always astonished at how vulnerable the human body can be, while at the same time astoundingly strong. I had a friend once who slipped on a leaf. Fell. Hit her head. She was twenty-four, and she died that night. You were shot twice, and you not only survived, but it looks from here as if you're thriving."

"It is a mystery. I tell people it must not have been my time, but that's just something easy to say. I'm not a religious man, or one who believes in fate. Nothing mystical or predestined. I guess I'm a pragmatist. I was in a dangerous profession, in a risky situation. It's no big surprise I was wounded. I lived because they got to me in time, got me to the right doctors. Thriving? Well, I wouldn't go that far, but I'm learning to accept my limitations. Oddly, there are fewer than I expected, with the notable exception of losing my career."

She didn't respond immediately, but she did lean in. She didn't even try to pretend she wasn't staring, wasn't taking his measure. "A pragmatist," she said eventually. "That's helpful, living in this city. This world."

"It is. What about you?" he asked. "What do you believe in?"

She smiled, leaned back in her chair. Her bangs were a bit in her eyes and he wanted to push them back to see her better. Not complaining, just sorta wishing.

"Boy, you don't fool around, do you?"

"Guess not. We can always talk about this damn cold front, if you'd prefer."

"I'm good," she said. "I like the tough questions."

"I didn't even ask, would you like something to eat? I

haven't looked at the menu, but I know they serve food here. Or we could go somewhere else for dinner."

"Oh, food. I'm not starving, but I could eat something. How about you?"

"I could do with more than the bologna sandwich I had around four. Busy day."

"I happen to know the menu here is excellent. Why don't you see if anything suits your fancy. Meanwhile I'll consider my answer to your very provocative question and finish my drink."

He nodded, grabbed the menu from the center of the table. Not much he didn't like. When he looked up again, she was still staring at him. He should have been unsettled. He wasn't used to undisguised interest. In fact, his life had depended on his blending in, fading into the background. Even the dark wasn't enough to hide behind, but instead of getting that crawling itch to run, he wanted her to look her fill. And he wanted her to like what she saw.

He passed her the menu, then finished his bourbon, signaling the waitress when he caught her eye. "There's nothing on there I wouldn't eat," he said to Rebecca. "Could live without the foie gras, but I like the meat and the fish selections. I think you should pick us out a few, and we'll have ourselves a small buffet while we go at least one step beyond the surface. How does that sound?"

"Fantastic."

Their order was taken, fresh drinks requested, and they were alone once more. It was all he could do not to call back the lovely girl and ask her to add a room with a king-size bed to the tab.

"I'm a mutt," Rebecca said, folding her hands on the shiny table. "Philosophically. I lean toward Buddhism, but I've got some roots in the church from when I was a kid. I mostly try to make a difference. Walk the walk, not just talk about it. I tend to connect to people who do the same."

That could have been a crock of bull, but his instincts said no. She was telling him the truth. It fit with her job, but that wasn't what he thought she was talking about. Another skill from his vice days was how to listen for the truth. Of course, in this instance, he had to factor in how badly he wanted to take Rebecca Thorpe to bed.

Which was really damn bad.

3

REBECCA LICKED THE TIP OF her thumb as she finished the last of her salt cod fritter. She'd decided to play hardball with the ordering—all of it finger food. Zucchini fritters, lollipop lamb chops, decadent French fries, even the crisp baby artichokes. She'd picked up a lollipop first thing, watching him watch her bring the food to her mouth, take a bite. Gauntlet thrown, she sipped her second drink and waited to see what he'd do.

He started with a couple of fries. Slow moving, deliberate, and his gaze on hers never wavered. As he chewed, his jaw muscle flexed in a way that made her blush. He couldn't tell, not in this light, yet his thick right eyebrow rose along with the corners of his mouth.

She grinned back, pleased he'd decided to play. Somehow the music had become smoky jazz, and the heat from the temperature-controlled floor slipped up her dress all the way to her very pretty, very naughty La Perla panties.

Through it all, the ordering, the waiting, the cute young waitress flirting with Jake as she set down their plates, Jake hadn't once lost the thread of their conversation. Rebecca wasn't sure if they were at the third or fourth level now that they'd reached ex-lovers territory.

"She was great," he said, using his napkin. "And I like to think I'm a reasonably adventurous guy, but when she started talking plushies…" He shook his head, grabbed a tiny artichoke.

"Plushies. You mean dressing up like stuffed animals plushies?"

"I do. I hope that's not your thing, but I'd have to say right up front that nope, not gonna go there. I like my partners to be human. It's a radical stance, but one I'm not going to budge on."

"Where do you stand on aliens who look humanoid?"

He thought a minute. "Depends. Do they really look like humans, or are they lizard people in disguise?"

"I see your point. I always draw the line at shape-shifters. I include vampires in that, by the way."

"Damn. There goes my plans for the rest of the night."

She laughed again, charmed. Not so much at the obvious quip but at his delivery. Very dry. Very…sexy. "Nothing wrong with a little nip here and there," she said.

He cleared his throat and shifted in his chair. "I agree," he said, putting his napkin on the table. "Now, if you'll excuse me."

As he walked away, Rebecca let herself linger on the breadth of his shoulders, the length of his legs. He might have a limp, but there was still a swagger to him that had her crossing her legs.

When he got back, she would bring up the room. They hadn't eaten too much and had only two drinks each. If they wanted dessert later they could order from room service. Everything about the evening led her to believe he was amenable, even though they hadn't yet touched.

While she could, she retrieved her mirror from her purse. After a fresh coat of lipstick, she stuck a breath strip in her mouth, realizing too late that it didn't go with vodka gimlets. At all. A quick shudder, then she closed her purse, aware of the room itself for the first time since she'd stepped off the elevator.

There was a sizable crowd for a Tuesday night. Most everyone was in business attire, upscale. While she saw people on the prowl, the atmosphere was not that of a pickup bar. Here, the desperation wouldn't start until around 3:00 a.m.

She wondered what Charlie and Bree were doing and almost got out her cell to text, but no, Bree could wait on Rebecca's report. Tonight felt private, different. In other circumstances, she'd have felt this evening was a beginning. She liked him a lot. More than anyone she'd been out with in years.

On the other hand, maybe knowing this was a singular event had made this ease possible. They weren't at a relationship audition. Sex, yes, but she figured they'd nailed that about five minutes in.

The conversation had gone from philosophy to her explaining the intricacies of preparing lunches and trading them at a church basement, and then somehow they'd landed at exes. Hers, she realized, had all fizzled due to boredom. No, that wasn't fair. There had been reasons she'd gone out with those few men for longer than a handful of months, but there had been no grand passions. Weirdly, she'd felt perfectly comfortable telling Jake just that.

There he was. Smiling from across the room. She watched as he maneuvered through people and tables.

When he sat down, he covered her hand with his. "I took the liberty of booking a room here tonight. I won't lie and say I wouldn't be disappointed if you don't want to join me, but I'll also take it like a man."

She turned her hand over and squeezed his fingers. "The only problem with that is I already have a room here. And since I'm the one who instigated this evening, I win the coin toss."

He studied her for a long minute. "Wow. That's… Full disclosure, though. I lied about taking it like a man."

She grinned. God, he was adorable. "If you're finished, why don't I put this on the tab, and we go down to cancel your reservation?"

He fetched his wallet from his pocket. "I'll be taking care of this. But thanks for the offer."

They wrapped it up, he put on a dark knee-length coat she hadn't even noticed, then held the back of her chair while she stood. An old-fashioned move, but one she didn't mind. Especially because she was a little wobbly. Not from the booze; she hadn't had enough to faze her. From the touching. The "any second now, don't know where things are going to go" touching.

After she picked up her purse, he slipped his hand around hers. It wasn't like the handshake, not at all. It was just…wonderful.

WALKING WITH REBECCA to the front desk reminded him of his prom. Not the dance, but afterward, going into the hotel in Brooklyn with Antoinette Fallucci on his arm. He'd been in a terrible borrowed tux that was too tight in the crotch even discounting the fact that he'd been seventeen, but Antoinette had looked like a princess in her strapless dress, and she'd been the homecoming queen, a cheerleader and without doubt the most beautiful and popular girl in his senior class. He'd strutted into that hotel. This time, he played it a little cooler, but he did feel that thrill, knowing he was with the best one, that every man in the place was jealous.

It had nothing to do with her being a Winslow. The subject hadn't come up and he didn't expect it to. Not when there were so many other interesting things to talk about.

He smiled as they waited for a desk clerk. She smiled in return and he wanted to kiss her. He'd stood close to her in the elevator, gotten a whiff of her perfume, and the effect still sizzled through his veins. He had no idea what the scent was, only that it made him want to spend a hell of a long time exploring that long, graceful neck of hers.

That they'd barely touched was both horrible and hot. He knew she'd be soft, but that was far too vague. How different soft was between the shell of an ear, the skin just under a belly button. His gaze drifted down as he realized there was no word for how it would feel to run his fingers across her inner thigh.

Shit, if he was going to be thinking like that, he should button his coat. Hide the evidence. Thankfully, the woman who'd made his reservation earlier called them to the desk.

"Is something wrong?" she asked.

"We double-booked. Miscommunication. I hope it's not too late to cancel."

"Mr. Donnelly, right?"

Surprised that she remembered his name, he nodded.

"I'll cancel that right now, sir. It'll be a moment."

Jake glanced at Rebecca. He liked that she was tall, five-eight, he'd guess? A six-inch difference was very doable. Not that anything couldn't be worked around.

He signed his name on the line, gave back the key card, and finally, they were free to leave.

"Thank you, Mr. Donnelly,"

"Yeah, thanks," he said, tearing his gaze from Rebecca, but he barely gave the other woman a second because his date, this amazing woman in the sleek black dress, tossed her hair behind her shoulder and tugged him along and it was as if the flag had been lowered in a race he hadn't known he was running. It took him two steps to catch up, and when they looked at each other, side by side, gripping each other's hands, they grinned like idiots. Who were going to have sex. Really, really soon.

"Should we order drinks?" she asked as they walked, their speed increasing with each step. "Champagne? Wine? Soda?"

"Wine? Do you like red? Although white would probably be better after vodka. Maybe we should just get some vodka."

"I like red." She pushed the elevator button three times, leaning into her thumb every time. "Besides, you're a bourbon man. Bourbon men don't drink vodka."

"Who told you such obvious lies? Whoever it was should be banished from ever tasting another shot of Stoli. And he shouldn't be able to look at a bottle of Elit."

The elevator dinged and opened. Finally. A couple walked out, ignoring them completely. It was Jake's turn to pull Rebecca inside.

"Then why did you order bourbon?" she asked.

He shrugged, astonished they were speaking in sentences when his brain and his body were one hundred percent focused on getting inside the goddamn room. "I like it."

"Okay." She pushed the button for the fifteenth floor. "What booze don't you like?"

He couldn't stand it, he pulled her until she was flush against him and he was staring down into her dark, wide eyes. "Boone's Farm."

She laughed as she pressed her breasts to his chest. He inhaled sharply at the feel of her, the reality of her. Then her hand, her right hand, slipped under his arm, around his waist and up his back. Without his permission, his hips jerked forward, his quickly hardening cock meeting the perfect resistance of her hip. Each floor they ascended felt like foreplay.

"What about you?" he asked, straining to pick up the thread of their conversation, although he was pretty sure if he started talking about pork belly futures neither of them would care. "Is there anything respectable you don't like?"

"Tons of things. But I suppose you're talking about liquor." Her breath whispered against his jaw, and that hand on his back was moving in small circles, the hint of friction electric. "Oddly," she said, her voice maybe half an octave lower than it had been a minute ago, "single malt Scotch whiskey. I know, it's very girlie of me, but I hate it. What's worse, I get very cranky when people get in my face about how superior it is. The age and what kind of barrel it was kept in. Which is ridiculous because I do the exact same thing with wine and champagne, so who the hell do I think I am? But there you have it. Completely irrational."

"Good to know," he said, now a few millimeters away from brushing his lips against hers. "I was going to seduce you with my knowledge of Glenlivet, but I won't now. Pity. I know a lot about Glenlivet, and I'm incredibly charming when I add the personal anecdotes."

"That's okay," she said, as they came to a smooth halt. "I already find you incredibly charming."

He'd have kissed her right then, right as they stepped out of the elevator, but he wanted it private. Not that anyone was in the hall. It didn't matter. He wasn't going to do anything to this woman until he had her alone and there was a bed nearby. He checked the wall plaque and followed the arrows to room 1562, at the very end of the hall. They didn't run, but they moved as quickly as his leg allowed.

She got the green light with her key card on the second try and he shoved the door open. His first impression of the room was that it was big for a Manhattan hotel and that it was very full with a sofa and chairs and coffee table, but it could have been the size of a pencil box and bright chartreuse and he wouldn't have cared. It was theirs, and while there wasn't a bed in front of him, there had to be one close. Rebecca walked in, but she didn't get far.

As he slammed the door shut behind him, he gave her a spin, a sweet little twirl that set her back against the door with him blocking her path.

Her smile said she didn't mind, and her lips parting as she raked his face with her very large eyes told him they were on the same page. She huffed softly as he slipped his hand behind her nape and his tongue in her mouth.

It was hot slick tongues and broken moans as they tried to get his coat off, both of them reaching at the same time. She scratched his wrist then shoved the coat off his shoulder while he was trying to remove the other side of the damn thing, and he twisted his shoulder in all the wrong ways.

He hissed as he drew back, hating his body so fucking much because he could be kissing her right now instead of this.

"I hurt you."

"You didn't. We did. I just have to be careful." He threw his coat with force onto one of the big chairs, then took off his jacket, as well. He turned his head as he reached for his shirt buttons, but her fingers on top of his made him look.

"We can be careful."

"It's the scars. Left shoulder, right thigh. I can keep my T-shirt on, turn off the lights—"

She slipped the top button through the hole. "Don't worry about my delicate sensibilities. I'm fine. As long as we can hurry up and get back to where we're getting naked together."

Scooping her into his arms, trapping her hands, he kissed her. Not that panic sloppy kissing, which was good, damn fine, but this was something else. This was a preview, a warning. He liked this part, and he was good at it. So he'd take it slow for the next few minutes, because soon, the moment he had that dress off her in fact, it was going to get crazy again. Messy, wet and hot, and while he couldn't do everything he used to, he could do plenty.

Her moan was low as she tussled with his tongue. He moved his hands under her hair until he found the top of her dress, the zipper hidden inconveniently behind a fold of material, but he was using his dominant hand, not the one with the intermittent quaver, so no problem. His cock hardened as the zipper lowered until it hit bottom. The feel of her skin beneath his palms made him groan, but when she pushed her hips against his aching erection, he decided the lesson was over, and all bets were off.

He pulled back, not letting her have another chance with his shirt.

"Fine," she said, chuckling, "be that way." Then she took two steps away and lifted her dress over her head and let it flutter to the floor.

Jake choked. It took him a minute of coughing to get his act together, and when he did, and he looked at her again, he had to consciously remember how to breathe. "Holy God."

"So you're a La Perla fan?"

"I have no idea what a La Perla is, but I'm over the moon about your underwear."

Her grin let him know she'd planned to knock him off his feet with the stunning bra and panties. Jesus, she was still wearing her heels, and the combination was enough to make a weaker man come without a touch.

The garments were sheerest white. Barely there, except for a small triangle that covered her pussy so he couldn't tell what she was hiding. He didn't give a damn. She could be hairy, bald as a cue ball or anything in between, it all worked as far as he was concerned. That he didn't know even with all that flesh on display made him insane.

The opposite was true on top. There was nothing but that sheer, sheer white covering her stunning breasts. Hard little nipples in the center of pink areolas like iced cupcakes with cherries on top.

And while staring at her was a wet dream all its own, there was so much more to be done. He tugged his shirt out from his trousers, toed off his shoes, then his socks, and by the time he'd unbuttoned the shirt with his right hand, his left had undone his belt and was working on his zipper.

Rebecca was most definitely not helping. In fact, she

was making it ridiculously harder to do this circus trick because whether she realized it or not, every move she made turned up the heat a notch. The sway of her hips as she took a single step, the roll of her shoulder, the shake of her head so her hair fluffed around her face. There wasn't a thing about her that didn't make him want to beg.

"You're killing me," he said, his voice as rough as sandpaper. He let his button-down fall, leaving him in his undershirt, and then his pants dropped and he kicked those out of the way.

Her gaze moved down to his thigh even as she ran her fingers over her bare tummy. Jake tensed as he waited for her verdict. She winced, but her hand didn't stop moving. He relaxed. She wasn't freaked out. His first date after had been, and he could never bring himself to blame her, but his gratitude that this woman hadn't run for the hills knew no bounds.

"Are you going to just stand there staring?" she asked.

"I don't know what to do first," he said. "You're stunning."

For all that she was driving him wild, the hint of a blush that warmed her cheeks was almost more than he could bear. "That's a pretty good place to start," she said as she covered the distance between them. "But an even better place would be in the actual bedroom."

He swung his arm around her neck and pulled her into a punishing kiss. His free hand went to the low line of her panties, the covered spot, and he slipped his fingers inside the material.

Ah. Not a full Brazilian then, but a landing strip. They needed to get to the bed before he came standing in his boxer briefs.

4

JAKE KISSED HER AS IF HE'D read her diary. All the things she hadn't written down. How that exact pressure made her shiver. How one of her favorite things was when it wasn't only thrusting, but teasing and nipping and licking and just plain wanting to feel *everything*.

His fingers brushing the small trail of hair made her quiver, and God, they needed to stop screwing around. She stepped back from the glorious kiss and took his hand out of her panties. "Now?" she asked. "Please?"

He laughed, dipped somewhat inelegantly to grab his slacks then pushed her along with his hand conveniently placed on her ass.

Finally, there was the king-size feather bed. It wasn't merely a gorgeous thing to sleep on. The plush headboard, which was actually a built-in feature of the wall, made for comfy bracing, if it should be needed. She hoped it would be needed.

"What are you grinning about?" he asked as he spun her around to face him.

"Happy. Excited. Wishing you were very much more naked than you are."

"I can do that," he said. "Here goes—if it's too much

a turnoff—well, I won't need therapy over it." He yanked his V-neck undershirt up his chest, quick, like taking off a bandage.

Rebecca was caught by the view of his slim waist, the lines of his abdominal muscles, the almost-but-not-quite-perfect four pack and the fact that he had actual hair on his chest. She swallowed at the blatant masculinity.

She, in turn, felt, well, gooey. Feminine. Small, hungry, attracted, girlie. She moved closer to him, unable to stop her fingers from touching his dark, slender line of hair that rose from just below his ribs until it spread to lightly cover his chest.

He gasped at the brush of her hand, and she watched his muscles shudder. Then he pulled the shirt off the rest of the way, revealing the scar at the top of his left shoulder. "The bullet barely missed the subclavian artery," he said. "Came in smooth, came out rough, but I was lucky. The doctor says eventually I should regain almost all my mobility."

She appreciated the heads-up. The small wound was puckered, red, shiny, but nothing horrific. Whereas his back, when he turned, wasn't nearly as neat. She exhaled hard, not from disgust but from sympathy. His skin was mottled; that same shiny red here though making it look more like a fresh burn than what it was. She raised her hand again, but paused an inch from his poor flesh.

Her gaze moved down to his thigh. That was a deep gouge, something ripped away, not like the torn and battered scarring on his shoulder. "Will it hurt?"

"To touch? No. It's mostly numb. Not a hundred percent, and sometimes something will press the wrong nerve. But you don't need to worry. That is, if you still want to—"

She leaned in then, letting her fingers brush the

strange terrain as she pressed her lips to the edge of his wound. "I'm sorry you were hurt."

"Me, too." He turned around slowly. "Onward?"

She was the one to cup his face, to ravish him with tongue and teeth and urgency.

"Well, damn." He kissed her again, once, hard, then stepped away, carefully maneuvering the waistband of his briefs over his straining cock. She couldn't look anywhere else but at his darkly flushed erection. There was moisture at the tip, his foreskin barely visible. "I'm going to start begging in a minute," he whispered.

She forced her gaze up. "We wouldn't want that."

He groaned low and loud, his cock jerking against his taut stomach. His hands went to her shoulders, gripping her firmly as he walked her to the bed. He paused before the back of her legs touched the mattress. "Okay, I can't... I love the..." He indicated her outfit with a sweeping glance up, down and up again. "That bra... Amazing. You're amazing. But it's got to go, because there isn't a thing I don't want to see. All right?"

She nodded, not able to do much more because he still held her arms.

Releasing her, he reached around and undid the bra's clasp. Then he kissed the curve of her neck with warm lips as he slipped the straps off her shoulders. The bra fell between them, floated down, touching her skin, and his, too, if his sharp hiss was anything to go by.

His gaze on her breasts, he huffed a breath before he swallowed. "Jesus. Rebecca."

She blushed again. The heat filled her cheeks and where was all her bravado and determination to be in charge of the night? She felt...shy? A little bit. Pleased, definitely. Not that she didn't want his praise, but in a moment she was going to duck her chin and twirl her hair because in all her fantasies of how things would go, she hadn't considered that she'd see him as so much more than the man on the card. She liked him, and even though there wasn't going to be a second date, she wanted him to like her in return. Not only the sex, but *her*.

She sent her panties to rest on top of her bra. The only thing he couldn't see now were her feet but that would change in a minute. He grinned, like he had in the hallway, and fell into a cloud of white down, bringing her along for the ride.

They kissed, deeper now, possessive and exploring and hungry. He sucked the very tip of her tongue, showing her how good he was with small things.

There were hands at play as well, hers brushing over his arms, his sides, down to the tapered waist and slim hips. She loved hip bones with their curves and shapes, but more than that she loved the unlimited access. She suspected he'd let her do anything, feel him anywhere. She could paint his toenails blue and he'd stay hard to the last little piggy. And if he wanted to return the favor? She'd probably quiver so much she'd have nail polish up to her ankles.

She laughed while he was teasing her lips, and he pulled slightly away. "What?"

"I'm already having the best time ever. You're…" She sighed. "You're fantastic."

The sound he made wasn't a word, but when he turned them both so she fell back on the feather bed, she gathered he liked the compliment.

"Condoms," he said. "Pocket." Then he rolled off the bed to his feet, and she got a show of his extraordinary butt as he rifled his trouser pockets.

"My," she said, when he turned around. His cock

looked exceptionally eager. It was well proportioned, longer and thicker than average, and it was straining so that with every move it tapped his belly, leaving a trail of liquid excitement behind.

She rose to her knees, unable to lay back passively when she was as eager as he was to discover the next sensation, to taste and to touch and to let herself be carried away.

He got back on the bed, ripping open the condom as he shuffled to the center, then he brought his lips so close to her ear she shivered with the warmth of his breath. "I want you to ride me. The first time. So I won't miss a thing."

Rebecca nodded. She'd thought it might be easier for him with his injuries, but that wasn't her main consideration at the moment. She wanted to watch him, as well. See the expression on his face as he entered her. "You need to put that on," she said, touching the rubber.

Jake slung another pillow where his head was likely to land, then eased the condom on his cock, hissing the whole time. As he straightened his legs, he put his hand on the base of his prick, holding it steady, and he eased back, his head canted so he would have a perfect view.

Rebecca wasn't particularly showy in bed, always a little too self-conscious, but something about Jake... Still on her parted knees, she took hold of her right nipple with her fingers. Two fingers. Her nips were hard enough that when she squeezed them, the tip poked out, swollen and dark pink.

"God damn," he said, his voice an endearing combination of breathless and raspy.

Her free hand moved slowly down her chest to her

tummy. She circled her belly button, then walked two fingers down and down until they reached her landing strip. She hadn't stopped with the nipple play, so Jake's gaze was going up and down, his lips parted as his breathing became more ragged.

He couldn't seem to help moving the hand on his cock. He stroked himself and it must have felt dangerous because the muscles in his jaw tightened and so did the tendons in his neck. Then he closed his eyes, groaning as if she were killing him dead. "Rebecca. I'm already going to embarrass myself with how fast I'm going to come. Do you really want that to happen before I'm inside you?"

She removed her hands from her body and she felt flushed with more than anticipation. She liked driving him crazy. Which was only fair. She was feeling kind of nuts herself.

"Point taken," she said. She crawled close to his body so she could kiss him one more time. It started slow and sensual, but it turned into hot and burning in seconds. "Ready?" she asked, her voice a breathy whisper.

"Dying."

She got into position, took over for his steadying hand by reaching behind and lowered herself so slowly her thighs trembled. Watching him every second.

His pupils were huge, his nostrils flared, his lips were parted and he sounded as if he'd just finished a marathon. It was fantastic.

She didn't want to look away from his face, but movement down below forced the issue. It was his muscles. Pectorals, abdominals. Clenching, trembling. Chest rising and falling like a piston, and there was a sheen of sweat that made her feel like the Vixen Queen of Planet Earth.

As much fun as it had been to watch him unravel, now all her attention had switched to her own body. Because, whoa. He wasn't lying there anymore, he was thrusting. Up. His hands had somehow gripped her hips when she wasn't looking, and he was moving her to suit himself. She didn't mind. At all.

"God, you're gorgeous," he whispered, and that was the voice she'd remember. The wobbly, wrecked croak that was just this side of recognizable speech. "Hot and wet and, Christ, when you grip me like that. Dammit... warn me next time. No, don't warn me. Do anything you want. Just make sure I haven't passed out. I don't want to miss any...ahhh."

That made her tighten like a vise and she leaned forward enough to where his cock rubbed her perfectly. She'd been so close that all it took was a slight thrust with her hips and she was coming, her head thrown back, her mouth open and gasping, keening in a pitch she didn't recognize.

When she could see again, she realized he'd come, too, and she'd wanted to watch. Dammit.

She fell sideways, sprawling, gasping away. She managed to turn her head to find him looking at her. Grinning like a very satisfied kid at Christmas. "That was..."

He nodded.

"Again?"

His eyebrows rose and he blinked at her. "I'm thirty-four, not seventeen."

"How long?"

He breathed for a while. Then grinned. "Give me half an hour. I'm feeling inspired."

"I'll order drinks."

"See if they have Red Bull."

She laughed. "I'm sure they can oblige."

Well, how was it?????

OMG, Bree! Lunch? Here? 1:30?

Ur making me wait? I HATE u!

U do not. Bring caffine & IV.

LOL. C U later.

REBECCA CLICKED OFF HER phone as she stared at her open briefcase. It felt as if she was forgetting something, but given the lack of any sensible amount of sleep, she had no chance of remembering. She shut the damn thing, aware of how much work she'd skipped in order to indulge her libido last night, then put on her coat. She'd meant to have been at the office for hours by now.

It had been worth it, though. She grabbed her purse and briefcase. There was no one in the elevator, but that would change as she headed down. It was eight-thirty already; she wanted the espresso she hadn't had time or patience to make for herself. The elevator stopped two floors down from her twenty-eighth-floor condo, and she exchanged the traditional noncommittal, no-need-to-speak smile with the man who was exceedingly proud of his Swiss watch. She had at one time known the brand, but all she could remember now was that it cost over a million bucks, and that this guy with his salt-and-pepper hair and his cashmere coat took every opportunity to flash his prize possession. It reminded her of a girl with a new engagement ring.

The elevator stopped at almost every floor, and everyone got very chummy by the time they reached the lobby. She was, of course, stuck in the back, and Mr. Swiss Watch's back was squishing her boobs. Thank goodness for the layers of coat and clothes between them because she only wanted to think about her boobs in terms of last night and Jake.

She smiled as she crossed the lobby, nodding at the concierge and the doorman before hitting the street. It was freezing even though there was no snow left on Madison Avenue.

What she should have done was immediately get in line for a cab, but what she did was cross the street, swimming with the tide of dark coats and clicking heels, to Starbucks. Inevitably there was a long line, but she was desperate.

While she waited, she took out her cell phone and called Dani, her assistant, who would be wondering where the hell Rebecca was. Dani would have called her by nine, but not before.

"You okay?" Dani asked immediately.

"Headache. Late night. Everything okay there?"

"Except for your to-do list, everything's great. Mr. Turner called, of course."

Rebecca sighed. Turner was in charge of catering at the Four Seasons. "What now?"

"Something to do with the gift baskets for the guests, but he wouldn't tell me what because I'm either a spy for another hotel or an idiot, I'm not quite sure."

"I'll call him when I get in. Do me a favor?"

"I'll start the coffee in fifteen minutes. Are you getting something to eat?"

"Yes, thanks."

"See you soon."

Rebecca tried not to yawn, which made her yawn, and then she decided, the hell with it, she was going to think about Jake. To say he'd left an impression was... well, leaving him at the crack of dawn had been ridiculously difficult.

They'd been outside, on a very public street, and still she hadn't been able to stop kissing him. She'd blamed him, of course, said it was all his fault, but it hadn't been. She'd gotten all tingly the moment her lips met his. Tingly. God, who even said that. No one, that's who.

The one very good thing he'd done was not ask for her phone number. Because that would have been stepping over the line. Last night was a one-night deal. Okay, so they'd technically had sex this morning in the shower, but that went under the rubric of one-night stand, so there was no need to get picky about it. The essence of the agreement, from both sides, had been that it was to be a singular event. Nothing more. One incredible, fantastic, amazing, toe-curling night. The end. Anything else was out of the question.

It would have been different if she was the kind of woman who regularly practiced recreational sex. She knew a lot who did, but she wasn't one of them. First of all, she had too much on her plate as it was, and second, it never worked, not really. *Sex and the City* tried to glorify it, but in the end, all that fooling around didn't amount to much.

She'd rather do without, thanks.

But goodness, if there was ever a man who appealed in a *Sex and the City* way, it was Jake. She closed her eyes as she pictured the way he'd looked at her with so much hunger she'd forgotten how to breathe. His hands on her bottom in the shower, such big hands, and such a very hard cock—

"Hey, lady, move it. Some of us got jobs to go to."

Rebecca's eyes jerked open, her face flushed with heat, even though she knew no one could tell what she'd been thinking, but her voice was firm and in control as she ordered the biggest espresso they made. And a lemon bar.

"LEAVE IT ALONE, OLD MAN."

"I didn't say a word." Mike Donnelly rolled himself out of the path of the coffeemaker.

"I'm in no mood," Jake said, filling his cup for the third time since he'd gotten up.

His father looked at his watch again. Jake knew it was noon. So he'd gone to bed the minute he'd gotten home, what of it. He wasn't missing out on a day of work. And he'd already called to reschedule his physio appointment.

"You're not gonna tell me anything? Not you had a good time, the dinner was crap, nothing?"

"The dinner was great, I had a terrific time and I'm not seeing her again, so what difference does it make?"

"Oh. What happened? She say something?" He leaned forward, his eyes wide. "You say something?"

"No. Neither of us said anything. It was the deal. That's all. It was never going to be more than the one night."

"Oh. So you work these things out ahead of time, huh? Like something in your day planner or your Black-Berry appointment book."

"I don't have a day planner or a BlackBerry. Pa, it's no big deal. It was a setup, we had a nice night. She was…great. Really great. But no more than that."

"Huh."

Jake let out a hell of a sigh. "What?" He sat down at the nook, his thigh killing him. Worth it, though. Every

ache and every pain. He'd do it again in a heartbeat.
Which wasn't an option.

"You liked her."

"I just said that, yeah."

"No. You *liked* her."

"Dad, you have guests out on the patio. Go play dominoes."

"Pete and Liam, guests? That'll be the day."

"What are you trying to tell me? I've got a headache,
and if I have to listen to you any longer, I'm gonna turn
around and go right back to bed."

"I'm not trying to tell you anything, big shot. I know
my boy, that's all."

Jake squinted at him over the rim of his mug. "Meaning?"

"Sometimes something prearranged can be rear-
ranged. That's all I'm saying."

"You been watching those soap operas again? I'm not
looking to rearrange my life."

"Okay, fine. Be that way. I'm going to have lunch
with my friends."

"Knock yourself out." Jake sipped his coffee until he
was alone in the kitchen. The stupid thing was he did
want to see her again. Ridiculous. The two of them, they
might have been great between the sheets, on top of the
sheets and in the shower, but outside of that, what did
they have in common?

Okay, except for film noir. That had been a hell of
a surprise, Rebecca loving those old black-and-white
movies. She knew a lot about them, too, and yet she
hadn't even heard of *Stranger on the Third Floor*. It was
the first film-noir thriller, and anybody who loved the
genre as much as Rebecca should have that in her collection.

And yeah, she'd been completely interested when he'd told her about the secrets of Manhattan. Lived there her whole life, never knew what was right under her feet. He'd told her a few of the places, like the whispering gallery in Grand Central Terminal and she'd barely scratched the surface of Central Park, especially the Ramble, his favorite spot.

He could hardly believe they'd spent so much time talking last night. The in-betweens had been for refueling, but for two people who'd just met, they'd gotten on like a house on fire. Maybe being naked helped. He'd like to do more of that. Not instead of the sex, because Jesus, that had been spectacular, but he hadn't connected with a woman, with anybody, like that since college.

He finished off his coffee, then got out his phone. He didn't have Kenny on speed dial, but it was close.

"Jake, my man. What's up?"

"You still doing that motorcycle messenger thing?"

"Nah, I'm designing webpages for geeks now."

"You wouldn't want to make a delivery to Midtown for, say, a fifty?"

"When?"

"Now."

Kenny turned off whatever the hell noise had been in the background. "Sure. Why not? The business is just getting started."

Jake knew "the business" was housed in Kenny's grandmother's basement, and if Kenny had a client, it was a relative or someone who owed him money. "Great. See you in ten."

5

ALL THE CAFFEINE IN THE world might have been enough to keep Rebecca from zoning out while she looked at the spreadsheet for donations to date, but she didn't have access. What she did have was about two minutes until Bree would arrive, and that would help.

Bree had already been a friend when Rebecca had decided to play matchmaker between Bree and Charlie, and now that they'd been a couple for almost a month, Bree and Rebecca had gotten even closer.

The best part of Bree was that she made Charlie so very happy. Of all the relatives, and God knew the Winslows did like to procreate, Charlie was the best of them. He was also the most notorious, being the editor in chief of *Naked New York,* a blog that virtually everyone in Manhattan depended on to find out what was happening in the city.

It was fascinating to watch the changes her cousin continued to go through during his weird courtship with Bree. He'd been an unswerving commitment-phobe, ready to die on his sword before he'd succumb to a romantic attachment. Until Bree.

Which was one of the big reasons Rebecca had decided to stop actively putting herself out there for dates. It was a very Zen decision. The universe would provide, and in the meantime she'd relax about the whole life-partner thing and enjoy herself with Jake. With men like Jake.

She sneaked yet another glance at his trading card picture, and her sleep-deprived mind went directly to the memory of riding Jake like a rodeo queen. Holy—

"Incoming."

Rebecca jerked at her assistant's voice coming over the intercom. Good. Bree had brought them lunch, including a Red Bull, which would keep Rebecca going for another couple of hours. She had to be on her game today. Every day. Last night had been a horrible lapse in judgment as far as work was concerned. Personally, she had no regrets. It had been the best blind date in her life. One of the hottest dates, period. Just thinking about him made her want to pick up the phone right this—

"Wow, you look like crap," Bree said as she crossed the office. "You must have had an incredible date."

Rebecca ignored the dig because it was completely true and concentrated on her friend. Bree was a tiny thing, maybe five feet, but she carried herself with such panache, dressed herself with so much bravado and flair, that her short stature was always a surprise.

Today she had on superskinny black jeans, four-inch black heels, a white single-button jacket, which was all well and good, but the kicker was the sizzling chartreuse satchel purse and a matching wraparound belt. The outfit was one hundred percent Bree, as was the new do. "Hey, you did stuff to your bangs."

"I did," Bree said. "Little teeny tie-dye at the edges." She put her big purse on Rebecca's desk, then dragged over the wing chair so they could share the space as they shared their lunch. "Wanna see?"

Rebecca stood up and leaned over while Bree did the same. There were at least four colors teasing at the tips, including the brilliant chartreuse, cerise, blue and white. "Fantastic. How long did that take you?"

"Forever." She pulled two Zabar's bags from her purse, a Red Bull, a Dr. Brown's cream soda and a stack of napkins. The unveiling of the meal was done sitting down. Pastrami and Swiss on rye with spicy mustard, a half-dozen dill pickles, a container of potato salad with two plastic forks and, for dessert, four chocolate rugelach.

Rebecca was tempted to start with the cookies; instead, she opened the energy drink.

"So talk to me," Bree said, taking her half of the sandwich and two pickles. "And let me see the card again."

Since the card was already next to her computer keyboard, Rebecca obliged before she grabbed her own food.

"Holy mother of pearl, this guy is so gorgeous I can't stand it." Bree looked up. "Was he even close?"

"Better," Rebecca said, and the sigh that came out after the word made Bree laugh.

"Details, woman."

"He's a cop. Was a cop. Shot, in the line of duty, if you can believe that."

"You're kidding."

"Nope. He wouldn't tell me too much about it, but he was hurt so badly he had the choice of early retirement or a desk job. He retired."

"Where?"

"To the family home, which he's remodeling for his father, who has something. Uh, wait, oh. Rheumatoid arthritis. Poor guy. Nice, though, huh, that Jake's fixing up the house?"

"I meant where was he shot?"

"Oh." Rebecca took a bite of her sandwich before moving on. She was clearly buzzed from the gobs of coffee she'd downed all morning, and now she was giving herself another big dose of caffeine. Eating was no longer optional. She couldn't be flying around the room when her two-o'clock arrived. She ate for a bit, even though she could see Bree was impatient, but finally, she said, "In the shoulder and the thigh."

"Ouch, ouch."

"I'll say. Not that he let it slow him down. Jeez Louise, he's got some stamina. And a killer body."

"Have you ever dated someone like him before?"

"What do you mean?"

Bree took a sip of her soda, then tilted her head to the right. "A blue-collar guy."

Rebecca shook her head. "It made a nice change."

"Did you talk at all?"

"Yes, we talked. What, you think I'm such a snob I can't talk to anyone without an Ivy League degree?"

"It wasn't about you being a snob. I'm wondering if there was any common ground."

Putting down her sandwich for a moment, Rebecca smiled. "We not only had a lot in common, but he was really interesting. Even without discussing his work."

"For example?"

"Films, for one."

"He likes those old black-and-white movies you're so annoying about?"

"A lot, it was— Hey!"

"Sorry to bother," Dani interrupted via the intercom. "But you've got a package."

Rebecca frowned. "It can't wait?"

"It's personal," Dani said. "And I think you're going to want to see it."

"Okay, come on back."

Not a minute later, the office door opened, and there was Dani, looking sharp in her Chanel-inspired suit, her dark hair pinned up in a very sixties chignon. More noteworthy was the vase she held, filled with what looked like a dozen white calla lilies.

Rebecca realized instantly who they were from. That sneak. She hadn't given him her cell number or her work address, although she supposed she was incredibly easy to find. What did it matter? He'd remembered.

"Wow, those are gorgeous," Bree said, as they watched Dani set the glass vase on the end of Rebecca's credenza. "Are they from him?"

"Have to be." Rebecca went around the desk to look for a card.

Dani handed her an oversized envelope. "This came with it."

Suddenly flushed, Rebecca turned just enough that she could see the beautiful flowers and keep her reaction private as she opened the package. God, it would really be embarrassing now if it turned out Jake hadn't been the one to send it, but nope, the moment she saw the DVD cover, she knew. *Stranger on the Third Floor,* starring Peter Lorre.

Jake had been surprised that she didn't own it. With a collection of film noirs like hers, she should have what he referred to as the first "true" example of the genre. The conversation had been as enthusiastic as two punch-drunk disgustingly horny people could manage, especially when one of them was fingering the other blissfully as he spoke. What shocked her even more were the flowers.

"So?" Bree asked from directly behind Rebecca. "What is it? Where did he even find calla lilies? It's still winter."

Rebecca handed her the DVD. "It's from the film," she said, pulling out the note that was still in the envelope.

"Calla lilies are featured in a Peter Lorre picture?"

"*Stage Door.* Katharine Hepburn. They're my favorite flowers."

"Ah," Bree said even as Dani said, "Wow," but Bree went on. "Ten bucks says he wants an encore."

"I'm not taking that bet," Dani said. "Who the hell is this guy?"

Rebecca opened the plain note card.

Hey, Rebecca,
How about we go crazy and try this thing one more time. Dinner? You say when and where? Jake.

His number followed. That was it. That was enough.

Bree was next to her now, and there was no way she hadn't seen Rebecca's grin or the way her cheeks must still be flushed with pink. "Oh, yeah. You owe me ten bucks," she said. "I like his style. You need to go out with him again."

Rebecca stuffed the note back in the envelope. "Not possible," she said, turning to face her friend. "We'd better finish up eating because I've got a fussy catering manager to deal with at two, and I need more sustenance. And more sugar." She went back to the desk, Bree following.

"No one's gonna tell me, huh?" Dani said. "Fine. No problem. I'm only the minion. I'll go clean the mirrors in the executive lounge or something. That'll be good."

Rebecca's first thought was to make sure Jake's trading card wasn't visible. Not because she didn't want Dani to know; their relationship was a good one, and while they didn't hang out together after work, they did their fair share of girl talk. But hot guys trading cards was like *Fight Club*. The first rule is that you don't talk about it. "He's a nice guy. A friend of a friend. Nothing serious. In fact, it's all in the past tense now."

"Those flowers seem pretty present to me," Bree said. "And a movie with Peter Lorre as The Stranger? That alone is worth at least one more round."

Rebecca took a large bite of sandwich as she sat down, purposefully ignoring the rolling eyes and shaking heads of her friends.

"Does Mr. Nothing Serious have a name at least?"

"Jake," Rebecca said, at the same time as Bree.

"Jake." Dani grinned as she went for the door. "Sounds hot."

That was the problem. He was too hot. And she had a banquet to coordinate and a foundation to run. There was a dinner at NYU she had to attend tonight, then tomorrow night she was going to have a preliminary crack at William West, her primary target for this year's new major donor at yet another fundraiser. The first night she'd even have free was Friday, and by then, if she lived that long, she'd have to pay through the nose to have her hairdresser come to her place so she could work while she was coifed.

It was impossible, that's all. Jake was a one-hit wonder. It was a damn shame, but there it was.

"WOULD YOU LIKE SOMETHING to drink? Coffee? I have some tea, I think, but I'd have to check. But coffee is already made and it's so nice of you to come over." Sally Quayle wrung her hands together. "I get so frightened, what with the news and the stories. Someone was robbed only three blocks away, did you hear? Albert Jester, he was robbed in broad daylight. Drug addicts. They're everywhere. They have no shame, no boundaries."

Jake hadn't had nearly enough sleep to be paying a house call, but he smiled as he gently herded his neighbor toward her kitchen. "Coffee would be nice, thanks. Then we can talk about security. How would that be?"

Sally pressed her hand to her chest as she nodded. "I'll fix you right up. It's freshly brewed, not even fifteen minutes ago."

"I'm sure it'll be great," he said, and he drew out a chair at the table and sat down. Everything still hurt this afternoon and he should have gone back to bed, but he'd never be able to sleep now that he'd sent the DVD to Rebecca. She would call. Why wouldn't she? Even if it was to tell him there wasn't a chance in hell, she wasn't the kind of woman to ignore him. Not after the night they'd had. Besides, she'd thank him for the flowers and the movie. At the very least.

He reached for his cell, twisting his bad shoulder in the process with a move that normally didn't hurt. He needed to make an appointment with Taye, who would read him the riot act while taking great joy in torturing Jake's poor muscles. He had to call soon, too, because lifting that new shower into place? Bending to fix the plaster and the pipes? Not gonna happen until he could move without wanting to punch a hole through a wall.

No calls. Which he already knew. He'd have heard the ring.

"Here you go, Jake." Sally put a big purple mug in front of him, then brought over a little plastic tray that had sugar and milk and a spoon. She took a seat, cradling her own mug in two slightly trembling hands. "My sister's brother-in-law says a Walther PPK pistol is the only way to go. It's what the secret agents use, and spies should know."

Jake put a couple of spoonfuls of sugar in his coffee, then added his milk, thinking about the best approach. She was scared right down to her toes, grieving a death that had happened thousands of miles away, that had to feel completely unreal, and there was no way he was going to let her get her hands on any kind of gun.

"Here's the thing about guns, Sally," he said. "Most people who own guns think they're safe…they figure they can handle anything that comes at them. So they don't bother with the extra dead bolt or the window blocks. And then, if someone does break in, because they've skipped over the houses that have obvious security, the gun owner is so scared, so terrified, either they end up shooting themselves or the perpetrator manages to take the gun from them."

"Oh, but—"

"Sally," he said, lowering his voice, making it as gentle as he could. "The very best way I know of, and remember, I've been a police officer for a long, long time, is to make sure no one ever gets into your house. Ever. We can do that, you and me. I have a friend who's an expert at putting together home security systems that are affordable, but most of all, they're reliable. What do you say we tackle this problem with the best information available, so that you can go to sleep knowing you're safe. Nothing is one hundred percent in this world, but this security system? It's got backups to the backups."

She stared at him for a long while, swallowing enough that he knew she was fighting off tears. Her husband had been a nice man. He shouldn't have died so young, left her on her own. At least she had family. And friends. Living on Howard Street, nobody was too alone, unless they made sure of it themselves, because this was a real neighborhood. As if it had been transported from another era, a time when checking up on one another was like getting groceries. Just something you did.

He took out his wallet, wincing as he moved his damn shoulder again, and brought out a card that had been sitting in there since he'd gotten out of the hospital. He pushed it across the table. "In case you feel the need to talk to someone. This guy? He's a grief counselor and he's supposed to be one of the best. He works with cops, and I've heard he also counsels spies."

Sally's smile told him she wasn't fooled by any of this. But maybe she'd make the call he hadn't been able to. "So what are window blocks?" she asked.

Jake took one last look at his phone, then put it aside as he started explaining the basics.

SHE WAS CRAZY. REBECCA WAS crazy and insane and she should have her head examined. She was also incredibly late, and Jake was going to be here in fifteen minutes, and she hadn't even showered yet.

Rebecca tossed her purse on her bed, kicked her shoes off then dashed to the bathroom, where she started the shower. In record time she'd stripped, put her hair up because there was no time and washed herself from the face down. She'd just shaved this morning, thank God. Shower off, she grabbed her towel and wrapped it around her body as she sat down at the vanity. She'd never done an elaborate job on her makeup except for special occa-

sions and it took her a minute to decide whether tonight's
encore presentation counted.

Nope. He'd clearly liked what he'd seen Tuesday
night, so she went with the regular. As she smoothed
on her blush, she went over what she had to do before
he arrived. The plan had been to make dinner together.
Homemade pasta with wild mushroom ragout, salad,
dessert, the whole nine yards.

That plan had been ditched at four this afternoon,
when the orchestra that was set to play for the donor
banquet, which was only five days away, had canceled.
The reasons were irrelevant, but her schedule, which
had included setting out everything so that the actual
cooking could be done quickly, had been replaced by
her purchase of a very excellent pappardelle with wild
mushroom sauce from Felidia in Midtown, and dessert
was now a tiramisu agli agrumi. She and Jake would
make the salad together. That could be cozy, right?

At the thought of his name, Rebecca shivered. A little
frisson that raced from her brain straight down until it
made her squeeze her legs together. It had been like that
since he'd sent the flowers. No, that wasn't true. It had
been like that since she'd sat down at the Kimberly Upstairs bar.

He was terribly distracting at the worst possible time.
Every minute her mind wasn't engaged on a specific
task, it was on Jake. His hands, the way he'd kissed
her, his ass—oh God, that butt was to die for. Unless
it was his laugh that stole her attention, or the way his
speech quickened when he was talking about the things
he loved, like secrets of New York, like films.

She had to get dressed. Now. She finished off her
makeup with a couple of swipes of mascara, then a matte

lipstick that would stay put. She bent over and shook out her oh-so-straight hair, then flipped it back and done.

Standing in front of the closet wasn't so simple. There were too many choices. Sexy with an eye toward a slower striptease? Something so low-cut the edge of her red lace bra would peek out? Skinny jeans and a loose sweater with mile-high heels?

She went with the loose-fitting but very low-cut pale gray sweater over black skinny jeans with black heels she wouldn't dare wear if she had to walk any real distance.

She had to suck it up to get the jeans zipped, but the package came together well. None of the mirror views were horrible, not even from the rear, and what was she forgetting?

Food, check. Wine. Wine! She rushed to the kitchen and got the bottle of cabernet from the rack. She uncorked it, wishing she'd thought of this before she'd showered, but she'd already planned on giving him some icy-cold vodka for the prep stage. Only one small glass, because neither of them needed to have a hangover, but she knew the vodka would be a hit.

She twirled around her kitchen, the big butcher-block island empty for the moment. Jake was probably minutes away, so she went fast.

First, though, music. A wonderful collection of movie soundtracks, themes from *Laura, Picnic, The Postman Always Rings Twice* and more. Then, the kitchen. The wooden salad bowl came out first, then the cutting board and knife. He said he was bringing everything for the salad, including the dressing. Then she got out plates, bowls, dessert plates, including two trays so they could eat and watch the movie at the same time. Wineglasses came down, and she willed the cabernet to breathe faster because the clock was ticking.

The call from the lobby stopped her halfway between the island and the fridge, where she'd meant to get out the wedge of parmigiana cheese, kicking up her heartbeat. He was here, and she was more nervous than she'd been for the blind date, more nervous than she'd been for her very first date.

She picked up the phone and told the front desk that yes, Mr. Donnelly was expected. She hung up and debated sneaking a quick shot of vodka to calm the hell down. How ridiculous. She already knew the night was going to be great. She'd do her best not to stay up too late because she had to work tomorrow even though it was a Saturday. He already knew what she looked like naked, and he probably couldn't have cared less about her decor or the food or anything but the chemistry they'd already established.

It was one more night. A bonus. That's all. Just for fun.

The bell rang, and she grabbed on to the back of the couch to steady herself before she walked over to the door.

6

Jake wiped his free hand down his jeans as he waited for Rebecca to open the door. Jesus, the building was incredible. He'd known it would be from the Madison Avenue address, but he'd had no real idea until he'd walked inside. It was a universe away from his old man's house. This was a high-rise with all the bells and whistles, and he couldn't imagine ever having enough money to live there. Only two condos per floor, for God's sake. A concierge. Museum-quality art in the lobby.

He hadn't thought about it much, her being a Winslow. She'd never known anything but luxury and extravagance. He'd met people in her tax bracket before, but they were mostly drug dealers, and there were typically a lot more automatic weapons involved. So his only frame of reference for this kind of life was the movies.

She didn't seem like someone ultrarich. Especially when she was naked and spread for him, pulling him down as she pushed herself into his thrusts.

Maybe he'd try not to greet her with a hard-on, that would be nice. Polite.

She opened the door and one look at her lost him that

battle. Christ, she was even more stunning than he remembered, and he had a great memory.

"Hey," she said, but she was grinning when she said it.

"Hey."

"Come on in."

He took a deep breath and went for it. God damn, but she was something in those heels, in that sweater. It wouldn't bother him at all if they skipped the dinner and went right to dessert.

"You can put that on the island," she said, nodding at the big grocery bag he'd brought. He was in charge of the salad, and he'd spared no expense. That thought made him chuckle as he put the bag down in a kitchen that would have looked at home on the cover of a magazine. With his hands free, he turned back to Rebecca and drew her close. "You're even more beautiful than I remember."

"It's only been three days."

"Extraordinarily more beautiful." He captured her lips in the act of smiling, knew without looking that her cheeks were flushed. She tasted clean and mint fresh, her tongue eager as they kissed as if they'd been apart for weeks.

Her hand moved to the back of his neck, her fingertips sneaking up his scalp, messing his hair and not helping the erection issue at all.

Sadly, she had on far too many clothes, and why were they making dinner when he could have brought a pizza with him? He didn't care about food, not when she was here and there was a bedroom so near.

She was the one to step back, although she paused before she did so. Her eyes were still closed as they breathed each other's breaths. It was all he could do not to close the distance, to take her mouth again and more, but this was her party. As she let go of him, a biting sharp pain shot through his shoulder.

Rebecca cleared her throat, looked over at the island and quickly back at him. "I can hang up your coat."

He obliged and while she went off to a closet in the foyer, he glanced around. The whole place was like something from *Architectural Digest*. Windows everywhere topped with white, scarlet-edged drapes that didn't block the view at all. He couldn't help stepping closer to the window past the dining room table. Spectacular. The Morgan Library was half a block away on 36th Street. When he turned his head to the right, there was the Empire State Building, its tower all lit up.

He then took in the living room. White furniture, white walls with that same brilliant red echoed in the pillows. The area rug was red and white geometric shapes that somehow made everything look cozier instead of just weird. On the wall over the couch was a giant painting, some abstract thing that was mostly deep blue. Not a drop of scarlet in it at all.

It was the kind of classy elegance he could appreciate from a distance. Up close, he had to admit it was intimidating. She was several galaxies outside of his orbit.

His gaze caught on a pair of sneakers half-hidden under a chair by the front door and he breathed easier.

"Vodka?" she asked, and he could tell she was a little nervous, too.

"Depends," he said, turning to face her. Again, it was like a body blow. A jolt made of desire and heat. "Is it the good stuff?"

"I'll let you decide," she said, opening the freezer door. She pulled out a bottle he recognized. Interestingly, it wasn't the very top of the line. Close, sure, but he had the feeling she was more concerned with liking the drink than impressing him. He hoped so.

She also took out two icy shot glasses, then a small bowl of lime wedges from the fridge. With a steady hand, she rimmed the glasses with the fruit, then poured them each a shot. He picked his up when she lifted hers, and they grinned at each other, which had become an actual thing. Between them. It wasn't something he did with many people, at least not since he'd been a kid.

He clicked her glass. "To second nights."

She nodded. "And calla lilies."

They drank and it went down smooth and cold, leaving him breathless and wanting to taste her again. "Put me to work," he said instead. The war between anticipation and action had moved from his head to his chest. She'd asked him to dinner. It wasn't the same thing as asking him to bed. "I'm good with a knife as long as there's enough room. Not so hot with measuring these days, but I can mix stuff."

"Confession time," she said. "We were going to make pasta. From scratch."

"You do that?"

"When I have time. Which I didn't tonight. So you're going to make me salad while I heat up the rest of dinner. If anyone gets to be the helper, it'll be me."

"It sounds like you've had a hell of a day. I'm decent with a microwave and takeout, unless there's something special about what you brought?"

She smiled at him as she shook her head. "Not a thing." Then she went to the fridge and brought out three different take-out containers. One was filled with pasta, one had a dark mushroom sauce and one she didn't open.

He located everything he'd need, particularly the wine, which he poured. He handed her a glass. "Sit down, relax, watch me tear lettuce to shreds. I like the music, by the way."

She inhaled deeply, let it out slowly, but rather than moving to the chair at the end of the island, she leaned in and kissed him. "Thank you. Work has been brutal."

When Rebecca turned, he could see a hint of red at the edge of the low-cut neckline. Like the edges of the curtains, the pillows on the couch. He was going to enjoy peeling away her layers.

He brought out his salad kit. Not that it was anything so studied or interesting. Four kinds of lettuce because according to his old friend Sal's mother only savages ate a salad with only romaine. Green onions were next, red peppers, cherry tomatoes, green olives, black olives and finally fresh basil from Sal's mother's kitchen window. Then came the grapeseed oil and balsamic vinegar he'd mixed up ahead of time, and finally, a lemon. He washed his hands, dried them on an incredibly soft kitchen towel, then went to work tearing lettuce as he stared at the gorgeous woman with the bared shoulder.

The sight was enough to make him thankful he hadn't picked up a knife yet. Her sweater had fallen to reveal one red bra strap across pale, perfect skin. Her legs in those tight black jeans were spread, one of her hands resting on the edge of her chair between her thighs. She raised a glass of dark wine to her lips and drank. When he was able to wrest his gaze from her lips, he found her staring at him, her pupils dark behind the fringe of bangs and eyelashes.

"How's the wine?" he asked, amazed his voice didn't break and that he'd said actual words.

"Good," she said. "Not as good as watching you man-handle that lettuce."

"The lettuce had it coming." He tore the last of the radicchio and picked up the escarole. "It must be demanding, running such a large foundation."

"It can be," she said, nodding as if the mere mention had reminded her again how exhausted she was. "Especially this week. I have no business doing this tonight."

"Why not? A girl's gotta eat."

She half smiled. "If that's all we're going to do tonight, then I think we need to have a talk."

"No, that's not all. But maybe we should postpone the movie."

She stilled, blinked at him.

Her reaction brought it home, what he'd suggested. This wasn't supposed to continue. Tonight was a one-off, a thank-you, he imagined, for the flowers and the DVD. "Or not."

She swallowed, even though she hadn't had any more wine. "No, that's a nice idea. The movie would be better if it happened after Wednesday night. After Thursday night, honestly, so I can finally get a decent night's sleep."

"What happens on Wednesday?"

"Big dinner. Huge dinner. It's where I flatter the hell out of our regular donors and woo the potentials. This year there's one very big fish I'm determined to land. He seems interested, but he's also playing coy. Teasing me along. But it'll be worth it. His contribution would end up in the tens of millions over the length of the endowment. That's game-changing money. That's schools and loans and medicine and lives saved. So many lives."

"No wonder you're exhausted. That's got to be a lot of pressure."

"Some things are worth it."

"I've always thought so."

"Hell, you were willing to put your life on the line. Talk about pressure."

He looked around the kitchen until he found the big chef's knife, then turned back to his salad and Rebecca. "Different kind, but yeah. Pressure was part of it. Not as much as deciding who gets what resources. That's tough. For everyone who gets, there are probably dozens, hundreds who don't."

She shifted on her chair, although thankfully she didn't adjust her sweater. He had to be careful because of the knife, but every chance he could, he'd look at that red strap, then her face. Holy shit.

"I don't have to make all those decisions," she said. "We have a board of directors. My job is to first make sure we're always refreshing our coffers and then to narrow down the choices of how we want to spend the money. So many need so much, it's not easy."

"I'll bet. I imagine you take into account what other groups are doing, try to spread the wealth?"

She nodded. "It's a triage system. Short- and long-term goals. Maximum benefit for the greatest number of people, things that hopefully turn out to be more than quick fixes. But I'd rather hear about your house and your father. You're doing a complete remodel?"

He grinned, thinking about what his dad would say walking into this joint. "Nope, just giving him living space on the ground floor. He has trouble with the stairs."

"You do a lot of that DIY stuff?"

"Nope. Learning as I go. Turns out the internet is a pretty useful thing. And DVDs. Lots of how-to DVDs." He finished the last of the chopping, put the salad together except for the dressing. He opened the containers of food, dividing the pasta and sauce between the two big plates.

Her hand on his shoulder made him jump. How had he not heard those heels click? Jesus, how rapidly his self-preservation instincts were devolving.

"I'll get this part," she said, so close to him that he felt the heat of her breath on his jaw.

Fast as that, he was all about Rebecca. The dinner could vanish for all he cared because her hand was still warm on his shoulder and her hip was pressing against him. He had his arms around her before he finished turning, his mouth on hers a second later.

Tasting her was better than anything on the menu. It was intimate and slow, their kiss, and maybe because he knew they were going to stop, that he wasn't going to drag her to the bedroom right this second, he paid attention to what was happening here, what he had.

She tasted like Rebecca. Jesus, how it compressed his chest to realize he knew that taste, could have picked her out of a crowd blindfolded. And while there were a dozen different places he wanted to memorize with his tongue, for now he slicked and slid against her in a slow back-and-forth, deep and shallow. Everything was what he wanted of this small, amazing part of her. Lips, tongue, teeth, breath, heat, wet.

He'd pushed his hips against her and it was the shock wave that brought him back to the room, to dinner. He pulled away, but only because he knew he would have her again soon.

SOMEHOW, REBECCA MANAGED to slow her heartbeat and stop her shaking long enough to heat up the entrée. Jake's salad was fantastic, and she ate more of that than the pasta. He did the reverse, so that worked out. The bottle of wine was almost finished and dessert waited, but Rebecca wasn't terribly interested in dessert.

"I could make coffee," he said. "There's that last box out on the counter."

She put down her wineglass and stood. "That's tiramisu, if you want some. Or we could just go back to my bedroom."

He looked up at her, and she almost laughed at the way his entire expression said there was no contest. "Where's the bedroom?" he asked, taking her hand in his, bringing it to his lips, where he kissed her palm.

"A hundred miles away."

He rose, pulled her into his body. "The couch isn't."

She shook her head, letting her lips brush his as she did. "Want you in my bed."

"Take me there."

It wasn't easy, letting go of him. So she didn't. She just slid her fingers into the waistband of his jeans and tugged him along, moving faster with each step and each thought of what came next.

The moment she crossed the threshold of her bedroom, her shoes were history. He was pulling up her sweater before she could get her hand out of his pants. They each worked on unbuttoning and unzipping, but he won the race by a mile. And then he tugged down, hard, pulling her jeans and her panties down to her knees.

"Oh, God," he said, and he ran his hands up the front of her thighs.

"Wait, wait. Do your shirt. I can't—"

"I don't care about my shirt. We have to get rid of your pants."

"I'm trying!"

"You suck at it." He batted her fumbling fingers away,

and they concentrated on divesting themselves of their own clothes. She shed her pants; his shirt had disappeared by the time she looked up, but when she reached behind her back to undo the clasp of her bra, he said, "Wait. Don't. Stop."

"Don't stop? Or Don't. Stop?"

"Leave it on." Then his trousers and boxer briefs hit the floor; his cock was as perfectly hard as she remembered. He whipped off his undershirt so swiftly he couldn't hide the wince as he stressed his shoulder.

He pressed up against her, his ability to control his hips apparently gone with his clothes, which she found extremely sexy.

After a kiss that nearly missed her mouth completely, he was pushing her backward toward the bed. "Sit," he said.

She did, wondering what he was up to.

It turned out he was going down on his knees. She worried for a moment, but he didn't seem to be in any pain, although she doubted he could kneel long. Then he had his hands on her knees, spreading her wide.

"Watch me," he said. His voice was unraveling. How much did she love that?"

He kept his gaze on hers as he bent forward. Her bed was high, and she had a nice view of the moment Jake switched his attention from her face to his new objective. Beginning with his lips on her inner thigh. Lips and tongue, a wicked combination. Hands and fingers, too, so that there was sensation all along the pathway to her pussy.

She wanted to press her legs together, but she couldn't, so she squeezed what was available. Jake must have noticed because he moaned low and long as he picked up the pace.

Finally, his hot breath painted her labia, and then, softly, he licked her from the bottom of her cleft to the top.

JAKE LOST HIMSELF IN THE taste of her, in the salt on his tongue, in the scent. His fingers spread her open, and he went to town. It was gorgeous, and she was amazing, and he'd loved every second of what she tasted like and the sounds she made when he pointed his tongue and fucked her with it.

Her hand was in his hair, and when he hit pay dirt, she let him know. His thigh hurt, but it was so worth it. The sad part was that he couldn't just move in, stay for the night. His cock was insistent, but his wound wouldn't leave him be, so he kept his tongue hard and pointed and worked fast on her full, hard clit.

That brought her other hand into his hair, and if he was half-bald at the end of this, well, hair grew back.

Her thighs pressed against his ears as her moans got louder, and when she started chanting his name, he went into fifth gear.

It was a race to see if he would suffocate or she would come first.

He lived.

It was a damn good thing she had the condom at the ready, because about one minute later, he was on the bed. He'd flipped her over so she was on her hands and knees, and he went to heaven as he thrust inside her.

She dropped to her elbows, her head on her pillow, and he'd never seen anything so erotic in his life. So proper on the outside, so cool and collected. In here, with him, wanton, abandoned and the sexiest thing alive. But dammit, he was going to come too fast. It's what she did to him.

He gripped her too tightly, his cock pistoned hard, hard, and he was swearing in his head because he couldn't even speak.

He meant to turn her over, to look her in the eyes, maybe kiss her as they came, but that would have to happen later because Rebecca stole a lot more than his composure. He came as if he'd never done it before, as if he'd do anything to be with her again.

7

THE ALARM WENT OFF AT the unholy hour of five, purposefully shrill. Rebecca threw her arm over to stop the beeping, but there was no way Jake could have slept through that. No one in a three-mile radius could have.

"That was…" Jake didn't finish the sentence.

"It's the only thing that gets me up. I just sleep through music or anything that doesn't make me want to rip out my ears."

"Next time, we're doing this on a weekend you don't have to work."

She turned over, kicking the duvet into something less restricting. They'd certainly been energetic last night. Despite her tiredness. At least they'd gotten five hours of sleep. "Next time?"

He turned to her, and while the draw was there, as urgent as it had been every time she got a look at him, they both played by morning-breath rules. "I keep doing that, don't I?"

She nodded. "Evidently, I don't mind."

"Excellent."

"I'm going to take a lot longer than you in the bathroom," she said. "Feel free to shower. There's a fresh toothbrush in the drawer under the rolled-up towels."

"I was kind of hoping for an in-home demo."

She brushed the back of her fingers across his cheekbone. "That would be a terribly risky thing to do."

"We're modern-day warriors," he said. "I have every faith."

Her laughter made her cover her mouth and start the day off better than she could have hoped. "Not when it comes to resisting you."

He hummed happily and planted his forehead against her chest above her breasts. His hand started petting her, long slow strokes that made what she had to do next very difficult.

"You have to get out of my bed."

"Harsh," he said, his sleep-roughened voice muffled.

"Vigilance is my only hope."

He sniffed. Moved himself back to the safe side of the bed. "Fine. I'll get out of your bed. I'll use your new toothbrush. But just know that I plan to make you a great omelet for when you've finished getting ready."

She laughed again. "Is that your idea of a threat?"

"Yeah, it's pretty weak. But it's all I've got. Too damn early in the morning." He threw back the covers and stood, his body still gorgeous, but she could see that some parts moved quicker than others. How much did those wounds hurt him every single day? She wished there was more to be done.

His cock certainly hadn't been affected. He was halfhard, and she knew it wouldn't take much to get him to attention. But work wasn't going anywhere. The thought of all she had to do today made her moan.

He walked to the end of the bed and collected his

clothes from the settee. "Anything you don't like in an omelet?"

She shook her head. "Everything in my fridge is fair game. Whatever you make will be wonderful. Oh, and the coffee should be ready in about five minutes."

He grinned and that quiver came back to her tummy. As she watched his butt while he walked to the bathroom, she wondered if she was being a complete idiot about all this. Letting him make her breakfast. Implying there'd be a next time. She was always careful about making friends too quickly, letting herself get too close. But kicking him out of her bed was hard enough. She just wasn't ready to kick him out of her life.

JAKE TOOK THE SUBWAY BACK to Brooklyn. It wasn't that crowded early on a Saturday morning so he was able to stretch out his leg. Of course, he did what he always did: scoped out the exits, every passenger who was in his car. Looked for signs of inebriation, of dilated pupils, of anything hinky. Then a sweep of the clothes, the hoodies in particular, the jeans. Possible weapon or cell phone? A loner paying too much attention to another passenger? It wasn't something he planned, it was the way he was. It didn't matter that he didn't have the badge, his brain had wired itself to the job. He never sat with his back to a wall, he always knew where the exits were, he was conscious of body language and facial ticks. A lot of good it did him now. Not only was he stuck with permanent injuries, he could also look forward to a lifetime of paranoia.

He was gonna have to get a little more serious about therapy if he wanted to keep up with Rebecca. And not just physical therapy.

He shook his head at his foolishness. Truth was, he

was playing with fire. Walking into that building last night had shown him everything he needed to know about him and Rebecca. Yeah, it was all fun and games and getting naked, but they'd also done a lot of other stuff. Stuff that didn't come with the normal one-night-stand package. Talked, for one thing. Talked a lot. Laughed. He'd cooked for her. She'd…opened wine.

He stared at the dark tunnel outside the subway window, everything speeding by. He would go home today, keep working on the downstairs bathroom. Listen to a ton of bad cop jokes. Watch his old man struggle to hold his fork, his mug, a domino. And parts of his body would burn angry at how he'd moved and strained and pushed too hard. But the other parts, the center of him, was glad he'd wrecked himself with Rebecca Thorpe, even if it never occurred to her that he might feel uncomfortable in a bed that cost more than he'd make in a year. Past tense. Made in a year.

Now, shit, disability. There was the house, eventually, but not for a long time, please God. And he had some savings. But he couldn't take her out to the type of places she was used to. Meals at some of those joints ran to the thousands. He could barely imagine what food could be worth that. Even with wine.

She was used to dealing in billions, he was looking for bargains at Greschlers' Hardware. He understood the part where they were naked, the sweaty part. He was having trouble with the talking. With liking her the way he did.

He rocked to the side at the curve, then settled. Being an undercover cop, being in with people who'd shoot him if he so much as looked at them funny, he'd learned to read people. It was survival, and it didn't go away once he was off the job. Rebecca liked him. She was comfortable with him, and she wanted him to like her back.

The women he'd been involved with, they were all
people whose lives he understood. If they weren't from
his neighborhood, they were from one just like it. Pizza
from the corner was a fine meal, getting together for
some green beer and corned beef on St. Paddy's Day,
watching Notre Dame at the corner bar. That's what he
knew. Not that he was embarrassed by his home or his
life, not at all. But it had given him his perspective. His
frame of reference.

Rebecca didn't fit outside of the bedroom. No two
ways about it. He didn't understand her motives, and
that could be a problem. Motives were important.

Hell, he barely understood why he was pushing this
thing, asking for more when it should have ended. He
might have come from a long line of cops, but he wasn't
just some mook who didn't understand what was what.
Until her. Until Madison Avenue and fucking wild mushroom ragout, for Christ's sake. What were they trying to
prove? Was he her good deed for the year? Her attempt
to get to know the little people? Was she his last-ditch
attempt to prove he was still all man and not just an unemployed cripple?

The train slowed, and he looked up, saw he had four
stops to go. But he watched the doors as they opened,
scanned the small groups of people as they entered,
chose seats. A couple of gangbangers sat front and center, so Jake would keep his wits about him, but he didn't
expect anything to happen. Except a train ride back to
his real life.

He'd think about her, no question there. And he'd see
her again, if he could figure out how to meet on neu-
tral territory. Not his place, because jeez, the old man?
Pete? Liam? They'd trip all over themselves trying to
impress her. But he didn't feel right about going back to

her place. Wouldn't, until he figured some things out. Like why he was already counting the minutes until he could be with her again.

REBECCA CLICKED THE TEXT function on her cell phone, clicked again on Bree's name and typed:

Donate my body to science

Not five seconds later, Bree responded:

Don't tell me you're still wrking

I will never not be wrking Bree. NEVER!

It'll get better. Tell me re BLUE EYES. Was 2nd as good as 1st?

He made me salad. Omelet this am. Yum. In every sense of the word.

Rebecca leaned back in her chair as she eyed the report spread out on her desk. She'd paused the demo that was currently on her screen and tried to get through the first page of the report three times, but she kept losing the thread. Thank God, the beep that told her Bree had texted her back saved her.

OMG. I can't stand it. U HAVE to invite him!

To what?

The donor dinner. Duh.

Rebecca blinked at the text, the message not fully computing for a full minute. She wasn't going to invite Jake to the donor dinner. He'd feel horribly out of place. Although she would certainly prefer sitting next to him rather than her cousin Reggie, not so affectionately known as Peckerhead, at least by Rebecca and Charlie. She took a sip of coffee before she set to typing again.

I can't invite him. Awkward.

For who?

Him!

Really? CW

Hey, who let you into this convo?

Sorry, he read over my shoulder. Stole my phone. I've slugged him.

Charlie, go away.

Is he a porn star? A gigolo? Missing teeth, perhaps? CW

Bite me.

Rebecca started typing instantly, before Charlie could get a text in edgewise.

It's not his kind of thing.

Says U. Ask.

Yeah, ask. I'm still betting missing teeth. Front uppers. CW

If I'd wanted a pain in the ass relative, I'd have had a brother. I have to go back to work.

Think about it. CW

Rebecca got out of her text screen and put her phone in her right-hand drawer. She glanced at the report, but didn't linger. Her mind was far too occupied by the notion of inviting Jake to the banquet. The idea had grown roots during that brief, weird conversation. Not all of them pleasant.

Jake in a tuxedo? That she could deal with. In fact, she wanted to see that very, very badly. Something tailored, fitting those broad shoulders and tapering to his waist. Black, almost traditional, but perhaps a hint of cerulean blue in his cuff links? It would have to be subtle, not even his pocket kerchief, a mere spot of blue. Maybe Burberry or Tom Ford, definitely single button and razor-sharp lapels.

She realized she was smiling when she reached for her coffee, but the grin faded quickly. What would an ex-policeman from Brooklyn do with a Tom Ford tux? The people she was hosting, these were men and women used to every luxury the world had to offer, and the most casual among them knew who was and wasn't one of them.

She'd grown up among the highest of the classes, and as much as their excesses bothered her, she had to be careful lest she not include herself. Just because she made it her mission to spread the wealth of the Winslow Foundation to a much broader and less-fashionable base, she didn't exactly live an ascetic's life. Her home was worth over three million dollars and that was just the space. She considered it a long-term investment, a clever buy at a time when the economy had taken a dive. But it was also what she was accustomed to.

She'd never lived in a building without a doorman. Never *had* to work. Her salary at the foundation was put right back into play as a donation, partly for the tax benefits, mostly to compensate for the guilt. It was convenient to think she was being generous when in truth, she could live extraordinarily well for the rest of her life on her trust fund. As it was, she barely touched the principal.

Her cup was almost empty, and she walked to the private lounge in a daze of sleep deprivation and hazy discomfort. Bree had come into her life, and therefore into Charlie's life, as a result of another pang of elitism. Rebecca had been invited to the lunch exchange by a professor she knew from NYU who no longer belonged to the group. They'd originally met in the park. Rebecca had never told Grace her last name, although she was fairly certain the English prof had recognized her. Grace had probably thought she was offering a chance for humility. Looking back, Rebecca agreed that she had.

Bree never spoke about it, about the disparity between their lifestyles. Rebecca imagined she and Charlie had talked. Knew they had, because he'd been so very famous as the creator and editor in chief of *Naked New York*. He was a celebrity in his own right, one who had used his wealth and influence to build his singular empire, one that had shouted clearly and loudly that he wasn't one of "those" Winslows.

As she poured a fresh cup of coffee, she thought about herself and Charlie, how they'd been so close growing up. Uncomfortable with the trappings of their heritage, but not enough to walk away, not completely. In Charlie's case, he'd replicated the success and influence, but in his own style. In hers, she'd decided to use her power for good. Going to law school had been hard, but worth it, as had learning everything she could about running a foundation and fundraising. Her sacrifices were tiny. Miniscule. Complaining about any of it unforgivable.

Which brought her in a roundabout way back to Jake and the question of his invitation. Once at her desk, she took out her purse and pulled out his trading card. God, he was ridiculously handsome, but his looks weren't what attracted her most now that she knew him. Maybe Charlie and Bree had been right to question her easy dismissal. Because it had been a knee-jerk reaction, that immediate no. Not, she realized, out of the goodness of her heart and concern for Jake.

She was honestly too tired to be having an existential crisis about her entire life. In another hour, she'd leave, go straight home to her mansion in the sky and put herself to bed. Tomorrow, when her brain wasn't packed with cotton, she'd think again.

"Okay, hit me," Jake said, taking a deep breath and letting his aggravation at being walkie-talkied to death wash over him like a passing breeze.

"What did the cop say to his belly button?"

"I don't know, Dad. What did the cop say to his belly button?"

"You're under a vest!"

Jake shook his head as he listened to the laughter coming from the front porch. After thirty or so seconds, he figured his old man was finished for the moment, and he could release the button. At least this joke hadn't made him groan. And where the hell they kept coming up with the vile things, Jake had no idea. He'd have guessed the internet, but not a one of them had a computer, or a cell phone with Wi-Fi. As for listening to anyone long enough to learn how to turn any internet-related device on, forgetaboutit. Stubborn old goats.

But, what the hell. He was something of a Luddite himself when it came right down to it. His needs were simple; he didn't have to have every new gadget that came down the pike. His laptop wasn't new, but it let him watch DVDs, get the scores, read the headlines and, from time to time, he'd even streamed a feature film. The screen was too small to make a habit of that last one, but it had come in handy when he'd been recuperating. Walking had been a real pain for quite some time, but as long as he had the laptop close, he didn't die of boredom. He was especially grateful for online books. They'd gotten him through some tough days.

Now, though, he wished like hell he'd never started this remodeling job. Putting up tile had to be the most tedious job in the world. It had all looked simple on paper but, as he couldn't escape learning, there was a great difference between remodeling and remodeling well. The bane of his existence wasn't the repetitive motions or the heavy lifting, even though those aggravated his wounds, it was the level. He could never tell when that water bubble was straight. He'd even sprung for one with a laser, and he still had trouble.

It made him long for the days of hiding in plain sight, hanging with drug dealers and fearing every breath would be his last.

The dreaded beep from the walkie-talkie interrupted his self-pity and he clicked on the button. "Got another one so soon?"

"Nope. Not quite."

It was Liam. Liam, who hardly ever used the walkie-talkie.

"We could use some help down here."

"What's wrong?" Jake dropped the trowel onto the tarp at his feet and hurried down the hallway, his senses on overdrive. He ignored the burn in his thigh as he raced through the living room to the front door. Throwing the door open, he saw the problem, and he had to stop himself from just lunging to his father, who was sprawled awkwardly on the sidewalk directly in front of the stairs that led up to the porch. He hadn't made the turn. It had happened once before, and Jake had promised to extend the porch but his dad had refused, insisted they would just move the damn card table they played on, move it back so he had more room.

"He's okay," Pete said. "I caught the chair before it hit his head."

Jake didn't see any blood. Liam was bent over, holding Mike's head in his big pale hands.

"I'm fine. Don't panic." Mike waved his crooked hand at Jake as if he was being a bother, and the way he glared at Liam it was clear the old moron hadn't wanted Jake to know.

Jake got down the steps faster than he had in weeks and squatted by his dad. "Anything hurt?"

"Yeah, my ego. Stupid ass wheelchair. I need to get me one of those sporty ones, the kind they race with."

"Yeah, that's exactly what you need." He put his arm behind his father's shoulders, the right arm because there was no way to use his left, not for this, not when a failure would matter so much. Screw it if the whole shower broke into a million pieces. Not this.

Liam helped, and together, they made one reasonably strong person able to lift Mike to his feet. The terrible claw of his hand grabbed on to Jake's upper arm, and while it hurt him, it had to be fiercely painful for his father.

"Come on. Let's get you in the chair you've got. See if it still works."

His dad nodded and took one unsteady step while Jake looked at him with every ounce of his attention. He didn't seem to be favoring anything more than usual, and he wasn't bleeding that Jake could see. But he'd still make an appointment with the doctor, get Mike checked over. So far, none of his spills had done anything too damaging, but it scared Jake to the bone each time it happened.

Whatever his own future held, it would include full-time care for his father. Maybe that would be Jake's job, and maybe it would last until he grew too old to get upstairs himself, but that was okay. He'd have plenty of breaks and time for himself, because they lived on Howard Street, in Windsor Terrace, and they were surrounded by a community who gave a shit when it counted.

Pete brought the wheelchair down the ramp, but not right up to Mike, which was good because Jake needed to watch him for a few more steps. Then they pushed him up. Pete and Liam did. The bastards slipped themselves into place, not giving Jake an option.

He could have made it up the ramp, goddammit, but it would have been a strain. He wasn't the man he used to be, not when it came to ramps or doing the job he was born to do or making love to a beautiful woman. He was a different Jake now, but the reality and his self-perception were still at war. Time, his physiotherapist had said. He had to give it time—

His cell rang, and as he limped up the steps after the old men, he put it to his ear. "Hello."

"Jake."

He paused, one foot on the porch. He felt a rush of heat down his back, settling low. "Rebecca."

"This is completely rude and please feel absolutely free to say no, but I'm actually in Brooklyn. Not far from your place, and I was wondering if you'd mind if I dropped by."

Every bit of his cop's instinct said it was a bad idea. Jake himself looked like a poor excuse for a day laborer. His father seemed to be okay now, but he'd be in a lot of discomfort and there was every possibility that seeing Rebecca Winslow Thorpe show up on his doorstep would be the final straw that did him in, and the house looked like shit. Not to mention Pete and Liam were about as tactful as three-year-olds. "Sure," he said, and with one word, he was doomed. "You know the address?"

"Well, yes. I know, creepy, but Google."

"It's okay. Come on over. Just be aware, you're gonna get what you get."

"That's all I want," she said. "I can be there in ten. Unless… I'm standing not five feet from Luigi's Pizza, which seems to be popular, given the crowd. I could bring one? Maybe some beer?"

Jake shook his head, more at the weird way this day was going than her offer. It was almost five, and he hadn't given a thought to dinner, knowing he'd either scrounge or they'd have something delivered. Rebecca didn't need to come with food, but as surreal as it was that she had called at all, it was also pretty brave, and she'd probably feel more comfortable if she came bearing gifts. "That'd be great, except there's four of us. My old man, his buddies, me. So how about you tell Gio behind the counter that the Donnellys need a couple pies and he can put it on our tab. Tell him to deliver 'cause it's gonna take him a little while if I know Sunday night at Luigi's. I got the beer covered, but if you want anything fancier than that, you're on your own."

She laughed. "I'll see you soon."

He clicked off, stared at his phone for a minute before he put it in his pocket. This was not his life.

8

REBECCA HAD ARRIVED IN picturesque Windsor Terrace, Brooklyn, at four-fifteen. Delivered by cab to what she guessed was the middle of town. It was certainly a busy street. Lots of people walking, businesses booming. Well, that was an exaggeration, if you didn't count Luigi's and the nearby bar.

But there were people on the streets moving at a pace that wasn't close to the speed of Manhattan, and there were families with strollers, dogs on leashes, dogs off leashes. Groups of teenagers, a startling number of whom were accessorized with not only tattoos, although those were plentiful, but metal. Industrial-looking rings embedded in earlobes, some stretching the skin so much it made her cringe. She couldn't help thinking of the long-term effects, but then that must be either a sign of her age, or that she was even more rigid and conservative than she'd thought.

The likelihood of her reaction coming from her class bias was mostly the reason she'd come to Brooklyn in the first place. After a long overdue excellent night's sleep, she'd continued to be bothered by the idea that she hadn't even considered asking Jake to be her date for the banquet.

After she'd run through all the reasonable issues—the fact that they didn't know each other that well outside of the bedroom, that they weren't technically dating and that he'd probably be bored out of his mind even if he did agree to go—she'd been left with a giant bundle of uncomfortable doubt. She honestly had no idea if she'd discounted him because she was being thoughtful or prejudiced.

It had taken her over an hour of walking up and down the big street to finally give in and call him, even though she was still confused and unsure. She could be calling him out of liberal guilt. She could be wanting him there because she liked him. What if it was both? What then?

No answers yet, but the deciding factor had been the pleasure she felt when she thought about him sitting next to her. Being able to look into his amazing blue eyes when she felt overwhelmed.

It was a novel sensation, liking him the way she did. Normally her turn-ons were more cerebral and practical. She liked brains, business acumen, elegance, good taste and a liberal bent. A sense of humor was a non-negotiable must-have, although difficult to find in combination with the rest of her requirements.

Jake was clever and he had a broad scope of interests. He made her laugh. She had no idea about the rest and hadn't cared that she hadn't known. Because he was for sex. Only, that wasn't how it was turning out.

She had arrived at the corner of Howard Street. One left turn, a few blocks, and she'd be there, at Jake's home. She'd meet his father. See the work Jake was doing on the house. There would be no sex involved. And while she was pretty sure she was going to ask him to be her date Wednesday night, she was leaving that option open.

The pizzas would arrive in the next ten or so minutes, according to Gio, who turned out to be the owner, so she should get a move on and stop stalling. Turning left, she looked at the row houses lining the wide street. The homes were virtually identical except for the front porches, which were wide and uniquely decorated, mostly with furniture that wouldn't be damaged by snow yet could be heavily used in more temperate months. She liked them, each of them, some with religious statues, some with art that gave a great deal away about the owners. The big old front porches were unheard of in Manhattan and she wondered what it would be like to grow up in a place like this.

The whole neighborhood felt as if it was from another era, and from what little she'd read about it in her Google searches, that was the point. The folks who lived here protected the ambience, and while they couldn't slow the gentrification of the main thoroughfares, they could maintain the residential streets in their old-fashioned glory.

She was nearing his place, and she hesitated again, her hands buried in the deep pockets of her thick wool coat, her boots clicking on the bumpy sidewalk and her nervous heart signaling her flight-or-fight response.

There were men on the porch, sitting at a card table. Old men, gray-headed and wrinkled, laughing at something. They weren't looking for her or even glancing in her direction. Jake hadn't told them? Okay. Fair enough, he knew the players.

She wasn't naive enough to think these men wouldn't know who she was. They would also have opinions about her family, and she would bet those opinions weren't favorable. The Winslows were not well-known for their charity and kindness despite the foundation.

She took another few steps and the laughing dimmed. The one with the most hair, the one facing her, had grown quiet. Seconds later, the two other men turned, making no effort whatsoever to hide their blatant curiosity.

She doubted they'd arrived at the Winslow part yet, but they would certainly know she was an outsider. "Hello," she said, smiling as she reached the front steps of the row house. "I'm here to see Jake."

"You are, huh?" The man who spoke was Jake's father. The one who'd spotted her first. This close, she could see he was in a wheelchair, see his gnarled hands. His accent, even with three small words, was epic.

"Yes, sir. He's expecting me."

"Then you'd better come on up," he said.

At the top of the steps, the appeal of the porch was made vividly clear. The large space heater did a terrific job of keeping out the bitter chill. She imagined only big storms would keep these troopers indoors. The card table was strewn with dominoes and coffee mugs, a couple of pens and a pad of paper. There were walkie-talkies, not cell phones, in front of each man, which must be their intercom system, a way to get Jake outside pronto.

The man sitting next to Jake's father raised his walkie-talkie to his mouth. "Jake."

"Yeah, Pete?" came the reply a few seconds later.

"Your friend is here."

"I'll be right out."

God, how they were staring. She felt a blush on her cheeks that made her even warmer. "I'm Rebecca

Thorpe," she said. "I was in the neighborhood, and Jake said it was all right if I came by."

"You come to this neighborhood often?" This from the biggest of the three, the one who had to twist around to see her. He had phenomenally bushy eyebrows.

"No. Never before today. It's a great street."

"We like it," Jake's father said, and it looked as if he was about to say more when the front door opened.

Jake wore jeans and a plaid flannel shirt, both looking as if they'd been with him a long time. She closed her hand into a fist to fight the urge to touch him, even though he was standing all the way across the porch. The tool belt hanging on his hips seemed a little newer than his clothes and the ensemble was surprisingly sexy. She couldn't hold back her grin, and neither, it seemed, could he. "You found it."

"I did."

"Gio give you any trouble?"

"Nope. But he also wouldn't tell me what kind of pizzas he was sending. I hope I didn't just get two pineapple and ham pies because that would be—"

"A travesty," he said, interrupting. "No. No pineapples have ever touched a pizza in this house."

"Okay, then. I guess I'll stay for a bit."

"Good."

Jake's father coughed. Loudly, and completely fake.

His son startled at the sound, as if he'd forgotten the old men were there. "Everybody, this is Rebecca. Thorpe."

"We know," his dad said.

"Ah. Recognized her, huh?"

"No, she had the manners God gave a child of five and introduced herself."

Jake, in the manner of kids from every walk of life,

rolled his eyes. "Rebecca, I'd like you to meet my father, Mike Donnelly, the emperor of Howard Street. To his left is family friend and classic car enthusiast Pete Baskin. The third gentleman is also an old family friend, Liam O'Hara. If you need any information about any of the *Die Hard* movies, he's your man."

"It's lovely to meet all of you, and I hope I haven't disturbed your game too much."

"Liam's cheating, anyway," Pete said at the exact same time Mike said, "Pete's cheating."

No one but Rebecca seemed to be surprised, but it made her laugh.

"Who's up for something to drink?" Jake asked. "The pizza should be arriving any minute."

Pete and Liam wanted beer, Mike coffee.

Jake held out his arm, inviting Rebecca into the house.

"Don't you hide her away in there, Jakey. We'll be wanting to talk to this beautiful young lady."

"Yes, Dad. I promise not to let her make a clean getaway."

"Hey, Rebecca," Pete said. "How many cops does it take to throw a man down the stairs?"

Jake groaned as all three men at the table smiled broadly, their wrinkles framing their grins like theater curtains.

"I don't know. How many?"

Pete laughed even before he said, "None. He fell."

The old men laughed. Hard. Full of wheezes and a couple of hiccups, it was impossible not to laugh with them. When she got a load of Jake's grimace, it all became funnier.

As she passed Jake and entered the house there was

no doubt she was not a native of this strange land, but a visitor on a guest pass.

The hallway was short, a little dark and had no photographs or flowers, only a place to hang coats and another to stash boots. Jake helped her off with her big wool monstrosity and hung it up, but he didn't ask her to remove her boots.

The front room was old-fashioned with a wooden fireplace, flowered wallpaper and a staircase leading to the second floor. There was a very nice hardwood floor. The furniture looked cozy with tables close at hand for cups or magazines. No TV though, but that mystery was cleared up when she was escorted into the living room. But before she could look around, Jake stepped close and pulled her into a kiss that went from welcome to "hi, there" in thirty seconds.

The flannel felt wonderful beneath her hands, or maybe that was knowing it was Jake she was touching. Unable to resist, she explored his manly tool belt and copped a grab of his ass for good measure.

He laughed as he kissed her, which was one heck of a nice thing.

When she drew back, she found his gaze, those blue eyes doing strange and wondrous things to her body. "I never just show up," she said. "Never. My entire family, including all my ancestors, are appalled. It's the height of rudeness."

"Boy, are you not from this neighborhood. No one calls ahead. They just barge the hell in, no matter what. It's a pain in the ass."

"It's a community."

"That, too."

"So it's all right that I'm here?" she asked even though she knew he would say yes no matter what.

"It's fantastic. And a surprise. I've been trying to figure out why since you called."

"Ah, that." She parted from him, took a look around. There was the big screen awkwardly hung half over very unique flowered wallpaper and half over the tallest wainscoting she'd ever seen. There was perhaps a foot of wallpaper showing, and the rest was green-and-white-striped wood with a small shelf thing running above the wainscoting across the length of the room. Here, too, were more comfy couches, two big recliners, more tables, but what really caught her interest were the photographs.

They were on every wall, on every tabletop. She started on the far wall over a console table. There was Jake as a kid, a little kid with a new bike complete with training wheels, smiling like he'd won the grandest prize of all. And there was his father, a young man standing proud in his NYPD uniform.

Her gaze stopped at an elegant picture of a woman with her dark hair in an updo, her makeup a little dated, but still tasteful, and Jake's eyes. That same blue, arresting, with dark, thick lashes Rebecca doubted were fake. She had a smile that was a little shy, but sweet, and there was a glow about her, as if she was looking at someone very special when the photographer had snapped the picture.

"She was a knockout," Jake said. "Oh, man, was my old man proud of her. He loved to take her dancing. There was a place in Park Slope that was an old-fashioned ballroom joint. No live orchestra, but they went there a lot. They were too young to be dancing like that, teased by all their friends, but they could dance. They won contests. Not a lot, nothing major. Didn't matter, that's not why they went."

"How long has she been gone?"

"Twelve years."

"I'm sorry."

Jake inhaled. "Me, too. She was a good mom. A little crazy. She liked to experiment with dinner. She sucked at that."

Rebecca laughed quietly as she put the picture back down. "Is there one of you in your uniform?"

He nodded, took her hand. They walked across the broad living room. It had the same hardwood flooring, but there was a big area rug in the center, deep green, which went with the wallpaper and the stripes. At the other end sat a bookcase, the lower shelves crammed with books. The upper two shelves had a few trinkets: a fancy candle, what looked like a music box, a set of those nesting dolls. And one large photograph in a silver frame of a much-younger Jake. His uniform was slightly different from his father's, but she couldn't have pinpointed how. The pride that came through in his posture and his eyes was identical.

"Oh, my," she said, "what is it about a man in uniform?"

"Depends on the man. I've known some butt-ugly cops."

She tugged him close. "Something tells me you had to fight them off with a stick wearing that NYPD blue."

"Hey, it wasn't the uniform."

"No." She looked at him squarely. "I'm sure it was your modesty."

"You're a riot."

She tilted her head toward the door. "If I'm not mistaken, dinner has arrived."

"I hope you like soy bacon and tofu and no tomato sauce."

"Ha."

The look he gave her made her worry that he wasn't kidding, but not for long. Not that he didn't try, but his eyes couldn't hide the smile that only teased his lips. Then he kissed her, slow and lush, until she forgot to be worried at all, and when he was through, he led her back to the Gang of Three.

THE PIZZA BOXES WERE EMPTY except for several discarded crusts courtesy of Liam, lying open on the coffee table in the living room. Jake's father was in his wheelchair, Liam and Pete were in the recliners and Rebecca sat on the couch next to Jake. They weren't pressed together, but they were close enough for their hands to brush. Every time that happened, a pulse of excitement surged through his body, particularly behind his fly. It wasn't critical—he wasn't seventeen any longer—but it made him hyperaware of her.

Even above the odor of pizza and pepperoni and garlic and onion, he had identified her scent. She wasn't one of those women who changed perfume as often as clothes, and for that he was grateful. This scent, something he couldn't name or even categorize, had made an impact. If he didn't see her for ten years, he'd still know it was her.

That was the good part. The bad part was that Mike had started telling stories. Embarrassing stories. Of Jake's childhood. Jake had given his father the glare of a lifetime, but no. Mike, the old bastard, was undaunted and unafraid. The first two had been uncomfortable, but they were kind of typical—peeing his pants at four, breaking an incredibly expensive vase at the police captain's house when Jake was seven. But this one...

"...he had one hell of a lisp," he father said, already

laughing. What's worse, Pete and Liam were laughing just as hard, and Rebecca, caught up in the moment, grinned at him as if it was all fun and games.

"Shut up, old man," Jake said. "It's not even funny."

"It's goddamn adorable, Jakey, so sit back and take it like a man."

Jake groaned, dropped his head in his hands. The only question was whether he should leave or stay. Staying meant utter humiliation. Running was cowardly, and he was still trying to impress the woman he wasn't supposed to be dating.

"So one day, my wife gets a call from his teacher. He's in second grade, mind you. Six." His dad had to pause for a minute to wipe his thumb under his eyes. "At first, see, my wife was worried. That his teacher was crying, she sounded so weird on the phone. But then, see, it turns out she was laughing."

"Oh, God," Liam said. "This kills me. Every fucking time." His eyes widened as he turned to Rebecca. "Excuse my language. I'm sorry."

"It's all right," she said. "I've heard the word before." Then she brushed Jake's hand as she leaned forward. "I've even said it a few times."

Liam nodded at her, then went back to staring at the storyteller, the father who had no concern whatsoever for his only child, the man who was single-handedly driving away any chance for a relationship with Rebecca.

"So she was laughing," his dad continued, "hard. Because my boy, my beautiful son, had been eaten alive by mosquitoes the night before. He was a mess, I gotta say, it wasn't pretty. But right in the middle of class, and remember this was a Catholic school and his teacher was a nun, so right in the middle, Jakey here stands up and yells, 'Thister, thethe methquito biteth are a pain in my ath.'" Mike had to stop and laugh for a while, and he wasn't alone. "So the sister says, 'What did you say?' and Jake just yells it again. The sister was calling my wife to tell her Jake had to go to the doctor because he had a pretty bad allergy, but damn, that story. It went all over the neighborhood like wildfire, and to this day, we can be walking down the block, and someone will yell out, 'Thethe methquito biteth are a pain in my ath!'"

Jake sighed, waiting for this hell to be over. Knowing that if he was really lucky, and he did get to see Rebecca again, she was going to bring up the lisp. No one could seem to help it.

Of course she laughed. Why wouldn't she? It was a riot. It wasn't his fault he hadn't had any front teeth. He was only in second grade, for God's sake, and weren't nuns supposed to be caring? Gentle? Twenty-nine years later, and he still kept hearing about the goddamn methquitoes.

Rebecca turned to Jake and held his face between her hands and kissed him, sitting right there on the living room couch. "It must have been awful," she said. "But so adorable I can't even…"

"Adorable. Just what a man wants to hear."

"You should want to," she said, keeping her voice low, as private as possible. "Because it's a wonderful thing. I'm so glad I came."

"Could have done without the show-and-tell."

She let him go, but didn't sit back. "That was the betht part."

Behind her, with laughter still lingering, Liam stood and started putting away the empty boxes. Rebecca noticed, then squeezed Jake's hand. "Walk me outside?"

"Walk you to 5th, you mean. Unless you want to call a cab from here."

"No, a walk would be good after all that pizza."

He stood back as she said her goodbyes, and he wasn't quite as bothered by the story being told. Of course, he'd get his revenge as soon as possible, but for tonight, it was fine. And wasn't she something as she spoke to his old man, touching his shoulder, getting personal. Jake didn't hear what she said, but he saw his father's face. Her visit made things more complicated, but that wasn't so horrible either. At least for now.

By the time he'd helped her on with her coat, Liam and Pete had helped Mike upstairs so Jake was able to leave comfortably. The two men would stick around until he got back. Now, though, he put on his own coat and went outside into the cold night.

They were quiet for a while, walking, her hand in his. It felt a little weird to have had such a domestic night when he'd never imagined her that way.

"I hope it wasn't too weird for you, me being there," she said.

"Interesting. Good interesting," he added, quickly. "I didn't expect…"

"I know. Me neither. I actually came here to ask you something."

"Okay."

"You know that dinner I've been bitching about?"

"Yep. Wednesday night, right?"

"Yes." She paused walking, faced him. "I wondered if you might like to come. As my date. But it's okay if you don't want to. It's black tie, and you know the kind of people who are going to be there, and it might turn out to be the most boring night of your life. Although my cousin Charlie and his girlfriend, Bree, will be there, and the food will be fantastic, but honestly, you don't have to say yes—"

"Yes," he said. "I'd love to come as your date."

"Really?"

Her wide dark eyes stared up at him with surprise, and he couldn't be sure but he thought she might be blushing.

"Really. It would be my honor. Where and when?"

She let out a big sigh, then grabbed the back of his neck and pulled him down into a kiss that should have waited for a much more private venue. He didn't mind.

9

OF ALL THE SKILLS REBECCA had learned from her parents, the ability to appear calm in virtually any circumstance was one of the most useful. It hadn't come easily, but over the years she'd found that she could separate her inner landscape from the outer facade. As she stood in the middle of the banquet room at the Four Seasons, those boundaries were being stretched to the limit.

It was early yet, with only staff in attendance, and the room buzzed with a controlled chaos. What had Rebecca sweating wasn't the catering or the orchestra or even the extravagant floral arrangements still being fussed with, but her own ability to let the people she'd hired do their jobs without her overseeing every last detail.

And Jake.

He hadn't arrived; it was two hours before anyone was expected. Dani was here, and the catering manager and one of the staff concierges and many, many hands to make sure every place setting was meticulous, that the food was superb in freshness, flavor and eye appeal. She had already checked into the room she'd booked for the night. If she had a lick of sense, she'd go upstairs immediately, lie down for at least twenty minutes, then begin her personal preparation. Dani was also going to use the room to change clothes so Rebecca's window of opportunity for a short nap was closing.

"Go. Everything's fine," Dani said, which illustrated perfectly the need for her to get the hell out of there.

Rebecca glanced around, still hesitating.

Dani, dressed in black pants, a striped shirt and low heels, crossed her arms over her chest. "You're making everyone nuts. If anything's going to crash and burn it'll be because we're all trying to impress you."

"Oh." Rebecca gave it a minute's thought and could see the point. "Fine. I'll rest. But I'm going to have my cell in my hand so call me if anything happens. I mean anything."

Dani's only response was to cross her heart, then stare pointedly at the door.

Rebecca took her leave and while she was certain she'd be unable to think of a thing besides the enormous checklist for the dinner, once she stepped into the elevator, it was Jake. All Jake.

She hadn't asked him about his tux, because that would have been unbearably awful, but she'd worried about it. Then she'd worried about worrying. He was altogether a difficult issue for her. Ever since her conversation with Bree and Charlie, Rebecca had played over every motive, every wish, every daydream she'd had in the short time she'd known Jake. Since she'd visited his home, her confusion had worsened. Yet hearing his voice instantly stifled her qualms, making it crystal clear how much she liked him. All the same, an hour later she was chock-full of self-doubt and second-guessing.

She entered the lovely deluxe hotel room. She was planning to spend the night there even though she lived quite close to the hotel, but she wasn't sure if Jake would stay. She hoped so now, but she might not later. A lot depended on the success of the evening, particularly her success with William West. When she'd met with him at the Gates Foundation dinner, he'd seemed interested, although she wasn't sure if his interest was in the Winslow Foundation or her.

He hadn't been overt, not at all, but the signs had all been there. Lingering eye contact, a kiss to the back of her hand that had made her uncomfortable. It was very likely that he was behaving the way he behaved with all women. He wouldn't be the first man she'd met who was like that. Under other circumstances, she wouldn't bother finding out the truth, but he had a substantial fortune he wanted to donate, and she was only one among many in line for it.

She just hoped she'd have a definitive read on him by the end of the evening. The last thing she wanted to do was waste time playing games.

She settled on the bed, her cell phone clutched in her right hand. She closed her eyes, but didn't expect to sleep. There would be dancing. The orchestra was fantastic, and they weren't going to go crazy with too modern a set because there wasn't a person attending who would know what to do to hip-hop. Well, maybe Bree and Charlie, but still. There would be slow numbers, mostly, and medium numbers, but nothing that would make anyone sweaty.

She had no idea how much of that, if any, Jake's leg could take. She'd prefer not to put him in an uncomfortable situation but that was unavoidable, wasn't it? And why was she even worried in the first place? If he had thought it was a bad idea, he'd have declined the invitation. He wasn't a child and he had nothing to prove to her.

God, they weren't even dating. Although they might as well be because there were going to be a hell of a lot of Winslows in The Cosmopolitan Suite. Her parents, to begin with. Her grandfather. Charlie. Andrew, her cousin on her mother's side, who was not terribly bright. He did, however, look great in photographs which was evidently all the family thought he needed to run for the New York senate. He'd be pressing the flesh, distracting and irritating everyone and taking the spotlight off the foundation.

She wouldn't think about that because there was nothing she could do about it. The Winslow family had her outvoted, and if she was honest with herself, she'd known keeping Andrew away was a lost cause before the discussion had come up.

She hated it, though. He was a jerk, and New York deserved so much better.

She moaned as she turned over. The nap was a farce, but maybe a shower would soothe her enough to deal with the rest of her night. She thought about asking her mother to bring one of her nice little calming pills with her, but rejected the notion immediately. If ever she needed to be sharp it was tonight.

She got her things together for her shower, made sure her dress and shoes were at the ready, then went into the bathroom, purposely leaving her cell phone on the bed-side table.

JAKE ENTERED THE FOUR SEASONS from the East 57th Street entrance and walked into the elevator that would take him down one level to The Cosmopolitan Suite, unashamed to admit that he was nervous. He knew how to behave with high-end company, that wasn't it. He wanted to impress Rebecca. At the very least, he wanted to be what she needed, although it didn't help that he wasn't sure what that would be.

First thing, he'd find himself a drink. Okay, second thing, because as he entered the banquet room, there she was. And she was a stunner.

Man, she looked like a movie star. Like a forties glamour girl, and he had to wonder if her choice in gowns had anything to do with their recent discussions of film noir. No, that was a ridiculous thought especially when he took into account that the style fit her to a T.

The dress was floor-length, a rich red that showed off her creamy shoulders and amazing curves. Her hair was pinned up, her lips red, and when she caught sight of him, there was nothing and no one else in the room. The smile that lit up her face got him moving. By the time he reached her, she had turned, and while he wanted to kiss her until the sun came up tomorrow, he stopped himself in the nick of time. Instead he followed her lead. She took one hand and squeezed it and kissed his cheek, then whispered, "I'm so glad you're here."

He nodded slightly, then forced himself to cool it as he realized they were most definitely not alone. Not five feet away, Jake recognized a guy who had his arm around a really petite, pretty girl. On further inspection, she wasn't that young. Just small. And decked out in a dress that made him blink. Not that she didn't look great in it, she did. It was just odd with pastel colors in a weirdly geometric jacket on top of a black-and-white-striped skirt and shoes that seemed to be made solely of straps.

"Jake Donnelly, this is my cousin Charlie Winslow, and my friend Bree Kingston. They'll be sitting with you when I'm roaming around shaking hands, so it would be better if you liked each other."

"Sure, no pressure," Jake said, as he shook hands with first Bree, then Charlie. "You're the blog guy. I don't know why I didn't make the connection."

"I am the blog guy, but in this room, I'm just Rebecca's cousin," Charlie said. "Nice to meet you."

Bree said, "You know what? I could use a drink. How about you boys go fetch us some?"

"It's all equality until someone needs a drink or there's a spider in the bathtub," Charlie said. "You want pineapple juice or something for grown-ups?"

Bree gave Charlie a quick glare. "A Sea Breeze, please."

Jake turned to Rebecca. "And you?"

"I don't dare start drinking this early. I'll have a tonic and lime. That'll fool everyone, right?"

"No one's going to notice. They'll all be too dazzled by how beautiful you are."

"Oh," Bree said as if she'd just seen a kitten. "Okay, you can stay."

He laughed to hide the embarrassment of having been such a cliché, but the look on Rebecca's face told him he hadn't crossed the unforgivable line. "Be right back."

He and Charlie went toward the nearest bar and Jake finally took a look at the joint. It was huge; there was a stage with a full orchestra playing something soft and jazzy, enormous vases with huge flower arrangements all around the many tables, each set up with more glittering silver and crystal than he'd seen in Macy's. It was a massive affair, this party, and he slowed his pace as he watched a row of servers enter the ballroom. They were in black and white, wore gloves and held silver platters with tiny hors d'oeuvres on them. Jesus. She'd said there were billions at stake but he only believed her now. She was playing in the majors.

"You used to be a cop?" Charlie asked as they reached the bar.

"Yeah. Got in right after college. Planned on staying until retirement. Didn't work out that way."

Since there wasn't much of a line yet, they were able to order pretty quickly. Charlie went first, then Jake put in his requests. He glanced back to find Bree and Rebecca huddled, both staring directly at him. Great.

"Don't worry," Charlie said. "You already passed. Rebecca wouldn't have invited you if you were even marginal. Tonight is huge for her. It's like the Super Bowl of fundraisers."

"She's amazing."

"That she is," Charlie said. "The only relative I like, which is something because we've got relatives crawling out of the woodwork. I'll do my best to help you avoid as many as possible."

"She told me her folks would be here."

"Her father isn't a Winslow by birth, but he might as well have been. He's got the entitlement thing down to a science." Charlie got his drinks and waited for Jake. "We all do, honestly. We grew up on the milk of privilege, but Rebecca has always handled it like a responsibility, not a game. She could have done anything with her life. The foundation used to be more of a tax dodge than a charitable enterprise, but she's changing all that. It's not easy, considering who's on the board."

It was Jake's turn to get his drinks, and he took advantage of the moment to take a good sip of his bourbon and water. Although he'd have to grab some of those appetizers before long. He wasn't about to get drunk, not tonight. "We haven't talked all that much about our respective careers," he said. "Although I checked out the foundation online. Seems to be doing a lot of good work."

Charlie brought them to the women, drinks were exchanged, but he didn't stop looking at Jake. "You can tell me to go jump in a lake," Charlie said, "but I've gotta ask the guy question. You got shot? Twice?"

Jake had been expecting that since he and Rebecca had met, but not from her cousin. It didn't bother him. Charlie was right. Every guy he knew had hit him up for details. He wondered though if it had been a setup. If Rebecca had wanted to know and asked Charlie to front the question. From the look on her face, he didn't think that was the case. She probably did want to know so he plunged ahead.

"Undercover operation. Didn't go so well. We trusted someone who didn't deserve it. There was a shoot-out like you see on cop shows on TV. I'd never seen anything like it before, and I didn't see it for long.

"I was lucky, I would have bled out if there hadn't been paramedics right there. The getting shot part wasn't at all like on TV. It hurt like a sonofabitch, and it didn't heal up by the next commercial. I still go to rehab, my left hand shakes from time to time and I'll be living with this limp for the rest of my life."

Charlie held up his drink. "Thank you for your service. I'm sorry it cost such a high price."

Rebecca had lost her smile, but she held her drink up in salute, as did Bree.

Jake wasn't good at this, and did what he always did, which was to look at his shoes. "Thanks." When he looked up again, it was at Rebecca. "How about them Yankees?"

Rebecca ignored Bree and Charlie completely. She kissed Jake on the lips. "I have to do things. I'll come back. I promise."

"Go," Jake said. "Knock 'em dead. As if you could help it."

A little "oh" let her know Bree had been listening, but Rebecca continued to ignore her friend. "I wish I didn't have to go. But duty calls." She pasted on a smile, went toward the entrance and began the fundraising portion of the evening.

While she welcomed guests that never failed to appear in *Time* magazine's 100 Most Influential People, some of them her own relatives, she couldn't resist sneaking glances back at Jake.

She wasn't sure of the designer of his tux, for all she knew it could be off the rack, but it didn't matter because the man wore the clothes, not the other way around. Did he ever.

It was traditional black, complete with bow tie and small pocket kerchief, white. The classic look was a fantastic frame for his face, his *eyes,* and she dared any woman in the room not to swoon over him after one sight.

"Rebecca." The strident voice couldn't be mistaken for any other.

Rebecca returned to her duties. "Hello, Mom. Dad." She bent for the air kisses and waited for the verdict. Both parents would have something to say about her, about the room, about the night, about every last little detail right down to the type of gloves worn by the waitstaff.

"You look very nice," her mother said. "Although you may want to rethink the strapless gowns when it comes to this particular event. You represent the entire family, and we wouldn't want anyone getting the wrong idea."

"I'm pretty certain everyone here would be able to tell I was a woman even if I wore a burka, Mother. And how's your hip, Dad? Better?"

Her father ignored the question. "The Bannerman Orchestra?" He sighed. It was all he needed to do.

"I like the way they rock the Hokey Pokey. Go get yourselves drinks. Have a good time. I made sure to have your favorite caviar to go with the Cristal Champagne. And don't annoy Charlie. He's in a mood."

Neither of them deigned to reply as they walked over to the bar. Rebecca had to admit they looked fantastic, but then the Winslows and the Thorpes had learned the art of presentation when they were toddlers.

And then she caught sight of Jake and he was looking at her, ignoring his companions, as far as she could tell. She smiled. He smiled back. When she held out her hand to Mr. and Mrs. Chandler, she knew she was blushing.

Time slipped by in a mixture of false bonhomie and genuine pleasure as she continued to schmooze the elite. The orchestra played old standards, reserving those best for dancing until later. Soon dinner would be served and while she couldn't wait for the seating, which would only come after she'd made her welcome speech, she was becoming concerned since William West hadn't arrived yet.

She'd felt sure he'd have come early, ready to continue the flirting he'd started last Thursday night. Well, she wouldn't really worry until halfway through dinner.

It wasn't a big surprise that Charlie was great. He was Rebecca's favorite cousin, and made it to the list of things they both liked. So far he'd added good vodka, pizza crusts, his salad-making expertise, a deep appreciation for her underwear, film noir and the kind of sex that could start wars. Bree was cool, too. She made him laugh, and he appreciated the way she was with Charlie. Easy, but connected. They hadn't been together long, but he'd wager the relationship would take.

His folks used to look at each other like these two did. As if the words were nice, but unnecessary.

Rebecca's voice on the stage snapped his gaze back to her. Dammit, the woman knocked him out. Not just the way she was gorgeous, but the way she held the attention of every person in the room. Yeah, he wasn't such a Brooklyn yahoo that he didn't recognize half the people in attendance. Christ, he read the papers. Watched the news. What the hell he was doing here, he had no idea.

That question was becoming something of a problem. Anyone with half a brain would know he and Rebecca were a temporary item. There was zero chance that he was anything more than a passing whim. The issue was that he was starting to care about that. About after.

Who was going to measure up to a woman like Rebecca Thorpe? It wasn't about the money thing, the hell with the money. But the woman? The heat between them? How he felt when he was with her? Yeah, who would he ever meet that would begin to compare?

The crowd laughed at something Rebecca had said and he found her looking at him instead of her audience. For a minute, she lost the gleam in her eye, and that was all on him. He hadn't been paying attention, and, dammit, that was his job, his only job. To support her. To make her feel like a million. Well, in this group, a billion. He smiled and hoped like hell he could put her back on track.

The next words out of her mouth were confident,

smooth. Amusing. She was back, and he wasn't going to think about the unknowable future. He was here, now, and he'd be a moron not to enjoy every last second.

10

Rebecca barely touched her sole meunière. Pity, because the food was unbelievably wonderful. She hated that her plate would go to waste.

If she could have she would have scooted her chair closer to Jake's until she could lean against him. She wanted his arm around her shoulders, his soft kiss in her hair. Instead, she contented herself with watching him enjoy his beef tenderloin, the sound of his laughter when Charlie or Bree said something amusing. It puzzled her, how much she enjoyed merely looking at him. At the funny and incredibly endearing way he would express himself with a quirk of his lips. He could transform from the essence of machismo to the picture of infinite kindness when he saw his father's hands.

She put another small bite into her mouth when Bree caught her eye. She pointedly glanced at Jake, then bit her lower lip as if Jake's pure awesomeness was too much to handle. Rebecca laughed, covering her mouth, trying not to choke.

"You okay?" Jake asked, his hand on her bare back above her dress.

She hissed at the contact even though his hand wasn't cold or a surprise.

He lifted it immediately at the sound, but she shook her head. "No, it's fine. I'm fine."

Jake was pulling away when her hand found his thigh. "It felt good," she said.

His smile unfolded slowly in all its slightly crooked glory as he touched her again. He kept his voice low, and she felt his breath on the shell of her ear. "You've nailed this," he said. "Listen. You can hear that people are enjoying themselves. I couldn't swear to it, but I bet for this crowd, that's unusual. Your fingerprints are all over this night. You should hit them hard as soon as the meal is over. They're pumped and primed."

She laughed again, but it was breathless at his compliments. She did as he'd suggested. She listened. The orchestra was on a break as she'd specified no music during dinner. She wanted people to talk. Above the clatter of silver, the clink of glasses, there was a steady mumble of voices, nothing distinct but the laughter.

She looked over her left shoulder to the nearest table. Not one of the guests was staring blankly while they ate. Everyone was engaged, participating. It was only one table, but indicative.

Her attention shifted to her immediate surroundings. Wine was being poured. Jake's hand rubbed a small circle on her back and her stomach tightened. Charlie asked Bree if she liked the amaranth; Bree told him she wasn't sure because she had no idea what amaranth was.

She hardly realized she had turned to face Jake, that she'd found his gaze and was staring, watching his pupils grow as his breathing quickened. "Thank you," she said. Then she kissed him on the lips. It was tempting to stay there, with his hand on her back and his words swimming in her head. But that would have to wait.

When she sat up, he drew away smoothly. He took up his fork and had another bite of the eggplant puree. His amaranth remained untouched. Perhaps it would have been wiser to go with a rice pilaf.

Rebecca was sidetracked by movement at the front door. William West had finally arrived. Although she couldn't make out the details, how he ripped off his coat told her everything about his mood. So much for getting him to commit to an endowment tonight.

Then again, maybe not. Once he'd turned back from getting his coat checked, all signs of tension had vanished and he appeared to be his usual confident self as his gaze swept the room. He found her quickly, giving her a courtly nod.

He wasn't much to look at. Average height, brown hair, a body that spoke of a golf hobby instead of a gym membership. He counted on his net worth to give him sex appeal.

Dani met him at the door, but West turned his back on her, which made Rebecca sit up damn straight. A woman Rebecca didn't recognize then entered, wearing what looked like a very politically incorrect full-length fur. She was tall and slim and beautiful, and she looked good as she smiled at Mr. West. She also looked very young, but that was par for the course in this crowd.

Interesting that while West had sent his RSVP in for two, he'd led her to believe that his CFO was going to join him. Well, perhaps the leggy brunette was the CFO.

West took the woman's arm and Dani led them to their table, making sure the waiter was on her heels with both wine and champagne.

Dani went from there directly to the kitchen. Rebecca

relaxed, knowing the next course would be delayed in order to give West and his guest time to catch up. Luckily, the fourth course was salad, and when it did arrive, the removal of plates would be handled perfectly. She may have begrudged spending the money on this particular ballroom, but the catering staff at the Four Seasons was impeccable, always.

For the first time that night, she lifted her wineglass. Part two of fundraising: the hard sell, would come all too soon, but she could handle it. Jake said so.

JAKE HAD LOST BOTH BREE and Charlie. Him to the bar in search of pineapple juice, and Bree to the ladies' room. Jake had watched in amazement as the banquet tables had been replaced by a dance floor and a number of cocktail tables had been set up on the periphery of the room. The entire operation hadn't taken ten minutes. Impressive.

He'd found a spot far enough away from the dancing to avoid being stepped on while leaving the tables for the more needful among the crowd. He normally didn't mind standing; he just wasn't sure how his leg was going to hold out.

A hand on his arm had him turning, expecting Bree. It was, in fact, a woman he'd noticed earlier. He'd place her age in her late fifties, mostly because of the obvious work she'd had done. He doubted very much lips that large had come direct from the factory, or that she'd been born looking so surprised. What had struck him before was that, according to the papers, she and her husband owned a large portion of Manhattan, so obviously the woman could have afforded the best in plastic surgeons. Hell, maybe she was actually in her eighties and the doctors had outdone themselves.

"I don't know you," she said, her words slurred with whiskey. He imagined she wore a very nice perfume, but it couldn't compete with the booze. "But you know Rebecca. Very well, I'm thinking."

"I'm glad to say she's a friend," he replied, smiling as pleasantly as he could.

"Friend, my ass. I'm Paulina."

"Nice to meet you," he said, holding out his hand. "Jake."

"You're the best-looking thing at this dinner. Did you know that?"

He bit back a laugh. "That's very kind of you."

"Oh, don't get excited," she said, waving her hand so that her jewels flashed against the lights. "I'm not going to do anything about it. My husband doesn't even mind. He knows I like to look."

"Paulina!"

Jake looked up at Charlie's voice, more grateful than he could say.

"We haven't seen each other in ages," Charlie said, taking her hand and spinning her away from Jake. "You get more beautiful every time I see you." He gave her two air kisses and a smile that looked one hundred percent real.

"Charlie. Honey. You're the best-looking thing at this dinner. Did you know that?"

"I did, Paulina, I did. There doesn't seem to be a damn thing I can do about it, though. I'm just that handsome."

She waved her hand again, laughing, and Charlie shoved a glass of juice at Jake before he guided the woman into the crowd.

"So he's thrown me over for another woman," Bree said, making Jake jump. The damn orchestra made it hard to know when people were approaching. "Is that my drink?"

He handed her the glass, then took a sip from his own. "He rescued me. Don't give him any grief."

"Well, damn, there goes my night."

"You're good together, you two."

She grinned happily. "I think so. It's weird though."

"What?"

"Him being Charlie Winslow. I'm from Ohio. Before I moved in with Charlie, I shared a tiny one-bedroom apartment with four people. Now we share a floor. A whole floor."

"It is kind of overwhelming," he said. "How really rich they are. But most of the time, I don't think about it."

"I ignored it when Charlie and I first started going out, but it's too big to ignore. It takes adjusting, on both our parts. He doesn't even get it half the time. What he has access to is insane. His normal is about fifty times grander than my wildest fantasies."

Jake thought about Rebecca's condo; the view alone let him know he was in over his head. "I don't think I'll be around long enough to have to adjust."

"Oh, no." Bree stepped in front of him, pouting. It was actually very cute. "Don't say that. Why did you say that? You guys are so great together."

"We're not even dating. Not for real. I have no idea why I'm here. We were a kind of setup thing. A mutual acquaintance. In theory, it was for one night only."

"Huh," Bree said, trying to hide her grin. "That's a familiar tale."

"Oh?"

"*Our* mutual acquaintance was Rebecca."

"Huh," he repeated.

Bree just wiggled her eyebrows.

Behind Bree, he caught sight of Rebecca, and the urge to join her was strong despite the fact that he knew she was working the room. She'd told him as much, apologetically, which he appreciated, but leaving no room for misinterpretation. Tonight was business, and he was... not.

On the other hand, her glass was empty. She kept bringing it up to her lips to drink, then lowering it as she recalled the tonic was gone.

"Charlie's on his way back," he said to Bree. "So if you'll excuse me."

"Sure," she said, glancing from him to Rebecca then back. "Go get her, tiger."

He ignored the crazy girl and went toward the bar. It took him longer than he'd like to get Rebecca's drink, but when he found her again, she was still talking to the same guy, and her glass was still empty. Jake's approach was stealthy, not wanting to disrupt the flow of her conversation, yet keeping the man's back to him so that Rebecca had a little warning.

Only, when he got close enough, he heard the guy laugh. The sound stopped Jake short. He'd heard that laugh before. One other time, twelve years ago. He'd never forgotten it, not a chance, because it had belonged to Vance Keegan.

"Lip" Keegan had been part of a very large drug bust. He'd escaped, along with about half a dozen others, when things had gone to hell. Unlike the other runners, Keegan had seemed to vanish into thin air.

Jake moved in slowly, trying to avoid Rebecca's attention until he could convince himself that he'd been mistaken. Even though the laugh was a dead ringer for Bender, a *Futurama* cartoon character, there had to be more than one person who sounded like that. Jake had been in charge of getting Keegan into the bus. He'd cuffed the guy, had him by the arm, and he'd let him get away. The piece of crap had laughed the whole way across the rooftop, a full block, right in Jake's ear. But that had happened a lifetime ago, when Jake had been a rookie.

The man with the uncanny laugh stepped closer to Rebecca. He reached over and touched her above the elbow. Jake moved in, right up between them, no excuses. Keegan stepped back, which was the point. Except it wasn't Keegan.

The face wasn't the same. The eyes were different, the shape of his jaw, his nose had been bigger. But shit, shit, under the mustache, this guy had been born with a cleft pallet. Same as Lip Keegan.

"Jake," Rebecca said. "Is everything all right?"

He forced himself to look at Rebecca. As soon as he did, the time and place came back to him with a jolt. He must have made a mistake, which was weird and embarrassing enough, but he'd intruded on what could have been a crucial moment. "I apologize. I lost my footing," he said, even more embarrassed that he was using his injuries to excuse himself. "I meant to refresh your drink."

His lame excuse, God, the pun made him wince, had done its job. Rebecca visibly relaxed and her smile wasn't at all forced.

"I'll leave you to it," he said, trading glasses with her.

"Wait," she said, touching his arm. "I'd like you to meet William West. The CEO of West Industries."

"Bill," he said. Dammit, that wasn't the same scar. Lip's scar had been jagged, a mess. "You are?"

Jake took the offered hand. "Jake Donnelly. A friend of Rebecca's." The handshake was tight, and Jake supposed he was fifty percent responsible, but all his instincts were telling him that West was not who he claimed to be. Jake thought about Paulina and her artificial face, and he wondered. With someone good on the end of a scalpel, it was possible.

"Thanks for the drink," Rebecca said, startling him again.

"My pleasure. I'll see you later." He nodded at West, then left, achingly aware of his limp and his confusion. He knew nothing about West Industries, but he did know that Keegan would have had twelve years to change his face, to reinvent himself.

On the other hand, the likelihood of Jake running into Vance Keegan at the Four Seasons was absurd. Still, he'd check it out, because even if the odds were he was as wrong as he could get, West was involved with Rebecca. If West did end up giving a grant or donation or whatever the hell people gave to foundations, Jake needed to be sure it wasn't blood money. Rebecca would never want that.

She would want him here. Thinking about her, instead of a long-shot hunch.

He ordered a bourbon at the bar, left a tip, then went straight back to Charlie and Bree, still standing near the dance floor. Charlie had his arms wrapped around her and they looked completely into each other. In love. Jake put aside his concerns and played his part as if his life depended on it.

THE ORCHESTRA CAME BACK from their break as Bill West kissed the back of Rebecca's hand. The gesture was creepy, but then the man was creepy, so what could she expect? It didn't matter whether she liked him or not, or that he'd flirted with her right in front of his girlfriend, companion, whatever she was. It wasn't difficult to see his *friend* hadn't been too thrilled. Rebecca wasn't either—not about the flirting, but how they'd ended the conversation. Even though West had said he was going to get involved with the foundation, no promise had been made, no dollar amount mentioned, and she'd needed both of those to happen tonight. On the plus side, they were going to meet privately later in the week. On the minus side, she'd have to see him privately.

Now the only pressing matter was finding Jake. She hadn't yet introduced him to her parents, and while that prospect wasn't thrilling, she figured she'd better. The last thing she'd want was for Jake to think she'd kept them apart. He'd never believe it was because she didn't want him to meet them, not the other way around.

She missed Jake, even though he was in the same room. She liked him. He'd brought her a tonic and lime because he'd noticed her glass was empty. Didn't sound like much, but in her experience it was almost unprecedented.

She spotted him on the other side of the dance floor. He'd been watching her. People kept blocking her line of sight, but only for seconds at a time as they danced by. He stayed where he was, watching, waiting. The room filled with the sound of strings, the violins romantic and dazzling, the cellos low and sexy.

They had to walk around the dance floor, but eventually, Jake was in front of her. She could reach out and touch him if she wanted.

She wanted.

Her hand went to the back of his neck and she drew him into a kiss. For a long moment there was nothing but his lips, the slide of his tongue, the warmth that spread through her body. He broke away, not far. She could still feel his breath on her chin.

"I'd sure like to do more of that," he said.

"Me, too. Will you stay the night? I have a room upstairs."

"Of course I will."

She brushed the back of his hand with hers. She wanted to steal him away, forget the party, the introductions, the good-nights.

"I know you have to go back to your duties," he said. "Dance with me first? Fair warning, it's not going to be pretty."

"Pretty is overrated."

They put their drinks on the nearest table and went to a corner of the dance floor, where Jake took her around her waist, drawing her close. Rebecca slipped her arms around his neck, rested her head on his shoulder. They didn't so much dance as sway, and even that was bumpy because Jake had to make adjustments.

It was altogether perfect.

The rest of the night would be so much more bearable knowing Jake would be there at the end.

_11_

AT ONE IN THE MORNING, there was absolutely nothing Jake wanted more than to get out of the ballroom, out of his tuxedo and into Rebecca. It didn't look like an escape was imminent, though.

He'd have figured the orchestra would have stopped playing by midnight, but nope. They kept on pumping out tunes, most of them a little peppier than the sleepy waltzes they'd featured when the crowd had been at its peak. Charlie and Bree had cut out over an hour ago, and William West had left an hour before them. Unfortunately, Rebecca was still being set upon by people who clearly didn't have work tomorrow. For God's sake, it was a Wednesday night.

Rebecca continued to look stunning. As if she'd just arrived. Not a hair out of place, her dress as beautiful and slinky as it had been when he'd first seen her. How did women do it? Stand up all night on tiptoe? High heels had to hurt like a sonofabitch.

He went over to the buffet table where they'd put out coffee and pastries a while ago. Since his leg was as tired as the rest of him, he was fingering one of his pain pills in his tux pocket. It didn't normally knock him out, but he didn't normally drink when he took the pill.

The coffee turned out to be a good idea. Sipping something hot and familiar made him feel more relaxed, let him give his obsessive mind a rest.

If he wasn't thinking about Rebecca, he was thinking about West. Keegan. That damn laugh, the lip. It was driving him crazy. That's what happened to a man when there wasn't a problem to solve that was more difficult than how to install bathroom tile. The mind turned to mush.

He was sinking into a really good sulk when he saw Rebecca coming toward him. He straightened, not giving a damn about his leg now, or his need for sleep. The nearer she got, the better his mood. Until he realized why the couple behind her looked so familiar. She'd said she was going to introduce him to her parents.

Fuck.

He put his coffee down on the buffet table and surreptitiously wiped his right hand on his slacks. Rebecca's smile would have put him at ease if her parents hadn't been right behind her.

"I'm sorry it's so late," she said, placing her hand on his arm and moving to his side. "I did want to introduce you to my parents before we left for the evening. Marjorie and Franklin, this is Jake Donnelly."

He shook their hands. He smiled, but only slightly, kept his cool because he had been trained by the best captain in the continental United States, and he did not give away the game under any kind of pressure. "Pleasure to meet you both."

"Rebecca hasn't told us much about you, Jake. What is it that you do?" Franklin's nonsmile reminded Jake of politicians and backstreet lawyers. He was unnaturally tan for March in New York, and he was fighting lean.

His wife was a beauty, and Rebecca favored her. Same honey-blond hair, same long face that sat right on the border of attractive in Marjorie's case.

"I'm unemployed at the moment," he said. "Doing some work on my father's house. Figuring out what comes next."

"Unemployed?" Franklin said.

"Yes, sir." Jake had been shot in the line of duty. He was under no obligation to explain himself. A glance at Rebecca told him she'd have no problem if he left it at that. But these were her folks. He didn't need to prove anything by being a dick, either. "I was in the NYPD. Major Case Squad detective. I was injured in the line of duty and took early retirement. I haven't decided yet where I'll land when I've healed up."

Franklin stopped looking at Jake as if he was infectious.

"That must have been terrible for you," Rebecca's mother said.

"It hasn't been a picnic, but I'm still here."

"And we're still *here*," Rebecca said, leaving his side to kiss her father on the cheek, then her mother. "It's late. Go home. I'm going to sleep soon."

"Tonight was very well done," Marjorie said.

"Thanks, Mom."

Franklin said nothing. He nodded, then took his wife's arm and went for the coat check.

Rebecca turned back to Jake. "Thank you. I probably should have prepared them."

"For what? That I'm so good-looking?"

She grinned. "That, too. They mean well. They're dinosaurs, you know? Stuck in time with very rigid boundaries. Charlie's parents, too. The whole family, actually. I think they stopped evolving when they got lucky during the thirties."

"Speaking of which," he said, sliding his hands around her waist. "That dress makes me think of smoky jazz clubs and men in fedoras."

"You'd look great in a hat."

"I have a hat."

"Really?"

"I'll wear it for you sometime."

"Do me a favor?" she asked.

"Whatever you want."

"Don't wear anything else when you show me."

He kissed her. Nothing too extravagant, not yet. Merely a preview of coming attractions.

Later, despite his best intentions and Rebecca's outstanding choice in underwear, she was so obviously exhausted when they finally climbed into the big hotel bed at two-twenty, that he couldn't do anything but hold her as she fell asleep.

By all rights, he should have been out like a light himself, but maybe it was the coffee, maybe how far out of his comfort zone he'd been all night, but he stared at the sliver of light coming in from the privacy drapes as his thoughts bounced around like a nine-ball off three rails.

If it wasn't about how much he wanted to see Rebecca again, it was about how stupid he was for wanting to see Rebecca again, and if neither of those made his gut tighten enough, he settled on the odds of William West being Vance Keegan 2.0, hiding his corrupt past with a fake identity and some excellent plastic surgery.

It took him a hell of a long time to get to sleep, but at least Rebecca was using his good shoulder for a pillow. That made up for a lot.

WAKING UP TO NO ALARM AND Jake wrapped around her like a warm blanket was everything a girl could want out of life. He must not have been up for too long if his fuzzy smile was anything to go by.

"Morning," she said, careful not to breathe in his direction.

He kissed her forehead. "Morning, gorgeous. I'm thinking about ordering up a lot of coffee. Maybe some French toast. You like French toast?"

She nodded, stifling a yawn. "I'll go do stuff," she said. "But save my shower for after."

"That's a hell of an idea."

"There are robes. In the bathroom. Big, thick white robes. I'll bring you one."

"Thanks. Anything else you want from room service?"

She shook her head, then felt him watch her ass as she walked away.

They lingered over food, teasing each other with cool feet sneaking up naked legs. Jake, aside from looking at her as if she was stunning despite her raccoon eyes and hair from her nightmares, continued to be amazing. Crazy amazing, like someone had built him to her exact specifications.

He did a recap of the evening that made her laugh and blush, showering her with kudos. Nothing would have pleased her more than spending the rest of the day in bed. And the night. Unfortunately, she did have to leave by two because as much as she deserved a day off, she wasn't going to get one. There were too many details to handle, her own notes and follow-up calls to enter on her calendar.

But it was only noon now. She put her cup down, then took his cup and put it on the room service tray. The edges of his lips curled up as she untied the robe's belt and pushed the thick terry cloth off his shoulders. She could only get so far, but Jake was quick, and he took over where she left off. She stripped herself bare, then rested once again on her knees.

Naked and mostly hard, Jake reached for her, cupping her cheek in his large hand. "You take my breath away," he said. "I want you all the time."

She turned her head to kiss his thumb. "Make love to me?"

"Yes." He shifted his hands to her shoulders and eased them both down on the bed until they were on their sides, inches apart, their gazes holding. "I never know where to start with you. If I go for the kiss, I can't see the rest of you. I don't have enough hands to touch every part of your body at once. I love being inside you, and believe me, I'm a big fan of coming, but then I have to rest, and that seems like such a waste."

It wasn't the same giddy shiver in her tummy. As strong, yes, but not the same. This was a warmth, deep down, that spread into her limbs and her chest and her throat and her hands. They met in a kiss, and he tasted like Jake beneath the maple and coffee.

As his hand ran down her arm, slowly, gently, tears built behind her closed lids. She liked him so much, she didn't know what to do with it. This was new. A part of herself hidden all these years. Triggered by his touch and how he saw her. So calm, so assured. He didn't care about her lineage or that she could be a snob or that she lived in a bubble of privilege. He had looked past all of it from that first night.

What surprised her even more was that she didn't care that he had no job, that his body was torn up, that he lived in a world she'd barely known existed.

His kiss deepened and she was on her back, with Jake settling between her legs. Everything felt slow as honey; even the light coming in from the terrace window steeped them in amber. She touched him, ran her palms down his back and over his shoulders and felt the muscles move beneath his skin. She breathed his breath and they rubbed against each other in a slow, easy dance that could have gone on forever. There was no rush to get to the finish line. This was enough. This was heaven.

She looked at his dark hair, mussed from sleep and her fingers, then down his strong back, so beautiful. Even the scar was a map of his character. He'd survived so much. He should have been bitter. Mad at the world. But that wasn't Jake.

He was a wonder. He'd expanded her world. He made her laugh and made her come and he was a terrible dancer. The way he talked to his father was something she'd dreamed of as a child. That she would wake up one day and her family would be close and they'd laugh together at silly things. That her dad would light up when she walked into a room. It was all so tempting.

Yet as much as Jake filled her with joy, she couldn't picture a future with him. But she wanted to. God, she wanted to.

She loved him. Oh, what had she done?

"You're trembling," he said.

Her fingers had gripped him so tightly, she had to be hurting him. She spread her thighs, lifted her hips with an urgency that hadn't been there a few moments ago. "Make love to me. Please."

He looked at her, his lips moist from her kisses, his eyes curious and a little worried. "Yes," he said again.

When he stretched to reach the condoms left on the bedside table, she clung to him even as she loosened her grip.

JAKE GOT HOME AT four-thirty that afternoon, still tired, leg and shoulder aching. The boys were on the porch, of course, giving him hell.

"My goodness, that was some party," Pete said, leaning back in his plastic chair. "I didn't think those fancy dress shindigs lasted all night."

"Maybe now he's been with hoi polloi," Liam added, "he doesn't want to hang out with us regular Joes."

Jake made it up the porch stairs and shook his head at the old busybodies. "Hoi polloi doesn't mean what you think it means," he said.

"Oh, so now we don't know English." Liam shifted. "Well, excuse me."

"I'm tired and cold and I need to get out of this damn monkey suit. But feel free to make fun of me in absentia."

The old men laughed, poking at each other as Jake hit the door. He gave his dad a grin, then went inside. Shower first, then he'd hit the computer. The downstairs unfinished bathroom made him groan with guilt. He'd get to it, but first, he had to see if there was any current record of Vance Keegan. Maybe the guy was in prison, maybe, more likely, he was long dead.

After another set of stairs, each step harder to climb, Jake started a hot bath, then went back to his room to put on some normal clothes. It wasn't as if he'd hated the party or felt overly uncomfortable. He just couldn't see making a habit of it.

That was the fundamental issue, wasn't it? Now that his uniform wasn't NYPD blue, it was worn jeans and comfortable shirts. He wore shoes he bought from the mall, he got his boxer briefs in a three-pack and his hair cut for five bucks at the local barber.

Rebecca and him? They were impossible. For a sprint, yeah, okay, but for the distance? No way.

He got into the tub even though there wasn't enough water yet and started massaging his thigh. Later he'd call about adding a therapy session. The muscles around the wound had gotten so damned tight it felt as if with the next step his whole thigh would tear in two. It was impossible to think when it got really bad, and according to the doctor, he was looking at a long rehab. Years. He'd never be the same, but if things went well, he eventually wouldn't have to depend on pain pills to get through a day.

Yet another reason he and Rebecca had a time limit. She could have anyone. The last thing she'd want to be saddled with was some broke ex-cop with no future.

He pressed down on his quadriceps with his thumb, digging into the worst of the pain. It hurt like a wildfire, spreading up, down, throughout his whole body. Why the hell was he even thinking about anything long-term? He had no clue what he was in for. What kind of life he could have, let alone what he wanted.

Rebecca was a slice of fantasy, that's all. He'd check on Keegan, make sure it was his imagination going off the deep end, and then, well, he'd see. She might not want to go out with him again, no matter how great this morning had been. He might wise up and end it before things got more complicated.

By the time he'd finished his soak and taken his damned pill, he'd changed his mind about hitting the computer. Instead, he went downstairs. His dad was in the kitchen, putting a piece of pumpkin pie on a paper plate.

"Did you eat dinner?"

"What are you, my mother?"

"Fine. Get rickets. See if I care. And cut me a piece, would ya?"

Jake reheated a cup of coffee then took both paper plates to the breakfast nook. Mike wheeled himself up to the table and managed his own cup.

"Where'd the boys go?"

He shrugged. "Liam wanted a lift to the mall. He needed some slippers or some damn thing."

Jake shoveled in some pie. "So I'm at this shindig, this party for millionaires, and I hear this guy laugh."

His father didn't look up. Ate. Drank.

"I recognize the laugh. Weird laugh, one you could ID easy, you know?"

The nod was noncommittal, but Jake hadn't gotten anywhere yet.

"The last time I heard it, I was on that joint task force. With the FBI and the ATF?"

"Your guy got away."

"Yeah. It was his laugh. That same weird fucking laugh."

His dad looked up at him. "That's what, a dozen years ago?"

Jake nodded. "I thought it was peculiar especially when I saw this guy from the front. He's got the same build, roughly, but the details are wrong. Hair, nose, eyes, jaw. But this guy, big shot, tons of money. Rebecca's trying to get him to donate a fortune. Anyway, he's got this cleft palate. Sewed up, but the scar is there. Like Stacy Keach."

"Yeah?"

"My guy had a cleft palate. It didn't look as good back then, but come on. The laugh and the lip?"

"Could be a coincidence."

"I know. It's more likely that it's nothing. That I got the laugh wrong. I mean, when's the last time you believed eyewitness testimony? It was years ago."

"He might have been in a fight. Been in a car wreck. Split his lip."

Jake nodded again. Ate some more pie.

"On the other hand," his father said, "you could have identified a fugitive. They had him on a murder charge, right?"

Jake sighed. Sat back and stretched out his leg. "Probably wouldn't hold up now. Evidence gone. Witnesses unreliable from the get-go."

"Might be worth a look."

"You think?" Jake asked, studying his old man's face. No way Mike Donnelly was going to toss him a bone. If Jake was full of crap, his father would say.

"What's your instinct tell you?"

"That he wasn't right."

"There's your answer."

"I could be completely wrong."

"That's true. So take your time. Be careful."

"I'm not a cop anymore."

"Jakey, you'll be a cop till the day you die."

REBECCA WALKED INTO HER condo just after nine-thirty, and she had enough energy to drag herself to her bedroom, strip, leaving her clothes in a heap, and fall into bed.

Things could have gone better at the office. She'd tried, she'd really tried to keep on task, but her thing with Jake had her tied up in knots.

Wasn't love supposed to be all rainbows and unicorns? All she felt was confused. It was supposed to have been a one-night stand. She hadn't meant to get involved with him. He was a wounded ex-cop from Brooklyn. She was…

She was exhausted. And scared. As unsure about what to do as she'd ever been. The idea of not seeing him again hurt. Physically hurt. But if she did see him again, what then? It would just exacerbate the problem. And if they wanted to take it to the next step?

He couldn't leave his father to come live with her. Besides, Jake was a proud man. He wouldn't want to live off her money. She wanted to believe she could become part of his life, but really? Commuting from Brooklyn? Living in a row house?

It was all too much, and her brains were scrambled from the banquet and Jake and the very real possibility that she'd become a person she didn't like very much. But she'd have to deal with it later. Maybe take a few days away from Jake, let things settle. She needed time. And some kind of miracle.

AT TEN-THIRTY, JAKE WAS AT the computer, his coffee fresh, and his leg had simmered down to bearable. There were a lot of hits when he typed in Vance Keegan's name in Google. But each link was about the past, the distant past. The biggest single subtopic was the missing money. They'd been expecting millions, and even the best forensic accountants hadn't been able to trace where all that loot had gone. The press had outdone themselves condemning the police, the FBI and the ATF. A separate task force had been put together to pinpoint the blame, and Jake's anger at reading about it was just as acute as it had been when it had happened.

But this wasn't about history, this was a mission of discovery. He wasn't having much luck. By the time the eleven o'clock news came on, he gave up on finding Keegan and started looking into West. Who was from Nevada. Henderson, born and raised.

The guy was worth a fortune. But he wasn't flashy with it and kept a relatively low profile. He was a venture capitalist who'd made some smart moves, including getting out of real estate before it had all come tumbling down. He was involved with a large number of limited partnerships that specialized in chains, everything from dry cleaning to mortuaries. There weren't a lot of articles about him.

According to the company bio, he was the same age as Keegan. Unmarried, no kids. He'd started his company with profits from a windfall, an inheritance from his uncle, his late father's brother. He'd invested the money, and the rest was a quiet success story.

Nothing hinted that West wasn't exactly who he said he was. But nothing eliminated the possibility either. What was really clear was that Jake didn't have near the access he needed. But he knew someone who could get deeper. A lot deeper.

Gary Summers was an old buddy, a guy Jake had known in college. Gary had been into computers, specifically hacking, since high school. He'd been approached by the government and decided that the good guys had the best toys so he'd signed up. He was an independent bastard, only taking on contract work that interested him. The two of them didn't talk about specifics, and that was probably why they were still friends.

Jake sent him a text. The answer came when he was downstairs helping his old man get ready for the stairs.

Come on up. Next week? Few days? U bring the beer. Send prelim info to 192.175.2.2.

Satisfied for the moment, Jake thought about calling Rebecca, just to hear her voice, but it was late, and he hoped she was sleeping. At the thought, his own exhaustion hit him like a truck. Waking up alone would be a bitch.

12

THE OFFICE WAS QUIET AS A crypt; she should have finished her work hours ago. To make matters worse, it was Sunday, day three of her self-prescribed time-out.

Jake had wanted to see her. He'd asked her to the movies, offered to feed her, even suggested a trip to a real Irish pub. She'd begged off each time, and while her reasons were legitimate, they weren't the whole truth.

Sadly, it turned out time away hadn't made her situation any less confusing. She missed him. Thought of him so often it was absurd. Why was it that even though *she'd* chosen to keep her distance, it felt as if she was being punished? Yearning, it seemed, wasn't just in storybooks, and it had a specific shape and weight right in the center of her chest.

She rubbed her eyes, stretched her neck, then pulled out Jake's trading card to look at his gorgeous face. She thought about her last phone conversation with him. He'd seemed tense. Probably because he could sense she wasn't telling him everything. They'd made love on Thursday morning. They'd bonded intensely, well, she had at least. Based on their phone conversations Jake's world hadn't been rocked off its axis. The two of them hadn't discussed it. By now he probably assumed she was withdrawing since the banquet was over. After she'd seen him in her native environment and found him lacking.

It would be much simpler if that were true.

She should call him.

Rebecca glanced at the clock. Ten minutes had passed since her last check, which had been ten minutes after the glance before. Ridiculous. She picked up the phone and hit speed dial 1. He'd moved up from speed dial 17 on Thursday before her self-imposed exile.

He answered after the first ring. "Hey."

"The thing is," she began, "if I finish answering the emails and writing up the last two reports, I can start tomorrow with a clean slate. All the work from the banquet will be finished on my end."

He paused, then said, "I see. How long do you think that'll take?"

"Longer than it should. I'm in slow motion."

"Any chance you'll be up for a visit at the end?"

Now it was her turn to be quiet.

"Fair enough," he said. "How about this? How about you and me and your clean slate go out to dinner tomorrow night? Early, so that you can get to sleep at a decent hour."

She thought for a second. Seeing him was all she wanted. Also dangerous. Screw it. "That's very doable. In fact, I think it's a great idea. Although, we could eat dinner at home, thereby eliminating a step."

"Tempting," he said, and she could picture him leaning against the wall in the bathroom. The one he was fixing up. She could tell he was in there from the echo. He did like to lean, but that probably had more to do with his bad leg than posing. He'd be wearing his tool belt, too. And jeans. Soft, worn jeans that curved around his most excellent behind.

"Okay," he said. "I'll bring dinner. No cooking. No movie watching. Dinner, then bed."

"Well, that's not going to help me sleep."

"Don't be silly," he said. "We'll have just finished eating. We'll work off dinner. Then you'll collapse in my arms and sleep the sleep of the just."

"Bible quotes?"

"Really?" he asked. "I thought that was from an Elvis Costello song."

She grinned, wanting him with her, right there in the office. Just sitting there so she could look over and see him. He'd smile at her, and she'd get wiggly. Of course then she'd have to go kiss him and her grand plan would bite the dust. "Right. Dinner, my place—"

Another call came on her line, which she would most likely ignore. "Hang on. I'll be right back. It could be work."

She clicked to the second call, a New York number she didn't recognize. "Hello?"

"Rebecca."

William West. She recognized his voice. "Mr. West."

"I thought we agreed on Bill."

"Bill. Can you hold on a moment? I'm on another call."

"I'll wait."

She clicked again, hating that she'd have to put off Jake. If it had been anyone else... "Crap, it is work," she said. "I won't be long. I hope. If it is, we'll talk tomorrow and settle times and stuff, okay?"

"Don't stay up too late. I don't want you falling asleep in the soup."

She smiled and almost blew him a kiss, which…jeez. She was overtired. "Later."

She clicked back to West. "What can I do for you, Bill?"

"I think it's a question of what I can do for you. I'd like to take you to dinner tomorrow evening. We can start the ball rolling on the endowment."

Holy… "Absolutely. Where and when?"

"I'll meet you in front of your office building at eight. The chef at Per Se owes me. We'll have a window seat."

Per Se was one of the most exclusive restaurants in Manhattan, and getting a table there in anything less than six months took an act of congress. "I'll meet you at the car."

Rebecca hung up, looked at her long list of emails, thought about all her options and quickly redialed Jake.

"Yeah?"

"Can you meet me tonight instead? In two hours?"

He was quiet for a minute. "Uh, sure. What changed?"

"William West. He's finally agreed to meet with me tomorrow night to talk actual money. It's not attorneys yet, but it's a major step closer. So I made the executive decision to scrap my noble plans for a clean slate Monday in favor of a delicious Sunday night."

Oddly there was silence again. She'd thought he'd be pleased. "Oh, wait. Is this about your father? We could make it Tuesday night. Give you time to set things up."

"No. No, my dad's fine. He's got friends on standby. Hell, half the neighborhood would volunteer to stay with him if I asked. So, no. It's no problem. I'll bring dinner?"

"That would be excellent."

"You like Chinese?"

"Love it. Especially dim sum. But brunch is probably over, so never mind."

"Never mind? I can get dim sum."

"Really? You're a magician. Oh, that would be… Maybe some extra char siu bao. And har gau. Oh, and spareribs."

Jake laughed. "Is that all? I can just order a couple of everything on the menu."

"I skipped lunch."

"I can't leave you alone for five minutes, can I?" he asked.

The tenderness in his voice made her sit back in her chair. It took her a second to respond, what with swallowing past the lump. "No, I guess you can't. I'll see you in two."

"Don't be late. Your concierge looked hungry the last time I was there."

JAKE WAS THE ONE WHO WAS almost late. Not because of dinner. Gary had called him while he'd been in the cab on the way to the Great Wall restaurant. It wasn't a long conversation, just enough to ruin Jake's mood. He ended up ordering all the dim sum appetizers, even though it was going to cost him a fortune, and he'd have to wait a hell of a long time for it. The wait was fine, and the money, well, he was pretty sure he was trying to prove something by draining his savings, but he couldn't worry about that now. Not when Gary had found something. It didn't necessarily make West a bad guy, but it didn't help.

Rebecca was meeting West tomorrow night. Getting ready to make a deal. What Jake had wouldn't prove anything. The man's laugh reminded Jake of a particular cartoon character. A lot of people were born with cleft palates. If the two things hadn't been combined, he'd have dismissed the notion with barely a second thought. But the two things had been connected.

He had to decide, before he got the food, before he got to Manhattan, whether he was going to ask her to postpone the meeting with West or not.

Dammit, he didn't want this thing with her to be over. Not yet. Yeah, yeah, it was inevitable, like death, like taxes, like his father driving him crazy, but not yet. He might not have a choice about that, though. Something had been off between them the past few days. Ever since Thursday afternoon. It wasn't her workload, that he got completely. She was her job, the way he'd been his, so he had no complaints about the hours she spent at the office. It was more subtle. Pauses when there shouldn't have been. An edginess to her voice.

She'd undoubtedly come to the same conclusion he had, that they were on borrowed time. That the more they saw each other, the more difficult the break would be.

She was the best thing that had happened to Jake in a long time. Even before he'd been shot, his life hadn't been all that spectacular. When he'd been working his way up the ranks, he hadn't wanted a relationship. When he'd gone under, he couldn't have one. And now? With no job, no idea what he was going to do? Even if she wasn't Rebecca Thorpe he'd have no chance in hell.

God, how he'd wanted deep cover assignments. It was always a choice, those, because of what they meant. It was dangerous as hell, obviously, but more than the prospect of being killed, the real long-term danger was getting lost.

He'd been on the edge of doing just that. He'd become Steve "Papo" Carniglia. A wannabe drug lord who'd worked his way up the ranks in the Far Rockaway Gang of Apes, getting close and tight with the man in charge because while he'd acted like a card-carrying member of the Queens' gang, he never played dumb.

As he sat on the really uncomfortable bench waiting for the food, he leaned his head back against the window and cursed his instincts. She had so much riding on West's money. Not just her, but all the people his money could help. The smart thing to do would be to let it go. Forget he'd ever heard that damn laugh. There were a lot of reasons it made sense to put the brakes on, but the one that had him tied up in knots was that she might be walking into something that could put her foundation in jeopardy.

Rebecca was doing everything in her power to elevate the image of the Winslow Foundation, to give it integrity and transparency. If he had a little more time, he could make sure who she was getting involved with. Then they could both rest easy. All he needed was a short reprieve.

He wanted to show her so much. Now that the banquet was over, she'd have time. First thing, he'd take her to the New York she'd never seen. The hidden city he'd spent so long exploring. He wanted to watch her face when she saw where she really lived.

He could have it, too. If she postponed that meeting. Or if he didn't bring up the subject of Keegan at all.

The host called Jake's name, and he shook his head at how overboard he'd gone in buying dinner for two. But he wanted Rebecca to have everything. Food, success, pride, honor, *everything*. How long he had before she came to her senses and showed him the door didn't matter in the end. Nothing mattered except Rebecca.

Well, there was his answer.

SHE OPENED THE DOOR AND laughed out loud when she saw the enormous bags he was carrying. "You dope," she said, taking one of the heavy bags. "You bought the whole restaurant?"

"You skipped lunch."

"Yeah, well, you're taking the leftovers home. That'll feed your dad and his buddies for a couple of weeks."

"Boy, do you not know my dad and his buddies. They may be old, but they eat like beat cops."

She watched him as he hung up his coat. He looked great, as always. No tool belt, dammit, but nice jeans, not quite as worn in, a little darker than the ones she'd declared her favorite, with a white oxford shirt tucked into them. She took another moment to admire his shoulder-to-waist ratio. She was a lucky, lucky woman.

"What's that goofy grin about?"

"You're very attractive," she said.

"That's it? Attractive?"

"That's a lot."

He shrugged.

"I'm not saying that's all you are."

He put his bag on the island, then took the one she was holding and dumped that, too. "What else am I?" he asked as he pulled her into his arms.

"Wow. Fish much?"

"From time to time. Come on." He kissed her, quick, teasing. "Give me something other than looks."

"As if you've never thought hot wasn't reason enough."

"I have, I'll admit it. But you're so much more than that," he said and then he really kissed her. It was as if he'd been starving, but for her. She felt his desperation in his hands and his lips and the way he thrummed with energy. She was helpless to do anything but kiss him back, to give as good as she got. When he finally drew back, she had to blink herself into the present, into the fact that the ache she'd felt for days had dissipated the moment she was in his arms. That she'd never felt like this before, not even dared to dream she could be madly, deeply in love, and that maybe, possibly, he felt… No, he was just being Jake. She'd know if he loved her.

She put some distance between them and the loss of his touch was like a slap. "Let's put out everything on the coffee table and grab whatever. Want a Sapporo?"

He didn't answer for a long minute, and she couldn't read him. Hesitance, and then a smile. His regular smile. "Sure. I'll start unpacking."

Rebecca got the beers, the plates and the good chopsticks. She also brought along her bottle of soy sauce because she had a tendency to squirt the packets all over herself and the furniture.

It looked like a modern sculpture, all the white boxes covering her coffee table. He'd had to put the magazines on the floor and the flowers on the side table.

"I'm going to have one of everything." she said, determined to keep things light. She handed him his beer. "Then decide about seconds."

"You'd better get a move on, because there's only three of each thing."

They sat next to each other on the couch. She had one leg curled under her butt; his legs were spread in that manly way that always amused. After he opened both beers, they grabbed their chopsticks, and it was on.

"Hey," she said, as she opened the third box. You cheated. This is the second box of char siu."

"Actually, I got three orders of those. And two each of the har gau and the ribs."

Before she could even think about it, she kissed him. "Thank you."

He kissed her back, lingering, until he came away with a sigh. "You're welcome. Don't eat them all."

"I wouldn't think of it," she said, deciding right then that the plan to keep her distance was ridiculous. She wasn't going to send him home after they ate. And she wasn't going to kick him out of her bed. Fighting it was a lost cause. Maybe the lesson here was to not be so damn logical about everything. So what if she didn't know where this would lead? That might turn out to be the best part. He'd already taught her so much. Who could say where he would take her next?

They didn't speak for the next while, but she managed to communicate quite well. Mostly by moaning. Taking a bite of the lobster after dipping it into a delicate sauce that was clearly made by the tears of angels, she made loud yummy noises as she chewed.

He laughed at her, looking at her as if she was extraordinary. It was the best dinner she'd had in ages. He stopped eating surprisingly quickly. Probably because he hadn't skipped lunch. Then he got himself another beer, and instead of sitting down again, he stood at the edge of the kitchen, watching her.

She smiled, but it faded after a minute. "I'm sorry about tomorrow night. I can't let this guy slip through my fingers. It's too important."

The words hadn't even finished coming out of her mouth when she saw Jake's demeanor change. His whole body tensed and he frowned, actively frowned.

"What?" she asked. "Are you okay?"

"Yeah. I'm fine," he said, but he burst into motion, leaning over to close the food cartons, avoiding her eyes.

"Jake, what just happened?"

He paused.

"You can't possibly think I have any interest in Bill West outside of his money."

"No. I don't." He stood, abandoning the boxes.

"So?"

"I'd like to ask you to postpone that meeting. With West."

"What? Why?"

He ran his hand through his hair, picked up his empty beer bottle and stared at it for a moment. "I have a bad feeling about him."

"I know. He's not my favorite person either. He flirted with me right in front of his girlfriend, or whoever she was. It was creepy. But I can handle myself."

"That's not it." Jake moved from behind the coffee table and walked over to the window. "Dammit, I wasn't ready to get into this yet."

Rebecca's stomach tightened and it wasn't pleasant. "What are you talking about, Jake? Tell me already."

He stared down into the street for too long before he turned to face her again. "I can't swear to it, but I'm pretty sure I've met West before."

The way he spoke, the way his voice lowered and his eyes grew cold made her very uncomfortable. "And?"

"It was a while ago. Before I did deep cover work. I think I met him at a drug bust."

"He was a junkie?"

"If he's who I think he is, he was a lot worse than that."

"Okay," she said, standing, walking toward him so she could see his face clearly. "I am so not understanding this."

"I have no proof, so this is going to sound crazy. And

I might be wrong. Really wrong. My gut, though. My gut is telling me there's something—"

She shook her head, waiting. Becoming more uneasy by the second.

"I recognized his laugh."

His laugh? She huffed her impatience and gave Jake a look. "Well, okay. It is…unique."

"Yeah. Not easy to forget. But that's not all. The guy I'm thinking of, Vance Keegan, he also had a scar from lip surgery."

"Am I supposed to understand?" she asked.

"No reason you should. He worked for a drug dealer named Luis Packard. A major drug trafficker who ran most of the East Coast for over ten years. Everything from heroin to coke to prescriptions. This guy Keegan was part of the organization, an office guy. Something with the money, although no one ever told me exactly what his role was. They killed a lot of people, sold a lot of drugs to a lot of kids.

"I was in on the bust. It was all over the news because when we were just about to lock it down, Packard's people hit us, hard. Smoke bombs, machine-gun fire. Packard was killed, and so were some of the good guys. The gun that killed Packard had Keegan's prints, among others. Keegan got away. Disappeared. Vanished. They looked for him, but he wasn't on the top-ten most wanted. They were more concerned with where the drug money had gone, all the millions of dollars that were supposedly in a panic room."

He kept talking, and Rebecca stared at him, barely comprehending what was happening. The whole thing was surreal. Jake sounded different, looked different… it was as if she'd stepped into one of their film noirs.

"I always believed Keegan's disappearance and the

missing money were connected. But that whole deal was way above my pay grade. Thing is, I was standing right next to Keegan, and he was laughing that weird laugh as we walked across the roof of the warehouse. He was laughing like he knew something, even though he was cuffed and surrounded by dozens of officers. Then he was gone."

Rebecca took a step back. "You think William West is really Vance Keegan? Wouldn't someone have noticed?"

"He hasn't been in New York in years. He claims to be from Nevada, has a home office there. He travels to Europe, to California, even to Africa and Asia, but he'd never been to New York until a few weeks ago. From everything I read, he's kept himself under the radar until last year. More importantly, he doesn't look the same. I think he had a bunch of surgery, reworked everything from his hairline to the shape of his jaw."

"Wait a minute—you've been investigating him?"

Jake moved a shoulder, his gaze unwavering. "I wouldn't say investigating," he said slowly. "Just searching online."

She had no idea what to do. Jake seemed dead serious. But West had a multimillion-dollar company. There was nothing shady about him, and her people had checked. "Jake, that's really a stretch, not to mention a serious accusation."

"I know. I told you it sounds crazy. And I'm not making an accusation. It's a hunch, but one that needs checking. That's why I'm asking for a postponement. Some time."

She needed some time herself. This was crazy information here, and if it had been anyone but Jake, she'd have laughed and dismissed the whole thing as some weird con. But it wasn't someone else. "I'm pretty certain there is a large percentage of people born with cleft palates."

"They called him Lip," Jake said, nodding. "That must have pissed him off. To be called that by Packard, who was a real piece of work. He was a vicious bastard, ran over anyone trying to get in on his territory. Didn't care who he took out in the process."

"Jake…"

"I know. That's why I decided to do some checking. I couldn't find anything, but my friend… This guy is a genius hacker. Works for Homeland Security. He told me tonight on my way to the restaurant that there's something fishy about the death of West's uncle. That's supposedly how West got his start-up funds. His uncle's estate. But the uncle was murdered. They never found out who did it. There are no other living relatives, and the uncle was a recluse. Lived way out in the desert with the scrub brush and the heat. His body wasn't discovered for almost two months."

Her stomach tightened; she wasn't liking the fact that someone else was involved. If West got wind of any of this… "I'm sorry, I don't see a connection between Keegan and a desert recluse."

"I wasn't gonna say anything. Because I know there are other explanations. I was undercover a long time, Rebecca. I survived by my instincts and training, but trust me, the instincts were more critical. Something clicked for me at the party. Something I can't ignore."

"I see," she said. But she didn't. Jake was wonderful, nearly perfect. But she hadn't even known him two weeks. This? This was kind of scary.

"I only need a week. That's all. Maybe less," Jake mumbled. He turned back to the window and his bad leg wobbled so much his hand shot to the wall for balance.

"But you're right. I'm probably going stir-crazy being stuck at home."

"I didn't say that. Honestly, the thought hadn't even crossed my mind." Unfortunately, it did now. She looked at his taut back, at his image in the mirror. She had the terrible feeling the next few minutes were going to have far-reaching repercussions.

So much for time to think things through. It was all down to *her* instincts now, and while there were many perfectly valid reasons to throw in the towel, and only one for sticking with Jake, she had to bet on the long shot. They might have been together only a short time, but she'd never had a connection like this with anyone. He wasn't crazy. In fact, he was the most down-to-earth, balanced man she'd ever met. Even as she knew her decision was final, she could barely believe it.

She stood behind him, placed her hand on his shoulder. "You're concerned for me," she said.

He faced her, all the ice gone from his gaze. Now his eyes were filled with doubt and fear, a very accurate echo of her own feelings. She couldn't picture a future for them, but she understood what was important to Jake now. Honor. Responsibility. All the things she'd fallen in love with.

"I am concerned for you," he said. "Very much."

"I could postpone, but I won't. Not because I don't believe there's a possibility you might be right. Admittedly, I think it's a very small chance, but anyway, I don't need to postpone because first of all, I'm not in any danger. Second, nothing is going to be signed tomorrow night. This type of deal takes time. The next step is only the negotiation to negotiate."

He nodded, but she doubted he was happy.

"The instant you have any proof, I'll stand with you

and we'll see him put away, but I need to tell you that every person who donates or participates in any meaningful way with the foundation is vetted by our security company. They have remarkable access, which is why they're astronomically expensive. They saw nothing wrong with West's background."

"I'm not surprised. If he did create himself on paper, he would have to have done a remarkably thorough job. I honestly do know how insane this sounds. It would be smarter to let it alone. But I don't think I can."

"Okay. Go with your gut. From what I know about you, I can't imagine you're taking any of this lightly."

He huffed a sad laugh. "So it's not a deal breaker?"

Rebecca ran her hand through his hair. "Nope. And that's why you need to see it through. Because nobody would give this up on a whim."

"Did I hear that right? Did you just tell me you're the hottest woman in New York?"

She laughed. "Now, that would be insane. No," she whispered, then kissed him. "But together, we're pretty incendiary, don't you think?"

His hands were on her now, confident, strong. Running down her back until they curved over her bottom. "Smokin'," he said and he bent to kiss her.

She put up a hand, stopping him. "Please, do not let West get wind of any of this. You have to promise me, Jake. He can't know."

Jake gave her his crooked smile. "You probably won't believe me, but I want to be wrong. I want you to win." Then his mouth was on hers, and she let herself relax against him, let herself trust him. There was an ache inside her and she wanted him badly. The way he'd looked at her, it made her heart hurt. No one had ever looked at her that way before. There'd been lust and hurt and greed and impatience. Even caring and concern and, yes, several kinds of love.

But his gaze had held more than she had words for. This man would slay dragons for her. There was no doubt at all about it. He would put her first over everything.

God, how she wanted him in her bed, in her arms. She wanted to be as close as two people could possibly get. When she tugged his hand, he followed after her, but this time, when they stood by her bed, it wasn't a race. They undressed slowly, one garment at a time, their gazes locked until the last possible second.

When they crawled into bed together, it was quiet. As they gathered each other, wrapping themselves in legs and arms and heat, she felt as safe as she'd ever been.

They kissed. No rush, just kissing. Slow, long touches and rubbing back and forth until the sounds of his breath and her own were only drowned out by the blood rushing in her head, by the beating of her heart.

When he entered her, she stilled him with a cry.

"Rebecca?" he whispered.

"It's good," she said, her lips against his. "Perfect."

13

STANDING OUTSIDE REBECCA'S building at seven-fifteen in the morning, Jake decided to hit a deli a few blocks down, have himself another coffee and try to put his head around what he was getting into.

That she'd made love to him last night, that they'd fooled around in the shower this morning was remarkable, considering, but not nearly as confusing as the fact that she'd made plans with him for Wednesday night. Future plans. When he'd told her his suspicions about West, Jake had seen the growing alarm on her face. He didn't blame her. It would have made so much more sense for her to cut her losses and be done with him.

As if he needed her to be even more incredible. Jesus. Not perfect though. He grinned as he crossed the street, letting the crowd swallow him and set the pace. She'd been cranky as hell this morning. Evidently, all this very fine dining was starting to get to her, and she'd been putting off yoga and the gym because of the donor thing, and she'd declared herself a disgusting slug this morning when her gray wool slacks were harder to zip than they should have been.

His repeated and heartfelt compliments about her

body, complete with kisses and petting, had been dismissed as irrelevant. Because he was a man. So, perfect? No. Which made her even better.

He walked over to 33rd to the 2nd Ave Deli and got himself a booth. He wished he had a notebook or something, but it was more important to have the coffee.

As he waited for the waitress, he tried like hell to organize his thoughts. The first option was to forget about Keegan. Leave it, ignore it. He had the feeling that's the option Rebecca would vote for, despite her support. She'd tell him he was doing the sensible thing. But he rarely did the sensible thing, and this was no exception. It would bother him to the end of his days if he didn't check it out to the best of his ability.

Second option, wait to see what Gary came up with. He knew his friend wasn't infallible, the internet did not have every answer in the world, and the man had a very demanding job. If Gary was discovered looking into anything suspicious, such as the background of William West, it could be bad for Gary.

Jake got his coffee, but before he did anything, he took out his phone. It rang once.

"I don't have anything else for you yet," Gary said.

"Not why I called. How much trouble can you get in for doing this stuff?"

"A lot. If I'm caught. But I won't be. And hell, now that I think of it, not that much trouble. I can always say I found something hinky and was doing my bit for the safety of our great nation."

"Do not bullshit me about this, dude. It's probably nothing. I'd really hate it if you were sent to prison."

Gary laughed. "I don't like you enough to go to prison. Stop worrying about it. I'll call you."

And that was that. Jake fixed up his coffee and as

he stirred, it occurred to him that he had another friend who might be helpful. Well, *friend* was stretching it, but the breakup hadn't been bad…hadn't been terrible at least. Crystal was great, but it was tricky, her being a lawyer and then becoming an assistant district attorney. Thing was, she worked in the Investigative Division of the D.A.'s office. Writing briefs, but still she was inside.

He didn't have her number any longer, but it would be better if he showed up in person, anyway. The one thing Jake had going for him was that he'd never been able to tell Crystal he was an undercover cop. Maybe now that he could, she'd understand why he'd been such a flake. If not, he'd play the sympathy card. She was a nice woman. It would bother her that he'd been shot, even if she had no desire to see him again.

So he'd go to her office. Ask to find out what she could about T-Mac, who was currently serving a life sentence in Sing Sing. He'd been part of the bust, took most of the heat after Keegan vanished and Luis Packard died. There was a chance T-Mac had some information on Keegan's whereabouts, although it was a slim chance.

At least Jake was already in the city. But first, he called his old man.

"You still shacking up with that gorgeous woman?" his father asked.

"Doesn't anybody say hello anymore?"

"Hello. You still shacking up with that gorgeous woman?"

"You're a riot. No. She's gone to work. But I'm gonna be a while. You doing okay?"

"I'm doing fine. The two domino cheaters are here with me, and everything's just peachy."

"Oh, God." Jake lowered his head, not in the least ready to hear about how Pete and Liam were conspiring against Mike to ruin his game. This happened at least once every couple of months and had more to do with the wheelchair knocking over the card table than duplicity and revenge. "You can tell me about it later. You need something for when I come home?"

"No. Yeah. Cookies."

"Chocolate chip or those oatmeal things?"

"Both."

"Maybe you should learn another game. I hear mahjongg is fun."

"Hey, Jakey? Go—"

Jake hung up. Then he got the number for the D.A.'s office and made sure Crystal was there. The odds weren't great that she'd speak to him, but he had nothing to lose. Story of his life.

THE LIMO WAS DIRECTLY IN front of the building, in the red zone; a female chauffeur wearing a traditional uniform opened the back door long before Rebecca reached the sidewalk, and William West stepped out of the car.

He was in a suit; she was sure it cost a bundle, but it wasn't anything special. Didn't particularly flatter him, but that didn't matter. He wasn't on display in this dance. She was.

She smiled and took his hand, then slid onto the seat. A few moments later, he got in on the other side. She'd had just enough time to remember why she was going to this dinner. No matter what ultimately happened, the best information she had right now was that West was a perfectly legitimate businessman who might be willing to donate a significant amount of money to her foundation. Many, many lives depended on those donations, and it was her job to help those people. She would use whatever tactics she believed would get the job done.

That meant manipulating West's attention. She'd be competing with the restaurant, the chef's tasting menu, the unbelievably fine service and the wine. She had to be more fascinating than all of that, and she had to make him feel as if he'd win something big by moving on to the next stage.

Not her. That was never, would never, be on the table, and they both knew that. This parlay was more subtle. It was a conversation. A tease. All about timing. She couldn't afford to think about Jake, about his instincts, about her feelings. Tonight she was fighting for inoculations, for clean water, for medical care, for food, for women and children.

"It's great to see you again so soon," West said. "I enjoyed the banquet, but this is even nicer, don't you think? A chance to get to know one another."

"It will be nice. I've been looking forward to it all day."

"Good. I called ahead. The chef's tasting menu tonight sounds fantastic."

"You know him?"

He nodded. "We've crossed paths."

"I didn't think you got to the city very often."

"Chef Keller travels to Las Vegas frequently."

"Ah, of course."

It was quiet for the rest of the drive, which wasn't long. Then they were at The Time Warner Center at Columbus Circle, and she was being escorted to the fourth-floor restaurant.

As soon as they were inside, the maître d' greeted them both by name. West walked behind her to take her coat. As it came away, she heard his soft gasp as he realized her dress was backless. Very backless. She allowed herself a tiny smile.

They were led to a window table with a gorgeous view of Central Park. She liked the restaurant, who wouldn't, as it was owned and run by the chef of the French Laundry, but the nine-course meal, even with tiny portions, was almost more than she could deal with after the week she'd had. It would have been so much better to be at Jake's place in Brooklyn, listening to his dad and friends, watching something on TV and eating a simple salad.

But she followed the rules of engagement. Nods at the wine, smiles and questions, letting him do most of the talking until the sixth course. She'd been judicious whereas West had been quick to refill his glasses of wine, different kinds, perfectly paired with each delicacy.

She excused herself, sure his gaze never left her back as she went to the ladies' room. Once there, she relaxed. It was just as elegant as one would expect. Spacious, beautiful, quiet. When she returned to the table, she'd get down to business, and she would get him to commit to a dollar amount.

So far she'd seen nothing suspicious about the man. He wasn't the most refined person she'd ever met but he wasn't in any way vulgar. He had no accent, not even a trace of New York. His laugh gave her chills, though she hadn't reacted, but she'd had to force her gaze away from his mouth more than once.

He rose as she approached the table on her return, then held her chair for her. As she was sitting, he bent in such a way that the light hit the edge of his hairline. That was when she saw it. A scar at his hairline, artfully masked by his dark hair. She'd seen enough face-lifts to know what she was looking at, and while it could be a remnant of his vanity, it might be something else completely.

As they continued on with little plates of perfect food, and talk swung to the endowment itself, she watched his face. Jake had said his jaw was different. Those scars were tricky, and not all could be hidden.

By course nine, she had him talking about five million a year for ten years. And she'd identified scar tissue just below his right ear.

That still meant nothing; half of her parents' friends had had work done. Although she'd apparently been giving him the wrong signals by watching him so carefully. The way he looked at her now spoke of a deal that had nothing to do with charity.

JAKE HADN'T EVEN TRIED TO sleep. It was eleven-thirty and he was bone tired but he was pacing the house like a caged animal. He hadn't asked her to call. But he couldn't imagine she wouldn't. She knew he was worried. The dinner probably wasn't over yet, so he should calm the hell down.

What he needed to do now was prepare himself. She had a lot riding on this deal. No reason for her to believe everything wasn't completely kosher, and if West had offered to give the foundation a ton of money, Rebecca would be pleased. And he'd be pleased for her.

Until proven guilty, West was nothing more than a victory for her and her foundation, and Jake could damn well keep anything else out of the conversation.

The TV was off, his old man was in bed, the place was quiet and Jake debated going to Midtown, waiting for her at her place. He dismissed the idea as beyond stupid, but man, he wished like hell she'd call.

He could call her. She'd know why. She was smart,

she was amazing, she'd be onto him in seconds. And she'd think he'd gone from being slightly nuts to tin-hat crazy.

He thought again about his afternoon at the D.A.'s office. He had no idea if it was going to pay off or not, but in the end it didn't matter what Crystal found out. He had already made arrangements with Pete to borrow his 1970 Barracuda. The car was the only thing, aside from dominoes and his friends, that Pete gave a crap about, and that he had given Jake the keys with no hesitation said a lot. That was one part of being home that had been great to relearn.

Of course cops watched out for each other, but when you're in deep cover, it was different. Any association with other law-enforcement personnel was dangerous for everyone involved. Jake hadn't realized just how empty his life had been for far too long. Filling it again was a privilege. He'd done pretty well with home and family. But that still left a lot of room.

Although it would play hell on his leg, he limped down the hall and grabbed his jacket. He wouldn't be gone long. He didn't like leaving his father alone, but Mike rarely woke up once he conked out. There was no reason for his father to go downstairs even if he did.

Soon, if Jake could ever get his life back on track, Mike wouldn't have to worry about stairs. Yet another reason this thing with Rebecca wasn't the best of ideas. Jake had his responsibilities at home and until he could figure out another way, that meant sticking close to Brooklyn.

He walked toward Fifth, taking his time, trying not to focus on his thigh but on his destination. There was a bar where a man could buy a beer. One beer, then he'd come back, get himself ready for bed.

When his cell rang in the middle of Howard and 4th, he jumped and grabbed for it so fast he almost dropped the damn thing. "Hello?"

"Did I wake you?"

Jake relaxed. Rebecca sounded good. Tired, but good. "I'm up. You okay?"

"He has some scars."

"What?"

"Scar tissue. One could have been from a face-lift, but there were several more, hard to see, and I might be wrong. I tried to dismiss it. I know a lot of people who've had work done, but I'll admit it's bothered me because it was a lot of scar tissue. It was behind his ear, but it wasn't like a face-lift scar. You said his jaw had been altered."

"Yeah, that's what I thought. The jaw, the nose, the hairline and his eyes."

"They weren't easy to spot. He had an amazingly good surgeon. And God knows a cosmetic scar isn't proof, or half my relatives would be arrested."

"No, they're not proof. But I may be able to get something more tomorrow. I'm taking Pete's car up to Sing Sing."

"Where's that?"

"Ossining. About an hour and a half drive. I'm going to visit one of the men who was working with Keegan. See what he can tell me."

"You're not a cop anymore," she said, and he could hear the soft movements of cloth against cloth. "Can you just show up like that?"

"I know a guy who knows a guy. Professional courtesy and all that. It shouldn't take too long. He'll either talk or not, but I figure he might be pretty unhappy to

be sitting in jail while Keegan's out and about making
so much money he can afford to give it away."

"If it's Keegan." She sounded tense.

"Right. If." He didn't feel much like getting that beer
now so he turned around. "And if he's William West,
how did your meeting go?"

"Look, Jake, you can't mention West's name tomorrow. Ask all you want about Keegan, but promise me
you won't try linking him to West."

"I won't. I never planned to. You have my word."

She sighed with relief. "Jesus, you've got me all crazy
and paranoid now."

He winced. Her words took a chunk out of him but
he sucked it up. He couldn't blame her for not blindly
jumping on the bandwagon. "Okay, for now we're as-
suming everything's copacetic with West. Tell me about
dinner."

"It went well. There's the chance we'll be getting five
million a year for ten years."

Jake whistled. "That's not chump change."

"I'm not holding my breath about it. There's a lot that
could still fall apart on this deal. The foundation will go
on, one way or another."

"I'm just glad you're okay."

"I am," she said. "Oh, and Jake?"

"Yeah?"

"You're considerate. Charming. Sexy. Funny. Decent.
Dedicated. Heroic. Did I mention sexy?"

He laughed. "What's that about?"

"Last night you asked me what I liked about you.
Aside from you being so very, very good-looking."

"I see," he said, flushing under the cold light from the
streetlamp, glad she hadn't thrown in that he was nuts.
"That was quite a list."

"All true."

"Sure you haven't mistaken me for an Eagle Scout?"

"Positive."

"Damn, woman. I wish you were a whole lot closer."

"Be glad I'm not. I'm so tired I can barely see. Do me a favor, check in with me tomorrow. I don't want to worry that you've been trapped in some prison riot or something."

"Okay. I will. And Rebecca? You're pretty goddamn fantastic yourself."

For a minute, he listened to her breath. "Good night, Jake. Drive safely. Be careful. Come back in one piece."

"I promise."

14

THE BARRACUDA WAS A BEAST in terms of power, but one hell of a beauty to drive. Now that Jake was almost at the prison, he turned down the factory-installed AM radio and went over his plan of action.

Crystal had come through, thankfully. She'd called him this morning with T-Mac's prison records and more importantly an overview of his phone records. Some of his calls had been from and to lawyers, but he had family. A mother and sister in Georgia. They didn't come by, only called. No calls to or from Nevada. As for T-Mac's life inside, he'd gone with the Bloods, which wasn't a surprise considering, and he wasn't classified as a high-risk inmate. He'd been there eleven years, time enough to get established, but not quite time enough for a chance at parole. They'd never been able to pin a murder on T-Mac.

His real name was Lantrel Wilson, and Jake had no idea where T-Mac had come from or what it meant. He'd been associated with Packard as a kid. Been arrested for selling drugs to other kids and sent to a juvenile facility three times before he was seventeen. He'd been thirty-four when he was busted in that raid, and according to testimony, which was highly suspect as it was given by other members of Packard's operation, T-Mac was not just an office guy, he was one of only three or four people who had access to the panic room safe.

The signs warning against picking up hitchhikers popped up frequently as he continued on toward Hunter St., the icy-blue Hudson to his left.

Then there was the rigmarole about getting inside. Crystal had come through on that, too, and he owed her now. Flowers. Expensive flowers. He kept his eyes and ears open as he went through check after check until he was finally admitted into one of the cubicles they used for attorney visits. It took fifteen minutes for the door to open, and T-Mac was led inside.

First eye contact was definitely a challenge, but this wasn't Jake's first rodeo so he ignored it, using the silence to note the changes eleven years had wrought. The man had some serious muscle now. Enough tattoos to decorate the cubicle walls a couple times over. And that was only what Jake could see. T-Mac wore his long hair in cornrows that looked greasy, had a Van Dyke beard and squinty little eyes.

"Who the fuck are you?" he asked, finally.

"You can't guess?"

"Cop?"

Jake smiled. "Ex-cop."

"So? What you want?"

"What can you tell me about Lip?"

T-Mac didn't blink. He looked uncomfortable, but that might have been because his chair was too small for his bulk. He could barely cross his arms. "Who?"

"Hey, you're the one that ended up taking the fall for Packard, for Lip, for everything. I would imagine

Lip getting away scot-free would be something to think about over the years."

"You don't know what I think about."

"I do not. You're correct. But I would like to find out what you know about Vance Keegan."

"For all I know, he's dead and gone. I got no word about him from nobody. Not for all the time I been here."

"Nothing? Not a sighting? Say, from someone in Nevada?"

That got Jake a wince and a look. "You think I got pen pals or somethin'? How'd you even get in here, ex-cop? What are you looking for?"

"I'm writing a book."

"Yeah, and I'm singing in a choir. That all?"

"I don't know. I have to wonder, though, if it turned out that Lip wasn't dead. That he was, say, living it up on the money that was supposed to be in the panic room. Making more money off that. Spending money. A lot of it. Would that clear up your memory some?"

"What the hell you talking about? Lip was nothing. Nobody. He got coffee and set up hookers."

"Yeah. That sounds about right. Packard. He was a real sonofabitch, wasn't he? Charging his own people twenty-percent interest? That had to sting."

That got a reaction. It had been a rumor, a note on a piece of paper that Crystal had found.

"It's time you left, ex-cop. I got nothing to say to you."

"Nothing to pass on if I should miraculously discover Lip is alive and well?"

T-Mac gave him a contemptuous look, then stood up. Jake found it was a lot faster to get out of the prison than in. Just as well…the trip had been nothing but a big waste of time.

IT FELT AS IF REBECCA hadn't been to the St. Marks church kitchen in months. Although they would meet next Monday to exchange lunches, today was a special gathering, a birthday party. Two women, an account rep for MetLife and a personal assistant of a famous author, were turning thirty. Rebecca couldn't always make it to the group get-togethers, but she'd been delighted to come to this one. Not only did she like Ally and Tricia, but left to her own devices while Jake was at the prison, she would have been a wreck.

It was too soon to expect a call, but she'd been on tenterhooks the whole morning. Her day, in fact, had been terrifically normal. Flowers delivered from Bill West, thanking her for the dinner. No meaning to it, just something men tended to do when they wanted to get into someone's pants. Or just to be polite, but that's not what West's gesture had been about. He wanted more. The way he'd looked at her at the end of the evening? It was as if he was doing everything in his power to figure her out, right down to how she liked her coffee in the morning. It had been an uncomfortable ride home, but maybe that was just her. What she knew about him, suspected about him, colored her perspective once the business of the evening had ended.

There was no proof. It was highly unlikely that he was a wanted man, a killer. If she eliminated that possibility entirely, what she was left with was a guy from Henderson, Nevada, who'd made a bundle and felt he wasn't getting enough attention. Or not enough attention from the right people. Why else come to New York to contribute his millions? He could have easily found worthy causes in Vegas or California.

No, he was looking for validation. He'd taken her to Per Se to impress her. That's why he'd brought a date to the banquet. He was preening, and that should have been her only consideration until there was more to go on than a couple of scars and an odd laugh.

"Well?"

Katy Groft stood in front of Rebecca. She'd changed her hair color to a softer brown with caramel highlights. It really suited her.

"You mean Jake."

"Yes, I mean Jake. How was it?"

"Great," she said, catching herself in the nick of time. Katy had gone out with Jake, too, and what was the proper etiquette for disclosure in the trading card world? She didn't know Katy that well. It might hurt her feelings that Jake and Rebecca had hit it off. Or she might be delighted. "He's a really nice guy."

"Nice guy, hell. He's gorgeous and funny and smart. He's the best date I've had this year. Wish it could've lasted longer with him, but *c'est la vie*."

Rebecca gave it up as a lost cause and told the truth. "You know what? Me, too. Best date in years. He's pretty amazing."

Katy stepped back two paces. "Oh," she said. "Why do I get the feeling it wasn't only one night with you two?"

Rebecca felt the warmth of her blush and was thrilled when she saw Bree approach. The lunch brigade were filing in now, and things would get moving soon. The cake was here, along with all the accoutrements. Instead of gifts, everyone was donating to the St. Marks kitchen, which, in addition to letting them cook, also served weekend meals to people in need. "It's been several more," she admitted. "And we're getting together tomorrow night."

"No," Katy said, her voice dropping low and loud. "You are kidding me."

"What?" Bree asked, not the least abashed by nosing in on the conversation. "Are we talking about Jake?"

"You know about Jake?" Katy asked.

"Met him. He's a dream. I swear, if I wasn't with Charlie—"

"You're still with Charlie Winslow?"

All three women turned at that voice. It was Shannon, of Hot Guys New York trading card fame, making her entrance with her usual flair, red hair flying, high heels clicking across the floor. "I should have charged money for these cards. The hits keep on coming."

"It was a stroke of genius," Bree said. "You should call the *Times*. Have them do an article."

Shannon gasped, her eyes wide and shocked. "No one is calling anyone, especially not the media. God, can you imagine? Men would be climbing all over themselves to get on the cards. And they'd all want to show off their *assets,* if you know what I mean." She held up her hand, index finger and thumb about two inches apart.

"Either that or they'd be lining up to sue you," Lacy said with a laugh.

Shannon shook her head. "For a dating circle? No one has that much free time."

"Besides," Katy said, "men are too vain. None of them would complain about using their pics without permission, especially if it got them on a date with one of us."

"Your lips to God's ears," Shannon said, with a glance toward the ceiling. "I want to keep playing with the deck. I'm certain I'm going to meet my Mr. Right through this plan. It's fated." She flipped her hair over her shoulder. "So let's all remember to keep this our little secret."

Rebecca grinned, but she agreed with Shannon in principle. The whole reason the trading cards worked was because it was a controlled environment. "Well, I'm thrilled that I'm part of it," she said. If Shannon couldn't get accolades from the press, she certainly deserved them from her. "I'm seeing someone really special."

"I didn't think we had any more gazillionaires in the stack," Shannon said. "Or was he posing as a regular guy?"

That stung. A lot. "No, he is a regular guy."

"Oh." Shannon frowned. "I'm sorry. I didn't mean—"

"Yes, you did. But it's okay. No reason not to. I was as surprised as anyone."

"Come on," Bree said, bumping her shoulder. "You're not like that. I'd know."

"No, I'm not looking for an escape clause," Rebecca said, touching Bree's hand. "I've had to do some real soul-searching over this. I never realized how accustomed I'd become to men of a certain class. It's been a real wake-up call. Yet another reason to be grateful for the trading cards."

Shannon wasn't frowning now. Her face softened, and her very pink lips curved into a smile. "That's good," she said. "Thank you for telling me that."

"I can't believe I let him get away," Katy said. "I had him first."

"You said it was all right."

Katy grinned at Rebecca. "Of course it's all right. I'm kidding. Jealous, but kidding. Now, return the favor and set me up with someone wonderful."

"I'll do my best," she said. She would, too. But there

wasn't a single man in her life, now that Charlie was taken, that she'd want to share with the women here. Her friends deserved better.

HE PULLED INTO A GAS STATION in Englewood to fill up the Barracuda. It took premium gas, for God's sake, and it drank like a lush. But, oh, how Pete loved this car.

Jake wasn't sure why—maybe he hadn't gotten the car gene—but he'd never been into them. Not even when he'd gotten his driver's license. He'd bought an old Toyota when he had enough money, learned enough to change the oil, change plugs and points, the basics, and that was fine. It was lucky he'd been a decent quarterback because he'd been harassed about that old bucket of bolts from day one.

Instead he'd become obsessed with guns. Not rifles, although he could handle one. Not hunting, he had no interest. He'd learned about guns at the shooting range, on a Smith & Wesson 36 revolver. He and his father had been like most teenagers and their dads, arguing, pissing each other off about everything, his hormones in charge, his father's patience stretched beyond the limit, but not at the range. There, Mike had been an extraordinary teacher, and Jake, an obedient and helpful son. That had lasted until Jake got two more bull's-eyes than his old man.

After he'd spent an ungodly amount on gasoline, Jake pulled the car into an empty space at the little food market, far from where anyone else would park. He was more afraid of wrecking Pete's car than he was of that prison riot Rebecca had warned him about.

He got himself a soda, found a seat on a bench where he could watch the Barracuda, which was worth a lot of money, not to mention Pete's well-being, and called Rebecca.

"Hi," she said. She sounded relieved, and that made him feel better than he'd expected, considering. "How did it go?"

"As far as concrete information? It sucked. But if you count inferences that could lead directly to the next step in the process, it also sucked."

"Oh, no," she said, but he could hear the relief in her tone. She probably assumed the poking around was over. That West was exactly who he said he was. She might be right.

"T-Mac wasn't forthcoming," he said. "The only undertone I got from him was his distinct wish that I would die. Soon."

"But I thought he was the one who got slammed with the whole deal." Rebecca sighed, and he could hear a murmur of voices in the background. "Wasn't he angry?"

"I couldn't tell. Probably. But then, the man's in prison for a hell of a long time. I don't think he has a lot of up days."

"No, I mean, shouldn't he have been more angry? Considering?"

It was Jake's turn to sigh. "I thought of that. But even if that's the case, there's nothing to do with the information. For all I know, Keegan's dead, T-Mac is just a guy in the joint and Packard had spent every last penny on a massive comic-book collection. I've got nothing."

"But you tried."

"Is that laughter I hear? Are you having fun while I'm moping?"

She giggled. "I'm at St. Marks. It's a birthday party, and it's almost over. I have to get back to the office."

"Ah, the frozen lunches. Put those together with the leftover dim sum, and you won't need to shop for a month."

"Ugh, food is the last thing I'm interested in. No lunches today though, only cake and ice cream. You want to come over tonight? Though it can't be too early because I have a meeting."

He was flat out grinning now. Had been since she'd said hello, for that matter, but that last question? That had been something else altogether. "I do," he said, tempted. No, he wasn't going to risk ruining his plan for tomorrow night. His leg had to be in full working order. "But I don't think I should."

"Oh?"

"I know it's very unmanly, but the truth is I'm exhausted. I need to do some work on my poor wounded body then get myself a full night's sleep. I won't do that if I'm with you."

"I give a pretty good massage."

Shit, her persistence was killing him, but did he want her to see how bad his leg was today? "Sweetheart, there is no way in the world I'm going to be in a bed with you and not keep us both up. Besides, you need to rest, too. I'm taking you somewhere special tomorrow evening."

"Where?"

"It's a surprise."

"No fair," she said, almost whining, which was pretty damn adorable. "Tell me."

"Nope. Wear something warm and comfortable. None of those lethal high heels."

"You like it when I wear high heels."

"Only when you're not wearing anything but your fancy underwear."

She didn't say anything for a minute. He could tell

she'd gone somewhere more private, quieter. "I'm sorry things didn't pan out about West. I'm happy for the foundation... You know what I mean."

"Yeah, I do. Although I'm not totally ready to throw in the towel. Unless that's what you want."

"How about we keep thinking it through," she said, her voice warm and sexy. "Who knows, together, we might come up with something that'll not only uncover the truth, but find all that missing money. Then I can negotiate a reward for the foundation."

He laughed. She really was good. "Yeah. Okay. We'll keep thinking. And if we don't uncover squat, we'll have given it a hell of a shot, right?"

"So tomorrow?" she asked.

"I'll pick you up at seven. Does that work?"

"Seven's great. Hey, Jake?"

"Yeah?"

"Sleep well. Take care of yourself."

"I..."

"Yeah?"

"Nothing. Thanks. You sleep well, too." He hung up his phone and stared at it as he took another big swig of soda. By the time he put the cell back in his pocket and climbed back into the car, he knew exactly how much trouble he was in.

He'd fallen for her. Fallen like a kid off a bicycle. Shit, he was in for a world of hurt.

15

WHOEVER THE HELL HAD invented full-length mirrors deserved to be sent to the same level of hell as shoe designers. The jeans Rebecca had on now were tight and made her look thinner, yet when she took them off they left a red indent around her waist, which Jake would see. Unless she wore a teddy under and didn't take that off until the lights were out and, oh, hell. Why was she so nervous?

She sucked it up to unzip, then traded the jeans for a different, looser pair. The solution to the whole problem turned out to be not looking in the mirror. Simple.

As per his instructions, she'd put on comfy boots that had virtually no heels at all, and a wonderful thick sweater she'd gotten for skiing. She had no idea where he planned to take her that would require walking in the cold March air, but for his sake she hoped there were plentiful rests and a nice place to snuggle when they got there.

The buzzer from the front desk caught her finishing her lipstick and speeded up her heart. She didn't even know how it could be more exciting to see him now than it had that first night. But it was. He made her pulse race, her insides tighten and her nipples get hard. What a fantastic superpower.

She couldn't even wait for the elevator to bring him up. Instead she stood outside by her open door, impatient and grinning.

At the sound of the ding she rose up on her toes, but settled before he stepped clear of his ride. His grin matched hers in intensity, and they sort of rushed at each other. It would have been ridiculous except for the kiss. That trumped everything. His hand cupped the back of her neck and she sneaked inside his coat to take hold of his hips. She pulled him in close so they were smooshed together thigh to chest and she filled herself up with his scent.

He went on kissing her, tasting her, the two of them greedy and eager as teenagers. When he moaned low and pushed his budding erection against her, she wondered if maybe they should skip the surprise and stay in bed for the next ten hours or so.

When he broke the kiss, he didn't go far. His forehead touched hers as he slowly exhaled, fingers still rubbing soft circles on her nape. "That was some welcome."

"Yeah, well, I love surprises."

"So it's the idea that's important, huh?" he asked. "For all you know I could be taking you for a pushcart falafel in the Village."

"It would depend on the cart." She needed to look at him. Still, she was disappointed when his hand fell away from her nape. "Come on, where are we going?"

"Get your coat. I'll show you."

She took hold of Jake's hand and led him into the house. Her coat and purse were ready. "You need to make a pit stop? Grab something to drink?"

He shook his head, his crooked smile melting her into a puddle of goo. "You continue to amaze me," he said.

She stopped short. "What? Why?"

"You surprise me every time we get together. Every time."

"How am I surprising you now?"

"You're like a kid on Christmas. I don't want to disappoint you. We're not going to Paris or anything."

She put her stuff back down on the table and walked to him. Hands on his shoulders made him look her straight in the eyes. "I don't care where we're going. Pushcart, Paris. Doesn't matter. I just want to hang out with you. And then screw like bunnies when we get back."

"Ah. I see. I hadn't thought of the screwing like bunnies part. I think I can change the itinerary. Anything for a friend."

"So, I'm a sacrifice now?"

He shook his head slowly. "You're the best thing that's ever happened to me." His voice had deepened and she heard him swallow, as if he hadn't meant to say that out loud.

She had to kiss him. Had to. She tried to make him see it was okay what he'd said. It was more than okay. Without scaring the pants off him. Or herself.

She was his best thing. She'd never been anyone's best thing before.

Wow.

JAKE TOOK HER HAND AS HE scooted into the cab beside her. "Brooklyn Bridge Station, please."

The cab took off, making its winding way to Broadway. Rebecca leaned against the window, the neck of her wool coat turned up, framing her face perfectly. "Brooklyn Bridge Station? Hmm."

"You won't guess."

"Let me think. What's around there?" She closed her eyes, and he wanted to kiss her. "It's the Financial District, so Bridge Café?"

"Naturally, you're going to think of restaurants. We're not going to a restaurant."

"Simply narrowing down the field." She grinned and fluttered her lashes at him, as if that had been her plan all along. "The Woolworth Building? South Street Seaport?"

"You're getting warm, but no. Not where we're going."

"New York Academy of Art?"

"How do you even know that?" he asked.

"Went to a fundraiser there. Oh, City Hall. Municipal buildings. Courts and things, right?"

"Yes. That's it. I'm taking you to courts and things."

She sighed as they waited in the crushing traffic. "I give up."

"Good. I bet you were hell on Christmas. Did you always find where your folks had hidden your gifts?"

Her smile faded a little. "No. Christmas wasn't like that at our house. My grandparents were taught to keep a rein on their emotions. That was a point of pride, and it was passed on. Drummed in. The trees were decorated by professionals. Christmas dinner was catered. I got mostly sensible gifts. Clothes, books. Charitable donations were made in my name."

"Wait. When you were a kid?"

She nodded. "Not only me. My cousins, too. It wasn't a horrible message. We'd been born into privilege and with that came responsibilities. When we were very young, we had chores around the house, and as soon as we were able, we were expected to do volunteer work in one form or another. It wasn't optional."

"But what about being a child? What happened to that part?"

"That was where Charlie came in. He was, just so you know, the devil incarnate. A rebel even in kindergarten. He gave me my first cigarette at eleven. Let's see. He helped me steal my first candy bar from a Duane Reade drugstore. We used to sneak into the liquor cabinets during the parties our parents would host and get absolutely smashed. I'm not sure why the nannies never busted us. I think they were glad to see us letting off steam. My family and his were really close, did everything together, until they caught us ditching school. We'd gone to Atlantic City when we were in seventh grade. I only saw him a couple of times a year after that. Well, officially, he remained my hero and we sneaked out all the time."

"I knew I liked him right off the bat."

"His parents were at the donor dinner."

"I didn't meet them."

"That's okay," she said. "They're…rigid. And the honest and horrible truth is, I don't think they like Charlie. Which is a shame because he's really something."

"I'm glad you had each other."

"Me, too. But when it came down to choosing what I was going to do with my life, the lessons of my parents had the most impact. I set my sights on the Winslow Foundation. We're doing good things."

He leaned over, helpless not to kiss her. "I was brought up the same way. Kind of."

"Yeah, I got that," she said, brushing her fingers over his cheek.

They swayed together with the stops and starts of the taxi. Rush-hour traffic was never easy. But that was okay. He was fine where he was. Jake brushed her lips with his one more time. "I never wanted to be anything but a cop. My family was full of heroes. I grew up believing that I could make a difference. I still do. My father, he was a tough sonofabitch. He didn't let me get away with much. But he worked like a dog to make sure I got into college, got my degree before I joined the force. I think he was hoping I'd grow up to be chief of police or something. I never wanted that. I needed to be on the street."

"You're pretty tough yourself."

"I was. I helped put away some bad people. I never took kindly to those bastards preying on the weak and the helpless. They destroyed families, kids. It was frustrating, because we'd get rid of one operation and another would take its place in a heartbeat. But you can't let that stop you. You do what's in front of you."

Rebecca's face was half in shadow, but he could see that she was staring at him, not grinning now, not moving. Just looking at him. "I admire you, Jake Donnelly. I admire your values and your courage and your willingness to take a stand."

He was pretty sure she couldn't see his blush. "I honored the job. Like my father did, and his father."

"Did you know you have a Brooklyn accent when you talk about your dad?"

"Is that so?"

"Yep." She leaned in, but the cab veered to the left and came to a jarring stop. "Brooklyn Bridge Station."

Jake had gone to the ATM before he'd picked up Rebecca, and even though he had to quit this crazy spending, he'd taken out a few hundred bucks. Just in case.

He paid the cabbie, then helped her out of the taxi. Now came the good part. It was brisk out, but not freezing. The air smelled clean for New York, and once they got free of the subway entrance, the street traffic thinned. "You ready to go on an adventure?"

"Oh, God, yes. Lead on, Macduff."

He grinned wide. "It's actually 'Lay on, Macduff.' But don't feel bad. It's misquoted all the time."

"I stand corrected," she said with a little bow.

He tried to leave it at that, but he couldn't. "That was on *Jeopardy* the other night."

She laughed and shook her head. "It still counts."

"Good." He took her hand again. "Follow me." He could have asked the cabbie to drop them closer to their ultimate destination, but he wanted it to be a surprise until the last minute. There was no rush. He'd accomplished what he'd needed to last night. Soaked for a long time, done the massage work, then he'd seen his physiotherapist for a session this morning. He'd needed it. Because tonight the pain was under control and his limp wasn't as noticeable. He figured he could get through the next couple of hours, no sweat.

Finally, in City Hall Park they came to another subway entrance: City Hall Station. When he pulled her to a halt, she gave him a sidelong glance. "Why did we go to the Brooklyn Bridge Station when we were coming here?"

"Because the subway doesn't stop here anymore. Well, that's not completely true. A train does come here, but only to turn around and leave again."

"Explain, please?"

"Let's explore the park. Do you mind?"

"Never. Adventure. Surprise. What could be better?"

She got closer to him, switched from holding his hand to putting her arm through his.

"In 1904, this was one of the first terminals of the IRT. This particular station was built as a showpiece. The city elders went all out. It was gorgeous, but it had two things that didn't work so well. One, not many people needed this stop when the Brooklyn Bridge platform was so close. Two, the trains back then were shorter than they are now, and the tracks here were con-figured in a pretty tight loop."

He led her to the park fountain, circled by flickering gas oil lamps, which made the water look magical. He pointed. "These are reconditioned lamps from the late nineteenth century, although some of them have been updated a little."

Jake watched Rebecca, her chin up, eyes wide as she took in the details of the old lighting fixtures. It was re-markably quiet around them, the swooping and falling of bursts of water onto the granite base of the fountain masking the traffic noise. He'd seen only a couple of people rushing across City Hall Park.

He was excited; he could feel his blood pumping and his adrenaline spike. He loved New York, especially Manhattan, and he'd become an urban explorer when he had time off, although he hadn't been able to do a lot of that since the shooting. He wanted her to see the hidden treasures all around her, and of course, it had to begin with City Hall Station.

He tugged at her arm and walked her around some greenery toward a circular tablet embedded in the side-walk in the south end of the park. Most people never noticed it as it wasn't well lit at night. But he'd prepared for that. He pulled out a flashlight to better illuminate it. There were carvings in the center, a time line of the history of City Hall, including the abandoned subway station.

"There used to be a big post office building here. They called it Mullet's Monstrosity. It was on Mail Street, which didn't survive."

He moved the flashlight to the right. "That's where it used to be. There's more than one street that vanished," he said. "Tyron Row disappeared, too. Park Row, where we are, is the only street in New York City called a row."

She crouched down, staring at the careful workmanship. "I love this. How many times have you been here?"

"More than I can count. I started exploring the old places when I was in college. A friend of mine who works for the IRT calls himself an urban historian. He's got a great blog. And something far more important."

She rose again and looked at him instead of the view. "What's that?"

"Keys to the kingdom."

"Where are you taking me, Jake?"

"Back in time," he said, then pulled her along, anxious now to retrace their steps to the subway entrance. They were still in City Hall Park though, and he didn't rush her because this part was good. It was great to have her outside, not at a restaurant, no parties, no pressure. From what he could tell, she was enjoying herself. Interested. There was so much to tell her, too. But tonight was something extraordinary. He was taking her for a private tour of the old City Hall subway station, refurbished for the 2004 centenary, but closed to the public. Tours were available, and they were fun, but he wanted the two of them to be alone for this.

"Huh," Rebecca said. "I don't even know what IRT stands for. I've lived here all my life, and I don't know that. I mean, obviously Rapid Transit."

"Interborough," he said. "Right around here was the start of subways in New York. The groundbreaking ceremony was held in 1900 and this platform opened in 1904."

She turned to face him. "I think this calls for a moment, don't you? Something to celebrate?"

"What did you have in mind?"

She looked up at him, her lips already parted. The kiss started slow. More breath than lips at first, then a brush, a tease. Jake let her run the show. Standing in the shadows, she was the tour guide now, and she seemed to know every important stop along the way, mapping his mouth with deliberate care, then begging entrance with a moist nudge. Of course he obliged. He wasn't a fool. And God, she tasted like everything he wanted.

He ran his hands underneath her coat, wanting to pull her blouse out of her pants so he could touch her skin, but if he did that, the tour would be over. She compelled him like that, made him want too much. But that had been true from the moment he'd set eyes on her. He couldn't get enough.

Her fingers slid up the back of his scalp and he gripped her tighter. The pressure kept building inside him, but he couldn't break away, not completely. Not yet. His mouth went to her jaw, her neck, and he kissed her there where he could breathe her scent and trail his tongue up to the shell of her ear.

"Wait," she said, stepping away. "Whoa. I'm getting a little carried away here."

He nodded, catching his breath, willing his heartbeat to slow.

"I really want to see the surprise," she said. "So here's the rule. No more fooling around until later. Okay?"

He was about to agree when he heard a sound that

triggered every internal red flag he had. Two pops, one then another, and he grabbed Rebecca and yanked her down to a crouch, then ran as fast as his gimp leg could take him until they'd reached the restraining wall that kept pedestrians from the City Hall building.

"What the—"

"Shh," he said, knowing he was freaking her out, but he had to get the message across fast and hard.

Rebecca froze as if he'd slapped her, which was good. He listened. For footsteps, for voices. There. To his left. Footsteps, heavy, moving slowly, coming right at them. He reached back and pulled Rebecca closer, put his coat across her face, then he tucked his head down, in case there were lights.

The footsteps got damn close, then continued on, still slow, still careful. Jake held steady until he could no longer hear them, then waited some more. Finally, he let her up.

"What the hell, Jake?" she whispered.

"Someone shot at us."

"What? I didn't hear anything."

"You didn't recognize the sound. It was suppressed. They used a silencer."

"Are you sure?"

He turned to face her. "I'd bet my life on it."

16

REBECCA HAD NO IDEA WHAT to make of any of this. She tried to remember the seconds before he'd pulled her down, but she couldn't recall any sounds at all. Jake seemed completely certain about the gunfire, but *gunfire?* Wasn't it more likely there were fireworks somewhere, or a car backfiring?

"Come on," he said, stepping over the barrier once again, holding her hand tight. "We have to get out of here now."

"Jake, wait. Just stop. I'm sure it sounded like a gunshot to you, but I swear, I didn't hear anything. We're in the middle of a park on a Wednesday night. Who would be shooting at us?"

He met her gaze, but only for a second. He was still scouring the shadows and the sidewalks, so focused she could feel the tremors in his hand. "You may be right, and I may be nuts, but I'm not willing to chance it, not with you here. We have to leave. Now. And we have to be quiet and quick."

She nodded. There was no point arguing. He kept them away from the lights, right against the barrier as they walked fast toward Broadway. Rebecca was the one who saw someone crouching by a fir tree. She yanked on Jake's hand, and when he glanced back, she pointed her chin.

He looked. "Shit," he said, then he was sprinting back from where they came, and this time, she heard it. A pop like a cork flying from a champagne bottle.

There was another pop, and this time, cement from the barricade in front of her splintered, making her gasp and cover her face as they ran. Jake pushed her over the barrier; his grunt when he landed next to her was a painful reminder of his limp and his pain.

"Keep down," he said. "I'll come get you in a second."

His hand disappeared and she panicked. "Jake." She remembered to whisper, but it didn't matter. He'd moved into an even deeper shadow between buildings. She covered her head with her arms, so afraid she could hardly breathe. Every second felt like her last, and she kept chanting his name over and over, trying to speed up time.

"Rebecca."

She jerked her head up. "Come on. Keep low."

Crouched over double, it was difficult as hell to walk, and it must have been ten times harder for Jake. He led her to the dark spot, and then he took her hand and brought it up against the wall.

The darkness was so complete she couldn't see spit, but she felt the edge of a doorway. Then nothing. A breeze. Startled, she jerked when he leaned in close to her head so he could whisper.

"I'm going to help you find the ladder that leads down from this doorway. You're not going to be able to see much when you start. In a minute though, you'll see blue. Those are the lights of the station below, and they'll stay on. They never go off. You'll adjust quickly to those lights, so don't be scared. I'll be right behind you, okay?"

She nodded. Then said, "Yes, okay."

It wasn't a simple thing, this maneuver. Because of the dark. Because she was shaking so badly. There was someone out there and he wasn't some random mugger. That gun had been aiming for her. For Jake. For both of them, either of them, it didn't matter. It was a real gun and real danger, and he was still out there.

The worst of it was the first step. It was as if nothing existed past the doorway. No staircase, no subway station, no earth at all. Nothing but a void, and all that was holding her from an endless fall was Jake, his hand steady, his voice so calm. "That's it. Easy does it. Just reach down with your right foot until you feel the step."

"I can't feel anything."

"Okay, okay. It's all right," he said, squeezing her hand. "Move your leg to the right. Swing it over nice and easy."

She obeyed him, but only because she was too petrified to do anything else. Then her foot hit against something metal. The thunk sounded thunderous.

"That's the ladder. That should help you get your bearings. Now you know where the side is, you can find the rung. Try again."

She did. She blinked trying to figure out if her eyes were open and maybe that was the scariest part. Not being able to tell. When her boot heel touched metal, she almost cried out, holding back the noise at the last second.

"Good, great. Firm your grip. The rest is simple, easy as can be. Really soon, there's going to be a blue light, and it'll come on gradually, but you'll see it, and you'll know you're halfway to the ground. Take your time, don't rush. You let me know when you're ready to let go, okay?"

She didn't think she'd ever be ready to let go of his hand, but this was no time to be a coward. He had to climb down, too. He must be terrified up there. And he knew what it felt like to get shot.

Oh, bad thought. She couldn't think about that now or she'd freeze. "Okay," she said and lowered herself until her left hand found the ladder. She'd never held on to anything so tightly.

"I'm right behind. I won't let anything happen to you. I swear."

"I know," she said, even though it felt as if her heart would beat straight out of her chest. But Jake had promised. He wasn't abandoning her; he was leading her to safety.

She stepped down with her other foot. Found the rung. Shifted her right hand. No turning back now, just down, just one step and another and the next and there. Blue. She didn't turn to find the source, just let the light filter into her field of vision. One step after another, and then she was seeing the wall, the ladder, her own hands. Miraculous. Weird. Real.

Looking up, she could make Jake out, too. Mostly his legs and his butt. By the time she got to the ground level, she felt more in control. She stepped away easily, even if she was more scared than she'd ever been in her life

Not thirty seconds later, Jake was beside her. "You okay?"

She nodded.

"Come on. I don't know how much they know about this station. But they're going to realize we came down at some point, so we'll head for the exit. I left the door open up there. If they try to get down the same way we did, it'll give us time to get out." He found her hand and turned.

"Wait," she said. "They?"

"Yeah. Two of them that I saw. I don't know if there are more."

She and Jake were speaking in whispers, but their voices echoed. In the distance, she heard a rumble. It was indistinct, more a feeling than a sound.

"But—"

"No time. We'll talk when we're safe. Stay close to me. The trains come through here. There are tracks, which means we have to be careful of the third rail, so no moving without me, got it? I can't use the flashlight. It's too dangerous. So stick close."

"Like glue," she said. She hadn't thought about the third rail. Despite not knowing what IRT stood for, she had taken the subway. She was a New Yorker, of course she had. So she'd known what the third rail was from the time she was a kid: Death. Big old nasty frying death.

So. Two gunmen. At least. Aiming for them. And now a third rail. Next time Jake asked her if she was ready for an adventure, she was going to say no. In the meantime, she slipped her free hand into his back pocket. That ought to keep her close enough.

JAKE IGNORED THE BURN IN his thigh and cursed himself for every kind of fool there'd ever been. He'd walked right into this. Shit. He'd been such an idiot.

T-Mac hadn't just taken the fall. He wasn't left there by accident. He'd made a deal with Keegan. He'd do the time for money. Had to be. That family in Georgia who called all the time? Jake had put out some feelers to find out about them, but hadn't gotten any return calls yet. He imagined they were living quite well.

Gary hadn't been able to dig up much of anything that wasn't on the official records about West, but he hadn't had a lot of free time to dedicate to the search. Why should he?

But Jake should have known better than to waltz into Sing Sing and announce his presence like a rank amateur. It hadn't even occurred to him that T-Mac and Keegan could have been in cahoots. Why not? Life with Packard and life in prison weren't that different except with prison there was a chance of parole. And when he got out, he'd be set. His family would be set. There was a money trail somewhere, and if Jake lived through this night, he was going to make it his business to find that trail and make sure both T-Mac and Keegan were tried for attempted murder.

First, though, he had to get Rebecca out of here in one piece. That's what made him the angriest. Not that he'd been an idiot—he'd been a dope plenty of times before. Never when it cost so much, and never, never when he had something so precious in his care.

He should have kept his suspicions to himself. He should have kept his mouth shut and done his digging on his own time.

The train that had been way the hell down the line was now coming on fast. There were still work lights up, so he could get them safely behind the concrete wall that kept the maintenance crews from accidentally getting run over.

He released her hand and covered her ears with his palms; the trains made an ungodly screech as they took the curve of this loop of track. The squeal of metal against metal echoed back on itself, bouncing off the tile walls of the station. Under that was the noise of the train itself, which sounded like an earthquake this close. He surrounded Rebecca as much as he could with his body and his hands as the train rumbled and screamed, and he felt her press in, gripping his back for all she was worth.

Jesus, she had to be okay. Whoever these guys were, they weren't sharpshooters, but he'd wager a great deal that they weren't willing to turn up empty-handed at the end of the night. West's whole world was being threatened, and he wasn't going to hire muscle on the cheap.

Jake would have to be smarter, that's all. Whoever they were, they didn't know this station. He did. Every nook and cranny, and that was what would save them. He already knew there was no cell phone reception in the station. But there were call boxes, if he could get to one.

He winced as the sound assaulted his ears, knowing it would take some time before they'd be able to hear each other. The worst of it passed and he slowly stepped back from Rebecca, checking to make sure she was all right.

She gave him a smile. Not a big one, but a brave one, and he kissed her, then guided her hand to his back pocket and they were on the move.

They got across the tracks fine, and then they followed the curve of the platform, hugging the walls. Halfway to the exit stairs, he saw one of the gunmen on the right edge of the stairs coming down, his gun held in both hands, his head moving so he could sweep the area. No flashlight, but then he didn't need one yet.

Quietly and smoothly, Jake moved backward about fifteen feet, guiding Rebecca. He felt his way to the alcove, a niche built into the wall that had been his favorite place to hide while showing his friends around, the better to scare the crap out of them when he jumped out. He'd been such an ass.

It was a tight fit for two, but that was okay. He turned her sideways, then pushed in himself. Face-to-face. He could look out beyond her to see where the gunmen were. If they weren't both down here, they would be soon. Now, Jake would listen. Wait. After a quick check to make sure he was in the clear, he bent and got a couple of good stones for throwing. Maybe he could get one of them to step on the tracks. Maybe he could get them close enough and push one of them himself.

In the meantime, he had to protect her as best he could. She was trembling like a leaf. He wasn't much better. No weapon, no way of reaching help. Her life depending on his wits and his speed. Standing here without much range of motion was about the worst thing he could do as far as his leg went.

He leaned in close to Rebecca's ear until his lips brushed the silky lobe. "We wait now," he whispered as softly as he could. "We have home turf advantage. We're going to be fine. I'm sorry I can't show you where you are. It's so beautiful, sweetheart. Colored glass, tiles of green, tan and white up to the ceiling in the four corners of the vault over the mezzanine. The skylights are amazing. Imagine great pools of natural light from up above, and when they're not enough, they brought in brass chandeliers," he said, trying to distract her but she was still shaking. "The architect who designed the arches was famous back then. A showman. His name was Rafael Guastavino."

Jake looked out again, hating the vulnerability of sticking his neck out, but he did it, and it was a damn good thing, because both men were down the stairs, and one of them was walking toward their alcove.

Jake ducked back, then pressed them both, hard, against the back of the cubbyhole. It was dark, very dark, and as long as the man didn't flash a light directly at them, he'd never know the alcove existed, let alone that they were hiding in it.

His footsteps seemed as loud as the train had been at its worst. Slow, taking his time. But then a real rumble started behind him. Another train. The man needed to hurry. Step up his pace. Get past them, well past them to the walkway leading down to the dark end of the tunnel.

He needed the man to be far enough that when the train came, he and Rebecca could make a break for the stairs. It would be so loud the gunmen would never hear them. Jake knew exactly where to go, where to hide, but he needed a few minutes' grace. It didn't seem like too much to ask for, so he did, until the sound of the train ground in his chest. He took hold of Rebecca's hand, squeezed it tight. Prayed he could move fast enough.

When the conductor's car was twenty feet away, Jake broke out, pulling her behind him. Not too fast, even though he wanted to sprint. Not until she caught up to him, and then they hauled ass. Fuck the leg, screw the pain, they were running up the stairs, the screech of the train filling the platform to the rafters. They were soundless, they were panting and then they were past the curve and up the second shorter set of stairs and he could see where those bastards had broken in. No locks to mess with meant he could get her out more quickly. Good. The final steps, leading up to the sidewalk, and she surged in front of him, pulling him with her, and thank God for that because his leg was about ready to quit.

He yanked his phone out of his pocket, but she

wouldn't stop. Not until they got to the street and she'd waved down a cab and shoved him inside.

While he called the 1st Precinct, she gave the cabbie an address. Jake told the desk who he was, including his old badge number, that there were armed men in the City Hall Station and that they'd be gone damn soon, so get there fast.

He hung up after giving his callback number, pulled her into a fierce kiss, squeezing her too tightly, and, shit, he couldn't breathe, but he didn't care. But *she* needed to breathe so he backed off and met her gaze. "You okay?"

"Scared out of my mind. I can hardly believe what just happened. It's insane."

"But you're okay. You're not hurt."

"Yes. Yes, I'm fine. We're going to Charlie's and we'll figure it all out there."

"Good," he said, then he bent over and pressed down on his thigh as he tried like hell not to scream. Her hand was on his back and she was talking.

"It's okay, honey. You were fantastic. You're going to be fine. You got us out. We're safe now. It's okay. Please, be okay."

JAKE DIDN'T RECOGNIZE THE building they were dropped at, but it didn't surprise him that it was where her cousin Charlie lived, considering it was directly across the street from the park on Central Park West.

Getting out of the cab and into the elevator was something he could have lived his whole life without, but Rebecca was a champ. She did all of the heavy lifting. He tried not to make any sounds, but then he'd step down and a muscle would spasm and it was like being shot all over again.

The elevator opened to Charlie and Bree looking worried. And confused.

"What's going on? You were pretty damn cryptic," Charlie said, but Bree shoved him to the side so she could put Jake's other arm around her shoulder and help him into the house. Apartment. Palace.

"Maybe we should call an ambulance," Bree said, trying to help him to the couch, but not succeeding very well.

"No. I don't need an ambulance. I need to take my pain medication. It's muscle and nerve damage from doing too much. It'll settle down."

Charlie left. Rebecca and Bree hovered. It was sweet, but what he needed was a few minutes alone. He was about to do some major cussing and there might even be some crying involved, and he'd prefer not to have any witnesses for that. Especially not Rebecca.

He got his pill bottle out of his pocket and winced at how his hand shook as he opened it. He wanted to take two, but that would make him groggy, and he couldn't afford that now. One wasn't going to kick this. Not without some serious muscle work, but it would help. Charlie came back with a glass. Jake didn't spill much, only on his jeans. Someone took the glass and he breathed as deeply as he could, trying to remember what Taye said about letting the pain in, not fighting it.

There were too many people, too many thoughts. He couldn't stop and he wasn't going to hold it together much longer.

Rebecca took a couple of steps back. "I need a drink," she said. "You two, come with me, and I'll catch you up."

"I'll be right there," Charlie said.

There might have been a struggle, but it was silent and Jake gave up trying to figure it out. When he opened his eyes again, Charlie was still there. "Do I need to call an attorney? My man on retainer is excellent."

Jake shook his head. "You need to get Rebecca somewhere safe. William West is an ex-drug trafficker I ran into a dozen years ago. It's too long a story to go into. But I recognized him. He sent a couple of guys to kill me. Rebecca was collateral damage." He looked up at Charlie. "I put her life in danger. I almost got her killed. You have to get her away, understand? Out of town. Out of the state."

Jake forced himself to his feet even though the pain threatened to shut him down for good. But he took hold of Charlie's shirt and looked him square in the eyes. "Goddammit, *I almost got her killed*." Charlie nodded. His face narrowed to a pinprick of light, then nothing.

17

REBECCA WAS SITTING NEXT to him on the couch. She looked pale and shaken as she held his hand. Shit. He must have blacked out for a minute. "What are you still doing here? You have to go."

She gently pushed him back down when he tried to get up. "It's okay. Calm down. Your pill hasn't kicked in yet."

"You don't get it. Keegan didn't just steal the money from Packard, he made a deal with T-Mac. The guy in Sing Sing. He paid T-Mac to take the fall. They've been working together all this time. I went in and spilled everything to T-Mac. He called West, and that's why those men were trying to kill us. Kill me. I'm sorry. I never should have said anything to you. I know, it's all my fault, but it doesn't matter now because Keegan knows you're with me so you're in danger. You have to leave. Now."

"Sweetie, it wasn't your fault," she said. "It wasn't you. It was me. The way I was staring at West over dinner. He knew I was looking for scars."

Jake sat up straighter and turned his hand so he was holding hers. He didn't think he'd been out long. Charlie was where he'd left him, but Bree was in his arms now. Fine. Good, but no one seemed to be getting the big picture. The danger wasn't over.

He turned back to Rebecca, mulling over what she'd said. "No way he would have made that connection," he murmured, knowing she wasn't necessarily wrong. Of course it wasn't her fault, but Keegan had to be paranoid returning to New York and anything could've set him off.

She shook her head. "But he did. I thought it was something else, I thought he was trying to figure out how to get in my pants. The way he stared at me. He knew something was wrong. I thought I was being subtle, but I wasn't. I was practically painting him a picture."

"It sounds like it was a combination of both those things," Charlie said, echoing Jake's thoughts. "The guy's been on the run for, what, twelve years? Anything could have tipped him off. Blame isn't the point. What do we do next?"

"We can't do anything until Jake can think without pain," Rebecca said. "Isn't there anything we can do for you?"

Jake shook his head, tried again to get up. How Keegan had put two and two together wasn't important now. Rebecca's safety was. "The only thing that will help me is for you to get the hell out of here. I mean it, Rebecca." He looked at Charlie. "What the fuck is wrong with you? I told you to get her out of the city."

Rebecca grabbed his chin and turned his head so he was facing her. "They're after you, too, goddammit, and I'm not leaving without you."

He'd never heard her swear like that and it stopped him. He glanced at Charlie, who had a faint smile tug-

ging at his mouth. What the hell was wrong with these
rich people? Did they think they were immune from
danger? "Those were real guns, with real ammo. They
meant you to die. They aren't finished. Your home isn't
safe. You're not safe. Do me a favor and go. Hire a car.
Don't go back to your place. Just get to the airport. Not
LaGuardia, go to Newark. Go anywhere. Pay cash.
And do it now please. I'm begging you. I have things
to do, and I can't even think straight while you're still
here."

"Ah," she said, nodding. "I get it now."

"Thank God," he said, putting his hand on his leg,
feeling instantly that it was way too soon to even try to
work on the muscle.

"But," Rebecca said, "I'm not leaving without you."

Jake stilled. What was it going to take? He ignored
her and looked to Charlie and Bree. "A little help would
be good here, people. I know you care about her. I can't
imagine any of you want to go to her funeral."

"Rebecca," Charlie said, releasing Bree from his hold.
"You're with me. Bree? Find out what this madman
needs, and let's get this show on the road. I don't want
to go to anyone's funeral."

Rebecca glared at him, then Charlie gave her a look
that spoke of years of collusion. She wasn't happy about
it, but she got up from the couch, squeezing Jake's hand
before she walked away with Charlie.

Jake leaned back on the couch. Now that he had an
ally, he could think clearly. At least that was his goal.

"What can I do?" Bree asked.

"I need to find out if the police got to those shooters.
And how we can connect the shooters to either T-Mac or
West, preferably both. I need to call Crystal Farrington.
She's an assistant D.A. who knows all about this." He

dug into his pocket for his wallet, the small movement making him wince. But there was her phone number. He'd call as soon as the spasm that was clawing through his quad let him go.

REBECCA TURNED ON HER cousin the minute the kitchen door swung shut. "I'm not leaving without him, Charlie. I don't know what you expect to accomplish, but changing my mind is not going to happen."

"Yeah, I got that," he said, smiling so smugly she wanted to slap him.

"Then what's with the 'Rebecca, you're with me' bull-crap?"

"Your cop needs to get his act together, and you being in his face wasn't helpful. The danger here is real, so we'd better figure out a way to get his goals accomplished while you're still in the house. Frankly, I don't like the idea that killers could be after you. You're the only relative I like. You're not checking out until we're old and decrepit."

"Oh. I thought you were going to argue with me."

"Nope. Before your little declaration there, I was going to tell you to fight for Jake. That he's the keeper you're always harping about. But you obviously have that covered, so now we can move on to practical matters. Like staying out of his way. At least for a while."

She hugged Charlie, real quick because they weren't the hugging type, and then she settled. "The way I see it, he only has a limited amount of focus at the moment. I'll keep back. Not away, because if something happens I need to be close, but I won't be obvious. I'll listen. So you'll have to be his sounding board. He'll know what to do, Charlie. He may not have his badge, but he's a damn good cop."

"Fine. You hang, I'll distract, and we'll get you both safe."

"THANKS, CRYSTAL. KEEP ME in the loop, and I'll do the same." Jake hung up the phone and looked at Charlie, who'd suddenly appeared in front of the couch.

"Who was in charge of the original operation?" Charlie asked.

"Wait your turn," Bree said before she addressed Jake. "I have a wet/dry heating pad. I'm thinking moist heat. Would that help?"

Jake looked at her, and he couldn't help smiling. She was wearing an obnoxiously bright orange sweater over a green skirt. "Yeah. Thanks. That would help." She hustled off, and he faced Charlie again. "She's not gone. I would know if she was gone."

"She's making the arrangements. Right now. So, tell me what you need to get West behind bars."

Jake had brought Crystal up to speed, and she was going to work on getting T-Mac's phone records, this time through legit channels because this time, they would need it in court. Dammit, how long did it take to get a car here to Central Park West? It wasn't like Brook— "Shit, I have to call my old man."

Blessedly, Charlie and Bree left him alone while he dialed his father. Jake had already asked the department to send a couple of uniforms to watch the house, but he wouldn't tell his father. That would just piss him off. He switched on the speaker since he thought he could work on his leg now. Besides, his dad knew about the Keegan/West connection, so there wasn't much to say, except that Jake might have put him in danger. Him and Pete and Liam.

"Don't you worry about us, Jakey," his father said, and it was like they were on the walkie-talkies. "We have about a hundred years of experience between us. And a goddamn arsenal. I hope those bastards do come here. We'll teach 'em what NYPD cops are made of."

"Don't take any chances, Dad." Jake used both thumbs on the peripheral muscles, working his way inward. "Please. Just, see if you can go stay with Liam, huh? Get out of there, at least until we know what to do."

"I'll tell you exactly what I'm going to do, son. I'm going to call Dan Reaves is what. He'll get a judge to sign the warrants to get into West's business, and the prison phone records, and damn near anything else he can once I tell him what's what. He's tried to live that bust down all his career. He wants Keegan. More than you do."

"He tried to kill Rebecca, old man. No one wants Keegan more than I do."

His father was quiet for a long moment, long enough for Jake to remember how she'd trembled in his arms, how brave she'd been. How he'd move heaven and earth for her if he could, but he was useless like this.

"You're right, Jake. Your job now is to keep her safe. I'll call Dan—we go way back. I'll keep you informed. He'll probably want to talk to you so make sure you have that phone on. And take a goddamn pill, I can hear the pain in your voice."

"Tell Reaves to get in touch with Crystal Farrington at the D.A.'s office. She's working on the phone records from Sing Sing, but she could use some backup."

"Farrington. Got it."

"Thanks, Dad," Jake said.

"No sweat."

"Hey, Pop, how many cops does it take to screw in a lightbulb?"

"How many?"

Jake smiled. "None. It turned itself in."

His father laughed as Jake hung up. Then he felt Rebecca's hand on his shoulder as she leaned over the couch and kissed him like she'd never let him go.

IT TOOK TWO HOURS, BUT Rebecca and Jake finally made it into the Town Car that Charlie had hired. Jake had walked without assistance, but his limp was awful and he still looked too pale. She'd packed some food for the ride. Nothing much, just some protein bars and juice; they'd grab something better at the airport.

She pressed herself against him, hardly believing everything that had happened in such a short period of time. The shooting, the trip down the ladder, the terrifying sound of echoing footsteps all felt more like something she'd read than something that she'd lived through.

But he'd brought her out safely. This amazing man. Listening as he'd talked to the two policeman who'd come to Charlie's had been an education in itself. Of course she'd known Jake was a cop; he'd demonstrated that in his every action tonight, in his instincts that had ferreted out a killer. But she'd been utterly captivated and impressed with his logic, his approach to finding the critical proof that would connect T-Mac to West.

"You're an incredible policeman," she said. "Not only were you right about everything—"

He opened his mouth in what she knew would be a protest, but she stopped him with two fingers on his lips.

"—but you saved my life."

"Your life shouldn't have been in danger in the first place," he said.

"Hmm. The correct response should have been 'You're welcome, Rebecca.'"

Jake ran his knuckles down her jaw. "The thought of losing you…"

"We're both here, and we're relatively fine. We'll be better once we're wherever we're going. Any thoughts on that?"

"I have no idea," he said. "Vegas is out."

She grinned. "No passports, so we can't leave the country. But those can be sent to us so our first destination doesn't have to be our last. We had talked about Paris."

"We probably won't be gone that long. Phone calls were made tonight, or an email, or whatever, which gives us a window of time to focus the search on how West and T-Mac connected. How West contacted the shooter. T-Mac is in Sing Sing. Somewhere, there's a record. As soon as they can latch on to anything concrete, then they'll go after Keegan with both barrels. That'll be our cue to come back. We could have that connection by morning."

"We wouldn't have to come back right away, would we?"

He smiled. "What did you have in mind?"

"Time. Alone with you. You know, to begin."

"Begin?"

She shifted in her seat until she was facing him. "You do realize that when I said I wasn't leaving without you, I meant forever."

Jake's smile vanished and his jaw slackened as he leaned toward her. "Rebecca."

"Oh, God. You don't want— I'm sorry, I thought—"

"No, no." He took both her hands and squeezed them. "I do. I…I didn't know you wanted—"

"I did. I do."

"How?" he asked, and it was so earnest and hopeful she teared up again.

"I couldn't see it before either," she said. "Even though I'd fallen totally in love with you, I couldn't see how we could make it work. And then tonight, I got it. All the things I was worried about were just logistics. Everything important is you. That we're together."

"But I don't have a job, I've got my Dad—"

"You've got disability, so that's fine. Look, if you'd cared about the money, this never would have happened. So we make it work. Oh."

"What?"

"We can't be gone for too long. Imagine what the boys are going to do to your place? It'll look like an armored frat house."

Jake smiled. "Yeah, pizza boxes to the ceiling." He touched her hair. "What about the foundation?"

"It's not going to fall apart. And we'll get your father's new bathroom in shape when we get back. Then we'll figure it out. Day by day. If you want to."

"*We'll* get Dad's bathroom in shape?"

"Yes, we."

"You trying to get into my tool belt?"

She traced his endearing crooked smile with the tip of her unsteady finger. To not have this face…this man in her life…was unthinkable. The thought terrified her more than the threat of West on their heels. "Always, and I'm quite good at getting my way."

He kissed her then, deeply. She kissed him back with every promise she could make. When she pulled back, it was only to tell him, "I'll never feel safer than in your arms."

"I'll never let anyone harm you," he whispered back. "You're all that matters. You're all that will ever matter to me."

* * * * *

Look what people are saying about this talented author...

"Shalvis thoroughly engages readers."
—*Publishers Weekly*

"Hot, sweet, fun and romantic! Pure pleasure!"
—Robyn Carr, *New York Times* bestselling author

"Witty, fun and sexy—the perfect romance!"
—Lori Foster, *New York Times* bestselling author

"Fast paced and deliciously fun. Jill Shalvis
sweeps you away!"
—Cherry Adair, *USA TODAY* bestselling author

"A fun, hot, sexy story of the redemptive powers
of love. Jill Shalvis sizzles."
—JoAnn Ross, *USA TODAY* bestselling author

Dear Reader,

Who doesn't love a sports hero? There's just something about a guy who'd lay it all on the line for the win. Mark Diego is an NHL head coach, and a lifelong athlete. He's used to winning, and getting his way. Too bad no one ever told Rainey Saunders that.

Rainey and Mark haven't seen each other in years when my story opens, but their past is indelibly imprinted in their minds.

These two were a challenge for me. Mark wanted things to go his way (and since he's a man, you can guess which way that was...). And Rainey was determined to call the shots. Sparks flew from my keyboard every day during the writing of this book. My fingers are still smoking.

This is my first Blaze® novel in a while, but it won't be my last. There is still a lot more heat left in the keyboard, so stay tuned. In the meantime, I hope you enjoy *Time Out*. I sure did.

Happy reading,

Jill Shalvis

http://www.jillshalvis.com

http://www.jillshalvis.com/blog (be sure to sign up for my newsletter on the right sidebar to keep up to date!)

http://www.twitter.com/jillshalvis

http://www.facebook.com/JillShalvis

TIME OUT

BY
JILL SHALVIS

First published in Great Britain 2012
by Mills & Boon, an imprint of Harlequin (UK) Limited,
Eton House, 18-24 Paradise Road, Richmond, Surrey TW9 1SR

© Jill Shalvis 2012

ISBN: 978 0 263 89373 1
ebook isbn: 978 1 408 96907 6

14-0512

Harlequin (UK) policy is to use papers that are natural, renewable and recyclable products and made from wood grown in sustainable forests. The logging and manufacturing processes conform to the legal environmental regulations of the country of origin.

Printed and bound in Spain
by Blackprint CPI, Barcelona

MILLS & BOON Book Club   2 Free Books!

 Get your free books now at
www.millsandboon.co.uk/freebookoffer

Or fill in the form below and post it back to us

Mrs/Miss/Ms/Mr (please circle)

First Name

Surname

Address

Postcode

E-mail

Send this completed page to: Mills & Boon Book Club, Free Book Offer, FREEPOST NAT 10298, Richmond, Surrey, TW9 1BR

Find out more at
www.millsandboon.co.uk/freebookoffer

Visit us Online

0112/K2XEA/REV

To Mary.
Thanks for always knowing what to say.

_1_

As ALWAYS, RAINEY'S brain was full, too full, but one thought kept rising to the top and wouldn't leave her alone. "Tell me again," she asked Lena. "*Why* do we like men?"

Her best friend and wingman—even though Lena was no longer technically single—laughed. "Oh, honey. We don't have enough time."

They both worked at the beleaguered North District Rec Center in Santa Rey, a small mid-California beach town. Lena handled the front desk. Rainey was the junior sports coordinator, and today she was running their biweekly car wash to raise funds for their desperate sports program. Sitting on a stool in the driveway of the rec building's parking lot, Rainey directed cars in and accepted customers' money, then sent them through to the teenagers who were doing the washing. She kept her laptop out for the slow times. In between cars she'd been working on the upcoming winter sports schedule while simultaneously discussing all things men. Rainey was nothing if not a most excellent multitasker.

And maybe the slightest bit of a control freak.

"I thought you were going to try that online dating service," Lena said.

"I did. I got lots of offers for hookups."

Lena laughed. "Well, what were you looking for?"

Coffee, a few laughs, a connection… A *real* connection, which Rainey was missing lately. Her last two boyfriends had been great but… not great enough. Lena thought she was picky. In truth, Rainey was looking for something that she'd only felt once before, a very long time ago, when she'd been sixteen and stupid. "Men suck."

"Mmm," Lena said. "If they're very good, they do. Listen, you've had a dry spell, is all. Get back in the pool, the water's warm."

"I haven't had a dry spell, I've just been busy." Okay, so she'd had a little bit of a dry spell. She'd been spending a lot of time at work, trying to keep the teens in the North District—the forgotten district—out of trouble. That alone was a full-time job. She turned to the next car. Mrs. Foster had the highest beehive in all the land, and had been Rainey's fourth grade teacher. "Thanks for supporting the rec center's car wash," Rainey said.

"You're welcome." Her beehive, bluer now than ever, still quivered. "I was going to go to South District since they're giving away ten minute back massages with each wash, but I'm glad I didn't. I overheard about your dry spell, dear. Let me get you a date with my grandson, Kyle."

Great. A pity date. "No, that's—"

"He's quite the catch, you know," Mrs. Foster said. "I'll have him call your mother for your number."

"Really, it's not necessary—"

But Mrs. Foster was already driving forward, where

her car was immediately attended to by a group of Rainey's well-behaved teens.

Okay, not all that well-behaved. Rainey had coerced them here on threat of death and dismemberment, but they desperately needed the money if they wanted a baseball and softball season.

"Score on Mrs. Foster's grandson," Lena said dryly. "Think Kyle still has buck teeth?"

"My mom won't give him my number." Probably. Okay, she totally would. Rainey had gone to school with Kyle, so her mother would think him safe enough. Plus, she'd turned thirty last week and now her mom was on a mission to get her married before it was "too late." Hot and sweaty, Rainey swiped her forehead. It might be only June, but it was ninety degrees, and she'd been sitting out here for hours. Her Anaheim Ducks ball cap shaded her face for the most part but she could feel that she'd still managed to sunburn her nose, and her sunglasses kept slipping down her damp face.

They'd fed the teens pizza about an hour ago, and the kids were using the fuel to scrub cars and squirt each other every chance they got. They were down a few bodies since Rainey had kicked four of the guys out, the same four who always gave her trouble. They'd been trying to coerce one of the younger teen girls into the woods with them.

Even long before the fires had devastated Santa Rey the previous summer, the North District had been steadily deteriorating, and that core group of four were hell-bent on deteriorating right along with the area. Working at the rec center was far more than a job for Rainey. She genuinely cared about this community and the kids, but those boys had no interest in her help. She

couldn't allow them back, not after today, and given that they'd called her a raging bitch as they'd vacated the premises, the hard feelings were mutual.

"Rick promised to take me out to dinner tonight," Lena said.

Rick was a lifelong friend of Rainey's as well as her boss, and also Lena's boyfriend. "Huh," she said. "He promised me some summer league coaches." Coaches who wouldn't quit when the going got rough, like the volunteer coaches tended to do. "It's three days before the start of the season."

"He's on it," Lena said, just as the man himself walked by, all dark eyes, dark hair, and a dark smile that never failed to get him what he wanted.

He flashed it at Rainey now. "I promised," Rick said. "And I'll deliver."

"Great," Rainey said. "But *when*—"

But nothing. He'd given Lena a quick, soft smile and was already gone, back inside the building to wield his power there.

"I hate it when he does that," Rainey grumbled.

Lena sighed dreamily. "If he hadn't tasked me with a hundred things more than I have time to manage this morning, I'd totally want to have his babies."

"Honey, you're dating him. You've been dating him for a year now. Chances are decent that you *will* be having his babies."

Lena beamed, ridiculously happy. Rainey wasn't jealous. Yes, Rick was hot, but they were friends, and had been since high school. Because of it, they knew far too much about each other. For instance, Rainey knew Rick had lost his virginity behind the high school football stands with their substitute P.E. teacher. In turn,

Rick knew that Rainey had *tried* to lose her virginity with his brother—the last guy she'd felt that elusive connection with—and been soundly rejected. At the humiliating years-old memory, she slumped in her seat. "What if my dry spell is like the Sahara Desert, never-ending?"

"All you have to do is take a man at face value. Don't go into it thinking you can change them. Men aren't fixer-uppers, not like a house or a car. You buy them as is."

"Well I haven't found one yet who's not in need of a little fixing."

Lena laughed. "No kidding, Ms. Control Freak."

"Hey."

"Face it, Rainey, you always have to have a plan with a start, a middle and an end. Definitely an end. You have to know everything before you even get into it. Dating doesn't work that way."

"Well, it should." Rainey gestured the next car through, accepting the money and handing out more change. The teens were moving the cars along at a good pace, and she was proud of them. "Everyone could benefit from a well executed plan."

"A love life doesn't work that way," Lena said. "And trust me, you need a love life."

"You can get a love life in a specialty shop nowadays, complete with a couple of batteries." Rainey took a moment to organize the cash box and quickly checked her work email on the laptop. "Thirty new emails," she groaned. All timely and critical, and she'd have to deal with them before the end of the day. Goody.

"I could help you with some of that," Lena offered.

"I've got it."

"See? Control freak."

Ignoring that painful truth, Rainey deleted a few emails and opened a few others. She loved her job, and was doing what she wanted. She'd gone to business school but she'd come back here to do this, to work with kids in need, and to give back. The work was crazy in the best of times. But these days, in the wake of the tragic California coast fires that had destroyed three out of four of their athletic fields last fall, not to mention both buildings where all their equipment had been housed, were not the best of times. Worse, the lease for the building they were in was up at the end of the year and they couldn't afford renewal.

Problem was, she had a hundred kids, many of them displaced from their own burned-out homes. She wanted to give them something to do after school that didn't involve loitering, shoplifting, drugs or sex. She'd just started to close her laptop when her gaze caught on the Yahoo news page. Hitting the volume key, she stared at a sports clip showing a seedy bar fight between some NHL players from the Anaheim Ducks and Sacramento Mammoths.

The clip had been playing all week, because…well, she hadn't figured out why, other than people seemed to love a sports scandal. The video was little more than a pile of well-known professional athletes wrestling each other to the ground in some L.A. bar, fists flying, dust rising.

Rainey gestured another car through, then turned back to the screen, riveted by the million-dollar limbs and titillating show of testosterone. On the day the footage had been taken, the two teams had been in the Stanley Cup finals. The game had been decided on

a controversial call in favor of the Ducks, killing the Mammoths' dreams.

That night at the bar, the Mammoth players had instigated the fight, holding their own against four Ducks until their head coach strode up out of nowhere. At thirty-four, Mark Diego was the youngest, most popular NHL head coach in the country.

And possibly even more gorgeous than his brother Rick.

On the tape, Mark's eyes narrowed in on the fight as he walked fearlessly into the fray, pulling his players out of the pile as though they weighed nothing. A fist flew near his face and he deflected it, leveling the sender of said fist a long, hard look.

The guy fell backwards trying to get away.

"That's the sexiest thing I've ever seen," Lena murmured, watching the clip over Rainey's shoulder.

Yeah. Yeah, it was. Rainey had seen Mark in action before, of course. He and Rick were close. And once upon a time, she'd been just as close, having grown up near the brothers. Back then, Mark had been tough, smart, and fiercely protective of those he cared about. He'd also had a wild streak a mile wide, and she'd seen him brawl plenty. It'd turned her on then, but it absolutely didn't now. She was grown-up, mature.

Or so she told herself in the light of day.

On the screen, hands on hips, Mark said something, something quiet but that nevertheless had the heaving mass of aggression screeching to a halt.

"Oh, yeah. Come to momma," Lena murmured. "Look at him, Rainey. Tall, dark, gorgeous. *Fearless.* I wouldn't mind him exerting his authority on me."

Rainey's belly quivered, and not because she'd in-

haled three pieces of pizza with the teens an hour ago. Mark was no longer a wild teenager, but a tightly controlled, complicated man. A stranger. How he "exerted his authority" was none of her business. "Lena, you're dating his brother." Just speaking about Mark had twisted open a wound in a small corner of her heart, a corner she didn't visit very often.

"I've never gotten to see the glory that would be the Diego brothers in stereo." Lena hadn't grown up in Santa Rey. "Mark hasn't come home since I've been with Rick. Being the youngest, baddest, sexiest head coach in all the NHL must be time-consuming."

"Trust me, he's not your type."

"Because he's rich and famous? Because he's tough as hell and cool as ice?"

"Because he's missing a vital organ."

Lena gasped in horror. "He doesn't have a d—"

"A heart! He's missing a heart! Jeez, get your mind out of the gutter."

Lena laughed. "How do you know he's missing a heart?" Her eyes widened. "You have a past! Of course you have a past, you grew up here with Rick. Is it sordid? Tell me!"

Rainey sighed. "I was younger, so Mark always thought of me as a…"

"Forbidden fruit?" Lena asked hopefully.

"Pest," Rainey corrected. "Look, I don't want to talk about it."

"I do!"

Knowing Lena wouldn't leave it alone, she caved. "Fine. I had a crush on him, and thought he was crushing back. Wrong. He didn't even know how I felt about

him, but before I figured that out, I managed to thoroughly humiliate myself. The end."

"Oh, I'm going to need much *more* than that."

Luckily Lena's cell phone chose that very moment to ring. God bless AT&T. Lena glanced at the ID and grimaced. "I've got to go." She pointed at Rainey. "This discussion is not over."

"Yeah, yeah. Later." Rainey waved her off. She purposely glanced away from her computer screen, but like a moth to a flame, she couldn't fight the pull, and turned back.

Mark was shoving his players ahead of him, away from the run-down L.A. bar and towards a black SUV, single-handedly taking care of the situation.

That had been three days ago. The fight had been all over the news, and the commission was thinking about suspending the players involved. Supposedly the two head coaches had stepped in and offered a solution that would involve giving back to the fans who'd supported the two teams.

She looked into Mark's implacable, uncompromising face on her laptop and the years fell away. She searched for the boy she'd once loved with all her sixteen-year-old heart, but couldn't find a hint of him.

TWO HOURS LATER, THEY'D gone through a satisfying amount of cars, fattening the rec center's empty coffers, and Rainey was ready to call it a day. She needed to help the teens clean up before the bus arrived. Many of them still had homework and other jobs to get to.

The parking lot was wet and soapy, with hoses crisscrossing the concrete, and buckets everywhere. With no more cars waiting, the teens were running around like

wild banshees, feeling free to squirt and torture one another. Rainey blew her whistle to get their attention. "We're done here," she called out. "Thanks so much for all your help today. The faster we clean up, the faster we can—" She broke off as the county bus rolled up and opened its doors. Dammit. All but a handful of the kids needed to get on that bus. It was their only ride.

When the bus pulled away, Rainey stared at the messy lot and the two kids she had left.

"More pizza?" Todd asked her hopefully. He was a lanky sixteen-year-old who had either a tapeworm or a bottomless stomach.

Rainey turned and looked through the pizza boxes. Empty. She opened her bag and pulled out her forgotten lunch. "I've got a PB&J—"

"Sweet," he said, and inhaled the sandwich in three bites. His gaze was locked on Sharee, a fellow high school junior, as she began rolling hoses. Sharee was all long, long mocha-colored limbs and grace. Another fire victim from the same neighborhood as Todd, she currently lived in a small trailer with her mother. When Sharee caught Todd staring, she leveled him with a haughty glare.

Todd merely grinned.

"Go help her," Rainey told him. "She can't do it all alone."

"Sure, I'll help her," Todd said, and the next thing Rainey knew, he was stalking a screaming Sharee with a bucket full of soapy water.

Sharee grabbed a hose and wielded it at him like a gun. "Drop the bucket and no one gets hurts. And by no one, I mean you."

Todd laughed at her and waved the bucket like a red flag in front of a bull.

"Okay, okay," Rainey said, stepping between them. "It's getting late." She knew for a fact that Todd still had to go work at his family's restaurant for several more hours. Sharee, on the cusp of not passing her classes, surely had a ton of homework. The girl also had a healing bruise high on one cheekbone and a set of matching bruises on both biceps, like someone had gripped her hard and shaken her.

Her father, Rainey guessed. Everyone knew Martin was a mean drunk but no one wanted to talk about it, least of all Sharee, who lived alone with her mother except for the nights her mother allowed the man into their trailer.

"He called me a scarecrow," Sharee said, pointing at Todd. "Now his sorry ass is going to pay."

"Language," Rainey said.

"Okay, his sorry butt. His sorry *butt* is going to pay."

"I said you have legs as long as a scarecrow," Todd said from behind Rainey. "Not that you *are* a scarecrow."

Sharee growled and lifted the hose.

"Stop!" Rainey said. "If you squirt him, you're leaving yourself wide open for retaliation."

"That's right," Todd said, nodding like a bobblehead. "Retaliation."

Rainey turned to shut Todd up just as Sharee let it rip with the hose and nailed him.

Rainey gave up. They had worked their asses off and deserved to let off a little steam. She stepped aside to leave them to it, but stopped short as a big, shiny black truck pulled into the lot.

Which was when the entire contents of Todd's bucket hit her. Sucking in a shocked gasp as the cold, soapy water rained over her, Rainey whipped around and stared at the sheepish teen, who was holding the offending empty bucket. "Oh, God," he said. "I'm so sorry, but you stepped right in its path!"

"You're in *big* trouble," Sharee told him. "You got her hair wet. You know how long it must take her to get that hair right?"

Sharee was right about the hair. Rainey shoved it out of her face, readjusting the Ducks hat on her head. Her wavy brown hair frizzed whenever it rained, or if the air was humid, or if she so much as breathed wrong. She had no doubt it resembled a squirrel's tail about now. "It's okay. Just...clean up," she said, watching as the black truck rolled to a stop.

"Look at that," Todd said reverently, Rainey's hair crisis forgotten. "That's one sweet truck."

Sneakers squishing, Rainy moved toward it. She could feel water running in rivulets down her body as the driver side window powered down. "I'm sorry," she said politely, feeling like a drowned rat. "We've closed up shop. We—" She broke off. The driver was wearing a Mammoth hat and reflective Oakleys, rendering him all but unrecognizable to the general public. But *she* recognized him just fine, and her heart stopped on a dime.

The man she'd just been watching on the news.

Mark Diego.

He wore a white button-down that was striking against his dark skin and stretched across broad shoulders. The hand-painted sign behind her said: Car

Wash—$10, but he pulled a hundred-dollar bill from his pocket. She stared down at it, boggled.

"No worries on the wash," he said in a low voice as smooth as aged whiskey, the same voice that had fueled her adolescent dreams.

He didn't recognize her.

Of course he didn't. She was wearing a ball cap, sunglasses, soap suds, and was drenched to the core, not to mention dressed like a complete slob. Unlike Mark, of course, who looked like sin-on-a-stick. Expensive sin-on-a-stick.

The bastard.

"I just need a place to park," he said with the smile that she knew probably melted panties and temperamental athletes with equal aplomb. "I'm here to see Rick Diego."

"You can park right where you are," Rainey said.

He turned off the engine and got out of the truck, six feet two inches of tough, rugged, leanly muscled grace. Two other guys got out as well, and beside her, Todd nearly swallowed his tongue. "Casey Reynolds! James Vasquez! Oh man, you guys rock!"

Casey, the Mammoths' right wing, was twenty-two and the youngest player on the team. He looked, walked and talked like the California surfer he was in his spare time. He wore loose basketball shorts, a T-shirt from some surf shop in the Caicos, and a backwards Mammoths' hat.

James was the team's left wing, and at twenty-four he was nearly as wild as Casey, but instead of looking like he belonged on a surfboard, James could have passed as a linebacker in the NFL. He was wearing

baggy blue jeans and a snug silk shirt that emphasized and outlined his every muscle.

If she hadn't known they were the two players who'd been in the big bar brawl, she could have guessed by Casey's nasty black eye and the bruise and cut on James's jaw. Still managing to look like million-dollar athletes, they smiled at Todd and shook his hand.

The kid looked like he might pass out.

Mark and his two players clearly had a longtime ease with each other, but just as clearly there was a hierarchy, with Mark at the top—and he hadn't taken his carefully observant eyes off Rainey.

Crap.

She turned away, but he snagged her hand and pulled her very wet self back around. She thought about tugging free.

Or kicking him.

As if he could read her mind, his lips twitched. "Easy," he murmured, and pulled off her sunglasses.

She narrowed her eyes against the sun and a wealth of unwelcome emotions as the very hint of a smile tugged at the corner of his sexy mouth.

"It's a little hard to tell with the raccoon eyes," he said. "But the bad 'tude's a dead giveaway. Rainey Saunders. Look at you."

The others were all still talking with a false sense of intimacy. Mark tapped the bill of Rainey's Ducks hat, giving a slow shake of his head, like he couldn't believe she'd be wearing anything other than the Mammoths' colors.

And suddenly she felt like that silly, love-struck teenager all over again. Having four years on her, he'd been clueless about the crush. He might never have

known at all if she hadn't made a fool of herself and sneaked into his apartment to strip for him. It'd all gone straight to hell since he'd been on the receiving end of a blow job at the time. She'd compounded the error with several more that evening, which she didn't want to think about. Ever. It'd all ended with her pride and confidence completely squashed.

Worse, the night had negated the years of friendship she and Mark had shared until then, all erased in one beat of stupidity.

Okay, several beats of stupidity.

She lifted her chin, which turned out to be a mistake because water had pooled on the bill and now dripped down her face. She blinked it away and tried to look cool—not easy under the best of circumstances, and this wasn't anywhere close to best.

Mark pointed to her nose. "You have a smudge of dirt."

Oh, good. Because she'd been under the illusion she was looking perfect. "Thought you liked dirty girls." The minute she said it, she could have cut out her tongue. He'd been on *GQ* last month, artfully stretched out on some L.A. beach, draped in sand.

And four naked, gorgeous, equally sandy women.

She'd bought the damn issue, which really chapped her ass. Mark clearly knew it, and his smile broke free. She rubbed at her nose but apparently this only made things worse because his smile widened.

"Here," he said, and ran a finger over the bridge of her nose himself.

Up this close and personal, it was hard to miss just how gorgeous he was.

Or how good he smelled.

Or how expensive he looked.

All of which was hugely irritating.

"Got it," he said. "Not much I can do about the soap all over you. Let's fix this too." Then, before she could stop him, he tugged off her drenched hat, flashed an amused glance at what was surely some scary-ass hair, then replaced her hat with the one from his own head. The Mammoths, of course. He ran a hand over his own silky, dark hair, leaving it slightly tousled and perfectly sexy.

She snatched back her hat. "I like the Ducks. They're my favorite team."

At this, both of his players turned from Todd and stared at her. Rainey didn't know if it was because of what she'd just said, or because no one dared sass their fearless leader. "No offense," she said to them.

"None taken," Casey said on a grin and held out his hand, introducing himself. James did the same.

Rainey instantly liked them both, and not just because they were famous, or cute as hell—which they were—but because they were quite harmless, as compared with their head coach. He wasn't the least bit harmless. Rainey squirmed a little, probably due to the soapy water running down her body.

Or the way Mark was studying her with the same quiet intensity he used on the ice—which she knew because she watched his games. All of them.

"So how do you know Coach?" James asked her.

Rainey looked into Mark's eyes. Well, not quite his eyes, since they were still behind the reflective Oakleys that probably cost more than her grocery bill for the month. "We go way back."

Mark's almost-smile made an appearance again.

"Rainey went to school with my brother Rick." He paused, clearly waiting for her to add something to the story.

No thank you, since the only thing she could add would be "and one time I threw myself at him and he turned me down flat."

They'd seen each other since, of course, on the few occasions when he'd come back to town to visit his dad and brother. Once when she'd been twenty-one, at a local police ball that Mark had helped chair. He'd slow danced with her and the air had crackled between them. Chemistry had abounded, and she could read in his dark eyes that he'd felt it too, and she'd melted at his interest. But she hadn't been able to swallow her mortification about the fiasco on her sixteenth birthday, so she'd made an excuse and bailed on him. She'd seen him again, several times, and each accidental run-in had been the same.

The laws of physics didn't change. The sun would come up. The sun would go down. And she would always be insanely attracted to Mark Diego.

The last chance encounter had been only two years ago. They'd had yet another near miss at a town Christmas ball when they'd again slow danced. He expressed interest in every hard line of his body, some harder than others, but she'd let self-preservation rule once more.

"So are you friends?" James asked her and Mark now. "Or...?" He waggled a finger back and forth between them with a matching waggle of his brow.

Mark gave him a single look, nothing more, and James zipped his lips.

Impressive. "Neither," she told James resolutely, trying to wring out the hem of her shirt while ignoring

how close Mark was standing to her, invading her personal space bubble.

"It's been a long time," he said. "You look…"

"All wet?" she asked.

His eyes heated, and something deep inside her quivered. Damn, he still had the power. He smiled, and she narrowed her eyes, daring him to go there, but his momma hadn't raised a fool.

"Different," he finally said. "You look different."

Yes, she imagined she looked quite different than the gorgeous women she'd seen hanging off his arm in magazines and blogs.

"It's good to see you," he said.

She wanted to believe that was true, but realized with some horror that she'd actually leaned into him, drawn in by that stupid magnetic charisma. But she was nothing if not a pro at hiding embarrassment. Spreading her arms, she gave him a hug, as if that'd been her intention all along. Squeezing his big, warm, hard body close, she made sure to spread as much of the suds and water from her shirt to his as she could. "It's good to see you as well," she said, her mouth against his ear, her lips brushing the lobe.

He went still at the contact, then instead of trying to pull free, merely folded her into his arms, trapping her against him. And damn if her body didn't burst to life, as if all this time it'd been just waiting for him to come back.

"Yeah, you're different," he murmured, doing as she had, pressing his mouth to her ear, giving her a shiver. "The little kitten grew up and got claws."

When she choked out a laugh, he closed his teeth over her earlobe.

She gasped, but then he soothed the ache with a quick touch of his tongue, yanking another shocked response from her. "You said you were looking for Rick," she managed to say, shoving free. "He's in his office." And then, with as much dignity as she could muster, she walked off, sneakers squishing, water dripping from her nose, and, she suspected, her shorts revealing a horrible, water-soaked wedgie.

2

AFTER CHECKING IN WITH his brother, Mark and his players got back into his truck, not heading back to the coast, but further up into the rolling hills.

Rainey Saunders, holy shit. Talk about a blast from his past. Seeing her had been like a sucker punch; her smile, her shorts. Those legs…

Once upon a time she'd been a definite sweet spot in his life. A friend of his younger brother, who always had a smile for him. He'd been fond of her, as much as any teenage guy could be fond of something other than himself. She'd hung out on the fringes of his world throughout school, and he'd thought of her as one of the pack. Until she'd changed things up by going from a cute little kid to a hot teenager.

The night she'd shown up in his college apartment had been both a shock and a loss. A shock because he'd honestly had no idea that she'd had a crush on him, at least not before she'd dropped her clothes for him without warning. Until then, she'd never let on, not once. And a loss because everything had changed afterwards. He'd never forget how she'd broken into his place and

found him in the throes with a coed. By the time he'd
caught up with her, she'd run off with the first guy she'd
found.

And that guy had been a real asshole who'd nearly
given her a birthday moment she hadn't counted on.
Mark had managed to stop it, and somehow *he'd* ended
up the bad guy.

Rainey had wanted Mark to notice her, to see her
as a woman, and hello, mission accomplished. Hell, he
could still picture her perfect body—but he'd been too
old for her. Even at twenty, he'd been smart enough to
know that. Too bad he hadn't been smart enough to
handle the situation correctly. Nope, he'd screwed it
up badly enough to affect their relationship to the point
that they'd no longer been friends.

It'd taken him a shamefully long time to figure that
out, though, and by then he'd been on his path and gone
from the area. Leaving Santa Rey had been his dream.
To go do something big, something to lift him out of
the poverty of his upbringing. He'd spent the next few
years climbing his way up the coaching staff ladder,
working in Toronto, New York, Boston…finally landing back on the west coast with a coveted head coaching position at the Mammoths.

He'd seen Rainey several times over the years since,
and on each occasion she'd definitely sparked his interest. As a bonus, they'd both been age suitable. But
though she'd flirted with him, nothing had ever come
of it. He had no idea what being with her would be like,
but he knew one thing. It would be interesting.

The Mammoths were officially off season now and
on vacation. Except for Casey and James, who were

damn lucky to still be a part of the team after their stupid bar fight.

He and the Ducks' coach had agreed to teach their players a lesson in how to be a role model by making them contribute to a struggling local community. Both coaches had chosen their own home communities, areas hit hard by fires and needing to heal. The players would be volunteer laborers at charity construction sites for most of the day, then after work they'd coach summer league ball. At the end of the summer league, the two rec centers would have a big game, with all the proceeds going directly to their programs. The community would benefit, the players could get their acts together, and everyone would feel like they'd made a difference.

All that was left was to tell his idiot players that they wouldn't be summering in style, but doing good old-fashioned hard work.

"Uh, Coach? Aren't we going home?" Casey asked from the passenger seat of the truck.

"Nope." Their asses were Mark's. They just didn't realize it yet. "We're staying in town."

"Where? At the Hard Rock Café?" This from James.

"We won't be at the beach." That was the South District, and they didn't need nearly as much help as the North District did. "We're heading to the very northern part of the county."

His two players exchanged glances. Mark smiled grimly and kept driving. He had a lot to think about—recruiting and trading for next season, not to mention hundreds of emails and phone calls waiting to be returned—but his brain kept skipping back to Rainey.

She'd grown up nice. The wet T-shirt had proved that. But it'd been far more than just a physical jolt

he'd gotten. One look into her fierce blue eyes and he'd felt…

Something. Not even in the finals had his heart taken such a hard leap as it had when he'd realized who she was. Or when she'd touched her mouth to his ear.

Or when he'd bitten hers and absorbed the sexy little startled gasp she'd made.

"Come on, Coach. We're sorry about the fight. We've said it a million times. But it was the big game, and we were robbed."

Just getting to the finals had been a sweet victory, considering the Mammoths were only a five-year-old franchise. It'd been a culmination of grit, determination, and hard work, and even thinking about the season had a surge of fierce pride going through him. But the bar fight—now viral on YouTube—had taken away from their amazing season, and was giving them nothing but bad press. Mark had been featured on *Sixty Minutes* and all the mornings shows, trying to put a positive spin on things. He'd been flown to New York in a helicopter to recite the *Top Ten Things That Had Gone Through His Mind After Losing The Stanley Cup*. He'd been on the *Ellen DeGeneres Show* and had plunged Ellen into the dunk tank for charity. And then there'd been the endless lower profile events filling his calendar: meet-and-greets, photo shoots and endless charity appearances.

And still all everyone wanted to talk about was the fight. It pissed him off. After working around the clock for seven months, he should be on vacation.

He'd seen the press of other players on Jay-Z's yacht in the Caribbean with a bunch of scantily-clad women. Mark wouldn't mind being on a sandy beach some-

where, a woman at his side, a drink in his hand. But no. Instead he was babysitting his two youngest players because apparently they thought with their fists instead of their brains.

That was going to change. It'd been handy having his brother as the director of the rec center. Casey and James would be working their asses off. Construction and coaching, and hopefully, if they were lucky, they'd manage to take in some positive publicity while they were at it. That would make the owners of the Mammoths happy, and Mark too.

As well as Rick.

Win-win, all around, and Mark was all about the win. Always.

James leaned forward from the backseat. "We stayed at the Santa Rey Resort last time, remember? Man, they have that great nightclub…." He sighed with fond memories.

Mark just kept driving. They weren't staying at the resort. Or the Four Seasons. Or anywhere that any of them were accustomed to. "You both agreed to do whatever it took to not be suspended, correct?"

Another long glance between the two players.

"Yeah," James said.

'You're going to work as volunteer construction crew on the fire rebuilds, then every afternoon you'll coach at the rec center."

"That sounds okay," James said. "Especially if the coach gig involves that hot little counselor they had running the car wash. What's her name… Rainey? Loved her wet T-shirt—you guys see that?"

Casey grinned. "I loved her whistle and clipboard,

and the way she barked orders like a little tyrant. Sexiest tyrant I've ever seen."

When James chuckled, Mark's fingers tightened on the steering wheel. "She's off limits." He ignored the third long look that James and Casey exchanged. But they had one thing right. Rainey *was* a tyrant, especially when she decided on something.

Or someone.

And once upon a time, she'd decided on him.

"So we're not going to the Biltmore?" James asked. "Cuz there's always plenty of hot babes there."

"James," Mark said. "What did I tell you about hot babes?"

James slumped in his seat. "That if I so much as look at one you're going to kick my ass."

"Do you doubt my ability to do so?"

James slouched even further. "No one in their right mind would doubt that, Coach."

"And anyway, you're not allowed back at the Biltmore," Casey reminded James. "That's where you got caught with that redhead by her husband. You had to jump out the window and sprained your knee and were out for three weeks."

"Oh yeah," James said on a fond sigh. "Madeline."

Mark felt a brain bleed coming on. He exited the highway, a good twenty miles from the beach and any "hot babes."

"Damn," James murmured, taking in the fire ravaged hills on either side of the narrow two-lane highway, then repeated the "damn" when Mark pulled up to a small, run-down-looking motel.

"Home sweet home for the next month," Mark told them grimly. "The Santa Rey Welcome Inn."

Casey and James just stared at the single story motel. The stucco walls were pea-green, the windows lined with wrought-iron grates. The yard was dead grass.

"They're on water restrictions," Mark said, and clapped them both on the backs. "You'll be reminded of that come shower time in the morning. There's a three-minute shower requirement here. Let's go," he said to their groans.

The Welcome Inn sign blinked on and off in flashing white lights. The door to the office was thrown open, letting out the scent of stale coffee and air freshener. Inside the office was a desk, a small couch, and a floor fan on full blast aimed at the woman behind the desk. Celia Anderson was sixty-something, and glued to the soap opera on the TV mounted on the wall—until she saw Mark. With a warm smile, she came around and squeezed him tight. "Aw, you're such a good boy," she said. "Throwing us your fancy business."

Boy? Casey mouthed to James.

"Sometimes homey is better than fancy," Mark said to Celia.

She patted his cheek gently. "Your father raised you right. I've got the three rooms you requested. Cash or credit?"

"Cash," he said, knowing how badly she needed the cash.

"I'll give you a discount."

"No," he said gently, putting his hand over hers when she went to punch a discounted rate into her computer. "Full price."

She beamed at him and handed over their room keys.

Which were actual keys. Casey looked at his like he didn't know what to do with it. They walked down the

outside hallway to their rooms. Each had a single bed, dresser and chair beneath the window. All of which had seen better days but were spotlessly clean.

"Coach, I think your assistant screwed up the reservations," Casey said.

James's head bobbled his agreement. "I don't think they even have cable."

"There's been no mistake," Mark said. "Unless you guys wanted to room together?"

They looked at the narrow bed and vehemently shook their heads, both wisely deciding to drop the subject.

Mark waited until he was alone to smile. Operation: *Ego Check* was in full swing.

For all of them.

RAINEY DIDN'T FALL ASLEEP until past midnight, and dreamed badly.

Sweet Sixteen, and she stood outside Mark's bedroom door, heart pounding inside her chest so loudly she was surprised she hadn't woken the entire apartment complex.

Mark had no idea she was here. No one did. She'd stolen his key from Rick and lied to her friends that she was too tired to go out. Wearing a pretty lacy teddy beneath her sweats, carrying a borrowed pair of sexy heels in her hand, she grinned. Tonight was the night. She was finally going to tell him she loved him, that she always had. They'd live happily ever after, just like in all the good chick flicks.

Quietly she opened his bedroom door and dropped her sweats. She stepped into the heels and fluffed her

*hair. She was just checking her boobs to make sure they
were even and perky when she heard it.*

A rough moan.

Whirling around, she got the shock of her life.

Mark wasn't sleeping. He wasn't even in his bed.

*He was sprawled in the beanbag chair beneath the
window, long legs spread for the woman on her knees
between his, head bobbing—Oh, God.*

*Mark's head was back, eyes closed, his perfect body
taut and his hands fisted in his date's hair as she...*

*Rainey must have made a sound, or maybe he'd
heard the crack of her heart as it split wide, because
Mark sat straight up so fast he nearly choked his date.
"Christ. Rainey—"*

*"Hey," his date complained, lifting her head with a
pissed-off frown. "I'm Melody."*

*Rainey turned to run away and ran smack into the
door—which didn't slow her down. Not that, or the
sprained ankle from her stupid heels.*

"Rainey!"

*The pounding of bare feet told her he was coming
after her. Not wanting to face him, she kicked her heels
off and raced barefoot out into the night like Cinderella
trying to beat the clock. Young and desperate, she'd
run off looking for a way to prove herself as grown up
as she imagined.*

*She'd been ripe for trouble, and unfortunately, she'd
found it.*

SITTING STRAIGHT UP in bed with a gasp, Rainey realized
it was dawn, and she blinked the dream away. Fourteen
years and she remembered every humiliating detail as if

it'd been yesterday. Especially what had happened next. But she wasn't going there, not now. Not ever.

By that afternoon, she'd nearly forgotten all about the dream *and* Mark. She was running laps with the group of teens who'd shown up after school, counting heads to make sure none had made off with each other into the bushes, when Sharee came up to her side.

Rainey's welcoming smile faded as she locked her gaze on the new bruise on the teen's jaw. "What happened?"

Sharee switched into her default expression—sullen. "Nothing."

"Sharee—"

"Walked into a door, no big deal."

"Where was your mother?"

Sharee lifted a shoulder. "Working."

Rainey would like to get Martin alone and walk *him* into a door, but that was a stupid idea. The man scared Rainey. "You know where I live, right?"

"The Northside town houses."

"Unit fifteen," Rainey said. "Next time your mother's working nights, come have a sleepover with me."

"Why?"

"So you don't walk into any more doors. We'll watch a movie and eat crap food. It'll be more fun than any date I've had in a while."

"How often do you date?" Sharee asked.

The easy answer was not much. But that was also the embarrassing answer. "Occasionally."

Sharee nodded, then went back to running laps. Rainey ran again too, until her cell phone buzzed an incoming text from Rick.

The help I promised you for the summer league is on their way. You've got two Mammoth players and their head coach, who I believe you've met. They work for you, Rainey. You're in charge.

She'd have to kill Rick later. For now, she grabbed her clipboard and blew her whistle. "Two more laps before we scrimmage," she called out, and began stretching to cool down. She'd figured Rick would get a few local college athletes. But nope, he'd gone all the way to the top.

And all she could think was that Mark would be around for three weeks.

Twenty-one days…

She lay on her back and stared at the puffy clouds floating lazily by, trying not to delve too deeply into how she felt about this. The first cloud looked sort of like a double-stuffed Oreo. She could really go for a handful of double-stuffed Oreos about now. The next cloud came into sight, resembling—"Mark?"

She blinked up at the cloud that wasn't a cloud at all as Mark flashed her his million-dollar smile.

"Heard you need me," he said. "Bad."

AT TWENTY-ONE, MARK had been long and leanly muscled, not a spare inch on him. Rainey's gaze ran down his thirty-four-year-old body and she had to admit he was even better now. In fact, the only way to improve on that body would be to dip it into chocolate.

He offered her a hand, his grip firm as he pulled her upright. She immediately brushed the dry grass from her behind and the backs of her legs, painfully aware of the fact that once again she was a complete mess and

he…he was not. He had all that perfect Latino skin, and the most amazing dark eyes that held more secrets than some developing countries. He had strong cheekbones and a mouth that always brought sinful thoughts to her mind, especially when he flashed that rare smile of his. He'd broken his nose twice in his wild and crazy youth, not that it dared to be anything less than aristocrat straight. But even better than his arresting face was everything else—his fierce passion, his drive, his smarts. And now for the first time, she supposed she could also appreciate his coaching skills firsthand. "We're running," she said.

"Really? Because it looked like you were napping."

Clearly he was in great shape. He could probably run a marathon without breaking a sweat. The thought of what else he might be able to do without breaking a sweat made her nipples hard.

Don't go there….

Too late. She closed her eyes so she couldn't stare at him, but as it turned out, he and his hot bod were imprinted on her brain. His world was about coaching million-dollar athletes, and he'd taken it upon himself to be as fit as they were. This meant he was six feet plus of hard sinew wrapped in testosterone, built to impress any guy and pretty much render any female a puddle of longing.

Except her.

Nope, there could be no melting, not for her. She was so over him. Completely. Over. Him.

Maybe.

Oh, God, she was in trouble. Because who was she kidding? She'd never gotten over him, never, and every

single guy she'd ever dated had been mentally measured up to him and found lacking.

It made no sense. Yes, she'd known him years ago. Back then she'd been insanely attracted to the way he cared deeply about those around him, his utter lack of fear of anything, and his truck. Apparently some things never changed.

He stepped closer, blocking the sun with his broad shoulders so that all she could see was him, and she forgot to breathe.

His fingertips brushed lightly over a cheek and something deep in her belly quivered. "You're getting sunburned," he said. "Where's your hat?"

The one he'd given her yesterday? She'd tried to toss it into her trash can last night. Twice.

It was sitting on her pillow at home.

But only because it would have been rude to let a gift go out with the week's trash. And that was the *only* reason she'd worn it to bed. "I'm wearing sunscreen."

He was just looking at her. His phone had vibrated no less than five times from the depths of his pockets, but he was ignoring it. She tried to imagine all he was responsible for on any given day, and couldn't.

"How have you been?" he asked.

"Good. And you? Congratulations on your season, by the way."

"Thanks. It really is good to see you, Rainey."

She laughed and spread her hands, indicating her state of dishevelment. "Yeah, well it gets better than this, I swear."

He smiled and looked past her to the girls. "Rick said to let you know the players and I are to report to you for coaching the kids. That's how both the Ducks and

the Mammoths are handling the fallout from the fight. We're trying to show that players can be role models and help our local communities at the same time. At the end of summer league, we'll have a big charity fund-raising game between the two rec centers and show that it doesn't have to end in a fight."

"Hmm." The idea was fantastic, and in truth, she really needed help. There'd been a time when she'd needed *him* too, not that she'd ever managed to get him.

And Rick had just given him to her on a silver platter. Oh, the irony. "That's great."

"Will the parents have a problem with us stepping in? Don't they usually coach for summer leagues?"

"Not in this part of town, they don't. They're all working, or not interested."

He eyed the teens on the field, specifically the boys, his sharp gaze already assessing. "How about you let us handle the entire boys' program?" He turned that gaze on her, and smiled. "It's been what, a few years?"

"Two." She clamped her lips shut when that slipped out, giving away the fact that she'd kept count.

His smile widened, and she arched a brow.

"I'll hug you hello again," she warned. "And this time I'm all sweaty."

He immediately stepped into her.

"No," she gasped. "I'll ruin your expensive shirt—"

Not listening, he wrapped his arms around her. "You can't ignore me this time, Rainey, though it's going to be fun watching you try. And you know what? I think I like you all hot and sweaty." He ran a hand down her back, smiling when she shivered. Stepping away, he gestured to the boys on the field. "Bring them in," he said. "Let's see what we've got."

While she blew the whistle, he eyed the two baseball diamonds. There were weeds growing in the lanes, no bases, and the lines had long ago been washed away.

"Why are they dressed like that?" he asked.

The boys were in a variety of baggy, saggy shorts and big T-shirts. Some of the girls wore just sports bras and oversize basketball shorts. Others wore tight T-shirts, or shirts so loose they were in danger of falling off. "We don't have practice jerseys."

He pulled out his cell phone and walked a few steps away, either to make or take a call, and Rainey absolutely did not watch his ass as he moved.

Much.

When he came back, she'd divided the teens up into boys and girls, and sent the boys to the further diamond to scrimmage because they were much better at self-regulating than the girls.

She'd split the girls into two bedraggled, short teams and Sharee was at bat. She hit a hard line drive up the first base line. Pepper, their pitcher, squeaked in fear and dropped to the mound.

"Nice hit," Mark said. "But why is the pitcher lying flat on the ground like there's been a fire drill?"

"Pepper's terrified of the ball."

He shook his head. "You've got your hands full with the girls, huh?"

First base grabbed the ball but Sharee was already rounding second.

First base threw, and...second base missed the catch.

Mark groaned.

"They'll get there," Rainey said. "I've been working with them while waiting on coaches."

At her defensive tone, he took a longer look at her. "You didn't know we were coming in to help you."

"No."

He grimaced. "Rick's an idiot."

"That idiot is my friend and boss."

"So you're okay with this? Working with me, even though you've done your best to ignore me all these years?"

"You're right," she decided. "Rick *is* an idiot."

He grinned.

And oh, God, that grin. He flashed white, straight teeth and a light of pure trouble in his eyes, and she helplessly responded.

Damn hormones.

"We're grown-ups," she said. "We can handle this— you working for me. Right? We can do it for all these kids."

Mark moved into her, a small movement that set her heart pounding. She refused to take a step back because she knew it would amuse him, and she'd done enough of that for a lifetime.

"Working *for* you?" he murmured in that bedroom voice.

"I'm the athletic director, so yeah. You coaching is you working for me. You're working under me and my command." She gave him a look. "You have a problem with that?"

"No problem at all." His gaze dropped to her mouth. "Though I'd much rather have *you* under *me*."

Jill Shalvis

3

RAINEY DID HER BEST to ignore all the parts of her body that were quivering and sending conflicting signals to her brain and drew a deep breath. "This is inappropriate," she finally said.

The corners of his mouth turned up slightly. "Only if someone overhears us."

She drew another deep breath. That one didn't work any better than the first, so she turned to the field, watching the girls silently for a few minutes. After three outs, the teams switched on the field.

"Uneven teams," Mark noted. "I'm going to go get a closer look at the boys."

She grabbed his hand to halt his progress. "This is rec league, Mark. It's not really about the competition."

"It's always about the competition."

"It's about having fun," she said.

His eyes met hers and held. The sun was beating down on them and Rainey resented that she was sweating and he was not.

"Winning *is* fun," he said.

Another little quiver where she had no business quivering.

Lila hit next and got a piece of the ball and screamed in surprise. Sharee sighted the ball and yelled *"mine!"*, diving for it, colliding hard with Kendra at second. Sharee managed to make the catch and the out.

Kendra rubbed her arm and glared at Sharee, who ignored her.

"Nice," Mark said. "She's got potential."

"This isn't hockey, Mark." But Rainey was talking to air because he'd walked onto the diamond like the superstar coach he was.

Sharee had her back to him, barking out orders at the other girls on the field like a drill sergeant. When she turned to face home plate, her eyes widened at the sight of Mark.

He held out his hand for the ball.

Sharee popped it into her mitt twice out of defiance, and only when Mark raised a single brow did she finally toss it to him, hard.

He caught it with seemingly no effort. "Name?"

"Sharee."

"What was that, Sharee?"

"A great pitch," she said, and popped her gum.

"After the pitch."

"A great play."

He nodded. "You're fast."

"The fastest."

He nodded again. "But you took yourself out of position and it wasn't your ball to go after. You could have let your team down."

Sharee stopped chewing her gum and frowned. She wasn't used to being told what to do, and she wasn't

much fond of men. "Kendra would have missed the out," she finally said.

"Then center field would have gotten it."

Sharee eyed the center fielder, who was busy braiding her hair, and snorted.

Mark just looked at Sharee for a long beat. "Do you know who I am?"

"Yeah. Head coach of the Mammoths."

"Do you know if I'm any good?" he asked.

"You're the best," Sharee said simply but grudgingly. "At hockey."

Mark smiled. "I played hockey *and* baseball in college, before I started coaching. My players listen to me, Sharee, and they listen because I get them results. But when they don't listen, they do push-ups. Lots of them."

Sharee blinked. "You make grown guys do push-ups?"

"I teach them to play hard or not at all. You're practicing for, what, maybe an hour a day? The least you can do is play hard for that entire time. As hard as you can, always."

"Or push-ups."

"That's right."

Sharee considered this. "I don't like push-ups."

"Then I'd listen real good. One hundred percent," he said to everyone. "I am asking for one hundred percent. It's effort. You don't have to have talent for effort. You," Mark said to the girl in center field, who was no longer braiding her hair but doing her best to be invisible. "What's your name?"

She opened her mouth but the only thing that came out was a squeak.

"It's Tina," Sharee said for her. "And she never catches the ball."

"Why not?"

Everyone looked at Tina, who squeaked again.

"Because she can't," Sharee said.

"So you make all the outs?" Mark asked.

"Most of 'em."

"That's what we call a ball hog." He tossed the ball back to her. "Let's see who else besides you can play."

"But—"

Again he arched a brow and she shut her mouth.

Rainey stared, mesmerized, as he coached the un-coachable Sharee through an inning, getting everyone involved.

Even Tina and Pepper.

When it was over, Rainey sent the kids back to the rec center building so that they wouldn't miss their buses home.

"Didn't mean to step on your toes," he said.

"I'm happy for the help. Nice job with them."

"Then why are you frowning?" he asked.

Because she was dripping sweat and he looked cool as ice. Because standing next to him brought back memories and yearnings she didn't want. Pick one. She grabbed her clipboard and started across the field, but Mark caught her by the back of her shirt and pulled her to him.

And there went her body again, quivering with all sorts of misfired signals to her brain. Her nipples went

hard, her thighs tingled, and most importantly, her ir-
ritation level skyrocketed.

"What's your hurry?" Mark asked, snaking an arm
around her to hold her in place. The kid were all gone.
She and Mark were hidden from view of the building by
the dugout. Knowing no one could see her, she closed
her eyes, absorbing the feeling of being this close to
him. Unattainable, she reminded herself. He was completely unattainable. "I just…" Her brain wasn't running on all cylinders.

"You just…" he repeated helpfully, his lips accidentally brushing her earlobe. Or at least she assumed it
was accidental. However it happened, her knees wobbled.

"I…" His hand was low on her belly, holding her in
place against him. "Wait—*what are you doing?*"

"We never really got to say hello in private." He
tightened his grip. "Hello, Rainey."

If his voice got any lower on the register, she'd probably orgasm on the spot.

"It's been too long," he murmured against her jaw.

Telling herself that no one could see them, she
pressed back against him just a little. "I don't know
about *too* long."

A soft chuckle gave her goose bumps, and then
he was gone so fast she nearly fell on her ass. When
she spun around, she got a good look at that gorgeous
face—the square jaw, the almost arrogant cheekbones,
the eyes that could be ice-cold or scorching-hot depending on his mood. And no matter what his mood was,
there was always the slight suggestion that maybe…
maybe he belonged on the dark side.

It was impossibly, annoyingly intriguing. *He* was

impossibly, annoyingly intriguing, and yet he called to the secret part of her that had never stopped craving him. She headed toward the building, and he easily kept pace. Between the field and the building was a full basketball court, with a ball sitting on the center line.

Mark nudged it with his foot in a way that had it leaping right into his hands. He tossed it to her, a light of challenge in his eyes. "One on one."

"Basketball's not your sport, Coach."

"And it's yours?"

"Maybe."

"Then play me," he dared.

"We're wearing the same color shirt. Someone's going to have to be skins." She had no idea why she said it, but he smiled.

"I guess that would be me."

She shrugged as if she could care less, while her inner slut said "yes please." "I guess—"

The words backed up in her throat when he reached over his head and yanked his shirt off in one economical movement, tossing it aside with no regard for the fact that it probably cost more than all her shirts added together.

Her eyes went directly to his chest. His skin was the color of the perfect mocha latte, and rippled with the strength just beneath it. She let her gaze drift down over his eight-pack, and—

"Keep looking at me like that," he said, "and we're going to have a problem."

She jerked her gaze away. "I wasn't looking at you like anything."

"Liar."

Yeah. She was a liar. She dribbled the ball, then bar-

reled past him to race down the court. She could hear his quick feet and knew he was right behind her, but then suddenly he was at her side, reaching in with a long arm to grab the ball away.

She shoved him, her hands sliding over his heated skin. Catching herself, she snatched the ball back, then executed a very poor shot that went in by sheer luck. Grinning, she turned to face him and plowed smack into his chest.

"Foul," he said.

"What are you, a girl?"

That made him smile. "Gee, wonder where Sharee gets her attitude from?"

"Actually, she gets that from her abusive alcoholic father."

Mark lost his smile and dribbled as he studied her. "It's a good thing...what you're doing here."

Feeling oddly uncomfortable with the compliment and the way his praise washed over her, she snatched the ball and went for another shot. Competitive to the bone, Mark shouldered his way into her space, grabbed the ball and sank a basket far more gracefully than she'd done. Dammit. She took the ball back and elbowed him when he crowded her.

He grinned, a very naughty grin that did things to her insides. "Is that how you want to play?" he asked. "Dirty?"

"Playing" with him at all was a very bad idea. But as always with Mark, her best judgment went out the window. Or in this case, down the court where she took the ball. Her feet were in the air for the layup when he grabbed her and spun her away from the basket.

Oh, no. Hell, no. She struggled, and they both fell to

the ground. He landed with a rough "oomph." Lying on top of him, she looked down into his face, extremely aware of how he felt sprawled beneath her.

His eyes were heat and raw power. "Foul number two. You play panicked, Rainey. Am I making you nervous?"

"Of course not." Face hot, fingers even hotter after bracing herself on his bare chest, she scrambled off him. She walked along the side of the rec building to the storage shed to put the ball away.

Mark had picked up his shirt and followed her, pulling it on as he did. Then he backed her to the shed.

"You really don't make me nervous," she said.

"You sure about that?"

Before she could answer, he kissed her, slipping a hand beneath her shirt at the base of her spine, trailing his fingers up her back. The kiss was long and slow and deep, and her hand came up to his chest for balance.

And absolutely not to explore the tight muscles there.

By the time he broke it off, she realized she'd let one of his legs thrust between hers, and she had both hands fisted in his shirt. Clearly she was sex-deprived. That was the only way to explain how she was riding his leg, breathing like a lunatic, still gripping him for all she was worth. She stared up at him, unable to access the correct brain synapses to make her mouth work. By the time she managed to speak, he'd smirked and begun walking away.

Dammit! "I'm not nervous," she called after him. "I'm annoyed, and I won our game!"

"You cheated." He shot her a look over his shoulder. "And payback is a bitch."

AFTER LEAVING THE FIELD, Mark attempted to put both Rainey and their kiss out of his head, which turned out to be surprisingly difficult.

Rainey had always had a way of worming beneath his skin and destroying his defenses, and apparently that hadn't changed. He'd missed her in his life—her sweet smile, her big heart, that way she'd had of making him want to be a better person than he was.

He picked up pizza and beer, and took it to the Welcome Inn.

As per their agreement, Casey and James had been at the construction site all day, just as their Duck counterparts were doing in their chosen community a couple hours south of them, just outside of Santa Barbara.

The two Mammoth players had been brought back to the inn by one of the workers. Mark had purposely stranded them in Santa Rey without a car, wanting them to be at his mercy—and out of trouble, with no chance of finding it. He located them in Casey's room, hunched over the yellow pages of the phone book arguing over food choices.

James looked up. "Did you know that there's no room service here?"

Mark lifted the three pizzas and twelve-pack. "I'm your room service tonight."

"Sweet." Casey looked very relieved as he tossed aside the phone book. He stretched and winced. "There's no whirlpool. No hot tub. No spa—"

"Nope." Mark took the sole chair in the room, turning it around to straddle it. "There's no amenities at all."

"Then why are we—"

"Because you two screwed up and are lucky to still have jobs."

They sighed in unison.

"And," Mark went on, "because the couple who owns this place lost their home in the fire last year. Business is down, way down."

"Shock," James muttered.

"You both agreed to this. The alternative is available to you—suspension." Mark stood. "So if this isn't something you can handle, don't be here when I come to pick you up in the morning."

He turned to the door, and just as he went through it, he heard James say, "Dude, sometimes it's okay to just shut the hell up."

AFTER DROPPING OFF THE pizza and ultimatum, Mark picked up his brother and drove the two of them up the highway another couple of miles, until the neighborhood deteriorated considerably.

"He's been looking forward to this for a long time," Rick said.

"I know." Last summer's fire had ravaged the area, and half the houses were destroyed. Of those, a good percentage had been cleared away and were in various stages of being rebuilt. The house Mark and Rick had grown up in was nearly finished now. Still small, still right on top of the neighbor's, but at least it was new. They got out of the truck and headed up the paved walk. The yard was landscaped and clearly well cared for. Before they could knock, the door opened.

"So the prodigal son finally returns," Ramon Diego said, a mirror image of Rick and Mark, plus two decades and some gray.

"I told you I was coming," Mark said. "I texted you."

Ramon made an annoyed sound. "Texting is for idiots on the hamster wheel."

Rick snorted.

Mark sighed, and his father's face softened. "Ah, *hijo,* it's good to see you." He pulled Mark in for a hard hug and a slap on the back.

"You too," Mark said, returning the hug. "The house looks good."

"Thanks to you." Ramon had migrated here from Mexico with his gardener father when he was seven years old. He'd grown up and become a gardener as well, and had lived here ever since. Forty-eight years and he still spoke with an accent. "Don't even try to tell me my insurance covered all the upgrades you had put in."

"Do you like it?" Mark asked.

"Yes, but you shouldn't waste your money on me. If you have that much money to spare, give up the job and come back to your home, your roots."

Mark's "roots" had been a tiny house crowded with his dad and brother, living hand to mouth. A one-way road for Mark as he grew up. A road to trouble.

Ramon gestured to the shiny truck in the driveway. "New?"

"You know damn well it is," Mark said. "It's the truck I bought for you for your birthday, and you had it sent back to me."

"Hmm," Ramon said noncommittally, possibly the most stubborn man on the planet. Mark knew his dad was proud of him, but he'd have been even more proud if Mark had stuck around and become a gardener too. Ramon had never understood Mark not living here in Santa Rey, using it as a home base.

"You should come home more often," Ramon said.

"I told you I wouldn't be able to come during the season."

"Bah. What kind of a job keeps a son from his home and family."

"The kind that makes him big bucks," Rick said.

They moved through the small living room and into the kitchen. "If you'd use the season tickets I bought you," Mark told his dad. "You could see me whenever you wanted."

"I saw you on TV breaking up that fight. You nearly took a left hook from that Ducks player. Getting soft?" He jabbed Mark's abs, then smiled. "Okay, maybe not. Come home, *hijo,* and stay. You've got all the money you could need now, yes? Come settle down, find someone to love you."

"Dad."

"I'm getting old. I need *nietos* to spoil."

Rick rolled his eyes and muttered, "Here we go. The bid for grandkids."

"Someone to take care of you," Ramon said, and smacked Rick on the back of the head.

"I take care of myself," Mark said. *And about a hundred others.*

Ramon sighed. "I suppose it's my fault. I harp on you about walking away from your humble beginnings and culture, and I divorced your mother when you were only five. Bad example."

"I've never walked away from my beginnings, Dad. I just have a job that requires a lot of traveling. And Mom divorced you. You drove her batshit crazy." His father was an incredibly hard worker, and incredibly old world

in his sensibilities. He'd driven his ambitious, wanna-be actress wife off years ago.

The living room was empty except for two beautiful potted plants. Same with the kitchen, though the cabinet doors were glass, revealing plates and cups on the shelves. "Where's the furniture? I sent money, and you've been back in this house for what, a few weeks now?"

"I liked my old furniture."

"I know, but it's all gone. You got out with the clothes on your back." Mark still shuddered to think how close he'd come to losing his dad.

"I'll get furniture eventually, as I find what suits me. Let's eat. You can tell me about your women."

There was only one at the moment, the one with the flashing eyes, a smart-ass mouth, and heart of gold. The one who still showed her every thought as it came to her. That had terrified him once upon a time.

Now it intrigued him.

His father was at the refrigerator, pulling out ingredients. "We'll have grilled quesadillas for dinner. It's a warm night. We'll sit on the patio."

"I'll take you out to dinner," Mark said.

"No, I'm not spending any more of your money. What if you get fired over this fight mess? Then you'll be broke. Save your money."

"I won't get fired, Dad. The players are working hard, making restitution."

"So you won't have to suspend them?"

"No, which is good since they've got more talent in their pinkie fingers than my entire line of offense, and I have a hot offense."

Ramon nodded his agreement to this. "The press has been relentless on you."

Rick nodded. "You were flashed on *Entertainment Tonight* with a woman from some reality show."

"That was a promo event," Mark said. "I told you, I don't need someone else to take care of right now."

"Love isn't a burden, *hijo*. You really think it'll soften you, make you that vulnerable?"

Mark sent his brother a feel-free-to-jump-in-here-and-redirect-the-converation-at-any-time look, but Rick just smirked, enjoying himself. "What happened to cooking?" Mark asked desperately.

"Your brother has someone," Ramon pointed out, not to be deterred.

Rick smiled smugly.

"You could at least have a home here in Santa Rey," his dad said. "And then maybe a family."

Mark sighed. "We're not going to agree on this issue."

"We would if you'd get over yourself. Chicken or carne quesadilla?"

No one in his world ever told Mark to get over himself. Instead they tripped over their feet to keep him happy. He supposed he should be thankful for the reminder to be humble. "Carne."

THE NEXT MORNING, BOTH James and Casey were ready to roll right on time. They were dressed for construction work and had a coffee for Mark.

Nice to know they could still suck up with the best of them. He wondered if either of them had talked the other out of bailing, but he didn't really give a shit. As

long as they were still here, willing to put in the time and maybe even learn something, he was good.

They worked until afternoon, showered, then attended the rec center's staff meeting, per Rick's request. This was held in a conference room, aka pre-school room, aka makeshift dance studio. Everyone sat at a large table, including Rainey, who didn't look directly at Mark. He knew that because *he* was looking directly at her.

Rick ran a surprisingly tight ship considering how laid-back he was. Assignments were passed out, the budget dealt with, and the sports schedule handled. When it came to that schedule and what was expected of Mark's players, Rick once again made it perfectly clear that Rainey was in charge.

Mark looked across the table and locked eyes with Rainey. He arched a brow and she flushed, but she definitely stared at his mouth before turning back to Rick attentively.

She was thinking about the kiss.

That made two of them. This was Mark's third time seeing her, and she was *still* a jolt on his system.

He realized that Rick and Rainey were speaking. Then Rainey stood up to reveal a poster that would be placed around town. It advertised the upcoming youth sports calendar and other events such as their biweekly car wash and the formal dinner and auction that would hopefully raise the desperately needed funds for a new rec building. She was looking around the room as she spoke, her eyes sharp and bright. She had an easy smile, an easy-to-listen-to voice, and who could forget that tight, toned yet curvy body.

She was in charge of her world.

Watching her, Mark felt something odd come over him. If he had to guess, he'd say it was a mix of warmth and pride and affection. He wasn't sentimental, and he sure as hell wasn't the most sensitive man on the planet. Or so he'd been told a time or a million....

But he'd missed her.

"The Mammoth players will be assisting me in this," she said, and he nodded, even though he wasn't listening so he had no idea what exactly they'd be assisting her with. He'd help her with whatever she wanted. He liked the jeans she was wearing today, which sat snug and low on her hips. Her top was a simple knit and shouldn't have been sexy at all, but somehow was. Maybe because it brought out her blue eyes. Maybe because it clung to her breasts enough to reveal she was feeling a little bit chilly—

"If it works into your schedule, that is," she said, and he realized with a jolt that she was looking right at him.

Everyone was looking right at him.

"That's fine," he said smoothly.

Casey and James both lifted their brows, but he ignored them. "We're here to serve."

James choked on the soda he was drinking.

Casey just continued staring at Mark like he'd lost his marbles.

His brother out-and-out grinned, which was his first clue.

"You just agreed to coach a girls' softball team," James whispered in his ear. "Me and Casey get the boys, but she gave you the girls."

Ah, hell.

Rainey was watching him, waiting for him to balk

and possibly leave, which was clearly what she'd been aiming for. Instead he nodded. "Great."

"Great?"

"Great," he repeated, refusing to let her beat him.

"The kids are going to love it," Rick said. "Tell him your plans, Rainey."

She was still looking a little shell-shocked that she hadn't gotten rid of him. Guess their kiss had shaken her up good.

That made two of them.

"Well, if you're really doing this…?" She stared at him, giving him another chance at a way out. But hell no. Diegos didn't take the out…ever.

"We're doing this," he said firmly. "All the way."

Color rose to her cheeks but she stayed professional. "Okay, well, the Mammoths are taking advantage of our needs in order to gain good publicity, so I figure it's only fair for us to take advantage of your celebrity status."

"Absolutely," Mark said. "How do you want to do that?"

Rainey glanced at Rick, who gave her the go-ahead to voice her thoughts. "You could let us auction off dates with you three," she said.

Mark was stunned. It was ingenious, but he should have expected no less. It was also just a little bit evil.

Seemed Rainey had grown some claws. He had no idea what it said about him that he liked it.

Casey grinned. "Sounds fun. And I'm sure the other guys would put their name on the ticket too."

"I'm in," James said agreeably, always up for something new, especially involving women. "As long as the ladies are single. No husbands with shotguns."

The meeting ended shortly after that and Rainey gathered her things, vacating quickly, the little sneak. Making his excuses, Mark followed after her. She was already halfway down the hall, moving at a fast clip. Obviously she had things to do, places to go. And people to avoid. He smiled grimly, thinking her ass looked sweet in those jeans. So did her attitude, with that whistle around her neck, the clipboard in her hands. She was running her show like...well, like he ran his. He picked up his stride until he was right behind her, and realized she was on her cell phone.

"This is all your fault, Lena," she hissed. "No. *No,* I'm most definitely *not* still crushing on him! That was a secret, by the way, and it was years ago— Yes, I've got eyes, I realize he's hot, thank you very much, but it's not all about looks. And anyway, I'm going out with Kyle Foster tonight, which is your fault too— Are you laughing? Stop laughing!" She paused, taking in whatever was being said to her. "You know what? Calling you was a bad idea. Listening to you in the first place was a bad bad idea. I have to go." She shoved her phone into her pocket and stood there, hands on hips.

"Hey," he said.

She jerked, swore, then started walking again, away from him, moving as if she hadn't heard him. Good tactic. He could totally see why it might work on some people—she moved like smoke. He could also see why she'd want to ignore him, but they had things to discuss. Slipping his fingers around her upper arm, he pulled her back to face him.

"I'm really busy," she said.

"Girls' softball?" he asked softly. "Really?"

"Not here," she said, and opened a door. Which she shut in his face.

Oh hell no, she didn't just do that. He hauled open the door, expecting an office, but instead found a small storage room lined with shelves.

Rainey was consulting her clipboard and searching the shelves.

He shut the door behind him, closing them in, making her gasp in surprise. "What are you doing—"

"You said not out there," he reminded her.

"I meant not out there, and not *anywhere*."

He stepped toward her. Her sultry voice would have made him hard as a rock—except he already was. *"Girls' softball?"* he repeated.

She took a step back and came up against the shelving unit. "You volunteered, remember? Now if you'll excuse me."

Already toe-to-toe, he put his hands on the shelf, bracketing her between his arms. He leaned in so that they were chest to chest, thigh to thigh…and everything in between. Her sweet little intake of air made him hard.

Or maybe that was just her. "Are you punishing me for what happened fourteen years ago?" he asked. "Or for kissing you yesterday?"

"Don't flatter yourself," she said, her hands coming up to fist his shirt, though it was unclear whether she planned to shove him away or hold him to her.

"Admit it," he said. "You gave me the girls to make me suffer."

"Maybe I gave you the girls because that's what's best for them. Not everything is about you, Mark."

Direct hit.

"So we used to know each other," she said. "So what. We're nothing to each other now." But her breathing was accelerated, and then there was the pulse fluttering wildly at the base of her throat. He set his thumb to it, his other fingers spanning her throat and although he was tempted to give it a squeeze, he tilted her head up to his.

Her hands tightened on him. "I mean it," she said. "We're not doing this."

"Define this."

"We're not going to be friends."

"Deal," he said.

"We're not going to even like each other."

"Obviously."

She stared into his eyes, hers turbulent and heated. "And no more kissing—"

He swallowed her words with his mouth, delving deeply, groaning at the taste of her. He heard her answering moan, and then her arms wound tight around his neck.

And for the first time since his arrival back in Santa Rey, they were on the same page.

4

RAINEY OPENED HER MOUTH to protest and Mark's tongue slid right in, so hot, so erotic, she moaned instead. God, the man could kiss. How was it that he looked as good as he did, was *that* sexy, and could kiss like heaven on earth? Talk about an unfair distribution of goods!

Just don't react, she told herself, but she might as well have tried to stop breathing, because this was Mark, big strong, badass *Mark*. The guy from her teenage fantasies. Her grown-up fantasies too, and resistance failed her.

Utterly.

So instead of resisting, she sank into him, and with a rough groan, he pressed her against the shelving unit, trapping her between the hard, cold steel at her back and the hard, hot body at her front. "Okay, wait," she gasped.

Pulling back the tiniest fraction, he looked at her from melting chocolate eyes.

"What are we doing?" she asked.

"Guess."

See, this was the problem with a guy like Mark.

There was a good reason that his players responded to him the way they did. He didn't make any excuses—about anything—and he knew how to get his way. Oh, how he knew, she thought as her hands slid into the silky dark hair at the nape of his neck. She pressed even closer, plastering herself to him, fighting the urge to wrap her legs around his waist as a low, very male sound rumbled in his throat. Her eyes drifted shut. *He isn't for you... He'll never be for you.*

"This doesn't mean anything," she panted, not letting go. So he wasn't for her. She would take what she could get from him. But only because here, with Mark, she felt alive, so damn alive. "You still drive me insane," she said.

He let out a groaning laugh, murmured something that might have been a "right back at you" and kissed her some more.

And God help her, she kissed him back until they had to break apart or suffocate.

"God, Rainey," he whispered hotly against her lips.

"I know—"

"Maybe you should throw your clipboard at me."

"Don't tempt me." She tightened her grip on his hair until he hissed out a breath, then it was her turn to do the same when he nipped at her throat, then worked his way up, along her jaw to her ear. She heard a low, desperate moan, and realized it was her own. She tried to keep the next one in but couldn't.

Nor could she make herself let go of him. Nope, she was going to instantly combust, and he hadn't even gotten into her pants. "I still don't like you," she gasped, sliding her hand beneath his shirt to run over his smooth, sleek back.

"I can work with that." Turning her, he pinned her flat against the storage room door, working his way back to her mouth. Their tongues tangled hotly as his hands yanked her shirt from her jeans and snaked beneath, his palms hot on her belly, heading north. When her knees wobbled, he pushed a muscled thigh between hers, holding her up.

"Wait," she managed to say.

His lips were trailing down the side of her face, along her jaw, dissolving her resolve as fast as she could build it up. "Wait…or stop?"

She had no idea.

He bit gently into her lower lip and tugged lightly, making her moan.

"Stop," she decided.

"Okay but you first."

She realized she was toying with the button of his jeans, the backs of her fingers brushing against the heat of his flat abs. *Crap!* Yanking her hands away, she drew a shaky breath. "Maybe we should go back to the not talking thing. That seems to work best for us."

He ran a finger down the side of her face, tucking a lock of hair behind her ear before pressing his mouth to her temple. "Good plan." His lips shifted down to her jaw. "No talking. We'll just—"

"Oh, no," she choked out with a gasping laugh and slid out from between him and the door. "No talking and no *anything* else either." Tugging the hem of her top down, she gave him one last pointed glare for emphasis and pulled open the door before she could change her mind. She rushed out and ran smack into James and Casey.

"Whoa there, killer," Casey said, steadying her.

"How are you on the ice? We could use you on the team." He looked at the man behind her. "Isn't that right, Coach?"

Rainey felt Mark's hand skim up her spine and settle on the nape of her neck. "Absolutely."

She shivered, then laughed to hide the reaction. "I'll have my people call your people," she quipped, then made her escape to the women's bathroom.

Lena came in while Rainey was still splashing cold water on her face, desperately trying to cool down her overheated, still humming body.

"This is all your fault," Rainey told her again. "Somehow."

"Really." Lena's gaze narrowed on Rainey's neck. "And how about the hickey on your neck. Whose fault is that?"

"Oh my God, I have a *hickey?*"

Lena was grinning wide. "Nah. I was just teasing."

"Dammit!"

"So does the coach kiss as good as he looks?"

"Yes," Rainey said miserably.

Lena laughed at her. "Maybe you found him."

"Found who?"

"You know. Him. Your keeper."

Rainey shook her head. "No way, not Mark. You know he's only got endgame in hockey, not women."

"But maybe…"

"No. No maybe." Rainey left, then stuck her head back in. "No," she said again, and shut the door on Lena's knowing laugh.

HOURS LATER, RAINEY left work and headed home. Halfway there, she made a pit stop at the string of trail-

ers that ran behind the railroad tracks dividing town. Sharee and her mother lived in one of them, towards the back.

No one answered Rainey's knock. She was just about to leave when Mona, Sharee's mother, appeared on the walk, still in her cocktail waitress uniform.

When she saw Rainey, she slowed to a stop and sighed. "You again."

"Hi, Mona."

"What now? Did Sharee get in another fight while I was at work?"

"No," Rainey said. "She walked into a door."

Mona's lips tightened.

"The last time I came out here," Rainey said quietly. "You told me that you and Martin were separated."

"We're working on things." Mona's gaze shifted away. "Look, I'm a single mom with a kid and a crap job, okay? Martin helps—he *should* help. He's an okay guy, he's just stressed, and Sharee's mouthy."

By all accounts, Martin wasn't an okay guy. He was angry and aggressive, and he made Rainey as uncomfortable as hell. "I think he hits her, Mona. If I knew it for sure, I'd report it. And then you might lose her."

Mona paled. "No."

"You tell Martin that, okay? Tell him I'll report him if he doesn't keep his hands off her."

Mona hugged herself and shook her head vehemently, and Rainey sighed. The authorities had been called out here no less than five times. But Sharee wouldn't admit to the abuse, and worse, every time she and Mona were questioned, Martin only got more "stressed."

"There are places you can go," Rainey said softly. "Places you can take Sharee and be safe."

Mona's face tightened. "We're fine."

Rainey just looked at her for a long moment, but in the end there was nothing more she could do. "Will you allow Sharee to stay at my place on the nights you're working?"

Without answering, Mona went inside.

Rainey went home. She made cookies because that's what she did when *she* was stressed—she ate cookies. Then she showered for her date with Kyle. It would be fun, she decided. And she needed fun. She would keep an open mind and stop thinking about Mark. Who knows, maybe Kyle would be The One to finally make her forget Mark altogether.

She heard the knock at precisely six o'clock. She waited for a zing of nerves. It was a first date. There should be nerves. But she felt nothing. She opened her door and went still.

Mark.

Now nerves flooded her. "What are you doing here?"

"We left a few things unfinished," he said.

"We always leave things unfinished!"

A car pulled up the street. *Kyle.* Inexplicably frantic, Rainey shoved at Mark's chest. "You have to go."

He didn't budge. "Hmm."

Hmm? What the hell did that mean? She looked around, considering shoving him into the bushes, but he leaned into her. "Don't even think about it." With his hands on her hips, he pushed her inside her town house and shut the door.

"You can't be here," she muttered. "I have a date."

He let go of her to look out the small window along-

side the front door, eyes focused on Kyle as he walked up the path. "I want to meet this guy."

"What? *No*."

The doorbell rang, and Mark turned his head to look at her, his eyes two pools of dark chocolate. "You still have shitty taste in men?"

"I— None of your business!"

The bell rang again, and in sheer panic, Rainey pushed Mark behind the door and out of sight, pointing at him to stay as she pasted a smile on her face and opened the door.

Kyle was medium height and build, with wind-tousled brown hair that curled over his collar and green eyes that had a light in them that suggested he might be thinking slightly NC-17 thoughts. Rainey stared at him in shock.

He smiled. "Surprised?"

Uh, yeah. He'd grown up and out, and had definitely lost the buck teeth. Plus he had a look of edge to him, a confidence, a blatant sexuality that shocked her. Kyle Foster had grown up to be a bad boy. "It's nice to see you," she said, surprised to find it true.

"Same goes." He looked her over. "You look good enough to eat."

From behind the door came a low growl.

Rainey didn't dare glance over, but she could feel the weight of Mark's stare. "Let me just grab my purse," she said quickly.

"What smells so good?" Kyle asked, trying to see past her and inside her place.

"I made chocolate chip cookies earlier."

"I love chocolate chip cookies," Kyle said.

Was it her imagination, or did Mark growl again?

Oh, God. "Burned them," she said quickly. Liar, liar, pants on fire. She had a glorious tray of cookies on her counter, to-die-for cookies, cookies that were better than an orgasm, but if she let him in, she'd be forced to introduce him to Mark. "Sorry. If you could just give me a sec." She shut the door on his face and winced. Then she glared at Mark.

"Let him in," he said. "You can introduce us." He said this in the tone the Big Bad Wolf had probably used on Little Red Riding Hood.

She pointed at him. "Shh!" She ran into the kitchen, grabbed her purse and strode past the six-foot-plus dark and annoyingly sexy man still standing in her entryway, throwing off enough attitude to light up a third world country.

"Your top's too tight," Mark said.

"No, it's not."

"Then your bra's too thin."

She stared down at herself. He was right—Nipple City. "Well, if you'd stop crowding me."

He smiled, dark and dangerous. He had no plans to stop crowding her. "And your jeans," he said.

"What's wrong with my jeans?"

"You have a stain on the ass."

She twisted around first one way, then the other, but saw nothing. "I can't see it."

"I can. Not exactly date pants, you know?"

"Fine! Don't move." She raced up the stairs and down the hallway to her bedroom, tore off the jeans, ripping through her dresser for another clean pair.

Nada.

Dammit! She yanked open her closet and settled on a short denim skirt, which meant she had to change

shoes, which also meant she had to redo her hair. Running back down the stairs, she came to a skidding halt at the bottom.

The front door was opened but Kyle was nowhere to be seen, and neither was his car. Eyes narrowed, she followed a faint sound into her kitchen, where she found Mark leaning back against her counter, Zen-calm, every muscle relaxed…eating her cookies.

"NICE SKIRT YOU'RE almost wearing," Mark said, and swallowed the last of his cookie. He brushed his fingers off, ignoring the death glare coming at him from the doorway. Rainey had changed out of the sexy jeans and into an even sexier short denim skirt, revealing perfectly toned legs that he wanted to nibble. He wanted to start at her toes and work his way up, up, up past her knees, past her thighs… to the heaven between them.

Something she most definitely wasn't ready to hear. "You're good at cookies," he said. "What else can you cook?"

She crossed her arms, which plumped up her breasts, and he revisited his thought. He wanted to nibble her all over.

Every single inch.

"Where's my date, Mark?"

He popped another cookie. "Funny thing about that."

Her eyes darkened, and she leaned against the doorway, arms still crossed as if maybe she didn't trust herself to come any further into the kitchen. He didn't know if that was because she wanted to kill him, or kiss him again.

He thought it was probably a good bet that it was the former. When he reached for yet another cookie, she let

out a sound of sheer temper and stalked across the room to snatch the plate away from him. "Those are mine."

Mark was aware that he was known for always being in control, for having a long fuse and rarely losing it, for being notoriously tight with his emotions. Rarely did he find himself in a situation where he wasn't perfectly at ease and didn't know exactly what he wanted the outcome to be.

But he was right now. He had no idea what the hell he was doing here.

None.

"Your date had to leave," he said. "Unexpectedly."

"Uh-huh. What did you do to him?"

In his world, people never questioned him. And it was a good place to be, his world. Apparently she hadn't gotten the memo. "Nothing."

Earlier, in the storage closet at the rec center, he'd stalked her, pressed her against the door. She did the same to him now, but this time her grip on his shirt wasn't passion. "Tell me, Mark."

The sound of his name on her tongue did something to him, something it shouldn't. "He waxes."

"What?"

"He waxes his body hair," he said.

She blinked. Paused. "And how did you get close enough to notice that?"

"I wasn't that close, I have excellent vision. He didn't have any hair on his arms."

"He's a swimmer. So he waxes, so what?"

Yeah, genius, so what? "He had a look in his eye. He was up to no good."

She gaped at him. "Tell me, was it like staring in a mirror?"

Well, maybe a little. But Mark had taken one look at the guy and seen a player. He'd asked the asshole what his plans were. Kyle had seemed amused by the question but had answered readily enough—candlelit dinner, dancing, capped off with a canyon drive to stargaze....

Bullshit the guy wanted to stargaze. No guy wanted to stargaze. Kyle wanted to get laid. In fact, Mark would bet his million-dollar bonus that the guy had a string of condoms at the ready. "I didn't like him."

"You didn't like him," Rainey repeated. "And I should care, *why?*"

"I'm an excellent judge of character."

She made a sound of disgust. "The last time you scared one of my dates off, I told you to never interfere in my life again."

He grabbed her as she went to pass by him. "The last time I scared off your date, it was because you were about six inches away from being raped."

She jerked as if he'd hit her, reminding him of one fact—they'd never talked about that night, about what had happened when he'd finally caught up with her.

Never.

And apparently they weren't going to do it now either, because she shoved at him hard and he let her go. She turned to her kitchen window, not moving, not speaking, just staring out at the backyard, her eyes clouded with bad memories.

Feeling lower than pond scum, he sighed. "Rainey—"

"Why are you here, Mark?"

"I..." He had no idea.

She turned to face him. "I agreed to go out with Kyle tonight because I'm looking for something. Someone.

Or at least I think I am. I'm…not lonely, that's not the right word. I love my life. But I want someone in it. It's been a while for me and I'm ready. I want to be in a relationship."

His gut hurt, and he had no idea why.

Her mouth curved, though the smile didn't meet her lips. "And I'm guessing by the panic on your face that a relationship is the last thing you're looking for."

He wasn't showing panic. He never showed panic.

"Fine," she said, rolling her eyes. "I made up the panic. God forbid you show an emotion."

"You think I don't have emotions?"

"I think you're miserly with them." She gave a faint smile. "But I do sense the slightest elevation in your blood pressure."

Now he rolled *his* eyes and she let out a low laugh. "Listen, I can't be like you, Mark, that's all. I'm not tough and cool as ice in any situation. That's not me. I want someone to care about me, someone who *wants* to be with me. Now I'm all dressed up with none of that in sight at the moment, so unless you want to be witness to something as messy as an uncontrolled emotion, you need to go."

"I would," he said quietly. "But—"

"But *what?*"

"I don't want to."

At that, she dropped her head between her shoulders and let out a sound that was either another laugh or something far too close to tears for his own comfort. "Mark, you *know* what broke up our friendship."

"Yes, you kicked me out of your life."

She sighed. "I didn't kick you out of my life. You left to go coach in Ontario, and I…"

"Stopped talking to me."

"It was temporary—I was mad," she said. "You remember why."

He let out a long breath. "Something about me being an interfering asshole."

"First, you rejected me. Then—"

"You were sixteen!"

"Then," she went on stubbornly. "You followed me on a date and beat the guy up."

"It wasn't a date. He picked you up after you ran out of my place. And in the ten minutes it took me to find you, he had you pinned in his backseat and was pulling off your clothes!"

Remembered humiliation flickered in her eyes. "Okay, so I acted stupid and immature, but I was hurting."

He blew out a breath and shoved his fingers in his hair. "It wasn't your fault. What he did to you wasn't your fault."

"What he was doing was consensual."

"You didn't know what you wanted."

"I wanted a friend and you turned into a Neanderthal."

He stared at her incredulously. "Well, what the hell did you want me to do, *let* him take you? You were a virgin!"

She flushed. "I wanted you to stop interfering as if I couldn't handle my own problems. I wanted you to listen to me. I wanted sympathy."

He must have given her a what-the-fuck look because she shook her head.

"I wanted a hug, Mark. I wanted you to hold my

hand and tell me I'd find someone else, someone better. I wanted understanding."

He just continued to stare at her, dumbstruck. Not a single one of those things had ever occurred to him.

The sound that escaped her told him she was just realizing that very fact. Brushing past him, she moved to the front door and held it open. A clear invite for him to get the hell out.

"Rainey—"

"I want to be alone."

Too damn bad. He slammed the door shut, hauled her up against him, closing his arms around her in a hug.

"It doesn't count now," she said stiffly, even as her body relaxed into his and she pressed her face into his shoulder. "Dammit, do you always smell good? That just really pisses me off."

"You know what pisses me off?" he asked. "That all I want to do is this." And then he pushed her up against the door and kissed her.

5

THE SECOND MARK LEANED into her, his hard body coming into contact with her own, Rainey knew she was in trouble. Her nipples immediately tightened into two beads against her soft top. But that was before his leg slid between hers, spreading her wide, his thigh rubbing against her core.

She wanted him.

She'd always wanted him.

Not yours, she told herself even as she clung to him. He's not yours and doesn't want to be. He's unattainable, unavailable... But he was clearly as aroused as she was, and that felt good. She turned him on, and being with him like this was the closest she'd get to what she might really want from him.

He shifted his thigh, rubbed it against her, and she let out a shockingly needy whimper. His lips grazed her earlobe, his breath hot along her skin, and a rush of heat shot through her. "Mark," she choked out as his fingers slid beneath her skirt to palm her bottom. It was all she could do not to wrap her legs around his waist and beg

him to get inside her now, now, now, and she mindlessly thrust her hips against his. "Please," she gasped.

"Anything." He held her against the door, his mouth sliding down her throat and over her collarbone, tugging her shirt aside to make room for himself. "Whatever you want, Rainey. Just tell me, it's yours." His hand slid beneath her top and cupped her breast, his thumb rubbing over her nipple until she quivered. "Do you want me to touch you like this? Do you want my mouth on you? What?"

"Yes." To all of it.

He tugged her shirt and her bra aside and drew her nipple into his mouth, sucking until she cried out. Lifting his head, he blew a soft breath over her wet flesh and she shivered in anticipation.

"What else, Rainey. What else do you want?"

"Everything," she gasped. "I want everything."

"Here? Now?"

"Here. Now. *Right* now."

He yanked her skirt up to her waist and her panties down to her knees. In complete contrast, his hand slid slowly up her inner thigh, taking its sweet time so that she was mindlessly rocking her hips, anticipating the touch long before his finger traced her folds. "Mmm, wet," he murmured, his mouth moving along her shoulder back to her collarbone, which he grazed with his teeth.

"Mark." She fisted her hands in his hair and pulled his mouth to hers, her entire world anchored on his finger. When it slid inside her, she thunked her head back against the door and panted. Then his thumb brushed her in a slow circle.

She cried out against his lips, arching into him,

yanking his hair. She couldn't help it. She was going up in flames. He merely pressed her hard to the door, locking her in place. Continuing the torture, he added another finger. She came hard and fast, the power of it sweeping over her like a tidal wave. And because he kept stroking, the aftershocks didn't fade away, but had her shuddering over and over....

"Christ, Rainey." He sucked her lower lip into his mouth, tangled his tongue with hers. "You are so gorgeous when you come."

All she could think about was him filling her, stretching her, making her come again. Her eyes flickered open and their gazes met. "In me," she demanded. "Now, God, now."

His eyes dilated black, filled with a staggering hunger...for her. She nearly stopped breathing. Instead she moved her hips against his, reveling in the feel of his muscles rippling beneath her touch. He'd pulled a condom from somewhere.

Thank God one of them could think.

After that, it was a blur of frenzied movements. She ripped his shirt off, he unzipped, and together they freed the essentials.

And oh God, the essentials...

It wasn't enough for him. "Everything off," he said, then lent his hands to the cause until she stood naked against the door. His gaze swept over her, hot and approving, as he lifted her up. "Wrap your legs around me— There. God, yeah, like that—" His voice was a low command, caressing her as much as his hands. "Hold on to me." Then his mouth crushed her own as he pushed her back against the door.

She threaded her hands into his hair as he thrust

deep inside of her. He made a rough sound of sheer male pleasure, his fingers digging into her soft flesh as she rocked into him. Again he thrust, slowly at first, teasing until she was begging. It was glorious torment, hot and demanding, just like the man kissing her.

They moved together, her breasts brushing his chest, tightening her nipples. She could feel his muscles bunching and flexing with each thrust, sending shock waves of pleasure straight to her core. When she came again, it was with his name on her lips as she pulsed hard around him, over and over again, taking him with her.

Still holding her, still buried deep inside, Mark sank to his knees. He looked as stunned as she felt and something deep inside her constricted. She pulled free. He grimaced but let her go without a word.

She pulled on her panties and his shirt, then leaned back against the door, knees still weak.

Mark got to his feet and handled the necessities of condom disposal and readjustment of clothing.

She had a hard time looking away from him. His pants were riding low on his hips, and he looked dangerous and primed for another round. *No,* she told herself firmly. *You may not have him again.* Not without a discussion about what this was, and what this wasn't, so that she didn't get hurt. *Her* terms, or no terms.

"I think we need some ground rules, Mark."

NO SHIT, MARK THOUGHT, still dazed.

"Rule number one. This—" She waggled her finger back and forth between them. "Happens only when and if I instigate it. If you do it, I might mistake it for some-

thing deeper and more emotional than it is. It'll mess with my head, Mark."

His gut hurt again. The last thing he ever wanted was to hurt her.

"Look," she said, more softly. "I get that we're stuck working together for the next month. We're grown-ups, we'll handle it. Right?"

He'd never in his life done less than handle anything that came his way. And he'd also never lost his ability to speak either, but he was having trouble now, so he nodded.

"Good," she said, looking relieved that he'd agreed to her terms. *Damn, Rainey, don't give me yourself on a silver platter and ask for nothing in return....*

"You should go now," she said.

She was making things easy, giving him the exit strategy. He should be ecstatic. Instead, he stepped toward her to... Hell, he didn't know. Hold her? Yeah, he wanted to hold her until the world stopped spinning.

But she gave a sharp jerk of her head and backed away.

Right. The rules. She was in charge of physical contact. Pretending that his legs weren't still wobbling, he did as she wanted and walked out.

He'd walked away plenty of times before. It should have been a no-brainer. Hell, he should have been *running,* far and fast, with relief filling his veins. Except it wasn't easy, and he felt no relief at all.

Plus, it was damn cold outside and she was still wearing his shirt.

THE NEXT DAY AT LUNCH, Rainey and Lena sat in the small café across the street from the rec center, each in-

haling a triple scoop ice cream sundae. Officially, it was a meeting about the upcoming charity auction. Unofficially, it was a discussion on their favorite topic. Men.

Specifically Mark.

"I'm surprised you didn't make me share a sundae with you," Lena said around a huge bite. "Usually you only allow yourself a single scoop."

"It's an entire sundae sort of day." Rainey ate one of the two cherries from the top. "It's got cherries on it so it's practically a fruit salad."

Lena grinned. "You know what I don't get? Why you aren't singing the 'Hallelujah Chorus.' I mean, you got lucky last night. Damn lucky by the looks of you."

Yeah, she had. It'd been everything she thought it would be, too.

And more. "I can't believe I slept with him. He chased off my date and I *still* got naked with him."

"Look, you can't blame yourself. The guy's got serious charisma. He's a walking fantasy. And you were past due." Lena paused. "Rick says you two have been past due for fourteen years."

"Rick? You talked to Rick about us?"

"Everyone's talking about you two."

"Why?"

"I don't know, Rainey, maybe because yesterday afternoon after the staff meeting you pulled Mark into the storage closet in the main hallway. And then today you come into work with that glow."

Rainey ate the other cherry and slumped in her seat.

Lena grinned. "This is going to be fun."

"No. Not fun. He's not my type."

"Right. Because he's not a fixer-upper," Lena said.

"You like the fixer-uppers so you can eventually let go of them for not being The One."

"Are you saying that Mark is perfect as is?"

"Mark is *oh-boy-howdy perfect,*" Lena said.

"No, he's not. He's bossy and domineering, and *way* too alpha."

"Mmm-hmm," Lena said dreamily. "I bet he likes to be in charge. Especially in bed, right?"

Rainey felt her cheeks go hot. *They hadn't made it to a bed….* "You're as impossible as he is."

Lena laughed and scooped up a big bite of ice cream, moaning in pleasure. "Some things just need to be appreciated for what they are, even the imperfect things. Like men. Hell, Rain. You accept the kids at the center every single day, just as is. Why not a man?"

Rainey stopped in the act of stuffing her face with a huge spoonful of ice cream and stared at Lena. Most of the time Lena's comments were sarcastic, but once in a while she said something so perfect it was shocking. "How did you get so wise?"

"Practice," Lena said. "And lots of kissing frogs before I found my prince. And you know what else? I think you found yours."

"I'm not going for Mark, Lena." It was a terrible idea. Terribly appealing…

She'd once read an article about him that said his talent in coaching came from the fact that he didn't so much inspire awe as he discouraged comfort.

She knew that to be true. Her comfort level was definitely at risk when he was around.

THAT AFTERNOON AFTER working on the construction site, Mark gathered his team on the bleachers and looked

them over. Twelve teenage girls, with more attitude than his million-dollar players combined.

Casey and James had their team on the far field. Boys. Boys who could really play, by the looks of them. How the hell his in-the-doghouse players had ended up with the easier task was beyond him.

Okay, he knew what had happened.

Rainey had happened.

And he knew no matter what the girls dished out, last night had been worth every minute.

His team wore a variety of outfits from short shorts that were better suited to pole dancing to basketball shorts so big they couldn't possibly stay up while the girls were running bases. Shirts ranged from oversized T-shirts that hung past the shorts to teeny tiny tank tops or snug tees. "First up," he said. "Everyone back to the locker room to change into appropriate gear."

No one moved.

"Ladies, I just gave you a direct order. Not obeying a direct order will get you personally acquainted with push-ups."

"We're already dressed out," one of them said, and when he gave her a long look, she added, "Coach, sir."

"Just Coach," he said, and went to the large duffle bag he'd brought with him. It was the warm-up T-shirts, shorts, and practice jerseys he'd had over-nighted. He had new equipment as well; bats, batting helmets, gloves… He handed the clothing out, then waited for them to run back to the building. Instead, they all stripped and dressed right there. "Jesus," he muttered, slamming his eyes shut. "Some warning!"

"Hey, we're covered," Sharee called out. "We're all in sports bras and spandex."

"From now on," he grated out, "you change inside. Always."

"Prude," someone muttered, probably Sharee.

Prude his ass, but swallowing the irony, he risked a peek and found them all suitably dressed. "Ground rules," he said. Now he sounded as anal as Rainey. "No ripping or cutting the sleeves off, no tying the shirts up high, no bras showing, and all shirts need to be neatly tucked in. And no sagging. There will be no asses on my field."

"We're not allowed to say asses." The timid voice belonged to the same girl who called him sir. "We're not supposed to swear."

Mark slid her a look. "Pepper, right?"

She gulped. "Yes."

"Well, Pepper. No swearing is a good rule. Tuck your shirts in."

More grumbling, but there was a flurry of movement as they obeyed. So far so good. "I want to see how you hit," Mark said. "Later, I'll get someone out here to videotape you so we can analyze your swing. We'll get stats both on you and also on the teams we're going to be playing so we can strategize, not just for your season but for the big fundraising game between us and Santa Barbara."

They were all just staring at him, mouths agape. Pepper raised her hand.

"Yes, Pepper."

"We don't have a video camera. Or stats."

"You have them now," Mark said.

"We're going to play Santa Barbara?" someone asked.

"We're going to *beat* Santa Barbara," he said. "The

boys' teams too." He pulled a clipboard from his duffle bag. "Come on, move your asses—" *Shit.* "Butts. Move your butts in close so you can see."

"You need a swear jar," one of the girls said to him. "By the end of the season, you could probably take us all out to dinner."

There were some giggles at this, and he looked at the amused faces. "How about this," he said. "I'll put a buck into a swear jar every time I swear, and you ladies have to put in a quarter every time you don't give me your all. Deal?"

"Deal," they said.

Mark spent the next twenty minutes outlining what he wanted to see, and then lined them up for drills. He started with them quick-catching the pop flies he sent out. Or theoretically quick-catching, because he didn't have much "quick" on his team. Three of the twelve could catch. Well, four if you counted Pepper, who tended to catch the balls with her shins, which made him doubly glad he'd brought shin guards. He had five or six who could hit, and a bunch more who tended to keep their eyes closed.

And then there was Sharee, who'd already dropped and given him push-ups for being rude and obnoxious to her teammates.

Twice.

He put them out in the field for field practice next. "Wait for your pitch," he told the first girl up. "Take two, then hit to the right."

"Huh?"

"Sharee's pitching, right?" he asked.

"Yeah. So?"

"So she gives it her best from the beginning, but she's only got two good ones in her."

"Hey," Sharee said from the mound. "I can hear you."

"Good. Learn from it." Mark turned back to the batter. "Take the third pitch and hit to the right."

"Why the right?"

He gestured to their first baseman and right fielder, both engaged in a discussion on what their plans were for the night. "They're not even looking at you. If you get any ball at all, you'll get all the way to second."

Which was exactly what happened.

Sharee threw down her glove in disgust.

"There's no temper tantrums in the big leagues," Mark told her. Which was a lie. There were plenty of tantrums in the big leagues, all of them, and you only had to watch ESPN to see them. "Here's a strategy for you, too. Watch the signs from your catcher instead of winging it. She'll be getting a signal from me on which pitch to throw. If you listen," he added as she opened her mouth to object, "you'll be a great pitcher. I can promise you that."

"And if I don't listen?"

"Then I'll bench you and put in Pepper."

Pepper squeaked, and he smiled at her. "You have an arm and you know it. You start practicing more, and you'll be ready to pitch at the game this weekend."

"I'm pitching at the game," Sharee said.

"Maybe. If you listen."

"Hmph."

At the end of practice, Mark gathered the girls in and looked them over. Bedraggled and hot and sweaty. "Decent effort," he said. "I'll see you tomorrow."

They all made their way toward the building. He turned to gather his gear and found Rainey sitting on the bleachers, watching him.

6

MARK HADN'T SEEN HER since the night before when he'd left her looking dewy and sated and pissed off at the both of them.

Today she was wearing a sweat suit, beat-up sneakers, and a ball cap.

The Ducks again.

Shaking his head, he walked over to the bleachers and sat. Stretching out his legs, he leaned back on the bench behind him and stared up at the sky.

"Long day?" she asked dryly.

"Hmm."

He slid her an assessing look. She was laughing at him, which should have ticked him off, but for one thing, he was too tired. And for another, she looked pretty when she was amused, even if it was at his expense.

"Should I drop and give you twenty?" she asked in a smart-ass tone.

Rainey humor. But he'd rather she drop and give him something else entirely. No doubt that, along with ev-

erything else he was thinking about doing to her, wasn't on the agenda for the day.

A tall blond guy wearing a suit poked his head out of the building and waved at Rainey. She smiled and got up, walking over to meet him halfway, where he handed her what looked like a stack of tickets. Rainey gave him a quick hug, which was returned with enthusiasm and an expression that Mark recognized all too well.

The guy wanted a lot more than the hug.

"Keep the top one for yourself," Mark heard him tell her. "That's the seat right next to mine."

A date. She had another damn date. His eye twitched. Probably due to the new brain bleed.

Rainey came back to the bleachers. "Lena's neighbor," she said. "Jacob works at the district office and brought tickets to the ballet tonight at the San Luis Obispo Theater for everyone here who wants to go."

He held out his hand.

She stared at him. "*You* want to go to the ballet."

Okay, true, he'd rather be dragged naked through town, but hell if he'd admit it. "Yes." And if he had to go, so did James and Casey. "I'll take three, unless this is a *private* date."

She slapped three tickets into his palm, and it did not escape his notice that she took them from the bottom of the pile. "It's not a date date," she said defensively. "And he's a nice guy. A non-fixer-upper, you know?"

No. He had no idea.

"And I told you," she said. "I'm looking for someone. Someone who wants me as is."

Hell, she killed him, he thought as she averted her face and let out a long, almost defeated breath. *Not*

friends, he reminded himself, even as something in his chest rolled over. "You're perfect as is, Rainey."

"Says the man who dates big-boobed blonde women from stupid reality shows."

He laughed. "That was a photo op, that's all."

"Every time?"

"Well, maybe not every time." He reached into her sweatshirt pocket and pulled out her phone, absolutely taking note that doing so caused her to suck in a breath when his fingers brushed her skin.

"What are you doing?" she asked.

"Programming myself in as your number one speed dial. In case you need another date rescue."

"I didn't need last night's rescue."

"You going to try to tell me last night didn't work out for you?"

Their gazes met, and she inhaled deeply. "Why are you doing this?"

No clue.

She looked at him for a long moment. "Are you jealous?"

Fuck, no.

Okay, yes. Yes, he was. "How can I be jealous of someone that's not a 'date date' to a *ballet?*"

She crossed her arms. "Okay, I'm sure I'm going to regret asking, but what's *your* idea of a good date?"

"Depends on the woman. With you it'd be a repeat of last night."

Color bloomed on her cheeks. "We're not going to discuss last night. Make that rule number two."

"Ah, yes. The rules of Rainey Saunders." He shook his head. "And people think *I'm* a control freak."

"Because you are."

"Hello, Mrs. Pot."

She made a sound of exasperation, and still seated, she leaned forward, stretching her fingers to her toes. Her sweatshirt rose up a little in the back, revealing a strip of smooth, creamy skin and a hint of twin dimples just above her ass, and the vague outline of a thong.

He didn't know which he wanted more, to trace that outline with his tongue or dip into the dimples. Before he could decide, she straightened, rolled her neck, and winced. "I have a kink."

"Yeah? Tell me all about it, slowly and in great detail."

She snorted. "Pervert."

Smiling, he slid over, behind her now, and put his hands on her shoulders. "You've got a rock quarry in here." He dug his fingers in, rubbing at her knots.

"I'm fine." But her head dropped forward, giving him better access. When he found a huge tension knot with his thumbs and began to work it out, she let out a soft moan that went straight through him. "Rainey."

"What?"

He pressed his face into her hair. *Go out with me instead of what's-his-name.* Before he could bare his pathetic soul, Rick came outside and saved him.

"She's home," Rick called out to Rainey. "I'm sending you over there with our famous backup." He waved Casey and James over. The guys had come from the gym, where they'd had their teams at the weights.

"Field trip," Rick said. "Rainey's in charge." He sent a grin in Mark's direction. "Need me to repeat?"

Mark flipped him off, and Rick's grin widened.

"Where are we going?" Casey asked.

"You'll see," Rick said.

Mark hated that answer.

"Shotgun." James leapt into the front seat of Rainey's car.

Casey got into the back.

Mark walked up to the passenger front door and gave James one long look.

James sighed, got out and slid into the back.

Rainey looked over her sunglasses at Mark. "Seriously?"

"No," he said, putting on his seat belt. "If I was serious, I'd have made you let me drive."

RAINEY'S CAR WAS FULL of more good-looking, great-smelling men than she had dollars in her wallet. Lena would be having an orgasm at just the thought. James and Casey were talking, keeping up a running dialogue about their day. But as she headed into the heart of the burned-out neighborhood, their chatter faded away.

From the shotgun position, Mark didn't say a word. He seemed to be in some sort of zone, with his game face on to boot. She wished she had a zone.

Or a game face.

Turning his head from where he'd been looking out the window, he met her gaze.

God, he had a set of eyes. Richly dark and deep, she got caught staring, and forced herself to look away before she drowned in him.

He slid on his cool sunglasses. She did the same. Good. With two layers between them now, she felt marginally better. "I don't know if any of you have seen the extent of the destruction," she said. "But it covers nearly 100,000 acres."

"I've been through it," Mark said. "My dad's new house isn't far from here."

Rainey glanced over at him again. "Your dad lost his house?"

"Yes. It's just been rebuilt."

"That was fast."

Mark nodded, and she understood that he'd expedited the building process. He'd pulled strings, spent his own money, done whatever he'd had to do to get his dad back into a place, and the knowledge had something quivering low in her belly.

And other parts, too, the parts that he'd had screaming for him last night. *Don't go there,* she told herself. *There's no need to go there.* Not with a man who was only here for one month at the most, a known player, and…and possessing the absolute power to embed himself deep inside her, and not just physically. He didn't want her hurt by a guy? Well the joke was on him because there was no one who could hurt her more.

When they got to the heart of the worst of the fire devastation, it was painful to see the blackened dead growth and destroyed homes where once the hills had been so green and alive.

"Damn," James said. "Damn."

"Besides doing the sports," Rainey said quietly, "I run the rec center's charity projects. We've been raising money all year to fund one of the rebuilds, the one you guys have been working on. There was a lotto drawing from the victims, and one lucky family won the place free and clear. We're going to go notify the winner."

"Mark has contacts you wouldn't believe," James said. "He can snap his fingers and make people drop money out their ass. You should have seen how much

money he raised for the Mammoths' charities over our last break. Maybe he could get another house funded for you."

Rainey glanced at Mark, surprised to find him looking a little bit uncomfortable, though he met her gaze and held it. "You good at raising money?" she asked. He was good at raising holy hell, or at least he had been. Probably Mark was good at raising whatever he wanted.

Casey grinned. "Yeah, he's good. He rented out our favorite club and he had a mud wrestling pit set up right in the center of the place, then invited a bunch of supermodels."

Rainey could imagine all the wild debauchery that must have gone on in that mud pit, each player getting a model for the night.

Or two...

Just thinking about it made her eye twitch, and she carefully put a finger to the lid to hold it still. "Interesting."

"Yeah, he raked in some big bucks that night," Casey said. "Our charities were real happy."

"Does all your fundraising involve mud pits and centerfolds?"

"Models," James corrected. "Though centerfolds would have been great too. Hey, Coach, you've got a bunch of centerfolds on auto-dial, right? Maybe—"

He trailed off when Casey drew an imaginary line across his throat for the universal "shut it." "Ix-nay on the enterfolds-say." Casey jerked his head in Mark's direction. "He's trying to impress."

"No worries," Rainey said dryly. "I've already got my impression. It's burned in my brain." She pulled into a trailer park and drove down a narrow street to

the end, where she parked in front of a very old, run-down trailer.

"Wow, that's the smallest trailer I've ever seen," Casey said. "Someone lives here?"

"Six someones," Rainey said. "We're here to tell them the good news, that they'll have a place by late summer." She smiled. "They're big hockey fans. Plus," she said, turning to Mark, "you've been coaching their daughter, Pepper."

The guys unfolded themselves out of her car and she looked them over, realizing that they were dripping with their usual air of privilege. "Do any of you ever look like anything less than a couple of million bucks?" she asked Mark.

James snickered, then choked on it when Mark glared at him. "I'm wearing sweats," he said calmly. "Same as you."

"Yes, but mine aren't flashy," she said. "Yours are from your corporate sponsor."

"Rainey, we're both wearing Nike."

"Yes, but yours probably cost more than I made last month."

James grinned. "Actually, you can't even buy what he's wearing. They made it just for him."

Mark let out a breath. "Should I strip?"

"No!" But as they walked through the muddy yard the size of a postage stamp to a tiny metal trailer that had seen better days in the last century, she slid him a look. "What if I'd said yes?" she whispered. "What would you have done?"

"You *didn't* say yes."

"But—"

Mark stopped and stepped into her personal space

bubble, bumping up against her as he put his mouth to her ear. "The next time we're alone," he said softly, "if you still want me to strip, all you have to do is...instigate. Or, as you so hotly did last night, demand. Careful, you're going to step on those geraniums."

She stared down at the flowers in the small pot near her feet, the only thing growing in the yard. They were beautiful, and at any other time it might have amused her that Mark Diego had known the name of the flower when she hadn't, but she was stuck on the stripping thing. She'd ask him to strip never.

Or later...

And great, now her nipples were hard. She slid him a gaze and found him watching her.

Eyes hot. Ignoring him, she moved to the door. "This trailer's just a loaner. They lost everything and have been borrowing this place from friends."

Karen Scott opened the door. She was in her midthirties but appeared older thanks to the pinched, worried look on her face, one that no doubt came from losing everything and having no control over an uncertain future.

"Karen," Rainey said gently. "I have a surprise for you—"

Karen took one look at Casey and James, and slapped a hand over her mouth. "Oh my God! *Oh my God!* You're—" She pointed at James. "And you! You're—"

James offered his hand. "James Vasquez."

"I know!" She bypassed his hand and threw herself at him, giving him a bear hug made all the more amusing because she was about a quarter of James's size.

Casey was treated to the next hug. "This is unbeliev-

able! We'd heard you were in town and Pepper's told us about you, Mr. Diego, but I never in a million years thought you'd be visiting us. The kids and John are all still at work—they're not going to believe this!" She moved back, revealing the interior of the trailer, which was maybe 125 square feet total, a hovel that had been put together in the seventies, and not well. Formica and steel and rusted parts, scrubbed to a desperate cleanliness.

Karen insisted they sit and let her serve them iced tea. Mark, James and Casey sat on the small built-in, fold-out couch, their big, muscled bodies squished into each other. Rainey watched James and Casey look around with horror as they realized that *six* people lived here. Mark didn't look surprised or horrified, but there was an empathy and a new gentleness she'd never seen from him before as he watched Karen bustle around the tiny three-by-three kitchenette. She was in perpetual motion, excited about the lovely surprise visit, and finally Rainey made her sit.

"Karen," she said. "The guys aren't the surprise. At least not the main one. You remember the housing project. Your name was drawn in the lottery for a new home."

Karen went utterly still. "What?"

"You and your family should be able to move in by the end of summer."

Karen gaped at her for a solid ten seconds, before letting out an ear-splitting whoop and throwing herself at Rainey.

They both hit the floor, laughing like loons.

Later, when Karen's family came home, there were more hugs and even tears. The guys spent some time

autographing everything the kids had and then Casey stripped off his hat and sweatshirt and gave them to an ecstatic Pepper, which prompted James to do the same for her brother.

The kids' sheer joy choked Rainey up. They'd had everything taken from them, everything, and yet they were so resilient. She turned away to give herself a minute, then found her gaze caught and held by Mark's. She had no idea how it was that he managed to catch her at her weakest every single time, but he did.

He didn't smirk, didn't even smile. Instead his eyes were steady and warm and somehow...somehow they made her feel the same.

MARK WAITED UNTIL CASEY and James had gotten into the back of Rainey's car before he took her hand and turned her to face him. "You're amazing," he said softly.

"I didn't do this."

"You do plenty. For everyone." He paused. "What do you do for yourself?"

"Tonight I'm going to the ballet."

Shit. He'd nearly forgotten about her date that wasn't a *date* date.

After refusing to let him drive, Rainey dropped him and the guys off at the rec center and promptly vanished. Mark took James and Casey back to the motel, and for the first time since they'd arrived, neither had a word of complaint about where they were staying. Compared with Pepper and her family's trailer, they had a palace, and James and Casey seemed very aware of it. The three of them ordered Thai takeout, and afterwards, Casey and James wanted to go out.

"Is there a club around here?" James asked. "We need some fun, man."

"I've got just the thing," Mark said, and drove them to the town's community theater.

James eyed the marquee and groaned. "No. No way. The last time a chick dragged me to the ballet, I fell asleep and she wouldn't put out after because she said I was snoring louder than the music. I'm not going in there and you can't make me."

"Consider it cultural education," Mark said, and gave him a shove towards the entry.

"This is about *him* getting laid," James whispered to Casey. "And how is *that* fair?"

"Dude, life's never fair."

AT THE BALLET, RAINEY sat with Jacob on one side, Lena on the other, surrounded by coworkers and friends. As the lights went down and the music began and the dancers took the stage, she could feel the tension within her slowly loosening its grip.

Mark wasn't going to show. Good, she thought. A huge relief hit her.

And the oddest, tiniest, most ridiculous bit of disappointment…

The lights dimmed even further, and Jacob slid his arm over the back of her chair, like he was stretching. But then his fingers settled on her shoulder. She waited for a zing, a thrill. But nothing happened. *Relax,* she ordered herself. He was cute. Nice. *Normal.*

His face nuzzled in her hair as he pulled her a little closer, but though she wished with all her might, she felt no zing, and definitely no thrill. When Mark so much as looked at her, her nipples hardened.

"You smell fantastic," Jacob said, and his hand nearly brushed the outside of her breast.

Her nipples didn't care.

Straightening, she pulled away with regret. "I'm sorry, can you excuse me a minute? I need to…" She waved vaguely to the exit and rose, stepping over Lena. On the other side of Lena was Rick, and on the other side of Rick sat…

Mark.

Oh, God. When had he showed up? She managed to get past the man without making eye contact, then found her way to the lobby to gulp in some air. A smattering of people were walking around looking glazed. She wondered if they were having a panic attack as well. Bypassing the bathrooms, she beelined straight for the bar. "Wine," she told the bartender, and slapped her credit card down. "Whatever you have." It didn't matter. She rarely drank wine because it tended to relax her right into a coma but she could use a coma about now. What was wrong with her that she'd been in the presence of two perfectly good guys in two days, and neither had produced a zing?

And just knowing that Mark was in the building had her so full of zing, her hair was practically smoking. The wine came and she gulped it down. "Another, please."

MARK CAME UP BEHIND Rainey. He looked at the two empty wine glasses in front of her and read a new relaxation in her body language—which was quite different from the body language she'd sported when she'd run out here—and smiled. "Better?" he asked.

Her shoulders stiffened, but she didn't look at him. "Go away."

"Can't."

"Why not?" She waved at the bartender, but he didn't see her, so she sighed. She had her hair up tonight, but a few golden-brown tendrils had escaped, brushing the nape of her neck.

She was heart-stoppingly beautiful to him, and just looking at her made him ache. He ran his finger down that nape and was rewarded by her full body shiver. Encouraged, he put his mouth to the spot just beneath her ear, smiling when she shivered again and sucked in a breath. "How's that not-a-date date with your non-fixer-upper going?" he asked.

"I think it's me." Looking morose, she propped her head on her hand. "I'm the fixer-upper."

Hating that she felt that way about herself, Mark swiveled her bar stool to face him. Her mascara was slightly smudged around her eyes, making them seem even more blue. She'd nibbled off her pretty gloss. She was wearing a little black dress, one strap slipping off her shoulder. Running a finger up her arm, he slid the strap back into place and left his hand on her. "I think you're perfect," he said softly. Beautiful, and achingly vulnerable, and…perfect.

She went still, then sighed and dropped her head to his chest, hard. "Now who's the liar?" she whispered.

With a low laugh, he tipped her head up and stared into her glossy eyes. She was half baked. "I mean it," he told her. "You don't need to change a goddamn thing."

Her gaze dropped from his eyes to his mouth, and her tongue darted out to lick her dry lips. The motion went straight through him like fire, heading south. She

stood up, her hands on his chest now, but he didn't flatter himself. She needed him for balance. Her high heels, black with a little bow around the ankles that he found sexy as hell, brought her mouth a lot closer to his. Her fingers dug in a little, fisting on the jacket of his suit.

He placed a hand on the small of her back, holding her to him, right there where he liked her best, when she murmured his name and sighed. "I'm going to instigate now."

His heart kicked. "Instigate away."

Just as their lips touched, a low, disbelieving male voice spoke behind them. *"Rainey?"*

They turned in unison to face Jacob, who was holding Rainey's shawl in his hands. Mouth grim, eyes hooded, he handed her the shawl, gave Mark an eat-shit-and-die look, and walked out of the theater.

7

THE BARTENDER BROUGHT Rainey a third glass of wine. She looked at it longingly but pushed it away. "All I want to know," she said to Mark, "is why. Why are you so hell-bent on sabotaging my dating life?"

Mark couldn't explain it to her. Hell, he couldn't explain it to himself. But apparently it was a rhetorical question because she began a conversation with her wineglass, something about men, stupidity, and the need for a vacation in the South Pacific. While she rambled on, Mark texted James.

Lobby. Now.

Mark then stole Rainey's keys from her purse, and when he saw James appear, he shifted out of earshot of Rainey. "When the ballet's over, take Rainey's car back to the motel."

"Do we have to wait until it's over?"

Mark handed him Rainey's keys. "Yes. I'll retrieve her car for her later."

James looked past Mark to see Rainey sitting at the bar. "What's the matter? Is she sick?"

"Indisposed."

James knew better than to try to get information from Mark when Mark didn't want to give it, but it didn't stop a sly smile from touching his lips. "I take it you're not going to be indisposed too."

Mark just looked at James, who sighed and left.

Mark turned back to Rainey, still seated at the bar, still talking to herself.

Nope, not to herself.

There was a guy seated beside her now, smiling a little too hard. "Hey, gorgeous," he said, leaning in so that his shoulder touched Rainey's bare one, making Mark grind his teeth. "How about I buy you another drink?" the slimeball asked.

"No, thank you," Rainey said. "I'm with someone."

"I don't see him."

"Right here." Mark stepped in between them, sliding an arm along Rainey's shoulders. "Let's go."

She stared up at him. "Not with you, you... you date wrecker."

The situation didn't get any better when he felt a tap on his shoulder. He turned and came face to face with Slimeball, who said, "I think the lady is making herself pretty clear."

"This doesn't involve you," Mark told him.

"She was just about to agree to come home with me."

"No she wasn't," Rainey said, shaking her head. At the movement, she put her fingers on her temples, as if she'd made herself dizzy. "Whoa."

Slimeball opened his mouth, but Mark gave a single shake of his head.

The guy was a couple of inches shorter than Mark and at least twenty pounds heavier. He was bulky muscle, the kind that would be slow in a fight, but Mark was pretty sure it wouldn't come to that. He waited, loose-limbed and ready...and sure enough, after a moment, the guy backed away.

"I'm taking you home, Rainey," Mark said. "Now."

"I've never been spoils of war before."

Shaking his head, Mark slipped an arm around her waist and guided her outside. The night was a cool one, and as they stepped into it, Rainey shivered in spite of her shawl. Shrugging out of his jacket, Mark wrapped it around her shoulders. "Pretty dress," he said.

"Don't."

"Don't tell you how beautiful you look?"

"I'm trying to stay mad at you." She wobbled, and he pulled her in tighter, breathing in her soft scent, which was some intoxicating combination of coconut and Rainey herself.

But she backed away. "Don't use those hands on me," she said, pointing at him. "Because they're magic hands." She pressed her own palms to her chest as if it ached. "They make me melt, and I refuse to melt over you, Mark Diego."

"Because...?"

"Because..." She pointed at him again. "Because you are very very very verrrrrrrryyyyyy bad for me."

He didn't have much to say to that. It happened to be a true statement. Even if he wanted to give her what she was looking for, how could he? The hockey season took up most of his year, during which time he traveled nonstop and was entrenched in the day-to-day running of an NHL team. If he wasn't at a game, he was think-

ing about the next one, or the last one, or he was dealing with his players, or planning game strategies, or
meeting with the owners or the other coaches... It was
endless. Endless and—

And it was bullshit.

The truth was he could make the time. If he wanted.

If a woman wanted...

Granted, a woman would have to want him pretty
damn bad to put up with the admittedly crazy schedule,
but others managed it. People all around him managed
it.

And Jesus, was he really thinking this? Maybe *he'd*
had the wine instead of Rainey. But ever since he'd
left Santa Rey all those years ago, he'd felt like he was
missing a part of himself.

Someone had once asked him if the NHL had disillusioned him at all, and he'd said no. He'd meant it. He
hadn't been disillusioned by fame and fortune in the
slightest. But he did have to admit, having a place to
step back from that world, a place where he was just a
regular guy, was nice. Real nice.

And wouldn't his dad love hearing that.

"You should have left me alone tonight," Rainey
said, standing there in the parking lot.

Looking down in her flushed face, he slowly nodded.
"I should have."

From the depths of her purse, her cell phone vibrated. It took her a minute to find it and then she
squinted at the readout. "Crap. It's my mom. Shh, don't
tell her I'm drunk."

He laughed softly as she stood there in the parking
lot and opened the phone.

"Hey, Mom, sorry I missed your call earlier, I was on

a date date. Or a not-so-date-date." She sighed. "Never mind." She paused. "No, I have no idea what I was thinking going out with a guy who has tickets to the ballet. You're right. And no, I'm not alone. I'm with Mark Diego— No, he's not still cute. He's…" Rainey looked Mark over from head to toe and back again, and her eyes darkened. "Never mind that either! What? No, I'm not going to bring him to dinner this week! Why? Because…because he's busy. Very busy."

Mark leaned in close. "Hi, Mrs. Saunders."

Rainey covered the phone with her hand and glared up at him. *"What are you doing?"*

He had no idea. "Does she still make that amazing lasagna—"

"Yes, not that you're going to taste it. Now *shh!* No, not you, Mom." She put her hand over Mark's face, pushing him away. "Uh oh, Mom, bad connection." She faked the sound of static. "Love you. Bye!"

Mark remembered Rainey's parents fondly. Her father was a trucker and traveled a lot. Her mother taught English at the high school. She was sweet and fun, and there was no doubt where Rainey had gotten her spirit from. "Your mom likes me."

"Yeah, but she likes everyone." She walked through the parking lot, then stopped short so unexpectedly he nearly plowed into the back of her. "I can't remember where I parked." Her phone rang again. "Oh for god's sake, Mom," she muttered, then frowned at the read-out. "Okay, not my mom. Hello?" Her body suddenly tensed, and she peered into the dark night. "Who is this?"

Mark shifted in closer, a hand at the small of her back as he eyed the lot around them.

"No," she said. "I didn't say that. And I certainly didn't threaten you then, but I am now. Keep your hands off Sharee, Martin, and don't ever call me again." She shoved the phone back into her purse.

"Who was that?"

"Sharee's father. Says I'm interfering where my interfering ass doesn't belong. I'm to shut up and be quiet—which I believe is a double negative." She looked around them and shivered. "And I still can't remember where I parked, dammit."

"Over here." He led her to his truck and got her into the passenger seat, leaning down to buckle her seat belt before locking her in. "Did he threaten you?" he asked when he was behind the wheel.

"No, I threatened him. And I'm really not supposed to do that."

"Your secret's safe with me," Mark said. "Tell me exactly what he said to you."

She sighed and sank into his leather seats, looking so fucking adorable, he felt his throat tighten. "It should piss me off when you get all possessive and protective," she said. "But it's oddly and disturbingly cute."

He stared at her. *"Cute?"*

"Yeah." She was quiet as he pulled out of the lot, and he wondered if she'd fallen asleep.

"Did you know I hadn't had sex in a year?" she asked, then sighed. "I really missed the orgasms."

Since he was dizzy with the subject change it took him a moment to formulate a response. "Orgasms are good."

"Better than lasagna."

"Damn A straight." He had them halfway home before she spoke again.

"Mark?"

"Yeah?"

She turned her head to look at him, her face hidden by the night. "My car isn't a truck."

"No?"

"And my car doesn't go this fast, and certainly not this smooth."

"Huh," he said.

"Wait." She sat straight up, restrained by the seat belt. "Are you kidnapping me?"

He slid her a look. "And if I was?"

"I don't know. I'm not tied up or anything."

"Did you want to be?"

"No, of course not." But her eyes glazed over and not from fear, making him both hard and amused at the same time.

RAINEY WAS STILL NICE and buzzed but she knew that she was mad at Mark. Somehow that made him all the more dark and sexy. She eyed his tie. He was so sexy in that tie. "I've been thinking…."

"Always dangerous."

"Maybe the other night wasn't as good as I remembered it."

"It was."

"I don't know…." She shrugged, and the jacket he'd wrapped around her slipped off her shoulders. "I might need a review."

He slid her a look that nearly had her going up in flames. He turned back to the road and took a deep breath. And then another when she leaned across the console and loosened his tie, slowly pulling it from around his neck, during which time her other hand

braced on his thigh, high enough to maybe accidentally even brush against his zipper.

"Christ, Rainey." His voice was strained in a new way, an extremely arousing way, egging her on. The next thing she knew, the truck swerved. She gripped the dash, laughing breathlessly as he whipped them to the side of the road and let her do as she wanted, which was crawl into his lap. His eyes dilated to solid black, his hands cupping her behind as she kissed him.

And kissed him...

She kissed him until she knew with certainty—it had been as good as she remembered.

Better.

RAINEY WOKE UP WITH A start and stared into two dark melted pools of... "Mmm," she said. "Chocolate."

"Wake up, Sleeping Beauty." Warm fingers ran over her forehead, brushing the hair from her face. "You're home."

She sat straight up in the passenger seat of his truck and stared around her. They were parked at her place. "I fell asleep?"

"Little bit." He was crouched at her side between her and the opened door.

She looked into his face and sighed. After a very sexy make out session, he'd gently put her back on her side of the truck and that was all she remembered before falling asleep. She knew that much of Mark's job involved taking care of people: his players, his management team, the press...everything. It all fell under his jurisdiction. And here he was, taking care of her.

That burned. She took care of herself. And to that

end, she unhooked her seat belt and turned to him. "Excuse me."

He obliged her by rising to his full height and offering her a hand. Which she only took so as not to be rude. And because she was just a little bit wobbly. And maybe because God, he looked so good. He was wearing a suit— Wait. Nope. *She* was wearing his jacket… and his tie. He was in just black slacks and a dark gray shirt shoved up to his elbows, revealing forearms that she knew from firsthand experience were warm and corded with strength.

The corners of his mouth tipped into an almost smile, a light of wicked naughtiness playing in his eyes. Suddenly suspicious, she ran her hands down her body, checking. Yep, she was still in her little black dress, bra and panties in place, though the latter seemed to have a telltale dampness…

His soft laugh brought her gaze back up to his.

"Relax." His voice was low and husky, the corners of his mouth twitching up into a smile. He set a hand at the base of her back and used his other to glide a fingertip slowly from her temple to her chin, the touch setting off a trail of sparks. "If we'd gotten naked again, you'd have woken up for it."

Her nipples tightened. "That's…cocky."

"That's fact," he assured her, and kissed her, slow and sensual.

"What was that?" she whispered when he pulled back.

"If you don't know, I'm doing something wrong."

Actually, he couldn't do it *less* wrong.

Mark propelled her up the path to her town house.

At the door, she stopped to fumble through her purse for her keys. "Where are they?"

"I gave them to James."

"You stole my keys? When?"

"When you were flirting with Dumbass at the bar."

"I wasn't flirting!"

He ran a hand along the top of the doorway, feeling the ledge.

She allowed herself to admire the flex of his shoulders and back muscles beneath his shirt. Not finding a key, Mark squatted low to peek beneath the mat while she peeked too—at his terrific ass.

"Where's your spare key?" he asked.

"How do you know I have one?"

"All women do."

She tore her gaze off his butt. "Excuse me. *All* women?"

He turned and eyed the potted plant besides the door before lifting the heavy ten gallon container with ease, smiling at the spare key lying there.

Dammit.

He calmly opened the door and nudged her in, turning on lights and looking curiously around. The town house was small, and given that she had a great job with crappy pay, it was also sparsely furnished. Most everything was reclaimed from various places, but she'd gathered them all herself, and it was home. "Thanks for the ride," she said.

He turned to her and slowly backed her to the door, resting his forearms along either side of her head. "That's not how you promised to thank me."

"Um—"

Shifting closer, he ran his hands down her body. "Don't tell me you've forgotten."

"Well…" A hint. She needed a hint.

"You talk in your sleep." He remained so close she was breathing his air, and he hers. "It was very enlightening," he said.

Oh, God. What had she said? Given the naughty dreams she'd had about him all week, it could have been anything.

He laughed softly, but then he moved away from her and into her kitchen. She managed to walk on trembly limbs to her couch and sink into it, listening to him help himself to her cupboards.

A minute later he came out with a full glass of water and a few aspirin, both of which he handed to her. "Drink the whole glass, just in case you have a morning hangover coming your way. 'Night, Rainey."

She stared in shock at his very fine ass as it walked to the front door. "You're…leaving?"

She saw his broad shoulders rise as he took a deep breath, and when he turned to face her, she realized he wasn't nearly as calm and relaxed as she'd thought. "Yes," he said.

"But—"

"Rainey, if I come an inch closer, I'm going to pick you up and rip that sexy dress off you, and then the bra and panties you were worried about earlier, leaving you in nothing but my tie and those heels, which, by the way, have been driving me crazy all night."

She felt her heart kick into gear.

"And then," he said. "I'm going to take you to your bedroom and do what you so sweetly begged me to do in your sleep."

"Wh-what did I ask you to do?" she whispered.

"Tie you up to your headboard and ravish you."

Oh, God. "I—I asked you to do that?"

"You asked me to do it until you screamed my name."

"I've never…" She broke off and squirmed a little on the couch. Her skin felt too tight, and her heart was thudding against her ribs. "Some of that would be… new." Some, as in all.

He looked at her for a long beat, then moved back to her. Slowly he crouched at her side and tugged playfully on the tie. "Go to bed, Rainey. Alone. Drink the water and I'll see you tomorrow."

Right. She nodded and closed her eyes.

She heard him move away, but the door didn't open. So she opened her eyes and found him standing in front of it, his hand on the doorknob, head bowed against the wood.

"What are you doing?" she asked.

"Trying to make myself leave." He lifted his head. "Because tomorrow you're going to remember that you don't like me, and I'm going to want to kick my own ass for not sticking around while you do."

In her tired state, that somehow made sense. Sad, sad sense. "You're right. Tomorrow I'll probably go back to being an uptight, bitchy control freak."

He smiled. "You're not bitchy."

"Just an uptight control freak?"

"Well, maybe a little."

She laughed. *Laughed.* And suddenly, she didn't want him to leave. She really really didn't. What she *did* want was him. Again. She wasn't sure exactly why she was still so attracted to him, but she had a nice buzz

going and decided it was okay not to think about it right now. So she stood up.

"What are you doing?"

"Instigating again." She climbed up on the coffee table. She wasn't sure why she did it exactly, except maybe because he was tall and sure and confident, and she needed to be those things too. Plus it just seemed like a striptease should be done from a tabletop. Reaching behind her, she unzipped her dress.

"Rainey."

His voice was hoarse, and very very serious, and ooh, she liked it.

She liked it a lot.

"You need to stop," he said, sounding very alpha.

She liked that too. She wondered if he'd boss her around when they got into bed.

She kind of hoped so.

She let the little straps slip off her shoulders, holding the material to her breasts. She thought she was being sexy as hell, so his telling her to stop confused her. "Why?"

"I'm not having drunk sex with you."

"I'm not drunk." She let the dress slowly slip from her breasts, revealing her pretty black lace push-up bra.

Mark appeared to stop breathing. "Rainey—"

"Whoops." She let go of her dress. "Look at that...."
She'd planned the dress sliding gracefully down her body to pool at her feet, but that's not what happened. It caught on her hips. She tried a little shimmy but her heels were much higher than her usual sneakers. Which meant that her ankle gave and she tumbled gracelessly to the floor.

"Jesus."

She heard Mark drop to his knees at her side, felt his hands run over her body. She could also feel that her dress had bunched at both the top and the bottom, ending up around her waist like a wadded belt. Probably she wasn't looking as sexy as she'd hoped.

"Rainey."

There was both a warning and a sexy growl to his voice, so she lay there, eyes closed, playing possum with those big, warm hands on her.

You just executed the most pathetic striptease ever, you idiot.

"Rainey."

She scrunched her eyes tighter, wondering what the chances were that he'd believe she'd died and would just go away.

"Dead women don't have hard nipples," he said, sounding amused. "Or wet panties."

With a gasp at his crudeness—and her body's traitorous reaction—she sat straight up and cracked her head on his chin.

He fell to his ass at her side and laughed, and when he straightened up, she shoved him. Staggering to her feet, she took stock. Now her dress was around her ankles. Perfect. Nice work on bringing the sexy. Turning away from him, she weeble-wobbled across the living room, dragging the dress behind her, limping on her left ankle.

From behind her, Mark made a sound that told her either he liked the view or he'd swallowed his tongue. She tried not to picture what she looked like as she went to her bedroom and slammed the door on his choked laugh.

Bastard.

Her ankle was really burning now. She probably needed ice, but since that meant walking back out there, she'd do without. Somehow—she wasn't sure how exactly—this was all Mark's fault. In fact, she was positive of it.

Crawling onto her bed, she proceeded to cover her head with her pillow, where she planned to stay forever and pretend the entire evening had been a bad dream.

8

RAINEY CAME AWAKE SLOWLY and lay very still, trying to figure out why she felt like she wasn't alone. What had she done last night? The ballet. Jacob. The wine. Mark… The entire evening came crashing back to her, and eyes still closed, she groaned miserably. "Oh, no."

"Oh, yes," said an amused male voice. Mark, of course.

Her eyes flew open. It was morning, which she knew because the sun was slanting in the windows across her face, making her eyeballs hurt. Mark was lying on top of her covers, head propped up on his hand, casual as he pleased. He wore only his slacks, unbuttoned, and was sprawled out for her viewing pleasure, all lean, hard planes and—

No. *Stop looking at him.* "What are you doing here?"

He leaned over her, and utterly without thinking, she ran her hands up his back with a little purr of sheer pleasure.

Mark went still, staring down at her in rare surprise while his arm kept moving, grabbing a mug of steam-

ing coffee from her nightstand. "I just wanted to make sure you were alive before I left," he said.

She forced her hands off him and tried to pretend she hadn't opened her legs to let him slip between them. She took the proffered coffee and drank away her embarrassment. "Thanks," she finally murmured, setting the mug down. Then casually lifted the covers to peek beneath.

She was still in her black lacy bra and panties. And his tie…

No heels.

Her left ankle was propped on a pillow with an ice pack. Ah, yes. Her oh-so-sexy striptease.

Mark had taken care of her. While she processed this, he rolled off the bed. She stared at his bare chest and felt the urge to lick him from his Adam's Apple to those perfect abs. And beyond too, down that faint silky happy trail to his—

"I'm pretty sure it's just a sprain, but you need to wrap it." He nodded to a still plastic-wrapped Ace bandage next to the coffee on the nightstand. "Figured you'd want to shower first."

Mouth dry, she nodded and very carefully sat up. He watched her as he reached for his shirt hanging off the back of her chair and shrugged into it. He tucked his shirt in, adjusting himself in the process before fastening his pants.

She swallowed hard at the intimate moment. "Thanks," she said. "For bringing me home."

He had a faint smile on his face as he studied her expression. "Anytime."

"I'm sorry if I was…a handful."

A small smile touched his lips. "Like I said. Anytime."

With a deep breath, she got out of the bed. She figured he'd turn away and give her a moment of privacy, but he didn't. He might not sleep with buzzed women, but he had no problem looking. He looked plenty as the sheet fell away.

"Pretty," he said, and came close when she winced at the weight on her ankle. Lifting her up, he carried her into the bathroom.

"I think I can manage from here," she said.

"Are you sure? I'm good in the shower."

Since he was good at everything, that wasn't a stretch. But she was definitely not at her best. "I'm sure."

With a slow nod, he left her alone.

Stripping off her bra and panties, she limped to the shower, turned it on, then proceeded to smack her ankle getting in. "Ouch, ouch, ouch, ouch. *Dammit.*"

And then suddenly Mark was back, whipping aside the shower curtain, expression concerned. "You okay?"

Was she? She had no idea. She was standing there, naked, wet. *Naked.* Lots of things were crowding for space in her brain, and oddly enough, not a one of them was embarrassment. "I'm instigating again," she whispered, and tugged him into the shower, clothes and all.

Without missing a beat, as if crazy naked women dragged him into their showers every day, his arms banded around her. His hair, dark brown and silky and drenched, fell over his forehead and nearly into his equally dark eyes. He clearly hadn't shaved and his jaw was rough with at least a day's growth. His shirt

was so wet as to be sheer, delineating every cut of every muscle on him. And there were a lot of muscles. He looked lethally gorgeous, and was lethally dangerous to her mental health as well, especially since all she could think about was ripping off his clothes to have her merry way with him. "Mark?"

"Yeah?"

"I'm naked."

One big, warm hand slid down to her butt and squeezed. The urge to lift her legs around his waist was so shockingly strong, she had to fight to remain still. "I'm naked," she said again. "And you're not."

"That could be fixed," he said, volleying the ball into her court, leaving the decision entirely up to her. He waited with the latent, powerful patience of a predator who had its prey cornered.

"You turned me down last night," she pointed out, smoothing a palm down his chest, taking in every well-defined muscle before sliding her hands under his shirt. "I'm not sure I could take a second rejection."

"Are you still under the influence?"

"No. Was that your only barrier?"

His eyes were two fathomless pools of heat. "For now."

"Then please," she whispered, lending her hands to the cause, tugging up his shirt. "Please fix your not-naked status."

With quick, smooth grace, he stripped out of his clothes, discarding them in a wet heap on the floor. God, he was so damn gorgeous. And that's when she knew. Even though she'd made the rules to keep herself from drowning in him, she was in over her head and going down for the count.

MARK STOOD THERE WITH Rainey in his arms, the water running down them, the air steamy and foggy, unable to believe how good she felt against him. She was looking at his body, and getting off on it—a fact he greatly appreciated because he enjoyed looking at her, too. So much he was currently hard enough to pound nails. "Are you going to instigate again?"

"I'm thinking about it," she said, water streaming over her in rivulets. "But for the record, this isn't about liking each other."

He traced the line of her spine down to her ass, slipping his fingers in between her legs, nearly detonating at the wet, creamy heat he found. "Because you don't. Like me," he clarified.

"Right."

He ignored the odd pang at that, and tipping her face up to his, he kissed her, kissed her long and deep and wet, until she was clutching at him, making soft little whimpers for more, and he'd damn well lay money down that she liked him now. He had no business caring one way or the other, but suddenly he wanted her to. Very much. "We can work on the like thing," he said. "We could start small."

"Yes, well, there's nothing *small* about you."

Laughing softly, he went on a little tour, kissing his way down her throat, over her collarbone, to a breast. Her nipples were tight, already hard when he ran his tongue over a puckered tip. "How about this, Rainey? Do you like this?"

She let out a barely there moan but didn't answer.

"Tell me." Sucking her into his mouth, he teased and kissed, absorbing her sexy whimper, but when she still didn't speak, he stopped and looked at her.

Her head was back, eyes closed, water streaming over her, so beautiful she took his breath.

Unhappy that he'd stopped, she lifted her head.

"Say it," he said.

"I liked that," she whispered.

"Good. How about this?" He gently clamped his teeth on her nipples and gave a light tug.

This ripped a throaty gasp from her and she tightened her fingers in his hair. "Mark—"

"Yes or no, Rainey?"

"Yes!"

"Okay, good, that's real good. Now let's see what else you like."

"I don't think—"

"No, we're addressing the problem, as you so smartly suggested." Dropping to his knees, he worked his way down her torso, kissing each rib, dipping his tongue into her belly button, making her squirm. "How about this," he asked. "Do you like this?"

When she said nothing, he once again stopped.

"I liked that!" she gasped, her hips rocking helplessly. "Please, don't stop."

Gripping her hips, he held her still and moved lower, pressing his mouth to her belly, then lower still, hovering right over her mound.

Above him, she stopped breathing.

With a smile, he reached up and extricated one of her hands from his hair, placing it against the tile wall at her side so she'd be better balanced.

"Mark—"

"And this? Do you like when I do this, Rainey?" He kissed her thigh, her knee.

"Y-yes," she whispered shakily. "I like that."

He gently kissed that same spot again, running his palm up her belly to graze a breast. "I'm glad." Carefully, he gripped her foot with the slightly swollen ankle and lifted it to the tub's ledge, which opened her up to him and gave him a heart-stopping view.

"Mark—"

Unable to resist, he leaned in and kissed first one inner thigh, and then the other.

And then in between.

"Yes," she gasped before he'd even asked, making him smile against her as his heart squeezed with a myriad of emotions so strong it shocked him. Affection, warmth, amusement and heat. There was so much heat, he could come from just listening to the sounds she made. He kissed a slow trail over her center, lingering in the spots that made her cry out. She took her other hand out of his hair and slapped it against the opposite wall so that both hands were straight out, bracing her, and still he felt her legs quiver.

"Oh, God—" Apparently unable to say more, she broke off, panting for breath.

Loving the taste of her, he parted her with his fingers, using his tongue, his teeth, to take her even higher, then closed his mouth over her and sucked, slipping first one finger and then another into her.

"Mark!"

Yeah, she liked that. And he loved the sound of his name on her lips. He wanted more. He wanted it all, which he realized just as she came, panting and shuddering for him, whispering his name over and over as she did.

RAINEY WOULD HAVE surely fallen to the floor of the shower if Mark hadn't caught her. She'd warned herself to hold back but that had proved difficult if not impossible. Still trembly and breathless, she found herself pressed between the cool hard tiles at her back and a hot, hard Mark at her front, the shower still pulsing hot water over them.

Before she could regroup, he cupped a breast, letting his thumb rub over her nipple as he slid a powerful thigh between hers, pressing in just enough to graze her heated, pulsing flesh, wrenching a moan from her.

"Rainey, look at me."

Her eyes flew open and she blinked away the water. "I like that," she heard herself murmur. *Way to hold back...* She leaned out of the shower and fumbled into her top vanity drawer for the sole condom she had there. A sample from somewhere. God bless samples.

His smile nearly made her come again. "Goal oriented," he said. "I like that." Dipping his dark, wet head, he pressed openmouthed kisses over her shoulder, nipping softly.

She slid her fingers into his hair and brought his head up, touching her tongue to his bottom lip, feeling the groan that rumbled from his chest to hers. Good. He was as gone as she was. It was her last thought as he took control of the kiss, cupping the back of her head in his big palm as his lower body ground into hers, sending shock waves of desire flooding through her.

She gasped when he pulled away, murmuring a protest at the loss of the contact, and then gasped again when he swiped everything off the wide tub edge at the opposite end from the shower head. Her shampoo, conditioner and face wash hit the shower floor, then

before she could blink he sat and pulled her on his lap. His long, inky black lashes were stuck together with little droplets of water, his eyes lit with a staggering hunger as he spread her thighs over his, opening her to him. The very tip of him sank into her, stretching her, making her gasp.

He went still, his face strained, his entire body tense as he struggled to give her time to adjust. It took only a heartbeat for her to need more, and she rocked her hips against him to let him know.

"Slow down," he rasped, voice rough. "I don't want to hurt you—"

"More."

With a low groan, he gave her another couple of inches and it was good, so good she sank all the way on him until he filled her up. The sensation was so incredible she cried out, but at the sound he went utterly still.

"Rainey, I'm sorry—"

"No, *I like!*"

He choked out a laugh at that, but she couldn't put a sentence together. She couldn't think past the deep quivering inside her that was spreading to every corner of her being. Instead, she rocked her hips again, mindless, trying to show him with her body how very okay she was.

Evidently he got the message because he began to move with her in slow, delicious thrusts, his big hands on her hips, controlling her movements.

He broke away from her mouth and locked his gaze with hers. His face was close, so close she saw something flicker in his eyes, something so intense it stole her breath. She couldn't name the emotion, she only

knew it matched what was going on inside her, and it was something new. "Mark, I need—"

"I know."

And he gave it to her, slow and sure, his thumb gliding over the spot where they joined, teasing, stroking... He drove her to the very brink, then held her suspended there, mindless, beyond desperate for her release before he finally allowed it. She came hard, which he clearly liked because he immediately followed her over, her name on his lips.

A long moment passed, or maybe a year, before he stirred against her, brushing his mouth across hers. "Next time, we do that in your bed," he murmured, still deep inside her.

Her body agreed with a shiver that made him drop his head to her shoulder and groan. They remained there, entwined, until the hot water suddenly gave way to cold, leaving Rainey gasping in shock and Mark laughing his ass off.

STILL GRINNING, MARK flicked off the water and eyed Rainey, who sat on the closed commode, chest still rising and falling as she tried to get her breath back.

He wasn't having much luck either. It was crazy. He ran five miles a day and could keep up with his world-class athletes just about any day of the week, and yet being with her had knocked his socks off.

And rocked his axis.

Grabbing a towel, he wrapped her in it, smiling when she just stared up at him. He liked the soft sated stupor in her eyes.

She shook her head. "I'm turning into a sex addict."

She rose to her feet and gingerly put weight on her ankle. "At least now we know."

"Know what?"

"That there's some crazy chemical thing going on here. It happens, I guess."

Yeah, it did happen. It happened a lot. But that wasn't all that what was happening here, and he was smart enough to know it. So was she. "Rainey—"

She turned towards him and kissed him, hard. Deep. And deliciously hot and wet. But when he groaned and reached for her, she shoved free. "Sorry. My fault. You've *got* to put clothes on." Pushing her wet hair from her face, she limped into her bedroom. With an impressive but frustrating talent, she managed to pull on clothes while keeping herself fully covered with the towel. "If I could stop kissing you, this wouldn't happen," she said. "When we kiss, I lose my inhibitions."

"Yeah?" he asked, intrigued. "All of them?"

"No, not all of them. But most."

A dare if he'd ever heard one. "Which ones don't you lose?"

She snatched her purse off the dresser, the tips of her ears bright red. "You know what? We are not discussing this."

"Can't be up-against-the-door sex," he said, enjoying teasing her. "Or shower sex. We've done both of those. Maybe you don't like to do it from behind. Or I know, you have an aversion to dirty talk. Are there dirty talk parameters we should discuss?"

"You made me dirty talk while we were having sex," she reminded him.

"You didn't use any dirty words. Maybe you have

some words that are okay, some that aren't. For instance, my penis. Would you want me to call it a dick, or a cock? Or how about your sweet spot? There are lots of names for that, like p—"

"Seriously?" She planted her hands on her hips. "Out of all of our issues, *this* is the one you want to discuss?"

"It's a good one."

She shook her head. "I'm leaving."

"This is your place."

"Right. God, you drive me nuts." She looked at her clock. "But I actually have to go to work." She moved out of the bedroom to the front door.

In nothing but the towel around his hips, he followed her. "Rainey."

"What?"

He maneuvered her to the door and kissed her. "Bye."

With a moan, she yanked him back and kissed him, running her hands over him as if she couldn't get enough before suddenly shoving him away. "Dammit, I said to put some clothes on!" She stormed out the front door, only to come to a skidding halt on her porch. "Crap!"

Her car wasn't there.

She sighed and turned back to him. "I need a ride to work."

When he smiled, she slapped her hands over her eyes. "Oh my God."

"What?"

"I'm adding smiling to the list. No smiling!"

"Why?" Pulling her back inside, he trapped her

against the door. "Do my smiles make you lose your inhibitions too? *All* of them?"

"Maybe."

"Okay, now you're just teasing me." He flicked his tongue over her earlobe and absorbed her soft moan.

"Argh!" Yanking free, she stormed back to the bedroom to grab his wet clothes, which she tossed into her dryer and turned it on. "You have to drive me to work. And you have to do it without making me want you. Got it?"

"I'll try. But I'm pretty irresistible when I put my mind to it."

9

MARK SPENT THE NEXT three days wielding a hammer alongside his players at the construction sites during the day, practicing with the teen girls in the late afternoons, and handling Mammoth business at night. He also had dinner with his dad, who'd gotten wind of Mark's interest in Rainey. *Thanks, Rick.* Ramon had told Mark that Rainey was a perfect fit for him, but they both knew what he really meant was *she'd keep you with one foot in Santa Rey, where you belong.*

Mark had his usual hundred balls in the air at all times, but in spite of doing the opposite of what his dad wanted, he couldn't stop thinking about Rainey.

He'd tried calling and had gotten her voice mail—twice—and a new and entirely foreign feeling had come over him.

She was avoiding him.

Four days after the ballet, he walked into the rec center and ran smack into her. She looked up from her clipboard, an apology on her lips, which tightened at the sight of him. "You."

Yeah. She'd been avoiding him. She was wearing

cargo shorts that emphasized the toned, tanned legs he'd loved having wrapped around him, a UCSB T-shirt and her favorite accessory—her whistle. And suddenly he wanted to see her wearing that whistle in his bed.

Just the whistle.

"You're early for practice," she said.

"Yeah, a little bit. Thought I could help out somehow." Or see you…

"Great." She slapped her clipboard to his chest. "Can you figure out which supplies we need to order?"

"What?"

"Check the list against the stock in the storage closet," she directed, and pointed to the same supply closet where only a week ago he'd kissed the both of them senseless. But before he could remind her of that, she was gone.

"Nice technique," Rick said as he came down the hallway. "Is that how you landed that Victoria's Secret model you dated last month?"

"Shut up." Mark looked down at the clipboard. "She wants me to be the supply boy."

"Huh. Probably she doesn't realize how important you are."

Mark sighed. "You're an ass."

"Are you sure that's me?"

Mark ignored this and opened the door to the closet, eyeing the shelf he'd pinned Rainey against. Clearly, he was losing his mind. It was obvious she didn't need him or even particularly like him. She didn't take his calls. She didn't seek him out.

And she wasn't just playing with him either, or being coy. That's not how she operated. What you saw was what you got with Rainey. She was the real deal.

And she didn't want him.

He wasn't sure how the shoe had gotten on the other foot, but it had and he needed to accept it and move on. Except...he couldn't seem to do that, which made no sense. He'd never been more on top of his world. His career was solid, his bank account was solid.

Maybe this vague unease was just from being back in Santa Rey, back with his father and brother, the two people in his life who didn't buy into his press. Yeah, that had to be it, being with family, with people who knew bullshit when they saw it and called him on it with no qualms. Here there was no snapping his fingers and getting his every need taken care of. Here no one looked at him to solve their every problem and deferred to him as if he were their god.

Here, he was the supply boy.

He supposed his dad was right about one thing— Santa Rey was home, since he hadn't bothered to get attached to anyplace else he'd been.

He thought briefly of his past girlfriends, or more accurately, lovers. He'd been with some incredibly beautiful women and yet he'd never gotten too attached for the sole reason that he hadn't wanted the additional responsibility.

It was possible he'd made a mistake there, that in trying to protect himself, he'd made it so he couldn't engage.

No, that wasn't it. He'd engaged with Rainey just fine. He'd engaged everything he had—body and heart and soul.

And maybe that was it. All this time he'd been just fine on his own with the occasional woman for fun and

diversion and stress release. But Rainey was shockingly different.

Why her? What was it about her that had so lowered his defenses? Because she was a nightmare waiting to happen to his life. She wasn't arm candy—not that she wasn't beautiful, because she was. She simply wasn't the type of woman to be content with the few crumbs he'd be able to give her, a mere side dish to the craziness of his life.

In fact, she had her own crazy life.

And what if *she* got attached? What then?

Except.

Except…she sure as hell didn't appear to be too attached.

He blew out another sigh and spent the next ten minutes comparing the list of needed supplies to what was on the shelves. There was no comparison, really. The center was short of everything, and he grabbed his phone. If he was doing this, then he was doing it right. He snapped a picture of the list and emailed it to the one person who could help him, then followed with a phone call.

Tony Ramirez answered with, "Yo, what can I get you?"

Tony was the Mammoths' supply manager. He stocked everything the players and staff needed, specifically the locker room, medical room and kitchen. It was a big job, and not an easy one. During the season, the team's needs varied on a day-to-day basis, from Ace bandages to the latest Xbox game to a turkey club sandwich on sourdough from the deli down the street, to a new Mammoths jersey on a moment's notice…

which meant that Tony was pretty much a world-class concierge service.

"Need some supplies," Mark said. "I'm in Santa Rey."

"Good for you, I'm in Cabo."

"Shit," Mark said. "Never mind."

"No, I've got my laptop. I can work my magic from anywhere, no worries. What do you need? Is it for Operation: Make The Mammoths Look Good Again, or for that chick that James and Casey tell me you're trying to impress?"

Mark pictured himself happily strangling his players.

"They make 'em pretty there in Santa Rey, huh?"

They did. They also made them feisty and sharp as hell, not to mention loyal and caring, and warm. So goddamn warm that Mark could still feel Rainey wrapped around him, the gentle heat of her breath on his throat as she pressed her face there, moaning his name. He could still feel the way she'd moved against him, driving him crazy. The way she'd shattered in his arms, clutching at him as if he was everything.

And then in the next moment she'd decided it didn't mean anything. Which he was fine with. Fucking fine. "The rec center here is in desperate need of some supplies. I just sent you the list."

"Didn't I just send you a bunch of baseball and softball equipment?"

"Yeah. This list is more for the rec center itself. Office supplies. But also, the kids I'm coaching are short on stuff I didn't anticipate. Running shoes, cleats, and…girlie stuff."

"Girlie stuff?"

"Sports bras."

"*Sports bras.* Are you shitting me?"

"You order jockstraps and compression shorts all the time."

"Yes," Tony said. "Because I know how to fit a dick into a cup. I have no knowledge of breasts—well, other than personal knowledge." He laughed to himself. "Where the hell am I supposed to get sports bras?"

"Hell, I don't know. The bra store? You said you were magic."

"Aw, man, you're going to owe me. The next blonde reality star that throws herself at you, you have to give to me. Make that the next *two* blondes."

"Yeah, yeah," Mark said. "Also get water bottles, enough for each kid and staff member because there's never enough water on the fields. Use the aluminum Mammoth ones if you want. And I want an iPad for stats, and—"

"An iPad?"

Turning, Mark came face to face with Rainey, who was standing in the doorway.

"We're barely budgeted for sports," she said dryly. "Pretty sure we're not budgeted for miracles."

Mark hung up on Tony. "Just trying to help."

"Or micromanaging," she suggested.

He smiled. "Again, hello, Mrs. Pot."

She sighed and shut the door, closing them in the closet. "It's very generous of you to do this," she said, staying firmly out of reach. A real feat in the small space.

"Yes, it is." Because she smelled amazing, he shifted closer without even thinking about it. "Feel free to thank me in any way you see fit."

Her mouth quirked, but she remained cool, calm and collected, in charge of her world.

It was a huge turn-on. Hell, everything about her was. Especially those shorts. Pressing her back against the door, he flattened his hands on either side of her head. "You've been avoiding me."

"I've been busy, is all." Her breasts brushed his chest and they both sucked in a breath.

Slowly he tipped his head down and watched as her nipples puckered and poked against the material of her shirt. "You're instigating again."

"My nipples have a mind of their own!"

Crowding her, he closed his teeth over her earlobe and tugged, not all that lightly.

She moaned and grabbed the fabric of his shirt. "No fair. I can't control my body's response to you."

Even better. He nipped his way down her jaw to her throat, nearly smiling when she tilted her head to make room for him. "God. Mark, stop." But even as she said it, she tightened her grip so he couldn't get away, tugging on a few chest hairs as she did. "Please," she said softly.

"I'll please anything you want, Rainey."

"Please don't do this. Don't make me want you."

Well, hell. He was a lot of things, but he wasn't a complete asshole. At least not when it came to her. He pulled back and met her gaze. "There are two of us in this, Rainey. Two of us wanting each other." With one last long look at her, he left the closet and made his way to practice, where he found the girls in various poses on the stands.

At least they were dressed in the gear he'd given them. Pepper was on the top row reading a book. Cindy

was sprawled across three benches, staring at the sky, twirling a strand of her hair, yammering on her cell phone. Kendra was at the bottom eating a candy bar and sucking a soda. The others were scattered in between, talking, laughing, doing each other's hair and texting.

Only Sharee was on the field, stretching.

Mark shot her a small smile, then walked up to the stands. "What's this?"

Every single one of the girls kept doing whatever they were doing. He mentally counted to three and asked again, using the voice that routinely terrified his world-class athletes in a blink.

The girls still didn't budge. With a sigh, he blew his whistle. With a variety of eye rolls, the teens made their way down to the grass in front of him.

"When you're dressed out," he said, "I expect to see you here running your drills. Not texting, not talking on the phone, not eating candy. You do all of that on your own time. This is *my* time."

Grumbling, they turned away to start their drills. "And what did I say about sagging?" he asked Kendra, whose shorts were so low he had no idea how she kept them up. "No shorts down past your ass—" Dammit. He pulled out a buck and handed it to Pepper, the keeper of the swear jar. "Or you won't play. Now start stretching, following the routine I showed you, or you'll be running laps."

They headed to join Sharee on the field. Mark watched them go, aware of Rainey coming up to his side. He waited for her to blast him about...hell, he didn't know what. Maybe breathing incorrectly.

Instead, she gave him an interminable look. "You do

realize that they're teenage girls, not grown men," she finally said.

"I have minimum requirements, regardless of the age or sex of the athlete. They're not difficult to meet."

"What are they?"

"Honesty, loyalty and one-hundred-percent participation."

She looked at him for a long moment. "Those are all good requirements," she said, and began walking back to the building.

Nice ass, he thought, and walked in the opposite direction, onto the field, handing Pepper another dollar.

"What's this for?" she asked.

"I thought a bad word."

RAINEY MADE HER WAY to her office, then stared out the window at the field. She had a million things to do and yet she was riveted in place, watching Mark coach the girls just as she'd occasionally watched him on TV. Hell, who was she kidding, she'd watched him more than occasionally. He had a way of standing at his team bench looking deceptively calm except for all that unfailing intensity and dogged aggression.

He was coaching the girls the same way he did his guys—hard and ruthless, and somehow also shockingly patient. And while not exactly kind, he had a way of being incredibly fair.

The girls, who'd given her and every other coach they'd had such endless grief, did everything in their power to please him.

"Rainey?"

She turned from the window to her office door and found Cliff from Accounting smiling at her. He was

lanky lean, with dark spiky hair and smiling eyes. He was shy as hell, but also one of the nicest guys she'd ever met. "Did I forget to sign my expense account again?" she asked.

Cliff laughed. They didn't have expense accounts. Hell, they were lucky to have salaries. "No." He looked behind them as if to make sure they were alone. "I was wondering if you wanted to go out sometime."

Some of her surprise must have shown on her face because he smiled with endearing self-consciousness and lifted a shoulder. "I know. We've worked together forever so why now, right? But—"

"Lena," Rainey guessed. "Lena put you up to this."

"She mentioned you were open to dating right now, but honestly I've always wanted to ask you out."

Aw. Dammit. And she *was* open to dating. Supposedly. And if it hadn't been for a certain alpha, obnoxious, annoying man outside on the field voluntarily helping her with the teens, the same alpha, obnoxious, annoying man she kept accidentally having sex with, she'd probably have said yes. "Cliff, I—"

"Just think about it," he said quickly, already backing away. "Don't give me your answer now. I'll call you sometime, okay?"

And then he was gone.

Rainey looked out the window again. Yep, Mark was still out there, batting pop flies to the girls for catching practice. He'd given them directions on how to improve and they were doing their best to follow.

And failing, a lot.

Never giving up, Mark kept at them, not afraid to get right in there to show them exactly what he wanted. He moved with easy grace and intensity, and she flashed

back to a few days prior, when he'd moved inside of her with that same grace and intensity.

The memory made her legs wobble. She pressed her forehead to the window. The girls were trying to do what Mark wanted, tossing him back the balls as soon as he hit them.

Sharee was the fastest and the best, even with the healing bruise on her face and sullen attitude. She'd missed a practice, then showed up today without a word of explanation. Rainey had tried to press the girl for details on what was going on at home, asking if she needed any help, interference, *anything,* but Sharee was an island.

Which might have something to do with the phone call Rainey had taken yesterday from the girl's father, the second extremely obnoxious "mind your own fucking business" phone call. Martin needed a new tune to sing.

Sharee rocketed a ball to Mark at the same time as Pepper. Mark caught Sharee's, and took Pepper's ball in the crotch.

Though she couldn't hear the collective gasp that went up from the entire team, Rainey sensed it as Mark bent at the waist. Whirling, she ran out of her office, hitting the field, pushing her way through the circle of girls around Mark. She put a hand on his shoulder. "Are you all right?"

He didn't answer, just sucked in another breath.

"Mark?"

Still bent over, hands on his thighs, he held up a finger indicating he needed a minute.

"What can I do?" she asked.

"Stop talking."

It was late enough to call practice, so Rainey excused the girls. As they shuffled by, they offered a chorus of "Sorry, Coach" and "get better, Coach."

When she was alone with Mark, Rainey asked, "Do you need a doctor? Ice for the swelling?"

With a slight groan, he finally straightened and sent her a dark glare.

"What?" she asked. "That's what you do for an injury. You ice it, right? It eases the pain and swelling."

"This is not the kind of pain and swelling I need you to manage for me," he grated out.

"Are you sure?"

He drew another deep breath and gained some of his color back as he walked stiffly past her. "I'm fine."

"I'm just trying to help. Offer a little TLC."

"Tell you what," he said. "If you really want to get your hands on my cock again, then—" He broke off at her surprised gasp. "Oh, sorry, we never did decide what you deemed an acceptable term for that particular body part, did we?"

She lifted her chin. "Clearly, you're feeling better."

At that, a hint of amusement came into his eyes. "Yeah. But any time you want to kiss it and make it all better, you know where I'm staying."

A FEW NIGHTS LATER, the Mammoths were scheduled for an exhibition game for a huge local charity event at home in Sacramento against the San Jose Sharks.

Rick drove Lena and Rainey to the game. Rainey didn't know what she'd expected, but it wasn't to sit with the players' girlfriends and wives, with a crystal-clear view of the ice and an even better one of the Mammoths' bench.

Mark was there with his players, of course, wearing his hat low, mouth grim as the tight game stayed tied all the way to the end, when his team pulled a goal out of nowhere in overtime.

Rainey was pretty sure she never took her eyes off Mark, not even when Casey was body checked into the end boards or when James took a flip pass to the head. Afterwards, Rick took her and Lena to the team room. There was a huge spread of food, reporters and players. Everyone was eating, relaxing, speaking to the media... having a good time.

Mark was in his big office off to the side, a large wall of glass revealing him standing at a huge desk, on his phone and laptop at the same time.

"Post game crap," Rick said, handing her a drink. "The Mammoths are working on their media coverage."

She nodded and continued to watch Mark in his element until he lifted his head and leveled his gaze unerringly on her.

She caught his surprise in the slight widening of his eyes before he left his office and came to her.

"You didn't know I was here," she said when he stood directly in front of her.

"Rick is a sneaky bastard."

"We had great seats," she said. "Usually I sit way up in the nose bleed section—" She broke off, but it was too late. Her secret was out. She met his gaze, his eyes full of laughter.

"You come to the games," he said.

She sighed. "Sometimes. But mostly I watch them on TV."

"To see me?"

"Well let's not go overboard."

"Admit it."

She sighed again. "Sometimes I really hate you."

His grin widened, and two players across the way gawked at him. So did the members of his coaching staff. In fact, everyone near them stared.

Apparently he didn't grin like that very often here at work.

"You don't hate me," he said, not paying the people around them any attention whatsoever. "You like me. And you know something else?" He leaned in. "You want me again, bad."

His mouth on her ear made her shiver but he was laughing, the bastard, his body shaking with it. She gave him a shove and stalked off to the food table. She needed meaningless calories, and lots of them.

Because yeah, she wanted him.

Bad.

She ate with Lena and Rick, then watched the team gather together and shove a present in Mark's hands.

"Just a little something from us, Coach," Casey said with far too much innocence. "To protect you when you're coaching the girls."

Mark gave him a long look and opened the box.

As his players hooted and hollered, he pulled out a jockstrap.

Mark's laughing eyes met Rainey's and heat bolted through her.

He'd rather have a box of condoms.

He didn't say it out loud, he didn't have to, but she felt her face heat. Because she wished he'd gotten a box of condoms too....

TWO DAYS LATER, MARK gathered the teenagers in the rec center parking lot. They'd had two home games so far, and had won one, lost the other. Today they were heading to their first away game against a neighboring rec league in Meadow Hills, twenty-five miles east of Santa Rey.

The guys took one bus, the girls another. Mark boarded after his last player, then stopped short at the sight of Rainey, sitting next to the driver.

"I try to go to as many of the away games as I can," she told him. "Especially the first one, in case a coach can't handle it."

He raised a brow. "Pretty sure I can handle it." He turned to take a seat but she pointed to the iPad in his hands. "What's that for?"

"I have stats I want to go over with the girls before the game." He pulled up a file for her. "See?"

She stared down at the numbers. "These stats aren't for our team."

"No, they're for the team we're playing today."

"How did you get them? We don't keep stats in our league. It's a noncompetitive league."

The word *noncompetitive* wasn't in Mark's vocabulary. "I had someone to go out and watch their games this week."

"You had…" She stared up at him for a full minute. "Okay, maybe you didn't get the memo. This is a *rec* league, and for *fun*."

"There's nothing wrong with being prepared."

"Mark." She appeared to pick her words carefully, and he let her, mostly because he was still standing over her and had a nice view right down her shirt.

"You can't coach these girls with the same fierce intensity you coach your players," she finally said.

He liked her pink lace bra. And he was pretty sure he could see the very faint outline of her nipples—

"Are you listening to me?" she asked.

"No," he said. "I stopped listening to you after you said noncompetitive."

She rolled her eyes. "You're a control freak."

Yeah, and it took one to know one. He was just about to say so when there was a tussle in the back of the bus between Sharee and Kendra. He strode down the aisle, eyes narrowed, but by the time he got to them, everyone was quiet and angelic. The bus began to move, forcing him to sit where he was—right in the middle of the team.

From her comfy seat up front all by herself, no kids near her, Rainey gave him a smirk.

The sexy tyrant...

"You need to switch over to thongs," Tina said to Cindy. "No VPL. Guys like that."

"VPL?" Cindy asked.

"Visible panty lines."

Mark shuddered and turned his head, only to catch another conversation.

"Ethan is such a jerk," Kendra was saying to Sharee on his other side, their earlier fight apparently forgotten. "He goes crazy when guys talk to me, and whenever I go out with anyone, he shows up."

To Mark, the guy sounded like a punk ass stalker. Except...

Except he'd essentially done the same to Rainey. Twice.

"What do you think, Coach?"

He blinked at Sharee.

"Should Kendra dump Ethan's sorry possessive butt?" she asked him.

"Yes," he said without hesitation. "Boys are like drugs, just say no."

Sharee rolled her eyes. "More like boys are like candy—yummy and good to eat."

Mark groaned. He was so far out of his comfort zone. "Aren't you fifteen?" he asked Kendra.

"Sixteen."

His mind spun, placing Ethan as one of the guys banned from the rec center. They'd been causing trouble in town, vandalizing, partying it up. From what he understood, most of the girls were scared of them. "*No* dating Ethan."

"You're not my dad."

"No, but I'm your coach. I control your field time."

Kendra narrowed her eyes. "That sounds like blackmail."

"Call it whatever you want. Date someone who's not an idiot."

Mark desperately tried to tune out all the chattering going on around him.

It didn't happen.

"Aiden is way hotter than Trevor," Tina said behind him.

"Definitely," Cindy agreed. "Aiden has facial hair. It means he's…mature."

"Mature how?" Tina wanted to know.

"Well, you know what they say about big feet, right? They say it about facial hair too. If he's got facial hair, he's got a big—"

Mark jammed his iPod earphones in his ears and

cranked his music, feeling like he was a hundred-year-old man. Jesus. These girls lived in a shockingly grown-up world for their age. They were already jaded, sarcastic, and in some cases, like Sharee, in daily danger.

He and Rick had grown up poor, but they'd been lucky to have Ramon's hardworking, caring influence. Some of these girls didn't have that, or any positive role model other than what they found at the rec center or at school in the way of coaches and teachers. That made it difficult, if not impossible, for a good guy to gain their trust.

He needed to try harder. He shut off the iPod and opened his eyes, then nearly jumped out of his skin when he saw Pepper staring at him.

She'd slid into the seat next to him. "Hi," she said.

"Hi. You okay?"

"Yeah." She looked down at her clasped hands. "But my, um…friend has a problem."

"Yeah?"

"Yeah. The guy she likes finally asked her out and they went, only now he's pretending she doesn't exist. So I'm wondering what could have happened. Do you know? Why he'd suddenly act so weird toward me—I mean my *friend?*"

Mark stared down at her bowed head. *Shit.* Yeah, he knew exactly why a guy would do that. Probably she hadn't put out, the bastard. He felt his heart squeeze with affection and worry. "The ass doesn't deserve you. Forget him."

Pepper held out her hand. Mark sighed and reached into his pocket for a dollar.

"Ryan likes you, Pepper," Sharee said. "Why don't you go for him?"

"Or stay single," Mark said desperately.

"She's not going to lose her virginity staying single," Sharee said.

Dear mother of God. "Abstinence is perfectly acceptable," he said firmly.

They all looked at him.

"Were *you* abstinent during your high school years?" Sharee wanted to know.

Fuck. He shoved his hands through his hair, and when he opened his eyes again, Pepper was once again holding out her hand. He'd said the word out loud. He fished in his pocket for another buck, but Pepper shook her head.

"The F-bomb is a five-dollar offense," she said.

He shoved a ten in her hand. "Keep the change. I'm going to need the credit."

10

AFTER WATCHING MARK coach the girls to a hard-earned win, Rainey went home and made brownies. Then she drove to the Welcome Inn Motel.

She wasn't quite sure what her goal was.

Okay, that was a big, fat lie. She knew *exactly* what her goal was. She was just conflicted about it. She'd watched Mark on that bus with those girls, completely out of his element and still completely one hundred percent committed.

It'd made him so damn attractive. *Too* attractive. Sitting in her car outside the motel, she called Lena. "Tell me to turn around and go home."

"Where are you?"

"Never mind that. Just tell me."

Lena cackled, the evil witch. "You're at Mark's," she guessed.

"Yes," Rainey said miserably.

"You're wearing good underwear, right? Something slinky?"

"Lena." She thunked her head against the steering

wheel. "I'm just here to deliver brownies as a thank-you."

"Uh-huh. And I'm the Easter Bunny. You should know that I put a condom in your purse the other day. Just in case. Side pocket. Magnum-sized. Ribbed for your pleasure."

"Oh my God."

"'Night, hon. Don't do anything I wouldn't do."

"There's *nothing* you wouldn't do!"

"Well, then you're in for a great night, aren't you?" Lena laughed and disconnected.

Rainey stared at the pristine black truck in the parking lot, sticking out among the beat-up cars and trucks around it. They weren't friends. They weren't having any sort of a relationship—hot sex aside—and yet…

And yet…

Somehow it felt like both of those things were happening in spite of themselves. She wasn't here to give him brownies. She and every single one of her hormones knew that. But she was already dangerously close to not being able to keep this casual. She wasn't good at going with the flow and letting things happen. Not when she knew in her heart that she could feel much more than simple lust for him.

That she already felt more.

And what if she gave in to it, what then? She'd have to deal with the consequences when he left—and he would—and she didn't have a game plan for that.

But then there was the fact that no matter what she threw at him, he managed it. Handled it. Even fixed it. She thought about earlier, how he'd managed to coach the girls to a strong win. How they listened to him. They *talked* to him.

A part of her wanted him for that alone. The rest of her wanted him because he was sharp and fearless and intelligent.

No, you want him because he oozes testosterone and pheromones.

Oh, yeah. That, too.

Blowing out a breath, she got out of her car and walked into the lobby, telling herself she was just going to give him the brownies and go.

Casey and James were in the lobby, reading trade magazines and newspapers, drinking beer, watching soap operas with the woman behind the front desk.

"Hey, Rainey, I smell chocolate," Casey said, pouncing on her brownies like he was starving, making her join them.

James showed her the calluses on his hands from all the hammering he'd been doing. Casey had a nice gash across his forehead after he'd apparently walked into a two-by-four on the job. The talk slipped to coaching the teens and Casey grinned. "Man, as many women as Coach always has throwing themselves at him, it's been fun watching him have to work at getting the chicks to like him."

Rainey's bite of brownie stuck like glue in her mouth at the thought of how many women loved Mark.

"You're an idiot," Casey told James.

"No, it's okay," Rainey assured him. "I'm perfectly aware of his reputation."

"I didn't mean it like that," James said earnestly. "It's not like he's a male ho or anything, I swear. It's just that...I don't know...he's sort of bigger than life, and women are curious, you know? Most of the time,

he doesn't even pay any attention to them leaving their phone numbers and panties on his hotel room door."

Rainey stood up, not needing to hear more. "So... where is he?"

"In his room making calls and doing some work," Casey said. "But he's grumpy."

"Huh," Rainey said. *Join the club.* "Think brownies'll help?"

They all looked at her like she was crazy, and she sighed. "Right. He can get anything he wants. Why would brownies help?"

"Um, Rainey?" Casey smiled gently. "We meant that no, the brownies won't help, but *you* will."

Two minutes later Rainey knocked on Mark's door, heart hammering in her throat. This was ridiculous, using brownies as a ruse to see him. So ridiculous. She turned to go, which of course was the exact moment the door opened. Walking away, she closed her eyes.

"Rainey." Even in that not-close-to-happy voice, the sound of her name on his lips made her nipples hard. Slowly she turned to face him. He wore a pair of Levi's and nothing else, half-buttoned and almost indecently low on his hips, revealing the perfect cut of his chest and abs.

And dammit, even his bare feet were beautiful.

He was holding a cell phone to his ear and his iPad in his hand. At her thorough inspection of his body, he arched a brow and tossed the iPad to the small desk. Still holding her gaze, he said into the phone, "I have to go, something just came up."

Without waiting for a reply, he disconnected and tossed the phone to the desk as well.

It immediately began vibrating, but Mark ignored it, eyes locked on her.

Fighting the twin urges to squirm and/or jump him, Rainey forced herself to stand there, cool and calm as could be. Because suddenly she accepted what she'd come here for.

Him.

She'd come here for him, any way that she could get him. "You busy?"

He didn't bother to answer that one, just leaned against the doorjamb.

Her eyes traveled the breadth of his shoulders down his bare torso, along the eight pack to the narrow silky trail of barely-there hair that vanished into the opened button fly of his jeans, and she felt her entire body respond. Was he wearing underwear? Because she couldn't see any... The thought of him commando under those jeans gave her a serious hot flash. Her brain tried to signal a warning that she was in over her head but she told herself she'd worry about the aftermath later.

Much later. "I brought brownies," she said. "I'm-sorry-for-being-an-ass brownies."

"My favorite," he said. He stepped back and gestured her in ahead of him, kicking the door closed.

She set the brownies on the desk next to his phone and iPad, then slid her hands to his biceps and turned him, pressing him back against the door.

His eyes went from unreadable to scorching as he permitted her to maneuver him. "You have plans," he murmured.

"Turns out that I do."

"Does it involve instigating? Or that TLC you promised me?"

"What if it does? What do I get in return?"

His smile was slow and sure and so sexy her bones melted. "Babe, you can have whatever your heart desires."

If only that were true, she thought, and stepped into him anyway, plastering herself to that body she dreamed about every night as she covered his mouth with hers.

The kiss ignited like a rocket flash. Not that this surprised her. Everything pertaining to Mark seemed to burn hot and fast. Frustration, lust…

His mouth was rough, hot and hungry on hers as he pulled her closer, taking control. She heard herself moan, kissing him with helpless desperation. If dessert was her usual drug of choice, it'd just been replaced because she couldn't seem to get enough of him.

Apparently feeling the same way, he gripped her hips, then slid his hands up to cup and mold her breasts. "I don't know exactly what your plan is," he murmured silkily. "But if it isn't me stripping you naked and then licking every square inch of you, you need to stop me now." His mouth got busy on her throat as his talented hands slid beneath her shirt, gliding up her belly, heading north.

All she managed was another moan, squirming a little, trying to encourage his hands to hurry. Obliging, he pushed up her shirt, tugged down her bra and ghosted the tips of his fingers over her nipples, leaving her body humming, throbbing for more.

His lips left hers for the barest breath. "Rainey."

"Yes." God, yes.

"Yes what?"

"Ohmigod, you and the dirty talk!"

He nipped her jaw. "Tell me," he murmured, voice husky. "Tell me you want me to strip you and lick you all over."

He wanted to hear the words from her, she got that. And in her daily life, she always had plenty of words, but he scrambled her brain. Plus, talking dirty felt...well, dirty. She nearly laughed, but Mark wasn't laughing. He was waiting for an answer with that same simmering intensity he gave to all aspects of his life, emitting a raw sensuality that made her feel sexy, so damn sexy. And he was like a drug, an addiction. A seductive addition... "Yes, I want that," she said. "What you said."

She'd have sworn his lips twitched, the smug bastard. "The stripping?" he asked.

"Yes, and the other." *Please to the other!*

"I can't remember what that was," he said.

Liar. He was such a liar. "I want the licking too," she whispered, and pressed her face to his chest.

He slid one arm around her waist, and lifted his other hand to run it down her hair, the gesture possessive and protective at the same time. "Anything else?"

"You really want me to say it?"

"Yes."

"Gah," she managed, and burrowed in even tighter, realizing she was nuzzling his chest, her nose pressed against a flat male nipple. He sucked in a breath through his teeth, nothing more than a low hiss that was the sexiest sound she'd ever heard. She opened her mouth on him, tempted to bite him, but as if he guessed

her intent, he wrapped his hand in her hair and tugged lightly until she looked up at him.

"After all we've done together," he said in amused disbelief. "How can you still be embarrassed?"

"I don't know!" She squeezed her eyes shut. "Can't we *just* do it?"

He reversed their positions, pressing her against the door now, and she promptly lost her train of thought because she could feel his every inch.

Every. Single. One.

He kissed her, sweeping his tongue over hers in a slow, languid stroke that melted her bones. She ran her hands up his sides and down again, sliding them into the back of his loose, low-slung jeans, and...

Oh, yeah. Commando.

She tried to get closer, and it still wasn't close enough. She'd have climbed inside him if she could, and she let out a low sound of frustration and need and desperation. His lips left hers for a bare second to whisper her name soothingly before hungrily devouring her again, until her entire body was trembling. Breathless, she tore her mouth free. "Mark, I can't... I can't stand up."

Almost before the words were out of her mouth, he lifted her and carried her to the bed. Then he stripped out of his jeans, shoving them down his thighs and off, his eyes never leaving hers.

At the sight of him, she gulped.

"Did you change your mind about the stripping or licking or..." His mouth curved, though his eyes remained serious. "Other stuff?"

"No."

He put a knee on the bed, then crawled up her body,

looking bigger and badder than she remembered, and with a momentary bout of nerves, she scooted backwards.

He immediately stopped stalking her. There in the middle of the bed on his knees, gloriously naked, gloriously hard, he went still. "You have all the power, Rainey. You know that, right?"

She didn't feel like that at all. This had started out as a way to have him, knowing that it wasn't real. For keeps. Even if she had *any* of the power, he was way too in control for her tastes. To even the playing field, she pulled off her shirt, then felt better when his eyes glazed over. She wriggled out of her jeans and panties, soaking up his appreciative groan. He was kneeling between her legs when he took one of her feet in his big hand and kissed her ankle, her calf, and then the inside of her knee.

At the soft sigh that escaped her, he looked at her from those smoking eyes. "Good?"

"So good. Don't stop."

"I won't." He set her foot flat on the bed, her knee bent, affording himself a front row center view of ground zero. "Mmm." The sound rumbled from his chest, and he slid his hands beneath her bottom and tugged her to him. Then he put his mouth on her, sending her flying with shocking ease.

When she'd stopped shuddering, he pushed up on his forearms. "I like that expression you're wearing."

"The one that says I no longer have a thought in my brain?"

"You have a thought. You want me inside you."

"More than my next breath." She hesitated, then ad-

mitted the rest of that truth. "There's a condom in my purse."

His smile was slow and sure and sexy as hell. "Brownies *and* a condom."

It took him less than ten seconds to locate it. And then he positioned himself above her and filled her in one smooth stroke, making her gasp and clutch at him. Her eyes closed involuntarily at the sensation of him pressing deep, so deep that she cried out from the sheer perfection of it, and then again when he stroked his thumb over her. "I'm—I need—"

"I know. I've got you." And he did. He brought her to another shattering climax, staying with her through it, then when she could open her eyes, she found his, black and scorching on hers. Still hard within her, he leaned over her, thrusting deep, sending her spiraling again, and this time he followed her.

RAINEY LAY THERE STARING at the ceiling, sucking air, trying to get her breath back. Mark appeared to be in the same state. After a minute, he rolled to his side and pulled her in close, fitting her against him so that she could feel the after-shock when it ran through his body. It caused the same tremor within her, so strong it was almost another orgasm—from nothing more than knowing she'd given him pleasure.

With a low, very male sound of satisfaction, he ran his fingers over her heated skin. Thriving on the touch, she had to fight the urge to crawl under the covers with him to fall asleep in his arms.

Definitely, she needed to go.

Sitting up, she slid off the bed and began to search for her clothing, not missing the irony—she'd told him

to stop interfering with her life, and yet she'd been the one to bring them to this point. The naked point. Which was about as deep into the interference of one's life as it got. At his soft chuckle, she looked up.

Mark was still sprawled across the bed, arms up behind his head, feet crossed, casual as could be, seeped in the supreme confidence of someone who didn't have to worry about whether or not he looked good naked.

Because he did.

So good.

So.

Damn.

Good.

"Why are you laughing?" she asked, wearing only her bra and one sock. "And where are my panties?"

He sat up, the muscles of his abs crunching and making her mouth go dry. In one fluid motion, he was off the bed and handing her the panties.

She reached for them, but with a wicked smile, he held them high above her head.

"Give me," she said.

"Don't you mean *please* give me?"

"You want me to beg?"

That smile spread slightly. "Nah. I just heard you beg plenty."

"I did not beg."

But she had. She so had.

Still grinning, still naked, he pulled her against him and pressed his mouth to her shoulder.

"My panties, Mark."

Eyes warm, he handed them to her, and then suddenly it was like her brain disconnected from her mouth

because she heard herself say, "Do I really have all the power?"

"After what we just did, you can doubt that?"

"I want the power to do something with this thing between you and me. Something more than just sex."

He went still, and her heart stopped. "Or not," she said. Feeling *very* exposed, she backed away. She shoved her legs into her panties and pulled them up. Then her jeans.

"Rainey—"

"No, you know what? That was leftover pheromones talking. Ignore it. Ignore me." Oh, God. "I gotta go."

He let out a long breath, then reached for her. "I thought you had me figured for a bad bet."

"You are. A really bad bet, at least for me, because you operate day-to-day."

And she operated long term. They both knew that. "I'm not a keeper, Rainey."

There was something in his voice, something terrifyingly regretful and terrifyingly firm.

Did he not realize that to her, he was the ultimate keeper? Sharply intelligent, funny as hell, hardworking, caring... But she wouldn't argue this, because as he'd pointed out, she'd already done her begging tonight. She went back to dressing, getting out of here her only plan. He'd told her that she had the power, but that was all wrong. *He* had the power, the power to stomp on her heart until it stopped functioning.

She turned to look for her shoes and bumped into his chest, which was a little like walking into a brick wall. "Excuse me," she said.

"I want to make sure you understand."

"I do."

"I don't think so," he said. "This isn't just sex for me, Rainey." He took her arms in his big hands to keep her from escaping and her belly quivered.

Stupid belly.

"I just don't have anything to offer more than what we have right now," he said quietly.

"Which is what, that day-to-day thing?"

"Yeah."

Okay, she got that. Loud and clear. Sex was great. More than sex…not so much.

"Where does that leave us?" he asked, his eyes serious.

"In the same place we've always been," she managed to say.

"So then… why exactly are we dressing?" His eyes were dark and focused on her breasts. "Because from here," he said softly, "going back to bed looks like a great idea."

"Because…" Hell. This was getting complicated. This had been all her doing, she should be fine. She wanted to be fine. But her feelings for him had deepened, and she was afraid. He was going to hurt her without even trying. "Excuse me a minute?" Vanishing into the bathroom, she locked herself in and whipped out her cell phone. "Lena," she whispered when her best friend picked up. "I need your help."

"What's the matter?"

Rainey sank to the closed toilet lid and dropped her head to her knees. "I'm with Mark."

"Nice."

"No, I mean I'm with him with him."

"Like I said, nice."

"Listen!" Rainey lowered her voice with effort. "He fooled me!"

"Huh?"

"You said I should go for a guy who *isn't* a fixer-upper, right? And I figured I was safe with Mark because he *is* a fixer-upper, the ultimate fixer-upper, actually. But I was wrong. He's not a fixer-upper at all. I like him just how he is. And now I'm screwed."

Lena laughed.

"I don't mean that in a good way! Okay, well it was good, but you know what I mean!"

"Ah, honey. You're afraid."

Yeah. She was. So deeply afraid she'd fallen in love—madly, irrevocably in love.

"Look, I realize I'm speaking Greek when I tell you this," Lena said. "But just enjoy the ride on this one." She paused. "Pun intended."

"But the plan was for this to be light!"

"Honey, you don't always have to have a plan."

Rainey sighed and hung up. God, what to do? Could she really just go with the flow and let this thing play out?

Yes, said her body.

No, said her brain. Hell, no. Because when he left, and he was going to, she'd be devastated. With a sound of frustration, she shoved her phone into her pocket, drew a deep breath, and stood up. Gathering her courage, she opened the door.

Standing there in the doorway, hands up over his head and latched onto the jamb, was six feet plus of pure testosterone wrapped in tough, rugged sinew.

They stared at each other for a long beat.

"She tell you to dump me?" he asked quietly.

"She told me to enjoy the ride."

His smile was slow and sure and sexy. Damn. She pointed at him. "None of that or my clothes will fall off again. Move. I need space to think."

He moved. He moved into her, sliding his arms around her and melting her damn knees.

11

A PART OF MARK HAD BEEN braced for Rainey to grab her purse and walk out of his motel room.

And out of his life.

He'd fully expected it. Hell, he deserved it. But she let him pull her in, even pressed her face to his throat and inhaled deeply, and relief flooded him. Knee-knocking, gut-squeezing relief. "Rainey—"

"I don't want to talk about it. You're not sticking around, we've never made each other any promises. There was no plan, so there's no reason for me to try to back you into one now." Her cell phone vibrated. "It's Lena," she muttered. "Probably apologizing for being a bad wingman." She opened her phone. "It's too late to help me now, I—" She broke off and came to immediate attention, straightening up. "Sharee?"

Mark watched the furrow across Rainey's brow. Her hair was wild, probably thanks to his fingers. Her make-up had smeared beneath her eyes a little and she had a whisker burn down her throat. Lifting his hand, he ran a thumb over the mark.

"Sharee?" Rainey said. "Honey, what's wrong?"

Mark shifted in closer and put a hand on her shoulder. She looked up at him, her eyes dark with concern, and surprised him even further when she leaned into him as she listened. "I'm coming right now," she said. "Stay in a lit area—Hello? *Sharee?*" She stared at her phone. "Dammit, her battery died. I've got to go."

Mark was already grabbing a shirt and keys. "I'll drive."

RAINEY'S NERVES WERE in her throat as she picked up her purse. She'd never heard Sharee upset before. Pissed-off, yes. Pure bravado, often. Upset and scared, no. "She's at the high school," Rainey told Mark. "She got dropped there after shopping with friends. Her mom was supposed to get her but isn't there yet and Sharee said those boys are there, the ones I kicked out of the rec center last week. They're harassing her because she's the one who told me who they were."

Mark opened the door for her, then followed her out. "Oh, you don't have to—"

"I'm driving," he repeated in that quiet but firm voice she'd heard him use in interviews, on the teens, and on his players. It was a voice that brooked no argument while at the same time instilled confidence and a belief that everything was going to be okay.

She wanted to believe it. They moved through the lobby. The guys were still there and waved at them.

"The walk of shame," Rainey murmured.

Mark's hand slid warmly to the back of her neck. "They won't say anything."

"Are you kidding? Look at me."

He pulled her around to look at her, and his eyes softened. "You look like you just—"

"Rolled around in bed? Had an orgasm?"

An affectionate smile crossed his face. "Or three."

She smacked him lightly in the abs—which didn't give—and he grabbed her hand, holding her at his side as they continued to walk.

True to Mark's word, Casey and James didn't say a thing, but that was because Mark was giving them a long look over her head, which she managed to just catch. She waited until they were outside heading to his truck. "What did you threaten them with?"

He slid her a glance. "You were standing right there. I didn't say anything."

"Uh-huh."

He smiled. "Push-ups. Laps. Sitting their ass on the bench. Pick one."

"They're grown-ups. You'd do that?"

"I don't care how old they are, their asses are mine."

She shook her head and laughed. "You sound like a dictator."

"I am."

"And you like it? All that power?"

He just shot her a look.

Yeah. He liked it.

They stepped out into the cool night. Rainey reached into her purse for her keys while Mark caught sight of her car and went utterly still.

Someone had spray-painted *Bitch* across the trunk.

"Huh," she said. "That's new." And unwelcome. And more than a little unnerving.

"The boys?" Mark asked, hands on hips, grim. Pissed off.

"I don't know."

Mark pulled out his phone.

"What are you doing?"

"Calling the police. We need to make a report."

"Later. We need to get Sharee first."

Not looking happy, he took her hand again and led her to his truck. As they drove, the moon slanted into the windshield at an angle, giving her only peeks at the man beside her. He took two calls and made one, though she missed out on eavesdropping because she was busy demon-dialing Sharee, who wasn't answering.

Mark slipped his phone away and continued driving with single-minded purpose, fast, but steady. In his zone. He pulled into the high school parking lot, where they found Sharee huddled on the front steps. Rainey ran out and hugged her. "You okay?"

Sharee allowed the contact for a brief moment before pulling back. "Yeah." She looked around uneasily. "I think they left."

Mark was alert, his eyes missing nothing as he scanned the lot, his posture both at ease and utterly ready for anything. "Let's get out of here."

Twenty minutes later, they pulled up to the trailer that Sharee shared with her mom.

It was dark.

Rainey turned to face the girl in the backseat. "Sharee—"

"I'll be fine," she said, getting out of the truck. "Thanks for the ride."

Mark got out with her and looked at Rainey. "Stay here."

Before she could say a word, he'd engaged the locks and walked Sharee to the door. He waited there, keeping both Rainey and Sharee in sight until lights were

on in the trailer. Then he came back to his truck and drove Rainey to the motel, where they met a police officer and filed a report about her car.

Then Mark followed her home and saw her to the door just as he had Sharee.

But the smoking hot kiss he laid on her was hers alone.

THE NEXT DAY MARK POKED his head into Rainey's office and surprised her. "Hungry?" he asked.

It was late afternoon and she'd worked through lunch. She was starving. "Maybe," she said. "Why?"

"Thought we'd go get dinner."

A date? She wasn't sure what that meant, not that it mattered. "I can't. I have plans."

Nothing about his body language changed. He was too good for that. But she sensed that her statement hadn't made him happy. "Plans?" he asked.

"I'm going to my parents' house."

"Are you taking a date with you?"

No. She'd decided she couldn't be dating while she was doing...whatever this was that she was doing with him. It wouldn't be fair to anyone else. She barely had the mental capacity to handle Mark, much less another man as well.

And...

And the truth was, she didn't have the emotional capacity either. Mark was currently using up all she had. "Would that bother you?"

"Hell yes."

Odd how that made her all soft and warm inside. "I'm not taking a date to my parents," she said quietly. "My plans to date are temporarily on hold."

He closed her office door behind him, then came around her desk and hauled her up to her toes, kissing her until she couldn't remember her own name. "Good," he said, and was gone.

RAINEY'S PARENTS LIVED in a small, modest home in an area that had been spared the fires but not the economic downturn. Here, the houses were tired, the yards were tired, *everything* was tired. In addition, thanks to the drought, they were under strict water restrictions. The grass hadn't survived but there were potted wild flowers on the porch, which made Rainey smile.

So did the fact that her mother stood in the front door, waiting with a warm hug. "Honey, it's so good to see you!"

"Mom, you just saw me a week ago."

"I know." Elizabeth Saunders was blonde with gray streaks, medium build like Rainey, with the softness that having two kids and then thirty years of happiness gave a woman. "You look different, honey." Her mom studied Rainey's face. "What is it?"

"Nothing." Lots of sex… "New face lotion."

"Well it's done something fantastic to your skin. You need to use it more often."

Rainey nodded. Keep having orgasms. Got it.

Her mom cupped Rainey's face, staring into it. "It really suits you."

Oh, for the love of—"What's for dinner?"

"Lasagna. And a *surprise*."

Rainey hoped it involved chocolate. She moved into the kitchen to check things out. Her younger sister Danica was there, stirring something on the stove. Danica was married to her high school sweetheart.

Zach was a marine, out on his second tour of duty at the moment. Rainey's seven-year-old niece sat on the counter sucking a Popsicle. Hope's mouth was purple, as were her lips and hands. Actually, just about everything was purple except for her dancing blue eyes. "Rainey!" she squealed in delight.

Rainey leaned in for a kiss and got a sloppy, wet smack right on the lips. "Yum. Grape."

Hope grinned.

Danica looked behind Rainey towards the doorway. "Where's your date?"

"I don't have one."

"Mom said you did."

"Nope."

"She said you were dating Mark Diego."

"Mom's crazy."

"Yeah. So?"

Rainey shook her head. "So I'm not dating Mark." *I'm just doing him.*

"Then can *I* date him?" Danica wanted to know.

"You're married."

Danica grinned. "Yes, but I'm not dead."

Rainey sighed. "He's not all that."

"Liar."

"Okay, he's all that with frosting on top." *Bastard.* Rainey plopped down in a kitchen chair, accepting the grape Popsicle that Hope pulled out of the freezer and handed her.

Danica waited until her daughter had gone looking for grandma. "So you're *not* doing Mark?" she whispered.

"Okay, that's not what you asked me."

"Honey," their mom called from the living room,

"your surprise arrived." She appeared in the kitchen doorway. "I ran into him today at the gas station," she whispered.

"I thought my surprise was chocolate," Rainey said, a very bad feeling coming over her.

"Nope. Better than chocolate." Her mother smiled, then turned and revealed...

Mark Diego.

MARK NEVER GAVE MUCH thought to his next meal. During the season, he ate at the Mammoths facilities, the same as his team. When he was on the road, there was room service and restaurants. Even off season, he usually went that route.

But one thing he rarely had—a home-cooked meal.

Rainey's mom had made lasagna and cheese bread, which was delicious, but his favorite part was afterwards, when Danica brought out the photo albums and showed him the old family pictures, including one of a two-year-old diaper-clad Rainey waddling away from the camera, diaper slipping low, thighs thick and chunky.

"Seriously?" Rainey asked.

"Oh, you don't like that one?" Danica flipped the pages to reveal a pre-teen Rainey in braces, looking... well, as annoyed as she was right now. Heart softening, Mark reached for her hand but she stood up.

And gave his feet a little nudge. Actually, it was more like a kick. "Mark has to go now," she said. "He's got a thing."

"A what?" Danica asked.

"A thing. Somewhere to be."

"I don't have a thing," Mark said, remaining seated, ignoring Rainey's dirty look.

"Okay," she said. "Then I have a thing."

Mark snagged her wrist. He was extremely aware that she thought that he was in this just for the sex, but she was wrong. He was in for more. He just wasn't sure what that more was. All he knew was that sitting in the slightly shabby living room surrounded by Rainey and her family made him feel more relaxed and calm than he could remember being in far too long.

Danica smiled at him and continued to flip through the photo album. "Uh-oh," she said. "Don't look now but here's Rainey's first boyfriend. You were what, like eighteen? Slow bloomer. Probably because you still had a crush on this one." She gestured to Mark, then grinned at him. "We all had a crush on you," she told him. "But I think Rainey's lasted a little longer than most."

Rainey tugged free of Mark's hold and headed to the door.

"Ah, don't get all butt-hurt and embarrassed," Danica called after her. "I'm sure Mark already knew—everyone knew."

The front door slammed.

Mark made his thank-yous and goodbyes, and got outside in time to see Rainey drive off. Given that she drove a POS and he didn't, he had no trouble keeping up with her. Especially since she stopped at a convenience store. He watched her go in and then come out five minutes later with a brown bag. He followed her to her town house and parked next to her.

"So," he said conversationally, following her up the

path to her door, gesturing to the brown bag. "Alcohol or sugar?"

"Sugar. I don't need an escort."

"There's some guy out there writing BITCH on your car, I'm walking you up."

She unlocked her door, stepped in, and tried to close it on him.

"I'm also coming in," he said.

"Fine, but we are *not* talking."

"Not talking is right up my alley." He moved through her place, checking out the rooms. Satisfied, he found her standing in the dark living room, staring out the window into the night. "Rainey."

She dropped her head to the window. "Don't."

He wasn't exactly sure what she was saying *don't* to, but had a feeling it was *don't* come close, *don't* talk, *don't* touch, *don't* so much as breathe. He was bound to disappoint her since he was going to insist on all of the above, and coming up behind her, he risked his neck by stroking a hand down her hair. "You okay?"

She made a soft sound, like a sigh. "She's right, you know. I've screwed up my love life, over and over again, because of how I felt for you. I think I compared every guy to you." She shook her head and let out a low laugh. "It was real nice of you to pretend you didn't know how I felt back then."

Catching her arm, he pulled her around to face him, unhappy to see the look in her eyes, the one that said she felt a little defeated, a little down, and definitely wary. "I wasn't pretending. I was really that slow, especially that night when you came to my apartment."

"Well of course you were slow that night. You were deep in the throes of getting…pleasured."

He let out a breath. "That's actually not the part of that whole nightmare of a night that I was referring to."

She crossed her arms. "Well, there's no other part of that night that I want to discuss. Ever." She looked away. "Certainly not why you felt the need to come after me if you didn't want me."

He stared at her bowed head and felt an unaccustomed squeeze in the region of his heart. "You were sixteen."

"I want to go back to the no-talking thing."

"I cared about you, Rainey. But you were off limits to me, with or without the girl in my bedroom that night. I didn't allow myself to look at you that way, and with good reason."

"I wasn't a child."

"You were a *felony*."

She seemed to stop breathing, which he took as a good sign. She was listening. "As for what happened after, I'm not sorry about that. He was drunk and being aggressive with you, and I don't care what you think of me now, surely you know I'd never walk away from that."

She said nothing.

"Never, Rainey. As far as I knew, you were innocent—"

She made a soft moan of protest, and he paused, taking in her profile, which wasn't giving much away. "And I'm not sorry I kicked his ass either."

At that, she looked up. "You did?"

He hesitated, knowing she wasn't going to thank him for this part. "After I made sure you got home, I went after him. I threatened to kill him if he ever went near you again."

Her eyes narrowed, and he raised a brow, daring her to protest. Finally, she blew out a breath, and even gave him a little smile. "Thanks." Pushing away from him, she headed for the kitchen.

Catching her by the waist, he turned her around and had to duck to look into her eyes. "And I didn't desert our friendship, I went to Ontario for a job. When I left, you weren't speaking to me."

"I'm not speaking to you now either."

He pulled her up against him. "I liked you," he said quietly. "A lot. You were fearless and a little wild, and a whole lot determined."

She snorted.

"I liked you," he repeated quietly, firmly. "But let's be honest. I liked all women back then. I wasn't much for commitment or a relationship beyond what I could get in the hours between dinner and breakfast. It was day-to-day for me."

"By all accounts, that hasn't changed much."

"Fair enough," he said. "I still tend towards the day-to-day. It suits my lifestyle." He hadn't given a lot of thought to having a deep, serious relationship in a while. He'd been there, done that, and it was more trouble than it was worth. He didn't play with women, he didn't lead them on. He enjoyed them. Made sure they enjoyed him. And then when things got sticky or uncomfortable, or too much to handle, he moved on.

Day to day...

"With my job, having a deep, meaningful, heavy relationship just hasn't been on my radar."

She nodded.

"None of that doesn't mean that I don't like the

woman you've become," he said. "Because I do. Very much."

"Even though I'm different?"

"Especially because you're different."

Her eyes lifted to his, revealing a vulnerability that cut him to the core. "Doesn't hurt that you're smart and smoking hot," he said.

"I'm a sure thing, Mark," she said on a low, embarrassed laugh. "You don't need to—"

"And fiercely protective about those you care about," he murmured. "And strong. So damn strong. I think that's what I like the best. Watching you run your world and make a difference while you're at it."

She shook her head. "If it's my turn to say I like you now, you're going to be disappointed. I got over liking you."

He grinned. "Aw, Rainey. You like me. You like me a whole hell of a lot."

"We really need to work on your self-confidence." But she blew out a breath and relaxed into him a little. "You've read your press, right? You know they call you a hard-ass." She lifted her hand and touched his face. "But they're wrong." She pressed her face to his throat and inhaled him in, like maybe he was her air and she needed more. And when her hands slid around his waist, beneath his shirt, and up his back, he knew he was a goner.

12

RAINEY WAS LOST IN MARK'S kiss when her phone vibrated.

Mark groaned.

"I'm sorry," she gasped. "I have to look." She pulled out her phone and eyed the text from a number she didn't recognize.

Are you up for a walk on the beach and dessert? Cliff

One of Mark's big hands cupped the back of hers and his thumb hit *delete*.

"Hey. Maybe I wanted dessert."

"I've got your dessert," he said, moving her backwards until the couch hit the backs of her knees and she dropped into it.

Following her down, he took both her hands in one of his and slowly drew them up over her head, pinning them there as he pressed his lower body into hers before hooking one of her legs around his waist, opening her up to him.

She moaned and he breathed out her name as he

cupped her breast, his thumb gliding over her nipple, causing her to arch up into him like a puppet on a string.

His mouth nipped at her ear, her jaw, then finally, oh God, finally, her mouth, and when he started to pull away, she whimpered.

"Shh," he murmured, and then her clothes were gone, and their hands were fighting to rip off his. He tackled the buttons on his shirt, shrugging out of it, revealing a torso and chest she wanted to rub her face against like a cat in heat. His short hair was mussed, his mouth wet, his eyes at half mast, a sexy heat to them that said her pleasure was his. She pushed him and then followed him to the floor, straddling him.

"And you say *I* have to be in charge," he murmured, chuckling low in his throat as his hands went to her butt. "You have a serious queen bee issue—Jesus!" he gasped when she slid down his body and licked him like a lollipop. She couldn't fit him all in her mouth but she gave it the old college try, and given the rough, raw sounds coming from him and the erotic way he writhed beneath her, she was doing more than okay. After a few minutes, he gasped, "Rainey, stop. I'm going to—"

She didn't stop. Swearing, he hauled her up his chest and rolled them again, pinning her beneath two hundred pounds of very determined Latino sex god. "You don't listen very well."

"Maybe I just wanted you to wrestle control away from me again."

He laughed roughly, then sank his teeth into her lower lip and tugged. "Rainey?"

"Yeah?"

"We're done playing."

"About time."

He produced a condom, then slowly entwined their fingers and drew her hands above her head, then he kissed her long and deep and hot. When they eventually tore apart to breathe, he stared down into her face. "Still mad I deleted Cliff's text?"

"Cliff who?"

With a smug smirk, he kissed her again, then slid into her. Pleasure flooded her, so intense it arched her back and had her crying out, clutching at him. The teasing and fun vanished in a blink, replaced by something so intense she could hardly breathe. Mark's eyes were dark and sultry, and she reared up to press her mouth to his. He took control of the kiss, making her melt into him all the more as he buried himself in her over and over, deeper, harder, faster, the entire time holding her gaze with his, letting her see everything she did to him.

It took her right over the edge. She was still quivering when he grabbed her hips and thrust one last time, holding himself tight against her as he came hard.

When she could think again, she realized he'd lain down beside her and was holding her close, running a hand over her heated, damp skin, waiting while she caught her breath. His wasn't all that steady either. It was her last thought before she drifted off to sleep, comforted by the sound of his heart beating wildly against her ear.

RAINEY WOKE UP ENTANGLED in a set of strong, warm arms. Dawn had come and gone. The sun crept in the window, highlighting the form of the man lying next to her.

His eyes were closed, his decadently inky black

lashes brushing against his cheeks. His dark hair was tousled, his jaw shadowed by a night's beard growth.

They hadn't slept much. Damn testosterone. In spite of herself, the need for him had called to her, over and over again.

It'd been an amazing night. She could replay every touch, every moan he'd wrenched from her, each moment of ecstasy.

And there'd been lots.

The sheet rode low on his hips and she soaked him up, the broad shoulders and wide chest tapering to that stomach she still, after licking every inch of him last night, wanted to press her mouth to. His chest was rising and falling steadily, but as if he sensed her perusal, he drew in a deep breath. The arm he had curled around her tightened, drawing her in closer. "Mmmm." The sound rumbled up from his chest as a hand slid into her hair. He had an obsession with her hair, she'd noticed, he loved touching it, burying his face in it.

His other hand slid down her back and gripped her butt, squeezing. She arched into the touch and felt herself practically purr with contentment.

And hence the danger. The sleeping portion of the night had given her a sense of intimacy—a *fake* intimacy. It'd brought contentment, warmth, affection. She didn't want to feel those things for him, but just like when she'd been a love-struck teenager, it'd happened. Only this time she'd known better.

This could be fixed, she hurried to assure herself. She just needed a time-out. *Now.*

He stirred when she slipped out of bed, opening his eyes. "Rainey." His voice was low and rough from sleep, and he was lying in her sheets like he belonged

there, long sinewy limbs at rest, eyes warm and getting warmer, heating all her parts equally.

"You need to stop giving me orgasms," she said.

"Aw, you don't mean that. Come here, I'll show you."

She actually took a step toward him before stopping short. "Oh my God. I think I'm actually addicted to you—"

This sentence ended with her letting out a startled scream because suddenly she was airborne. Mark had risen from the bed and tossed her to the mattress. He followed her down, crawling up her body. They were both naked, and at the contact, she arched up and moaned.

His smile was pure trouble.

"Oh, no," she said, scooting backwards. "I'm going to work."

He grabbed her ankles and tugged.

She landed flat on her back, legs spread wide, held open by him. "I'm not playing," she said, having to try real hard not to be turned on. "We're having another car wash today, and I have a staff meeting about the formal dinner and auction next Saturday. Busy day," she said, breathless from just the way he was looking at her. "And besides, you wanted a day to day, right? Well it's a new day and I have plans. Gotta go."

"I think I'm missing something," he said, slipping his hand into her hair, tugging lightly until she looked into his eyes. "What's the real problem here?"

"The problem is that I have thirty minutes to get into work! Let go." She attempted to leave the bed, but he merely tightened his grip, pulling her to him until their faces were so close that she could feel his warm breath on her lips. She could see the heat in his eyes,

and also a curiosity. Probably the man had never been kicked out of a woman's bed before. "It's nothing personal," she said.

"Bullshit."

She sighed. "Okay, you're right. It's personal. It's just that...remember when I said I had to instigate or I'd get screwed up?"

"Yeah."

"Well, it happened anyway. I'm screwed up."

"What are you screwed up about?"

The fact that I've fallen in love with you... She fought to get free and rolled off the bed. "I have to go, Mark. Don't make this harder than it is."

"I'm not making this anything," he said, sitting up, watching her from inscrutable eyes. "That's all you. If things veer off the path of your plan in any way, you panic, like now. Things happen, Rainey. You know that."

"Hey, *you're* the one with the plan," she said. "The plan that can't go more than a day in advance. I'm not even sure why, except that it leaves you open in case something better comes along."

"Is that what you think?" He caught her before she could grab her clothes—damn he was fast—and pulled her back to his chest. "Rainey, there's no one else. Not while we're..."

"Having all the sex?" She crossed her arms, doing her best to ignore that her butt was pressed into his groin. But then he stirred. Hardened. "Are you kidding me? *Now?*"

With a sigh, he let her go. "I can't help it. You're naked. And hot. I'm hard-wired to react."

They both looked at his erection. A little part of her wanted to push him back down to the bed and jump him.

Okay, a big part of her.

"I'm seriously late," she said. "We can finish this tonight."

"Can't. I'm flying to New York after the car wash, doing some press. I'll be gone three or four days."

"Oh," she said, hopefully hiding her disappointment.

"I'll see you when I get back," he murmured, watching her body with avid attention as she gathered some clothes.

"Can you make plans that far out?"

"Ha ha." He pulled out his phone and opened his calendar file, flipping through the days with his thumb. "Shit. Five days. I'll be back Saturday, just in time for the auction and the big games on Sunday."

"That's almost a whole week," she said. "I might find another non-fixer upper by then. Gotta leave my options open." She went into the bathroom, carefully avoiding the mirror and her rosy oversexed complexion as she got into the shower. When she went back into the bedroom to dress, she didn't look at Mark's oversexed self either, still naked and sprawled out on her bed, working on his phone. She grabbed her purse and turned to the door, only to be forced back around by Mark's firm hands on her arms.

"Lunch," he said. "Today."

"Can't."

"Can't? Or won't?"

"Can't. I have a meeting. And won't. I need a little space, Mark."

He stared at her as if it hadn't occurred to him that she wouldn't want him.

"Tell me you've been turned down before," she said.

"Sure. In fifth grade Serena Gutierrez said she'd go out with me, but then I found out she'd also said yes to five other guys. She broke my heart."

Hands on hips, she narrowed her eyes. "Something past puberty."

"I was dumped right before my high school prom and had to go stag."

"Yes, and you ended up with three dates once you got there," she reminded him. "Three girls who were also solo."

"Oh yeah," he said with a fond smile.

Whirling, she headed down the hallway to the front door.

"Okay, okay," he said on a laugh, following her. "I've been dumped plenty. I work twenty-four/seven, and I travel all the time. I don't have a lot left to give to a relationship. Women don't tend to like that."

"Hence the day-to-day thing?"

"Don't fix what isn't broke," he said.

Right. She nodded, throat tight. "Good idea." Too bad it was too late. She was already broke. "Goodbye, Mark," she said softly, and walked out the door.

MARK STARED AT THE CLOSED door and felt cold to the bone. That hadn't felt like an "I'll see you in five days" goodbye. That had felt like a *goodbye* goodbye.

Which meant he'd messed up. It'd been a while since he'd done that, and even longer since he'd faced a problem that he had no idea how to fix.

Needing to try, he yanked the door open and stepped onto the porch, just in time to see Rainey's taillights vanish down the road.

"Damn," he muttered, and shoved his fingers through his hair. He was the biggest dumbass on the planet.

A female gasp interrupted his musings, and had him turning to face a woman standing on the next porch over. She was in her forties, looking completely shell-shocked as she stared at him.

"You're...*naked*."

Shit. Yes, he was. Bare-assed naked, giving her the full Monty. With as much dignity as he could, he turned to go back inside, but the door had shut behind him.

And locked.

Mark once again faced the woman, who let out a low, inarticulate sound at the sight of him. "I'm going to need to borrow your phone," he said.

13

MARK WAS SITTING OUT front of Rainey's town house with the neighbor's towel around his hips when Rick drove up and honked.

"Shut up," Mark muttered as he walked to the car.

"Watch the towel, man, these are leather seats."

Mark flipped him off.

"Aw," Rick said with a tsk. "Rough day already?"

"I don't want to talk about it. Ever."

"I bet." Rick drove off with lots of grinning and the occasional snicker, which Mark ignored.

They went to the motel so Mark could get clothes, and then to the construction site, where he spent the next few hours compartmentalizing. Swinging a hammer, wielding his phone for Mammoth business, and…thinking about Rainey dumping his sorry ass.

Don't go there….

Late afternoon he left the construction site and headed to the rec center for the car wash. Casey and James helped staff members set up but there was a lot of chaos, and for that Mark was glad because it gave him something to do other than think too hard. His softball

team straggled in one by one, dropped off by parents or riding in with friends who had a license, and for a minute, Mark's spirits rose. The girls would annoy him in no time flat, taking his attention away from himself.

They weren't in their uniforms today. Nope, they'd come dressed as they pleased, which was hardly dressed at all. Bikinis, low-riding shorts, tight yoga pants…the combination made his head spin. "Okay, no," he said. "Go add layers. *Lots* of them."

When he turned around, Rick was standing there, holding two sodas. "You do realize that they're not your million-dollar guys, being paid to be bossed by you, right?"

"You brought me here to clean up their act and make players out of them."

"No, I brought you here so your players could clean up their act."

Oh, yeah. Right. "Well, we'll kill two birds with one stone."

Rick shook his head and offered him one of the sodas. "You look like hell, man. So how did you end up the one dumped? And has that ever even happened before?"

"What part of I don't want to talk about it don't you get?" He let out a breath when Rainey came out of the building wearing denim shorts and a tee, and…

Mark's ball cap.

She was finally wearing *his* ball cap. Ignoring the pain in his chest, he looked her over as indifferently as he could manage. A ponytail stuck out the back of the hat, her beat-up sneakers were sans socks, and she looked every bit as young as his softball team. Across

the parking lot, their gazes met. Hers was wary, uncertain, vulnerable, and... hell.

Sad.

He imagined his was more of the same, minus the vulnerable part. He didn't do vulnerable.

"Want my advice?" Rick asked.

"No."

His brother clapped a hand on Mark's shoulder. "Gonna give it to you anyway. Whatever it is, whatever stupid ass thing you've done, suck it up and apologize. Even if you weren't wrong. Works every time, and as a bonus, you get make-up sex."

"*That's* your advice?" Mark asked. "To grovel?"

"You got anything better?"

"No."

Rick laughed and walked off, heading for Lena, who greeted him with a sweet smile and a kiss.

Rainey was still looking at Mark. Raising her chin slightly, she headed right for him, and his heart, abused all damn morning, kicked hard. For the first time in his entire life, he actually had to fight a flight response but he forced himself to hold his ground as more cars pulled in.

Guys. Teenage guys. The ones James and Casey were working with. They piled out of their cars with greetings for Rainey and his girls, who were coming back outside, only slightly more covered than they'd been when they arrived.

"Mark."

Sharee hadn't changed out of her short shorts and she was sauntering up to Todd, who had his eyes locked on her body.

"Mark," Rainey repeated.

"What the hell are they wearing?"

"Who?"

"The girls. Look at them, do you call that a swim-suit?" he asked. "Because I call it floss."

She made a choked reply, and he turned to look at her. She was laughing at him. This morning she'd walked away from him and now she was laughing at him. "How is this funny?" he demanded.

"You're micromanaging. Listen, Coach, all you have to do this afternoon is stand around and look pretty."

"What?" he asked incredulously, but then he was distracted by Todd, who was running a finger over Sha-ree's shoulder. What the hell?

Rainey moved in front of Mark and waited until he tore his attention away from the teens. "It's a car wash, Mark. A summer car wash for the teenagers' sports pro-gram. We do this biweekly. They're having fun, as they should."

He tried to look over her head but she merely went up on her tiptoes and held eye contact. "You going to tell me what happened this morning?"

"We…" He refused to say they broke up. One, they hadn't had that kind of a relationship, and two, even if they had, he sure as hell didn't want to admit it was over. "Had a difference of opinion."

She blinked, then took a step back. "I meant about you getting locked out on my porch naked."

Shit. "I don't know what you're talking about."

"Nice," she said, nodding. "And I can see how you manage to fool people with that voice. It's absolutely authoritative." She pulled out her phone, brought up a picture, and showed it to him.

It was him. Bare ass. On her porch.

"It's a little blurry," she said, staring at it. "Because Stacy—my neighbor—was extremely nervous. She was also impressed. It was chilly this morning."

His jaw set. "She sent this to you?"

"Yes. She was worried about the naked guy trying to break into my place." Mercifully she put her phone away. "Now, about that 'difference of opinion'."

Oh, hell. He braced himself. "You walked away from me."

"Yes, because I had to go to work." She paused again, her eyes on his. "And…you thought I walked away from you." She waited a beat. "You actually thought I'd—" Now she shook her head. "It was an argument, Mark. And I'm guessing by your reaction that you don't have many of them. Of course not." She smacked her own forehead. "Because in your world, you're the dictator. Well, Mark, welcome to the *real* world. Where I get to be right some of the time, and that means you have to be wrong occasionally."

"Wrong," he repeated slowly.

"Yeah, wrong," she said on a mirthless laugh. "Even the word sounds foreign coming off your tongue." She was hands on hips, pissed off. "So is that what usually happens? You just write off anyone who disagrees with you?"

Actually, very few people ever disagreed with him. He was paid the big bucks to be in charge, in control, and to make small decisions, and he was good at those things. He didn't have much of a margin of error, and frankly, he'd surrounded himself with people who knew this and were either always in line with his way of thinking, or they kept their opinions to themselves.

"Wow, you are so spoiled." Her smile had vanished,

and now she just looked disappointed in him. That was new too.

New and entirely uncomfortable. "Rainey—"

"Tell me this. You came here this morning thinking what, that we were totally over?" She stared at him, obviously catching the answer in his eyes. "I see," she said slowly. "How convenient that must have been for you."

"It didn't feel convenient," he said. "It felt like a knife in my chest."

She absorbed that silently, without any hint of how she felt about it. Fair enough, he supposed, since he'd kept his feelings from her often enough.

THEY MADE FIVE thousand dollars at the car wash, Mark made sure of it. He called in favors and made nonnegotiable requests of everyone he could think of, and the cars poured in.

When it was over, Rick pulled him aside. "I take back every shitty thing I said about you."

Mark slid him a look.

"Well, for today anyway." Rick grinned, hauling him in for a guy hug. Mark shoved free and wrote the rec center a check, matching the funds as he'd promised to do. "How's it going finding a new building?"

"It's not." Rick's smile faded. "But we still have until the end of the year. Hopefully something will work out or we're out of a lot of jobs, not to mention what will happen if the kids end up with no programs to keep them busy."

Mark nodded.

"How about you and Rainey?"

"What about us?" Mark asked.

"You forget what I said about groveling?"

"I'm not groveling, Rick."

"Right, because that would be too big a step for you. You try the supply closet? That seems to work well for you two."

"Hey, we were *talking* in that closet."

"Uh-huh. Listen, I love you, man," Rick said. "Love you like a brother…"

Mark rolled his eyes.

"But you can't screw with Rainey like you do your other women."

"I don't screw with women."

"No, you screw 'em and leave 'em. We all watch *Entertainment Tonight,* you know."

"It was a photo shoot!"

"Rainey's a sweetheart," Rick said. "She's strong and tough and fiercely protective, and she takes care of those she cares about, but sometimes she forgets to take care of herself."

"I know that."

"And did you also know that in her world, being with you, sleeping with you, is a relationship? She's invested."

"We've discussed it," Mark said tightly. "We're taking it day-to-day."

Rick's eyebrows went up, then he shook his head. "Day to day? Are you kidding me? You let a woman like Rainey hang on your whim?"

Mark pulled out his phone but for once it wasn't ringing. That was great.

"You're an even bigger idiot than I thought," Rick said.

"Thanks."

"Hey, I'm trying to help here. Figured since I'm the only one of us in a successful relationship, I should spread the wealth of knowledge."

"You had nothing to do with your *relationship*. Lena set her sights on you, and you just happened to be smart enough to let her."

"Which begs the question," Rick said. "Why aren't you just as smart?"

ON THE WAY TO THE AIRPORT, Mark made a drive-by past Rainey's place. She wasn't in, which just about killed him. He took the red-eye to New York and hit the ground running the next day. In his hotel room that night, he stared at the ceiling. He'd told himself he'd been too busy to think of Rainey, but that was a lie, and one thing he never did was lie to himself.

He'd thought of her.

And as stupid as it seemed given that he'd just seen her the day before, all wet and soapy and having a great time at the car wash, he missed her. It wasn't a physical ache. Okay, it was. But hell, she'd looked damn good in those shorts and tee, better than any of the teenagers and their newfound sexuality.

Rainey had looked comfortable in her skin. Happy with herself and what she'd chosen to do with her life. Sure of herself.

It had been the sexiest thing he'd ever seen, and yeah, now he was lying in bed with a hard-on the size of Montana, but he missed more than her body.

He'd be back in Santa Rey in a few days, he told himself. Just in time for the black-tie dinner and auction, and then the big games against Santa Barbara the next day. Every penny that was donated was going

to the rec center, and Mark had made sure that there would be a lot of pennies. The Mammoths had donated the money for the event, the supplies, the ads, and the ballroom at the Four Seasons—everything, and all the players had agreed to get auctioned off.

The money should be huge, and then there were the games the next day. After that, Mark and the guys could leave town knowing they'd done their best to give back to a community that had badly needed the help.

And Rainey…Rainey would go back to dating. Hell, maybe she was out on a date right now. Which would be no one's fault but his own.

Rick had been right. Mark was an idiot. If he'd played his cards better, he could have postponed the trip and right this minute be gliding into Rainey's sweet, hot, tight heat, listening to those sexy little sounds she made when she got close, the ones that made him want to come just thinking about it.

Shoving up from his bed, he hit the shower, standing there at two-thirty in the morning beneath the hot water, his only company his regrets and his soapy fist.

RAINEY WALKED INTO the auction, her stomach in knots. She'd come with Lena and Rick, the three of them dressed to the hilt. She was wearing a little black dress and heels that bolstered her courage.

The ballroom glittered with the rich and famous. Santa Rey was four hours north of Hollywood and Malibu, and thanks to Mark offering up all the Mammoth players for auction, celebrities had flocked to the event. Casey was up on the block first, and was bought by a blonde television starlet. James went up next. Lena started to bid on him but Rick yanked her back into her

seat. James ended up going to some cute young twenty-something, happily spending her daddy's money.

And so it went, with Rainey dazzled by the money pouring in.

After the last player was auctioned off, the entire team of Mammoth players dragged Mark up onto the stage. She knew he'd just come back into town and had to be exhausted, but he looked incredible in a tux. He didn't look thrilled about being auctioned off, but resigned to his fate, he stood there as the bidding started. And the crowd wasn't shy either. Rainey's heart started pounding, and her palms went sweaty as she lifted her bid paddle.

One hundred dollars. She'd just bid one hundred dollars on a man she was more than a little pissed at. Three women were in the bidding with her. One hundred twenty five. One hundred fifty. One hundred seventy-five... Unable to sit calmly, Rainey stood up and shouted her next bid. "*Two* hundred." It was all she had left on her Visa. Maybe if she didn't eat for the next month she could go to three hundred.

The next bidder was from Los Angeles. A woman producer, someone whispered. She bid a thousand dollars and Rainey sagged back in her seat. Probably for the best. It'd been silly to even think about bidding on him.

She felt a tap on her shoulder. Turning, she found James, crouched down low so he couldn't be seen. "Here," he said, and shoved something into her hand.

She looked down and her eyes almost fell out of her head. It was a wad of hundreds. "James—"

"It's from the guys. You can't turn it down, you'll insult them. Plus, we all voted. We need you to win

him, Rainey, *bad*. He's been a complete ass this week, even from three thousand miles away. Only you can soften him up. Please win him and do whatever it is you do to make him nice again."

She looked across the ballroom at the players, who were all watching her hopefully. "How much is here?" she asked.

"Five grand."

"Five *grand?*"

James smiled. "Just hedging our bets. Plus, it's a write-off. Don't second-guess it, beautiful. It's lunch money for some of these guys."

"Mark Diego, going for thirty-five hundred," the auctioneer said. "Once, twice—"

"Five thousand!" Rainey shouted.

The players cheered and hooted and hollered.

Lena leapt up and hugged her tight.

Rick was looking pleased.

James just grinned from ear to ear.

And from the stage, Mark's gaze narrowed on Rainey, unreadable as ever.

WHEN THE AUCTION ENDED, Rainey headed out to her car and found a certain big shot NHL coach leaning against the hood, watching her walk toward him with dark, speculative eyes.

Up close and personal, he took her breath. Like his expensive players, he was looking GQ Corporate Hot tonight in that very sexy tux, black shirt, black on black tie, and those badass eyes glinting with pure trouble. It was a cool evening, and yet she felt herself begin to perspire.

She'd purchased him. Good Lord. She'd fought for

him tooth and nail and she'd won, and all she wanted
to do was tear off that suit with her teeth.

And then lick him head to toe.

Not good. She'd already licked him from head to toe
and knew that he tasted better than any of her favorite
foods. She knew that he felt the same about her.

And she knew something else too. She knew by the
way that her heart was pounding, pounding, pounding,
threatening to burst out of her ribs, that this was no
simple thing that she'd be getting over anytime soon.

The closer she got, the more her stomach jangled. It
was crazy, her reaction was crazy. He was just a guy, a
bossy, demanding, alpha guy she'd once known....

And yet somewhere along the way, maybe when he'd
so readily and willingly stepped up to the plate to help,
becoming a true role model for the team, she'd realized
how much more he was. Watching him step outside his
comfort zone only intensified the experience.

You could do the same, a little voice said. Take a real
risk for once. Step outside the box, veer from the plan...

Don't let your fear hang you up. Take a risk on him.

His eyes never wavered from hers, and she hoped
like hell she wasn't broadcasting her thoughts because
she really wasn't ready for him to know them. "Hey."

His smile went a little tight, but he gave her a soft
"hey" and backed her to her car, pressing up against
her, slipping his hands in her hair to tip her face up to
his. "I missed you," he said.

Her heart squeezed. "Are you sure? Because before
you left, I thought maybe I was driving you a little
nuts."

"Definitely, you're driving me nuts."

She thought about getting annoyed at his present

tense except he pressed his mouth to her temple, then took a tour along to her ear. Taking the lobe lightly in his teeth, he tugged.

She clutched at him, the bones in her knees vanishing. "Mark."

"I have something I want to show you."

"I know," she said, feeling his erection press into her belly.

He snorted. "Not that. Come on, let's go."

Easier said than done. The parking lot was mobbed by everyone trying to leave the auction.

"Excuse me, Mark Diego!"

They both turned and faced two guys in their early twenties, carrying cameras that flashed brightly in their faces.

Rainey grimaced and covered her eyes.

Mark didn't so much as flinch, but grabbed Rainey's hand and kept them moving.

"Sorry about the Stanley Cup, man," one of them said, keeping pace. "Is this your girlfriend? What's your name, sweetheart?"

Rainey opened her mouth but Mark spoke up. "No comment," he said, and walked her toward his truck so fast she could barely keep up, damn her four-inch heels. Mark opened the passenger side door for her, then stood practically on top of her as she attempted to get in. But his truck was high and her little black dress was short. And snug. "Back up," she said. "I need some room for this."

"Babe, I'm the only thing blocking the money shot."

Rainey realized he was right. Without his protection, the photographers could get a picture of her crotch.

"It's either me or them," he said. "And somehow I think you'd rather it be me than the entire free world."

"Fine. But don't look."

"I won't," he said as she slid in, and he totally looked.

"Hey!"

She caught his quick, bad boy grin before he shut the truck door, locking her inside.

MARK DROVE RAINEY UP the highway a few miles, into the burned-out area of the county, nerves eating at his gut. He was more nervous now than he'd been at the finals. When he turned off the paved road and onto what was little more than a field of dirt, he stopped the truck and got out, walking around for Rainey.

She eyed the large trailer in front of them. "What's this?"

Saying nothing, he unlocked the trailer and led her inside and hit the light switch.

Rainey looked around at the office equipment and architectural plans spread across one of the desks. "Mark?"

"Look out there." Heart pounding, he pointed to the window as he flicked another switch and the land on the other side of the trailer lit up. "That's where it'll go."

She moved to the window and stood highlighted there in her little black dress and heels, the elegance of her outfit clashing with her hair, which was trailing out of the twist she'd had it in, brushing her shoulders and neck. "Where what will go?" she asked, pressing her nose to the glass.

"The new parks and rec center."

She turned and looked at him, eyes shocked. "What?"

"Yeah, I bought and donated this land to the rec center. By this same time next year you'll be in your new office."

She stared at him for a long beat. "Did you do this so I'd sleep with you again?"

"Is that even a possibility?"

She just stared at him some more, taking a page out of his own play book with a damn good game face.

"No," she said, her eyes on his mouth. "I'm not going to sleep with you again."

He went icy cold and couldn't breathe. "No?"

"No. Sleeping with you is what went wrong. Sleeping with you makes me want more than you can give."

He let out a breath and nodded. He understood but it felt like he'd just taken a full body hit.

"But," she said, taking a step closer to him, "the not sleeping part—that works for me." She was breathing a little hard and her nipples were pebbled against that mouthwatering black dress.

He wanted to strip her out of it and leave her in just the hot heels, but she was throwing more than a little 'tude, and the shoes might be detrimental to his health. Nope, it all had to go, everything, leaving her gloriously naked. Then his gaze locked on the pulse frantically beating at the base of her neck and he knew he wasn't alone. Reaching out, he cupped her throat, his thumb brushing over the spot. She was flushed, and the low cut of her dress was affording him a view that made his mouth water.

"Does it work for you?" she asked.

"Hell, yes."

14

THE WORDS WEREN'T OUT of Mark's mouth before Rainey pretty much flung herself at him. She couldn't help it, there wasn't a woman in all the land who could have helped it.

He caught her. Of course he caught her. He always caught whatever was thrown at him, but he was also protective and warm and caring, and had the biggest heart of anyone she'd ever known. She backed him to the waist-high window she'd just been staring out and kissed him, long and deep, and when his hands came up to hold her, a rough groan vibrating from his chest, she tore her mouth free to kiss his throat while she pushed his jacket off his broad shoulders. He tossed it aside while she worked open the buttons on his shirt. Clearly relishing her touch, he held himself still, his hands tight on her arms, as if it was costing him to give her the reins.

But when she licked his nipple, he appeared to lose his tenuous grip. He whipped her around so that she was against the window now, the wood sill pressing into the small of her back. His eyes were dark, scorch-

ing, and as his hands skimmed up her thighs, bringing the material of her dress with them, she shivered, a flash of excitement going through her.

"Hold this," he commanded, peeling her hands from his shoulders, forcing her to hold her dress bunched at her waist.

"I'm in the window!"

"No one's here. You're so beautiful, Rainey."

Her stomach quivered, and she was glad she'd worn her sexiest black silky thong. "It's the dress."

"Mmmm." His eyes ran up the shimmery material she was holding at her waist, at her panties, and darkened. "Love the dress."

"And the heels. It's the heels, too."

He ran a hand over the delicate ankle strap and hummed another agreement. "Definitely love the heels."

"And—"

"Rainey."

"Yeah?"

He smiled that wicked smile again and kissed her, then cupped her face and said against her mouth, "It's you. It's all you. I'm going to take you here."

"Here?"

"Here." That said, he dropped to his knees and put a big hand on each of her thighs, pushing her legs apart.

"Um, the window—"

He kissed her hipbone.

"I—" God, she couldn't remember what she'd wanted to say.

He skimmed his fingers up her legs, playing with the tiny strings on her hips.

"Oh," she breathed, when his mouth brushed from

one hip to the other, low on her belly, just above the material of her thong.

"So pretty." He stroked over the wet silk.

"But this was supposed to be *your* pleasure—ohmigod," she gasped when he nipped her skin, catching the silk in his teeth and very slowly tugging. "Mark—"

"Hmm?"

She started to drop the hem of her dress but he covered her hands with his, indicating he wanted her to keep it out of his way.

Then he let his fingers take over the task of pulling the thong down to midthigh, groaning at the sight he'd unveiled for himself. "Trust me, Rainey. This *is* my pleasure."

Acutely aware of the glass at her back, she tried to squeeze her legs together but he was on his knees between them. "Someone could come."

"Yes, and that someone's going to be you."

Oh, God. He sent her a wicked smile. His hands, still on her hips, spread wide, allowing his thumbs to meet, glancing over her center.

Her head hit the glass. She was already panting. "But…"

Another slow, purposeful stroke of his thumb had her moaning.

He was right. She was going to come. Her hands went into his hair. "Mark— We've been here too long already. Someone might show up to investigate the lights."

"Tell you what," he said silkily, pushing her onto the ledge so that it was more like a narrowed seat. "You keep a watch and let me know if you see anyone."

"Okay." Except the back of her head was against the glass. And her eyes were closed.

And...*oh*. He was gliding his fingers over her while his mouth—

God, his mouth. Beneath his tongue and hands she writhed, unable to stay still.

"I'm going to make you come with my fingers, Rainey. And then I'm going to make you come with my mouth. And then I'm going to bury myself in your body. I won't be able to stroke you hard and deep though. I'll barely move, so that if someone drove by, they wouldn't be able to tell what we're doing. But you'll know. I'm going to make love to you until neither of us can remember our names. All while you sit right here and look beautiful and elegant and untouchable to anyone who happens by."

He slid a finger into her and she nearly jerked off the ledge.

"Hold still, Rainey. We don't want to have to stop."

"No." She tightened her grip on his hair. "Please don't stop."

He kissed first one inner thigh and then the other, and she could feel his hot breath against her. She wanted to rock up into him but she managed to stay still.

"Good girl," he whispered against her, his thumb purposely brushing over her in a steady rhythm now, her rhythm.

Holding still was the hardest thing she'd ever done. Her toes were curling, her belly quivering, and when he increased the pace of his fingers, her eyes crossed behind her closed lids. She didn't even realize her hips were rocking helplessly until he set a hand on them.

206

"If you stop," she said. "I'll hurt you."

He laughed softly, then pulled her thong off entirely, gently pushing her thighs open even more. When he added another finger, she bit her lower lip to keep her cry in.

"No, I want to hear you," he whispered against her skin, and stroked his tongue over ground zero.

She cried out again and sank her fingers into his hair for balance.

"Yeah, like that," he said huskily. "Do you know what it does to me to hear those sexy sounds?"

She was beside herself, utterly incapable of answering him, lost in the sensations he was sending rocketing through her. "It makes me crazy," he told her. "Crazy for you."

Crazy worked.

She felt crazy, too.

"Come for me, Rainey. I want to taste you when you're coming."

She pretty much lost it then. First to his fingers, then to his mouth, and then he sank into her silken wet heat. As he'd promised, he barely moved within her, and yet took her to a place she'd never been.

It was the hottest, most erotic experience of her life.

THE NIGHT WAS DARK AND chilly, but inside his truck on the way back into town, with the heater on low and Rainey next to him, all snuggled into his suit jacket, rumpled and sexy as hell, the oddest feeling came over Mark.

Comfort.

Bliss.

Contentment.

Reaching out, he took her hand and brought it to his mouth, then settled it on his thigh as he glanced at her. She was out cold, breathing deep and slow, dreaming....

Of him?

Her mouth curved slightly, and his did the same. He hoped she was dreaming of him.

His dreams were certainly filled with her often enough. Of course his dreams didn't necessarily make him smile sweetly the way she did. More like they made him groan and wake up hard as a rock. He hadn't jacked off so much since middle school.

But it was more than that. He couldn't believe how much she'd come to mean to him. So damn much...

He pulled up to her place and stroked a strand of hair from her face. She let out a low purr of pleasure and stretched. "How come I always fall asleep in your truck?" she murmured.

"It's a mystery." But it wasn't. Even he knew why. Because no matter how much sexual tension there was between them, there was still an ease, a very natural one.

He walked with her up the path to her town house. At the door, she cupped his face in her hands, and stroked his jaw gently. "I love what you did," she told him. "Buying that land, getting plans drawn for the rec center. You're helping so many people, Mark. You're changing lives." Her thumb ran over his bottom lip, making it tingle before she leaned in and brushed her mouth over his in a sweet, far too short kiss. "You've changed my life, too."

He started to deny this but she stopped him. "You did," she said very softly. "You don't even realize how

much. I've always let Mr. Wrong work for me because it gave me something to do—fix him. Which was merely a way to avoid the truth that I myself was the real fixer-upper."

"Rainey, no. You're perfect."

"No, I'm not." She ran her fingers over his lips, gently shushing him. "I'm flawed, and far from perfect. I pick men that aren't right for me and then try to scare them off."

"You're not that scary."

"Give me some time," she quipped.

"I still won't find you scary."

"That's because you'll be gone," she reminded him. "Back to your whirlwind life."

"I get to Santa Rey occasionally."

She smiled but there was something different in her gaze now, something sad. "Good night, Mark."

"Rainey." He couldn't explain his sudden panic, but it was like he'd missed something. "Why do I feel like you really mean goodbye?"

"It used to be," she said with a terrifying quietness, "that I'd take any scrap bit of affection from you I could get. That was the sixteen-year-old in me, the pathetic, loser sixteen-year-old who didn't respect or love herself. I realize that it didn't start out all that different this time either. I mean, I played a good game, but we both know my crush is still in painful existence." She shook her head. "The bad news is that it's grown even past that." Again, she leaned in and brushed her lips to his, clinging for a minute. He could feel her tremor and tried to tighten his grip on her, but she wriggled loose, closing her eyes when he pressed his mouth to her forehead. "Tonight was amazing. I'll never forget it. Or you."

"Rainey—"

"I love you, Mark," she whispered, and then slid out of his embrace and inside, leaving him standing there wondering what the fuck had just happened.

THE NEXT DAY DAWNED BRIGHT and sunny. Perfect game weather. The Santa Barbara rec center teams had arrived by bus. The girls played first. Rainey sat with Lena, watching from the sidelines as Mark coached the teens in a tight game. The stands were filled. The entire town had turned out, it seemed, and a good number of people had come from Santa Barbara too. The mood of the crowd was fun and boisterous.

In between plays, Rainey told Lena the whole story of the night before, leaving out a whole bunch of what had happened in the trailer, much to Lena's annoyance.

"A real friend would give details," Lena said. "Like size, stamina…"

"Hey. Can we focus on the real problem here?"

"Yeah, I'm not seeing the *real* problem," Lena said. "Mark's rescued you from crappy dates, pretty much single-handedly saved your job, and he's been there whenever you've needed him, for whatever you've needed. What a complete ass, huh?"

"Look, I know he's been there." Always, no matter what she needed. "But he doesn't want a relationship. Nothing changes that fact."

Casey, James and Rick had been sitting with the boys but they came over and joined the two of them for a few minutes. "So what are we talking about?" Rick asked.

"Nothing," Rainey said.

"How perfect Mark is for her," Lena said.

"Aw," Casey said, disappointed. "That's not news."

"If they're so perfect for each other, then why does he look like shit?" James asked. "I don't think he's slept."

"Mark never looks like hell," Lena said reverently. "Unless you mean *hot* as hell."

"Sitting right here," Rick said to Lena.

Lena smiled and kissed him. "The hotness runs in the family."

Rainey hadn't slept either. She looked at Mark standing just outside the dugout, but if he was tired, hurting, unhappy, he gave no sign of it as he coached the girls through a three-run inning. At the break, he left the dugout and walked to the stands, ignoring everyone to stop in front of Rainey. He wore a pair of beat-up Nikes and a pair of threadbare jeans, soft and loose on his hips, still managing to define the best body she'd ever had the pleasure of tasting. His T-shirt was sweat-dampened and sticking to the hard muscles of his arms and chest. It'd been given to him by the girls, and was bedazzled and fabric painted with a big *COACH* on the front.

He should have looked ridiculous. Instead, with his expensive sunglasses and all the testosterone he wore like aftershave, he looked...

Perfect.

"Hey," he said, sliding off his glasses, his gaze intense as it ran over her.

She became incredibly aware that the entire Santa Rey side of the stands had gone silent, trying to catch their conversation. "Hey."

"I want to talk to you after the game," he said. "You busy?"

She did her best to look cool in front of their avid audience and shook her head. "Nope. Not busy."

"Good." He strode back to the game, and she might or might not have been staring at his very fine ass when Lena nudged her in the side with her elbow.

"Do you think 'talk' is a euphemism for—"

Rainey stood up. "Going to the snack bar."

IT WAS A TIME-OUT AND Mark stood in the dugout talking to the girls.

Or rather, the girls were talking to him.

"We can tell you're having a bad day, Coach," Pepper said. "Did you get dumped?"

"This is a time-out," he said. "We are going to discuss the game."

"Aw. You did." Pepper put her hand on his shoulder. "What'd you do? Because Rainey's a really great person, you know? Probably if you just said you were sorry, she'd take you back."

Mark shook his head. Never once in his entire professional career had he had a time-out like this one. In his world, his players lived and breathed for his words and never questioned him. "We're in the dugout," he said. "In the middle of a very important game." The press was there, which had been Mark's intention all along. But he found he could care less about the press. It was about these girls. "We're talking about the game."

"That's not as much fun," Kendra said. "I bet if you tell us what you screwed up, we could tell you how to fix it."

"How do you know he screwed up?" Cindy asked.

"Please," Sharee said. "Rainey wouldn't have

screwed up. She never screws anything up. She's on top of things, always."

Mark scrubbed his hands over his face. How the hell had this gotten so out of control? He couldn't even wrangle in a handful of teenage girls.

Oh, who the hell was he kidding. He'd lost control weeks ago, his first day back in Santa Rey. They wanted to know what he'd screwed up, and he had no way to tell them that he'd screwed up a damn long time ago.

She loved him. She saw right through him and still loved his sorry ass. The words had slipped out of her mouth so easily, so naturally, words he'd never dreamed he'd hear directed at him from a woman like her. A woman he could trust in, believe in, a woman with whom he could be himself. She was so amazing, so much more than he deserved, and she was meant to be his.

He also knew that things didn't always work out the way they should.

Pepper put her hand on Mark's. "My dad says it's okay to make mistakes," she said very quietly.

Mark's dad had often told him the same thing. In fact, Ramon was right this minute out there in the stands cheering his son on, which he'd do no matter what mistakes Mark made.

"Everyone makes them," the girl said. "But only the very brave fix their mistakes."

Mark lifted his head and looked her into her old-soul eyes. "You're right." He'd pulled Rainey in even as he'd pushed her away. He was good at that, the push/pull. Standing, he locked eyes with Rainey. She stood off to

the side between the bleachers and the snack bar. Close enough to have heard the entire conversation.

The ump whistled that the time out was over. Sharee went off to bat, and the other girls plopped back down on the bench of the dugout.

Mark didn't move, didn't break eye contact with Rainey. He had no idea how long they could have kept that up, communicating their longing without a word, when the sharp crack of Sharee connecting with the ball surprised them both.

SHAREE'S HIT WENT STRAIGHT up the line and Rainey watched as the girl took off running. The teen still had an attitude the size of the diamond, but she had it under control these days. There were fewer blowups and hardly a single bad word out of her all week.

Of course that might have been because Todd was in the stands watching her, cheering her on.

Sharee glanced at the teen and blushed.

Todd, already in uniform for his game, grinned.

Watching them caused both a pang in Rainey's heart and a smile on her face.

But that faded fast as she caught sight of the man in dirty jeans and wrinkled shirt walking toward the field from the parking lot. He staggered a bit, but his eyes stayed focused on the diamond.

Martin, Sharee's father.

Drunk.

Just what Sharee needed, for her father to humiliate her today.

Rainey moved towards him, wanting to run the other way, but she couldn't let him ruin the game for Sharee. "Martin, wait."

"Gettoutta my way."

He smelled like a brewery and looked like he'd slept in one. "Did you come to see the game?" she asked.

"I came to see my daughter," he slurred, blinking slowly like an owl. "She stole money from my wallet. She's going to pay for that."

Rainey's gut tightened. "I have your money in my office," she said, gesturing in the opposite direction of the field. No way was she letting him out there to embarrass Sharee.

Not that Rainey was going to take him to her office either. Hell, no. He was a mean drunk, and her unease had turned to fear. She led him around the side of the building, heading back toward the parking lot, her phone in her hand to call Rick for help if necessary, when suddenly she was slammed up against the brick building, hard enough that she saw stars. But that wasn't her biggest problem. That would be the forearm across her throat, blocking her airway.

Her fear turned to terror.

"You told her to call the police on me," Martin hissed, his fingers biting into Rainey's arms. "Didn't you, bitch?"

Bitch… It *hadn't* been those kids who'd painted her car. It'd been Martin. Rainey blinked the spots from her eyes and looked around.

There was no one in sight. They were all watching the game. She wasn't quite in view of the parking lot, and was out of view of the stands. In succeeding to get him away from the field, she'd screwed herself. "Martin, I can't…breathe."

"Because of you, Sharee called the police on me

the other night. I went to jail, and lost my job when I couldn't make bail."

"You shouldn't...hit her."

Martin gave Rainey another shove against the brick wall, and her head snapped against it, hard. More stars. She'd have slid to the ground if he hadn't been holding her up. He pressed harder against her throat and her vision shrank to a pinpoint. "Stay away from my kid," he gritted out. "Stay away from me. You hear me?"

She heard him, barely, over the rush of blood pounding through her ears. Unable to draw a breath, she clawed at his hands.

"Answer me, bitch!"

She answered in the only way she could. With a knee to his crotch.

His scream was high-pitched, and thankfully very loud as he let go and they both hit the ground.

Martin bellowed in pain again.

Someone hear him, she thought. *Please, someone hear...*

Pounding footsteps sounded, and cool hands reached for her. "Jesus. *Rainey.*"

Mark.

"I've got you," he said firmly, pulling her against him, his voice raw with emotion. "I've got you, Rainey."

There were others with him, the whole field by the sounds of it, but she could only sigh in relief as the spots claimed her.

15

RAINEY BLINKED AND FOUND herself staring up at a white ceiling. She was in the hospital.

"You're okay." Mark's voice, then his face, appeared in front of her, looking more fierce and intense than she'd ever seen him.

"You have a concussion," he said. "And your wind-pipe is strained." As was his voice. "You're going to hurt like hell, but you're okay."

She nodded and held his gaze. It was blazing with bare emotion. She tried to say his name, but nothing came out.

"Don't," he murmured. He leaned over her, one arm braced at her far hip, the other stroking her hair back from her face. "Talking will just hurt." Turning, he reached for a cup with a straw and helped her drink. "You're supposed to just lie there quiet until morning," he said.

She felt surrounded by him, in a really warm way. She swallowed and winced. "Martin—"

"In jail," he said tightly, and dropped his head, eyes closed for a beat. Then he met her gaze. "You did great,

Rainey. You took a really bad situation and handled it. Do you have any idea how amazing you are?"

"Did you win?"

He stared at her in shock for a beat, before an exhausted but warm smile crossed his face. "Yeah. I won." He pressed his forehead to hers. "But not the game. We declared a tie. God, Rainey. I thought I'd lost you. I just found you and I thought you were gone."

She remembered how he'd looked earlier, in his sunglasses, hat low over his game face, letting nothing ruffle him.

Nothing.

In fact, she'd never seen anything ruffle the man... except her.

She got to him. And there was a good reason for that. He loved her, too.

And if she hadn't already been head over heels, she'd have fallen for him right then and there, even as she watched the pain and hurt flash in his eyes, neither of which he tried to hold back from her. "Sixty-five seconds," he said. "You weren't breathing for sixty-five seconds after we found you. I lived and died during each one of them." He let out a breath. "Never again."

Her heart stopped. Never again...?

"Never again do I want to be without you."

Her heart had barely kicked back on when Mark cupped her face and peered deeply into her eyes. "I want to be with you tonight," he said.

"Here in the hospital?"

"Here. And tomorrow night. The next night, too."

She swallowed hard. "What happened to day-to-day?"

"It went to hell," he said. "Do you have any idea how

addicting you are? The minute I'm away from you I'm already thinking about the next time I'm going to see you. Touch you. Taste you."

"That sounds like sex."

"It's always been more than sex, Rainey. Always. You said you love me." He gently set his finger on her lips when she would have spoken. "That threw me. You throw me. You were unexpected, and you've changed my endgame. And then you—" His eyes burned hot emotion. She was surprised when he wrapped his arms around her and buried his face between her breasts, breathing deeply. "You could have died before I could tell you." His grip on her tightened. It wasn't something he'd ever done before, taking comfort from her instead of offering it. Eyes burning, she wrapped her arms around him and pulled him in even closer.

"I can't remember my life before this summer," he said, lifting his face. "Before you came back into my world. I don't want to be without you, Rainey. I've known that for a while, before what happened to you today, but I guess I thought knowing it made me weak."

And he wasn't a man who had any patience with weaknesses, especially his own. She laid her cheek on top of his silky hair. "And now?"

He let her see everything he was feeling. "I don't give a shit whether it makes me weak or not. You're the only thing I care about. I love you, Rainey. I think I always have. You make me feel."

"What do I make you feel?"

"Everything. You make me feel everything."

* * * * *

A sneaky peek at next month...

Blaze®

SCORCHING HOT, SEXY READS

My wish list for next month's titles...

In stores from 18th May 2012:

❏ Want Me – Jo Leigh

& Night After Night... – Kathy Lyons

❏ Rub It In – Kira Sinclair

& Just One Kiss – Isabel Sharpe

Available at WHSmith, Tesco, Asda, Eason, Amazon and Apple

Just can't wait?

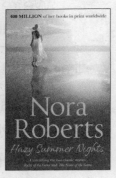